MW00872518

The Druid Queen

Path of the Ranger, Book 16

Pedro Urvi

COMMUNITY:
Mail: pedrourvi@hotmail.com
Facebook: https://www.facebook.com/PedroUrviAuthor/
My Website: http://pedrourvi.com
Twitter: https://twitter.com/PedroUrvi

Copyright ©2023 Pedro Urvi
All rights reserved

Translation by:
Christy Cox

Edited by:
Mallory Brandon Bingham

DEDICATION

To my good friend Guiller.

Thank you for all your support since day one.

Content

Content..4

MAP..6

Chapter 1 7

Chapter 2 14

Chapter 3 23

Chapter 4 30

Chapter 5 41

Chapter 6 48

Chapter 7 57

Chapter 8 66

Chapter 9 77

Chapter 10 88

Chapter 11 99

Chapter 12 104

Chapter 13 110

Chapter 14 121

Chapter 15 130

Chapter 16 142

Chapter 17 150

Chapter 18 158

Chapter 19 168

Chapter 20 179

Chapter 21 186

Chapter 22 193

Chapter 23 201

Chapter 24 ....*208*

Chapter 25 ....*221*

Chapter 26 ....*230*

Chapter 27 ....*237*

Chapter 28 ....*245*

Chapter 29 ....*255*

Chapter 30 ....*262*

Chapter 31 ....*271*

Chapter 32 ....*279*

Chapter 33 ....*288*

Chapter 34 ....*297*

Chapter 35 ....*303*

Chapter 36 ....*310*

Chapter 37 ....*319*

Chapter 38 ....*327*

Chapter 39 ....*336*

Chapter 40 ....*345*

Chapter 41 ....*353*

Chapter 42 ....*359*

Chapter 43 ....*367*

Chapter 44 ....*377*

The adventure continues in the next book of the saga:............*385*

The Secret of the Dragon (Path of the Ranger, Book 17).........*386*

Note from the author:..*387*

Author *388*

Other Series by Pedro Urvi *389*

MAP

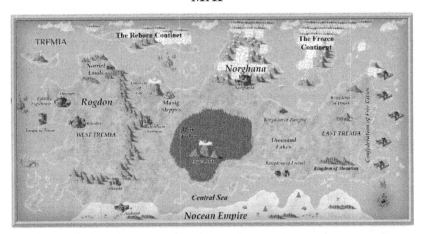

Chapter 1

"Three to the east!" Astrid warned in a whisper loaded with urgency, and she vanished swiftly through the wet underbrush of the forest, which was already shedding the snow that had fallen during the winter.

"Three more in the west," Lasgol called out as well as he located them using his *Hawk's Eye* skill. Astrid has already vanished in the underbrush, but Lasgol knew she had heard him. The Assassin's instincts were well developed and she was always on the alert.

Ona growled with her gaze on the north.

Lasgol got down beside the panther and watched in the direction she was indicating. *Can you detect more in the north?* he transmitted to her. The great, half-crumbled, rocky building prevented him from seeing what might be behind it.

The Snow Panther chirped once.

I not catch power, Camu messaged right behind Lasgol's back.

That's not a good sign. If the dragon is here, you should be able to feel his power. The information Egil received indicates suspicious activity in this area.

I know. Egil good information always, I not catch power, Camu messaged.

The fact that the creature was unable to pick up Dergha-Sho-Blaska's power was not a good omen. Yet Egil had received relevant information, so they had to check the place. They were northeast of the capital, between the city of Olstran and the village of the Four Winds.

Let's move cautiously. If they find out we're approaching we'll have to fight, and I'd rather know what we're up against beforehand, Lasgol transmitted.

Okay, was Camu's message.

Ona growled once.

They made their way through the forest bushes without a noise. In a plain further ahead they could see a huge ruinous building with, at its right, a pretty big hunting cabin. This type of cabin was used to hunt large predators such as bears, or snow panthers. A stream ran beside the cabin, a cabin which must have been able to hold about a dozen hunters. Behind the ruined building and the cabin rose an impressive mountain with snow-covered peaks and sides, already melting with the arrival of spring.

Lasgol moved to the last trees before the plain and stopped, crouching. Ona and Camu stopped beside him and lay on the ground, waiting for his orders.

I can see the ones in the north, there are two. Thanks for the warning, Ona.

The panther made no sound; she was carefully watching from the bushes what was going on before them between the two buildings.

Funny group, Lasgol transmitted, looking at the men working on the ruined building. From what he could tell it appeared to have been a manor destroyed some time ago, by man or by nature. Several half-crumbled walls were still holding up stoically against the passing of time. He could see the plan of the building and what had been the rooms back in the day from the remains. There was half a tower still standing as if by magic on the northwestern corner, but it looked as if it could collapse at any moment.

A number of men were working, digging up dirt in one of the inner halls and carrying it away in wheelbarrows to deposit on one side of the cabin. Judging by the amount of dirt they had dug up, the depth of the hole they were digging, and the remains, Lasgol guessed they had been there for some time, over a week.

What are they doing? he wondered, more to himself than to his companions, but since he was using his *Animal Communication* skill they both received it.

Ona chirped twice, indicating she did not know.

Look treasure? Camu suggested.

Looking for treasure? Have you been talking about gold with Viggo again?

I talk Viggo about gold, silver, and treasures. Much interesting.

It's not very interesting. Wealth shouldn't interest you at all.

Yes interesting. Viggo say much interesting get treasures.

If you keep talking to Viggo you're going to end up badly, you'll see.

Viggo funny. One day treasure.

Yeah, you go and believe everything he tells you and see how well you do. And why on earth would you want silver? You haven't told me yet.

I tell when I know.

Lasgol rolled his eyes. Camu did not even know what he wanted silver for. In any case, knowing him, it did not surprise Lasgol in the least.

Ona growled, pointing eastward.

Lasgol squinted in that direction to see through the brush and trees.

A patrol of two is coming, he transmitted the warning to his friends.

Camouflage? Camu messaged.

Yeah, hide us. Ona, be still and silent, we'll be in camouflage, Lasgol transmitted. The panther stood stone still.

Camu flashed silver and the three vanished from the sight of any human eye that might try to find them.

Two watchmen armed with short bows were approaching slowly from the west. They were alert to their surroundings, looking for anything that might be suspicious. Lasgol saw that their clothes were not very good quality and they wore light leather padded armor over them. They each carried a knife and a short axe at their waists. By their attire they looked more like bandits than anything else. For a moment Lasgol had thought they might be mercenaries or deserters, but those usually wore stolen clothes and armor, which was not the case here.

The watchmen went by behind them without seeing them. Lasgol waited until the men had their backs to them.

Now! he transmitted to his friends.

Lasgol lunged at the back of the man more to the right and Ona jumped at the one on the left. A dull blow with the hilt of his knife rendered the man unconscious. He turned to Ona and saw that she was gripping the bandit's neck with her fangs. The man was still on the ground, his eyes wide open. Panic was beginning to show in them.

Strangle, not kill, Lasgol transmitted to Ona.

The panther glanced at Lasgol and obeyed. She gripped harder and the bandit was left without air, unable to fill his lungs because of the pressure Ona was putting on his neck. The man's eyes closed as he lost consciousness and Ona let go of him.

Lasgol went over to check that he was still alive.

Very well done, he told Ona. He had been training her in several types of attack for a while now. He had realized that the more he advanced in his dominion of his magic, the better she understood him when he transmitted things to her. They had improved both communication and understanding so much that now Lasgol could tell her to perform very specific attacks and movements, which the panther executed exactly as he had taught her without any mistake.

Tie quickly, movement camp, Camu messaged in warning.

Lasgol hastened to tie and gag the two watchmen and then watched what was going on.

What movement? he transmitted to Camu.

Leader come, Camu messaged.

Lasgol did not need to look hard, he was able to identify him clearly. He was a large, strong man, with a red beard and long hair. If it were not for how scruffy he was and the brutish Norghanian look, he might have passed for a man from Irinel. The leader barked some orders to two of his henchmen and they vanished: one inside the cabin and the other into the hole they were digging. From the way he went down into the hole, Lasgol guessed they were carving out steps in order to go down, which he found curious.

The one that had gone into the cabin reappeared a moment later, followed by two other henchmen who were dragging two men whose hands were tied. The men threw the prisoners roughly at their leader's feet.

"Where is it?" the leader asked in a stern, deep voice.

"We... don't know..." one of the prisoners said from the ground. They both had their hands tied behind their backs and looked terrible. They had been beaten savagely.

"It had better be down there where we're digging, or you'll suffer more than you've done so far," the leader threatened them, pointing his finger at them. There was coldness in his look that manifested the cruelty he was capable of.

"It's... down there..." the other prisoner said, his voice shaking. He was broken, and fear made him speak.

"What should we do?" one of the henchmen asked.

"Keep digging!" the leader ordered his men.

The man nodded.

"And dig faster. I want it now, and when I say now, I mean right away!"

Lasgol felt bad for the two unfortunate men. He had no idea who they were, but he was sure they did not deserve to be in that situation. No-one deserved that, although they might not be trustworthy—something that would not surprise him. Thieves and outlaws tended to surround themselves and deal with people of the same kind.

From the two prisoners' clothing, or what was left of it, torn and bloodied, Lasgol guessed they were of pretty good standing and with some gold. Their boots and breeches were of good quality, as were their belts, and their hands, although not fine, were also not weathered by hard work. Their faces, covered in bruises and blood, seemed to Lasgol to be those of middle or high-classed Norghanians.

"It had better be down there, or else you'll pay dearly," the leader threatened them again, and this time he delivered a couple of kicks to the men's sides as they were lying on the ground.

Can you tell whether the leader has power? Lasgol transmitted to Camu, fearing he might be a warlock who somehow had something to do with the Visionaries, even if his attire did not seem to indicate so.

Not feel, but not know.

Yeah, I can't tell whether he's a mage. He's still a little too far away for me to be able to assure he isn't.

Thanks to Eicewald's teachings, they were now alert to any mage and tried to ascertain their rank and level. They had done it with the King's Ice Magi, and the truth was they did pretty well. If done unobtrusively and without using too much power, the Magi did not even notice, which prevented conflict. They would soon be able to tell quite accurately the rank of a mage and how powerful he or she was, and therefore how dangerous the mage might become for them if they were to confront him or her. This was essential knowledge, since it avoided possible unpleasant surprises.

Not believe any is magical.

Lasgol nodded. He did not think any of them had the Gift.

They don't look like Visionaries or Defenders either... he said ruefully.

Ona growled twice, she did not think they were either.

Unless it was a ruse, which it might be. If it was not, it would be a shame that they did not belong to either of the two sects that served the Immortal Dragon. They had spent the whole harsh Norghanian winter searching for the dragon, chasing after every clue Egil got. So far, they had managed to catch only a few Defenders and Visionaries who had been left behind. Lasgol had hoped that the fanatics might lead them to their all-powerful lord, Dergha-Sho-Blaska, but that had not been the case. The dragon seemed to have vanished in the sky after reincarnating and leaving the Sizzling Wrath volcano on Cinders Island. His followers did not know where he was, and neither did the Panthers.

The Snow Panthers were aware that the dragon had not vanished into thin air, but they could not find any trace that might lead them to the mythical creature. They were all wondering what the dragon was planning. What had driven him into hiding. They could only speculate and guess based on what they had seen and the knowledge they had. What they did know for sure was that sooner or later Dergha-Sho-Blaska would make an appearance, and then they would have to stand up to the creature and defeat it, something they had not figured out how to do yet. If everything that was said about dragons was true, and from what they had witnessed, they were not so wrong in their assumption that it was going to be practically impossible to achieve.

Lasgol heaved a sigh. Half-impossible missions were a part of his life, but this one in particular hunting and killing an immortal dragon, gave him gooseflesh. Not for what might happen to him, but for what might happen to his friends and fellow Panthers. According to documents, and Egil had read all he had found about dragons, men could not even scratch a dragon with their steel weapons. What was obviously more terrifying still was the immense magical and physical power of these fearsome creatures. The more he thought about it, the more Lasgol believed that stopping Dergha-Sho-Blaska was going to be a suicide mission.

He wrinkled his nose and drove those negative thoughts out of his mind. They had an extremely important mission to do and they would carry it out. Thinking about death did not change the situation. He focused on the task at hand: the fact that the men they were watching did not seem to be fanatics of either of the two sects was not a good sign either. The fact that they were digging gave him some hope, but not much. One of Egil's theories was that the dragon might be hiding underground, in some deep cave with the intention of recovering. It was a theory that Lasgol agreed with, since he had not appeared in the skies of Norghana, which is what everyone had been waiting for.

He cheered up. They might find the entrance to the lair where the dragon was hiding in this ruinous place. If they found him weak and recovering, in a lethargic state, they might be able to finish him off before he had all his power available—this was the group's hope. But if they did not find him before he was fully recovered with all his power, things were going to get very ugly. The fact that there were no signs of him so far was good news, and it provided them with hope to keep looking for the dragon.

In any case, whatever was going on here, it did not look legal. Their duty as Rangers was to investigate, more so when there were people being tortured and threatened with death.

The hoot of an owl warned Lasgol that Astrid was already in position and waiting for his signal to take action.

We're going to intervene, he transmitted to Ona and Camu.

I ready.

Ona growled once.

Very well. We deal with the leader first, then we free the prisoners.

Okay.

They got ready to assault the settlement.

Chapter 2

Nilsa was coming down from fetching the messages from pigeons and owls at the top of the Tower of the Rangers. She was taking the stairs two at a time, skipping and hopping. The best way to conquer her clumsy instincts was to take them to the limit, and that was what Nilsa did every day. She was cheerful. She wanted to deliver the messages to Gondabar as soon as possible in order to find out whether there was some interesting piece of news.

She took the last steps down to the floor below in a long jump and was close to not being able to stop in time and colliding with and knocking over a Ranger on duty at the door that gave access to what was the last floor of the tower.

"Ranger Liaison!" the guard cried out as he stepped aside, startled.

"Good morning, Ranger on duty!" Nilsa greeted him as she recovered her balance and passed by without even brushing against him.

She went on down the stairs, pleased with herself for correcting her course and not colliding with the guard. Every day she felt a little bit nimbler and more coordinated. She no longer got nervous or as upset as she used to, which helped a lot with her clumsiness, which was growing less every day. It was fading from her daily activity but not from her memory; she always kept it in mind and made real efforts not to be clumsy.

She continued down the stairs as fast as she could, heading to the floor where Gondabar's study was. She took long leaps with momentum or pushing off the rock walls. She always tried to startle the Rangers in duty at every level of the tower. She liked to do this to keep fit and improve her coordination and balance. She sought the latter in particular. Leaping up and down the stairs fast and with an occasional pirouette was great for her. The Rangers on duty were not too pleased since they were pretty startled. Luckily Nilsa was well liked by practically all Rangers in the Tower and they forgave her for it.

She arrived on the floor where Gondabar's study was and went in after greeting the two Rangers at the door. She did not try to startle them since they were in no mood for games. They guarded the Leader of the Rangers' rooms and his assistants, and they took their task seriously. She passed by the assistants' desks as they worked without pause. They always seemed to have their noses buried in some letter or tome, and sometimes both.

Seeing them working, Nilsa wondered how her colleagues were doing and how their missions were going. She had not seen them for weeks and she could not help worrying about their fate. She was the only Snow Panther who had remained in the Royal Castle. It was not her choice either, since she would rather be with her friends, but Gondabar had not let her. He had requested her to stay and help him.

Since their return to Norghania after what had happened at the Sizzling Wrath Volcano on Cinders Island, things had changed for the Panthers. After explaining to Gondabar and the First Ranger Raner Olsen what had happened and after they had questioned the prisoners of the sects, they had brought back with them, the vision of both men had changed. Up till then, both leaders of the Rangers had treated the matter as a serious possible danger that might occur, but more in relation with the sects and the danger they posed without fully believing in the possibility of the existence of Dergha-Sho-Blaska, the immortal dragon.

Still, after the questionings the prisoners rescued from the volcano had been subjected to, besides the detailed explanations of the Snow Panthers, it seemed that the possible existence of the dragon had sunk in at last for both Gondabar and Raner. Their concern was not only for the two sects, but also the dragon itself. This was an important step, because they were going to need all the support from the Rangers if they wanted to stop the dragon.

Unfortunately, it was not all good news regarding the support the Panthers would have. The only evidence of the dragon's existence was the testimony of those who were present during its reincarnation, and Gondabar did not dare go to King Thoran with only that. No matter how much the Panthers had tried to persuade him that he must alert the King, they had not managed to do so. Without more tangible evidence he did not seem inclined to either.

The Panthers understood his reluctance. The King was not exactly an open-minded person, easy to persuade, rather the opposite.

Gondabar feared that Thoran would blame the whole thing on a collective hallucination or madness, due to inhalation of the volcano's fumes or something like that. He was not going to believe such a story, and neither would his brother. Besides, he would not take it well. Gondabar did not want to be at odds with Thoran—that would not be good for the Kingdom. Knowing him as Gondabar did, he could not go to the King with such a story without irrefutable evidence. Both the monarch and his brother would laugh at him, and their anger would ensue if he insisted.

Since there had not been any more sightings of the dragon, or attacks that might unequivocally be from such a creature, Gondabar remained cautious regarding telling the King. For now, he would rather investigate clues and information until there was physical and demonstrable proof of the dragon's existence. Then he would go to the King, but not a moment sooner. Gondabar was prudent by nature, and with King Thoran by necessity. The King's temperament was not one to put to the test—outrageous stories about a reborn dragon would not be believed or well received by Thoran.

On the other hand, Gondabar had told the rest of the Rangers' leaders and they had taken the threat seriously. Both Sigrid at the Shelter and Dolbarar at the Camp were in the know and collaborating in the search for the dragon. Gondabar had requested great efforts from all of them and asked them to prioritize the search for the dragon over other businesses of the Rangers without fully neglecting the Kingdom's protection. If the Rangers already had a lot of work, now they would have even more.

Managing communications, gathering information and related news about possible sightings, checking stories, and other additional tasks was going to require a lot of coordination and someone who had Gondabar's full trust and had integrity, and he had chosen none other than Nilsa.

She was pleased to have been given such responsibility. The only negative point was that she would not be able to be out on field missions with her friends. Gondabar had reinstated her in her post as Liaison, only now her main job was to coordinate and organize all the intelligence and all efforts that had to do with Dergha-Sho-Blaska's destruction.

Besides, Nilsa suspected there was some other reason for Gondabar to have given her this post. The Leader of the Rangers could not cope with all the required work. Nilsa could see with growing clarity that something was wrong with Gondabar. She could not tell whether it was the weight of his years or an illness he was trying to hide, but he looked pretty bad. He tired easily and had to withdraw to his chamber often. This had her worried.

She knocked on the door.

"Liaison Nilsa reporting with communications."

"Come in, Liaison," Gondabar's voice came from inside.

Nilsa went in and saw that the leader of the Rangers was accompanied by the First Ranger Raner. They were discussing something over a map of the realm where they had stuck a number of little flags made of wood and cloth of different colors. Nilsa did not know what they meant and was intrigued.

"My lords," Nilsa greeted them with a slight bow.

"Liaison," Raner replied.

"Do we have any important mail?" asked Gondabar.

"We do," Nilsa confirmed, offering him two rolled and sealed letters.

Gondabar took them, and after checking the seals he opened the first one, read it carefully, and then was thoughtful.

"It's from the Mother Specialist Sigrid,"

"Is there news at the Shelter?" Raner asked, raising an eyebrow.

"Nothing significant. The White Pearl hasn't been activated. Sigrid's asking for several Ranger Specialists to watch over it day and night. Right now, it's being watched by the Master Specialists, but that's interfering with the formation of the new Specialists."

"Aren't Loke, Enduald, and Galdason doing that?"

"Sigrid has sent Loke to investigate a possible lead in the south, outside the Shelter. Enduald and Galdason are studying the Pearl and also the cave where the Dragon Orb had been hibernating. They can't be at both places at once, night and day. If the Pearl activates and the dragon or members of the sect came out of it, everyone in the Shelter would be in great danger. That Pearl must be closely watched day and night."

"In that case we'd better send some Ranger Specialists," Raner said, agreeing with Sigrid's request.

"Yes, I agree. I don't want the formation of the future specialists to be hampered in the long run. We have several serious problems, but we must keep training at the Camp and Shelter in order to strengthen the Rangers' Corps. Choose three Specialists, Raner, and send them. Since it's only surveillance work, they'd better be of Nature."

"Fine. I'll make a selection and send them over at once."

Gondabar opened the other letter.

"It's from my good friend Dolbarar," he announced and went on reading.

"Does he need help at the Camp?" Raner asked.

"He tells me they've tracked all around the Camp with no luck. There's no trace of the dragon. They're also tracking north. I asked him to go into the Frozen Territories, beyond the Unreachable Mountains."

Raner was thoughtful.

"That's a good place to hide. Mountains, caves, and eternal snow."

"That's what Dolbarar and I thought. That's why we sent Rangers to check."

"That might provoke an altercation with the Wild Peoples of the Ice…"

"It might, yes… but we have to explore all of our territory to make sure the dragon isn't hiding in Norghana. The north is still ours, although the Wild Ones of the Ice are in the coldest area."

"Let's hope there isn't a confrontation…" Raner said, sounding doubtful.

"I asked Dolbarar to send competent, experienced Rangers who will avoid any confrontation. We want to find out whether the dragon is in those territories, not start another war with the Peoples of the Frozen Continent."

"Maybe we could ask them?" suggested Nilsa.

Gondabar and Raner looked at her blankly.

"Ask who?" Gondabar asked, staring at Nilsa.

"The Peoples of the Frozen Continent, their leader."

"We don't know who their leaders are now," said Raner.

"It's a mystery who's in charge now," Gondabar explained.

"We might try to find out," Nilsa said.

"We? Who do you mean?" Gondabar looked at her questioningly.

"The Snow Panthers."

"Oh… do you have any contacts there?"

"We believe so, although we haven't spoken to him in a long

time."

"We lose nothing by trying," Gondabar said.

"I'll ask the others as soon as they return from their current missions."

Gondabar nodded.

"Any news from the Panthers? Have they found out anything?"

"Nothing so far, which means their missions haven't been fruitful or that they haven't finished yet. If they had found out anything they would've sent news at once."

That's true," Gondabar nodded again.

"The rest of the Rangers we have combing the east and west and both coasts haven't reported anything unusual, have they?" Raner asked.

"Nothing, sir. All the reports they've sent back are negative," Nilsa confirmed, "Although they don't really know what they're looking for, sir."

"They've been told to look for signs of the presence of a dangerous beast of great size and capable of flying and killing a man easily," said Gondabar. "I preferred not to use the word 'dragon,' several rumors are already spreading among the people because of the terrifying message the sect of the visionaries was spreading throughout the realm."

"Wouldn't it be better to tell them frankly that we are looking for a dragon?" Nilsa suggested.

Gondabar and Raner looked at one another for a moment and then shook their heads.

"Dangerous flying beast of great size is a pretty accurate description that avoids hysteria," Gondabar said.

"Besides, persuading the Rangers that they're chasing an immortal dragon would be very difficult, if not impossible, and it creates doubts about the rational integrity of command," Raner stated.

"I don't understand, sir…"

"Raner means that the Rangers might think we've lost our minds if we tell them they have to find a dragon," Gondabar explained.

"Oh, I see…"

"We already have trouble coming to grips with the idea of it, so imagine a veteran Ranger," Gondabar went on, spreading his arms open, meaning it was not credible.

"We'd lose a lot of credibility. It's better to avoid that as much as possible," Raner stated.

"But Sigrid and the Master Specialists and Dolbarar and the Elder Rangers believe us, don't they?" Nilsa asked, wondering whether or not they really had the support she believed they did.

Gondabar sighed deeply.

"They want to believe us, which is different," he said.

"As you can understand, Nilsa, those of us who haven't seen it find it hard to accept that such a mythical creature exists," Raner admitted. "We're taking a leap of faith here, on your word."

"Well put," Gondabar agreed. "It's a blind bet and against our beliefs, the fact that we're in grave danger because a creature with an unequaled destructive power has appeared. We're betting you're right and that you're not part of a ruse against us."

"I see. But I can promise we're not part of any scheme against the Rangers or the King. Thank you for trusting our word, sir," Nilsa felt honored that their leaders trusted them like that.

"And your judgment," Gondabar added with a slight smile.

"Don't think we don't trust you. On the contrary, we trust you completely. The doubt we'll always have is whether you've been tricked somehow. That's going to be hard to cope with," Raner explained.

"Until you see the dragon yourselves. Then all doubts will vanish," Nilsa said in a prophetic tone. "It's only a matter of time," she added.

Gondabar nodded slowly several times.

"I hope that what we see is the dead body of the dragon. Before it commits any atrocity. That's my wish."

"A wish I share. And if I can be one of those who kill it, even better," Raner said.

Nilsa nodded.

"Once we find it, we won't let it escape," she said wishfully, making a tight fist.

"Until that moment comes, we have to keep looking. We have to cover the whole kingdom, from east to west and north to south. I don't want it to get away if it's hiding here," Gondabar said.

"I'll coordinate that, sir," Nilsa promised.

"Very well. I trust you and your skills completely."

"We must consider the possibility that it might be hiding somewhere else in Tremia, sir," Raner said.

"I wish it were so. But for that we first have to make sure it's not in our territory," said Gondabar. "Once we're sure I'll feel a lot easier. I don't like the fact that all this started because the orb was frozen in the Shelter. It makes me uneasy and gives me the shivers. I'm not one to believe in premonitions, superstitions, and things like that, but I don't like that it woke up here, in the heart of Norghana. Maybe it's somehow linked to our land, and that doesn't help me sleep at night."

"It might be. The theory that it's hiding here because it has something to do with our land is worth considering."

"It could also use the Pearl at the Shelter to come back here," Nilsa suggested.

"True, that's why we have to watch it. There are no more Pearls in Norghana, are there?" Gondabar asked.

"Not that we know of, but we haven't been actively searching for them," Nilsa replied.

"That means there could be another one to find?" Gondabar said, frowning.

"It wouldn't make much sense. If they were using them, as we believe they were, to travel great distances without needing to fly, why put two so close?" Raner reasoned as he moved a finger on the map on the table beside them.

"That's what we think too," Nilsa joined him at the table.

"Well, better that way," Gondabar relaxed a little.

"We have another important matter to deal with. The prisoners we rescued are all recuperated and in good health. We can't hold them any longer. So far, we used the excuse that it was for their own good, but the whole winter season has passed and they're demanding their freedom," Raner said.

"I know..." Gondabar said thoughtfully. "Do you believe we'll get anything else of relevance from any of them?"

Raner wrinkled his nose.

"I doubt it. No matter how often we've asked them their answers haven't been of much help. The fanatic ones continue proclaiming the end of the days of men and the arrival of the all-powerful, which we guess is the reborn dragon. The prisoners forced to work inside the volcano don't understand what happened to them, and many barely saw what went on from the terror they felt. The ones who saw the creature and realized what was happening, in spite of the horror,

21

confirmed they had seen a dragon come out of the wall, fall into the pit with liquid silver, and afterward fly out to the skies after tearing down the ceiling of the great cavern. All of their individual accounts agree. The details mentioned by the different people are the same, so we have to take them as truth, although they don't provide much light on the solution to the problem."

"Multiple people describing an event with similar details is considered a fact or a possible truth," Gondabar nodded. "That's why we believed what you've told us" he said to Nilsa.

"Thank you, sir." Nilsa realized the importance of the slaves having witnessed the rebirth of the dragon. Otherwise, the Panthers would have had a tough job convincing Gondabar and Raner, given there was no trace of the dragon and the expected attack bringing death and destruction had not occurred all winter.

"We've already held them long enough. Let them go," Gondabar ordered.

Raner nodded, "Very well, sir."

"Nilsa, make sure they are well taken care of and that each one receives a small amount of gold so they can go on with their lives and recover from such a traumatic experience. My assistants will provide you with the gold."

"That's very honorable, sir," Nilsa said, grateful for the gesture of the Leader of the Rangers. It was not common at all to compensate with gold, least of all among the Rangers where the pay was rather scarce and they seldom had any extra.

"We should have protected them better. We should have prevented what they've gone through at the hands of these slavers," said Gondabar.

"It won't happen again. I have several trustworthy Rangers devoted exclusively to seeking out sects and similar clandestine organizations in Norghana. We'll prevent it from ever happening again," Raner promised.

"I certainly hope so," Gondabar said, nodding repeatedly.

"I'll make sure to start preparations so they can resume their lives right away," Nilsa said.

"I'll come with you and help, Nilsa," Raner said.

"Good. Go and organize it all. If you hear news about the dragon or its sects I want to know at once."

"At your command, sir!" Nilsa said.

"Yes, sir, of course," Raner said as well.

The First Ranger and Nilsa left Gondabar's study. Nilsa had the feeling that they wouldn't be long in coming back to report, and it would not be good news.

Chapter 3

Ingrid and Viggo were riding together toward the city of Ostangor. Viggo was grumpier than usual, which surprised Ingrid. Lately he had been very cheerful with these "bug hunting" expeditions, as he called them, but for some reason he did not like this one, and Ingrid wondered why. They were outdoors, enjoying the beginning of spring on a "hunting operation," as Egil had called their outings and which, from what they had already experienced so far, often ended in a fight. There was no reason for the Assassin to be in a bad mood.

"Beautiful day for hunting, isn't it?" she said from her saddle as she inhaled the sweet, aromatic scent of the breeze that blew from the east.

"I just don't understand why we have to investigate each and every one of the alleged sightings of dragons or similar monsters Egil's agents tell him about," Viggo protested, frowning.

"Because one of those sightings could be Dergha-Sho-Blaska. Is it so hard to understand?"

"The thing is, it's never him. How many have we already checked out, twenty sightings? And what always happens? They're not bloody Dergha-Sho-Blaska!"

"Even so, we have to investigate every case because one of them could be him. We have to be thorough. Our chance to find and destroy him might be in any rumor of some wayward beast sighted."

"Sure, that's what the know-it-all says, which isn't necessarily true. So far, he's been proven wrong. Let me remind you that we haven't found the dragon, and my butt's flat from so much riding up and down chasing after unsubstantial rumors."

"No one said it would be easy. Egil's right, and I agree with him. We have to follow up on and check every possible occurrence. If, on the other hand, we only investigate some sightings, the more likely ones, the monster will escape."

"But it's always some Troll, giant lizard, colossal hairy spider, enraged albino bear, or pure fantasy of some lunatic who thinks he's seen a dragon," Viggo protested, waving his arms so much he

24

frightened his horse. "I never thought there were so many lunatics around seeing dragons and other nightmare creatures," he said as he pulled on the reins to calm his mount.

Ingrid shook her head. "The fact that two sects have been spreading apocalyptic messages of destruction throughout the kingdom is responsible for this. Those who hear and believe them start imagining things, or even seeing them."

"Because they're crazy as loons. It'd be best to tie and gag all of them and take them to Zangria, for instance, and set them all loose there so they can pester the Zangrians. Subversive war I'd call it," Viggo smiled, pleased with his idea.

"You're forgetting that they don't speak Zangrian. Your plan would fail."

"Bah, a small, insignificant detail. They'd pester them all the same, and since the Zangrians wouldn't understand them, it would only mean even more pestering for them."

"The Zangrians would most likely kill them all for spying or something like that. Remember, we're practically at war with the Zangrians, even if it hasn't been declared."

"All the better, that would be the end of the lunatic problem for us."

"You can't kill all the crazy people who come across a monster in Norghana."

"I'm not going to kill them, the Zangrians will."

"Yeah, yeah, but because you sent them there. Don't hide behind such a lame excuse," Ingrid scolded, wagging her finger at him.

"I'd be sending them on an excursion with my best wishes," Viggo replied, looking saintly. "If those Zangrian brutes killed them it wouldn't be my fault," he replied, shrugging with a look of pure innocence.

"Your thought process is completely twisted."

"Me? But I'm full of nothing but love," Viggo said, blowing her a kiss as he blinked rapidly.

"You're a pumpkin head, that's what you are."

"I love you too," Viggo replied lovingly.

Ingrid snorted and shook her head.

"The Ice Gods are punishing me for something I did in a previous life," she said, looking toward the snow-peaked mountains.

"On the contrary, they're rewarding you with my love and

devotion for something incredibly good you did," Viggo said, pointing both thumbs at himself.

"Yeah, sure, exactly," Ingrid snorted again and stroked her white horse's mane.

Viggo reined his mount in and looked to the west. Then he turned east and finally south. He nodded to himself.

"We're getting close. Krystall Lake, where there's been a supposed dragon sighting, is a little more to the north," he said, squinting as if trying to see it.

"I see you know this area of Norghana pretty well," Ingrid tried to elicit the reason from him. "It's unknown to me. I've never set foot in these valleys."

"You're not missing anything. The only important thing here is the city of Ostangor."

Ingrid knew that Ostangor was the second largest city in Norghana after the capital, although she had never visited it. She remembered hearing it mentioned for some reason.

"Why does this city ring a bell?"

"No reason, I think," Viggo replied instantly.

"Aren't you from here?" she asked him, beginning to remember that it had been Viggo himself who had mentioned Ostangor.

"Maybe, so what?"

"Hmmm… is that why you're in such a bad mood? Because we're returning to your home city?"

"No, not at all," Viggo said, lifting his chin. "The whole city can burn for all I care, and with all its inhabitants too. I'd set fire to it myself and would lock all the doors from outside so no one could get out."

"I know you didn't have a happy childhood, so I understand you're not thrilled to be back here," she said kindly.

"'Unhappy' doesn't even begin to describe my childhood. Don't make me talk about it, 'cause I don't feel like it…"

"That's exactly what I want. Tell me what happened to you as a child, you never explained much. I'd like to know, to understand…"

"I'm not in the mood for horror stories, least of all my own. Maybe some other time when I feel more cheerful. But I'll need a whole case of wine or a keg of beer to be able to tell you."

"Very well, I won't insist. But if you want a friendly ear, I'm here."

Viggo looked at her for an instant. He seemed to be about to say something but did not. He nodded and pointed to the hillock in front of them which the path led to.

"We'll see the city of Ostangor once we're up there."

"Good, we'll see what that city of yours looks like," said Ingrid and spurred her mount up the hill at a gallop.

"I don't understand the rush... it's not like there's anything to see..." Viggo commented as he followed her uphill, not in any hurry to reach the top.

Ingrid was watching the city in the distance with her hand shading her eyes from the sun. The temperature was great and even the sun was shining intensely in an ever-clearer sky. The winds were pushing the clouds toward the mountains, clearing the plain that began at the foot of the hill and in whose center the city stood.

"It doesn't look that bad. I thought it'd be, oh, I don't know, grimmer," Ingrid commented as Viggo came up the hill at a turtle's pace. He seemed to be making his poor horse go as slowly as it could.

"If you say so..." he muttered under his breath.

"It's the typical Norghanian city, robust, rustic, rocky, and a little dark, of sizeable proportions. It doesn't look that dangerous to me," Ingrid went on while she checked the city in the distance.

"Wait until night falls and you'll see whether it's dangerous or not."

"I guess that means it is," Ingrid glanced back, waiting for Viggo's reply.

"I couldn't tell you if it is now, only that it used to be, extremely dangerous, when I was a boy. I hope things have improved a little, but I doubt it."

"Why's that? It's been a long time, the King's law must have brought some order in the city."

Viggo smiled and let out a small guffaw.

"Have I ever told you how beautiful you become when you get so gullible?"

"What do you mean by gullible? I'm not gullible at all!"

Viggo moved his mount to her side, smiled at her, and gave her a lovelorn gaze.

"You believe in good, honor, and justice. That the King, his nobles, and their soldiers will fulfill their duties."

"Of course, I believe that."

Viggo nodded several times.

"That's why I'm saying you're gullible. Thank goodness you have me…"

"To make my life impossible?" Ingrid snapped in a tone that implied she had not liked the insinuation.

"To save you from yourself and your lofty ideals, which are completely unrealistic. Kings, nobles, and soldiers… all will disappoint you. You should know by now with everything we've lived through and what we've seen."

"I know all too well what they're like. And we've all lived through the same experiences, don't think I don't see it. Still, I keep hoping that one day it won't be like this."

"Dreaming is free, but keep in mind that your dreams may end up as nightmares. In any case, I'll keep your dreams and defend you from your nightmares."

"Wow, you're showing the troubadour vein in you again," Ingrid looked at him, surprised.

"Can't help it when I'm beside you, my beautiful northern-tempered blonde."

Ingrid rolled her eyes. Then she stared at him and said firmly, "One day kings, nobles, and soldiers will honor their subjects and will do their duty with honor, as they should."

"You're adorable," Viggo said lovingly.

"And you're a scatterbrain."

"But I'm your scatterbrain."

"Always," Ingrid snapped back, but her gaze went from angry to loving. "Come here and kiss me with those roguish lips of yours."

Viggo smiled, his eyes shining bright.

"Right away, my warrior beauty," and he kissed her passionately.

The spring skies bore witness to a love scene as deep as it was unlikely. Two such different people who, in spite of all odds and with everything against them and their own marked differences, could not help but love one another. A force that was greater than them, that of their feelings, drove them inexorably to a love which nothing could stop. They both knew that nothing would ever break them apart, no matter what. Their hearts were one and so it would be forever, although no one might understand how that could be.

"If anyone had ever told me that I would fall in love with you…"

"You'd have punched them in the jaw," Viggo interrupted.

"Absolutely," she smiled.

"I like seeing you smile, you do it too seldom."

"I'm not a person who smiles easily, I know. The bitter life I've lived has made me so. But my heart is joyful, and you make me smile."

"In that case I'll try to make you smile every day of your life. I'll make it a goal of mine."

Ingrid frowned thoughtfully.

"Thinking again, you don't need to make the effort."

"I've already said it, I can't take it back. You'll smile every day, at least once, or I won't be doing my job properly."

"Your job? And what's that then?"

"Being in love with you, of course," Viggo replied with a serious face.

Ingrid could not help but smile at those words, which touched her deeply.

"Kiss me again, my love."

"I will, happy and gladly," he said and kissed her again.

They stayed on the hill looking at the city in the distance for a while longer, happy and in love. They were aware that the moment they went into the metropolis that sweet moment they were sharing would vanish and they would be two Rangers once again, carrying out an official mission.

After a while Ingrid sighed and half-closed her eyes.

"Let's go into the city and find out information from the local authorities," she said in her usual determined tone.

Viggo wrinkled his nose and snorted.

"We'd better go straight to the lake, I know where it is. We don't need to go into the city."

"We have to speak to the authorities and get all the information they have before going to the lake. Besides, we should ask for reinforcements, Gondabar's orders."

"Yeah, our old and ailing leader doesn't want us to face a dragon on our own. Although, on the other hand, he doesn't fully believe the dragon is real. I guess it must be his age and ailments."

"Don't be bitter, I can see you coming."

"I'm not being bitter. I say things as I see them. He probably thinks we're crazy anyway and that's why he wants us to have reinforcements, to ask them what happened afterward."

Ingrid bowed her head.

"I don't think that's a bad precaution. If someone came to me and told me such an unlikely story as ours, I'd also want to make sure there was no foul play behind it."

"Rather than unlikely, the story is outrageous. I say that because every time we tell someone new you only need to see the way they react. Their face takes on a look of being addressed by total lunatics."

"Yeah, it would be better not to tell others unless absolutely necessary. And now, let's go to the city. I don't know why you don't want to visit it, since you grew up here, but it doesn't matter. We'll follow Gondabar's protocol and investigate with local support, never on our own."

Viggo muttered something under his breath and then looked at Ingrid.

"As you wish. But I'm telling you that it's not worth entering the city, and you won't find any help, rather the very opposite."

"It can't be that bad."

"No, it'll be worse, you'll see," Viggo warned her as he started down the hill toward the city.

Ingrid was thoughtful for a moment. Viggo's words sounded like a bad omen and she was not used to that. She shrugged the feeling off—whatever they found, they would deal with it. She was confident. Besides, she was curious to see the city where Viggo had been born and grown up. Perhaps by visiting it she might understand his personality better. She cheered up. It was going to be an interesting visit. She followed Viggo to the city.

Chapter 4

They entered the big city through the southern entrance. The city was surrounded by a robust wall about thirty-six feet tall by nine wide, not the tallest but robust indeed. It had no moat or large defensive towers, nor a very elaborate battlement; the wall was protected by a dozen small turrets located at regular intervals along the whole perimeter and the battlement was a long parapet of unpolished rock. They had built that wall to serve as defense but without any filigree. It was functional and rough, like many Norghanian buildings.

From what Ingrid knew, it was a city that lived off the mines and trade of the raw material obtained from them, as well as the tools and personnel needed to operate them. As any good commercial city, the gates were wide open, and all kind of traders, peddlers, merchants, and the like came and went through the city with their mule- or oxen-driven carts in a steady transit that provided the city with all kinds of merchandise. They could also see peasants and farmers coming to the city to sell their produce and bring their cattle for slaughter.

The guards at the gate were more concerned with the flow of traffic than possible threats, so Ingrid and Viggo were able to get in without having to stop and present themselves. They went along the main street slowly, following a trader that was leading three riding horses. There were people coming and going in both directions and the passersby crossed from one side of the street to the other.

"Is it always so busy?" Ingrid asked Viggo.

"Yeah, as far as I remember. The city is prosperous commercially, but decadent in other aspects…"

"What do you mean?" Ingrid looked around, trying to understand.

"Don't worry, you'll find out. It's an interesting city…"

"I'm not sure I like what your tone's implying."

Viggo grinned. "Let's not get ahead of ourselves. Look around and let the city seduce you with its charm."

Ingrid made a face.

"I never let anything seduce me."

"That's why you're my beautiful warrior."

A snort and a glare were the answer Viggo got for his flattery.

As they went further along Ostangor's streets, Ingrid noticed that for a large commercial and populated city it did look quite decadent. The houses were unpainted and uncared for—she could see filth and neglect in the façades. The balconies looked as if they could fall if the winter wind blew strong. The roofs did not look any better, they did not look as if they could withstand one more snowfall.

"Why do the houses here look like that? Are we in a bad neighborhood?" she asked as she watched people wandering from one end to the other. They looked like regular Norghanian workers, the kind you found in all the cities in the realm. They had no out-of-the-ordinary characteristics, although they might look a little dirtier, but Ingrid put it down to the mines and all the filth they produced.

Viggo choked, laughing.

"Bad neighborhood? This is one of the good ones, with working people."

Ingrid kept looking around as they rode along the street with its irregular cobblestones, which caused the horses to slip.

"Why are the houses so neglected?" she said, indicating one to her right that had a balcony hanging half off one end.

"It's because of the maintenance tax."

"I don't remember hearing about any maintenance tax on a house," Ingrid was puzzled.

"It's been in existence for a long time, as well as many other taxes. They fill the Magistrate's chests. He rules the city, and he in turn fills those of Duke Pilman Wrotoson, who owns the city since it's in the middle of his duchy."

"A city doesn't belong to any noble. He has rights on it but it's not his," Ingrid replied.

"Well, you can explain that to Wrotoson, but he's not the kind who likes to listen. Him or his two sons: Lars and Angus. He's certainly behaved as if the city were his, and his sons do the same. When I was a child, they were already freely abusing their power, and they were only a few years older than I was. After all these years... I don't even want to imagine."

"Pity. It's awful that the nobles and their families take advantage of their privileged situations for personal ends. And the fact that they're despots makes it even worse."

"I don't wholly agree with you."

"Who rules the city?"

"Unless it's changed, which it might have, since I haven't been here since I entered the Rangers, that would be Magistrate Mustrel and his city guard."

"The Duke's soldiers?"

"Not exactly. The Duke and his soldiers live in the castle his lordship has further north, near the great mines."

"So, then it's the Magistrate who governs the city?"

"As a front for the Duke and the King, yes, but in reality, this city is ruled by a couple of underworld syndicates."

Ingrid looked at Viggo, frowning.

"Explain what you mean by that. Outlaws and thieves don't govern cities, least of all one as big and rich as this one."

Viggo smiled tenderly, looking at Ingrid.

"There's a lot you still don't know about this tough and cruel world, and I hate to be the one to show it to you."

"Whatever I need to know and understand, I will. I'd rather you explained, I trust you completely. If I had to learn it any other way it might be worse."

Viggo nodded and was thoughtful.

"Fine. I'll explain as we come across them. Although I feel like someone ruining a little girl's birthday."

"Don't worry, this little girl will give you a black eye if you don't explain in full detail," Ingrid said, showing him her right fist.

"I'm suddenly over any qualms I might have had, why do you think that might be?" The irony of the comment was clear.

"Where are the soldiers stationed in the city?" Ingrid asked, rising in her stirrups to see better.

"A little more to the northwest, in the highest part of the city. There's a fort with a regiment there. Beside the fortress there's another military-looking building but which is really a large prison. They put anyone they catch in there."

"That's more like it."

"Well, you wait and see, then you tell me."

Ingrid was intrigued by his reply.

They went on along the streets of the great city. Viggo guided Ingrid and took shortcuts he remembered down or up less busy streets to avoid the people wandering everywhere. The streets he picked were narrower and less favored by traders, which allowed them to ride more comfortably. Not that the people got in their way on purpose, but they prevented the horses from keeping a steady pace.

Viggo took a left turn and they went down a street until they came to an empty area crowded with stalls.

"And this is the great central market," Viggo announced with a wave of his hand that took in the whole square.

"It's huge," Ingrid swept her gaze across the enormous square.

"They say it's one of the largest markets in Norghana, if not the largest."

"It's certainly the biggest one I've ever seen."

"It's not only big, but also this busy and crowded every three days. We've arrived on market day, so you'll be able to enjoy it. Tomorrow and the day after most of the stalls will be gone to return on the third day."

"That's a curious system," Ingrid nodded thoughtfully.

"It's so they have time to replenish the goods they want to sell. There's so much trade that most of the products vanish in a single day."

Ingrid listened to Viggo's explanations as she looked at the place. They had stopped their horses at the entrance of the great market and had stood aside so the people and the carts could go by—they all seemed eager to get to the square. The more she watched the place the bigger it looked to her, not only in size but in people. It was undoubtedly enormous. There were hundreds, or rather a thousand stalls, where all kind of wares were traded.

"Is it just me, or is everything organized in quadrants?" Ingrid commented as she squinted, trying to take in all the details of the busy place.

"You've got a good eye, although now there are many more quadrants than I remember, from what I'm seeing."

At the upper left corner there were farming stalls, selling a variety of local vegetables, some fruits, wheat, other cereals, and the like. The residents came to the stalls for fresh produce. Those with more money could also indulge in a little sweet fruit, but the rest made do with the basics: lots of legumes, carrots, and onions mainly.

Beside the fruit and vegetables stalls they saw the meat. Here you could see miners looking for a good joint of meat to put in their stomachs. They were unmistakable since they were dirty from head to toe, wrapped in dark cloaks that only revealed their eyes. Pork sausages and knuckle as well as ribs seem to be the favorite among the hungry workers, or it might be that the steak was too expensive for them. Funnily enough, chicken and other domestic fowl did not have as much success with the miners.

At the upper right corner, the farmers used small corrals to show their horses, cows, oxen, mules, donkeys, and other animals to prospective buyers. The Rangers did not see miners here—the customers looked cleaner and better dressed. It was obviously a wealthier social group.

Viggo and Ingrid went over to look at the animals on sale.

"This section is one I like less. It always smells horrible, like horse, cow, and ox manure," Viggo said with a look of disgust in his face.

"You should be used to it; we spend half our lives on horses."

"Yeah, but ours are the only ones, and they're not pooping all the time in the same spot like all these," he said, pointing at the horses nickering behind the fence.

Ingrid bent over to look at a cow delivering a smelly load.

"In this case I'm totally right, let's keep going." Viggo made a comical face, pinching his nose with two fingers, and they continued making their way through the market.

At the lower left corner were the bakers. Their breads, cakes, and desserts were the delight of many, especially the younger crowd. Many citizens came for bread, mostly the cheapest kind, and some even bought stale bread to make a kind of soup. They put it in milk and it was a powerful breakfast or supper. The delicious desserts were only within reach of the wealthiest.

At the lower right corner, business over the mining produce was conducted. It was the largest section and clearly defined by the piles of ore recently extracted on display by the stalls. There were silver, lead, copper, zinc, and iron piles that would be made into domestic utensils, all kinds of weapons, precious jewels, and also coin. A swarm of traders surrounded these stalls and seemed to be negotiating at the top of their voices. There were dozens of them, since the minerals stalls attracted the most people in the whole market.

"I see that the most important trade is focused on mining."

"And that's always been the case. This city is rich and populous thanks to the northern mines. They're not far from the city, near the north gate, which had to be divided into four so as to facilitate the mining transit. The gate gives access to the roads that lead to the mines. I don't recommend visiting—you swallow a lot of dust and filth and it smells awful."

Ingrid nodded.

"I'm not particularly interested in mines. But I do find the way they sell precious minerals here curious."

"Curious? I find it natural, shouting at the top of your voice."

"I'd never seen it done this way."

"Since the production of mineral varies in quantity and quality, especially from one mine to the next, they bring it all here to compete for prices. The traders who buy it examine the quality thoroughly and look for the competition so the prices go down, hence all the yelling and agitated gestures of the buyers. If you look carefully, you'll see that the traders barely react. They try to maintain the high price, ignoring the bidding. I've always found it most entertaining."

"Sure, because of the uproar. If they were buying dresses you'd be immediately bored."

"The clothes stalls are in the upper middle section. Would you like to take a look? I'd love to give you a pretty gala dress. You'd look beautiful."

Ingrid glared at him.

"You'd better not be making fun of me."

Viggo raised both hands.

"I wouldn't dare. I mean it. I've never seen you in a dress. You must be a real sight, a vision, a spirit of beauty from the realm of the Gods, and icy, with that northern beauty of yours so hard and cold."

"Hard and cold like the steel that I *do* want to see. Where are the weapons stalls?"

"Really, how can you be so heartless? You don't appreciate my bard's soul."

"It's not that I don't appreciate it, it's that you're such a bad poet. And your flattering verses are horrible."

Viggo snorted and mimicked stabbing his own heart.

The weapons stalls were in the lower center of the square.

"Let's leave the horses over there, in front of that inn, and let's go over to look at them," Ingrid suggested.

"Then no dresses, only weapons," Viggo commented with a look of dismay on his face.

"Exactly. Don't you ever forget it. If you wanted a pretty damsel of the nobility dressed in beautiful dresses and jewels, you picked the wrong woman."

"I can swear without an ounce of doubt that I don't. I have the perfect woman for me," Viggo smiled at her mischievously.

"You'd better," Ingrid replied, dismounting.

Viggo spoke to the inn's stable boy and gave him a coin so he would look after the horses. Before the boy walked away Viggo grabbed his arm and whispered in his ear.

"If anything happens to the horses, I'll slit your throat."

The boy opened his eyes wide.

"Nothing will happen to them... sir..."

"Mark my words," Viggo turned to Ingrid and let the boy leave.

"What did you say that made him look so scared?" she asked.

"Nothing, I was paying him for his service. I was only reminding him to do it properly."

Ingrid understood and her face showed it. She nodded at Viggo so he would follow her. They walked over to the weapons stalls, making their way through the crowd that seemed to want to see everything, although they were not doing much buying. Ingrid elbowed her way through without qualms and Viggo followed her, smiling. They reached a stall with Norghanian axes and Ingrid stopped to admire the craftsmanship of several of the weapons.

"Nothing like holding a good weapon in your hand to feel better," she said, holding the axe firmly as she looked at it appreciatively.

"Whenever I hear you talk like that, I remember why I love you so much," Viggo said, smiling as he picked another axe and studied it.

"Now say I'm not romantic," Ingrid replied.

Viggo burst out laughing.

"You're absolutely right."

Ingrid left the axe she had in her hand and picked up a larger one while the salesman gave her all kinds of explanations and details about how exceptional the weapon was. All of a sudden, Viggo slid toward Ingrid as if he was going to put his arm around her, but what he grabbed was someone else's arm.

Ingrid noticed the movement and turned swiftly, brandishing the axe.

"What's this?" she asked, looking at Viggo holding a boy not over ten years old by the wrist.

"Let me go, I haven't done anything!" the boy pleaded. His hair was blond like the sun's rays and his skin was white as snow, although covered in filth. All of him was filthy; he seemed to have just come out of the mine.

"Of course, you've done something," Viggo argued, squeezing his arm harder.

"I haven't done anything!" the boy insisted, trying to get away and pulling back, but his arm was tightly held.

"What have you done?" Ingrid asked in a hard tone.

"Nothing at all!" the boy cried while trying to free his arm from Viggo's grip.

"Return the pouch," Viggo said seriously.

"I don't have a pouch!"

Several people had turned to look and were watching the scene with curiosity, although they did not intervene. The trader also craned his neck to see what was going on, and so did one of his helpers.

"If you don't return the pouch and I find it on you after stripping you naked right here, I'll cut off this arm," Viggo threatened with such a murderous tone that the boy froze. He stopped trying to escape and no longer tried to deny anything.

Ingrid reached her free hand to her Ranger's belt for the pouch with her pay and did not find it.

"You little thief!" she cried angrily. "You stole it! You've just gotten yourself in a deep mess!"

"A thief!" cried one of the customers at the next stall, and more people came to see what the fuss was about.

"Here it is," the boy said, and with his free hand he produced the pouch as if it were a magic trick.

Ingrid took the pouch and looked at the little crook in disbelief.

"You're just a kid."

"Don't you believe that. He's a professional thief, he's been doing this for years," Viggo said.

"No, sir, this is my first time, they made me do it," he said, sobbing.

"Don't believe him, he's lying, it's all fake," Viggo said, shaking his head.

"Bloody thieves, they're a plague worse than rats!" cried one of the onlookers.

"Hand him over to the Magistrate, let him hang the thief!" said the trader. "I'm tired of them robbing my customers and not letting me do business in peace."

Ingrid looked at Viggo.

"Don't tell me they'll hang him for this? They'll just send him to jail for a while..."

"Not here. There are too many like him. When thieves are caught the city makes an example of them, it's always been like that."

"So they learn!" said another buyer.

"It's the best thing to do with them!" said another.

"Let me go, sir!" the boy begged Viggo, looking him in the eyes. He was now weeping with tears that looked real.

"If I hand you over to the guards or this mob," Viggo said with a nod at those who were already asking for the boy's head, "you won't see another day."

"No, please! Let me go!"

"First tell me who you're working for."

"For no one sir, I swear it!"

"You're lying again," Viggo pulled the boy closer.

"I'm not lying!" he tried to break loose and escape but he could not.

"They all lie. They're all liars and thieves, from the cradle!" a man shouted.

Viggo grabbed the boy by the neck with his arm and whispered so that no one else might hear.

"Do you work for the Red Fox's Syndicate or for the Crazy Crow's?"

The boy stopped struggling. He looked up at Viggo, trying to decipher who he was and how he knew those names.

"I..."

"You can tell me. I was once like you," Viggo whispered.

"No, that's not possible."

"There's a life after the gang, you can get out. Don't think it's impossible. I am living proof."

The boy was staring at Viggo and it was clear he did not trust him, that his words did not convince him.

Viggo turned him around hard toward the side where there were no people shouting. He showed him the mark in the inner side of his left arm.

"See the mark of the gang?"

The boy saw the tattoo in the shape of a black circle.

"You're from the Crazy Crow's Syndicate!" he muffled a cry.

"I was, yes. What's your syndicate?" Viggo asked, turning him around again as if he were struggling with him so the onlookers would not notice what they were up to.

"The Red Fox's."

"Show me."

The boy rolled up his sleeve and showed him the tattoo of a red circle.

"I see we begin to understand one another," Viggo whispered. "What do they call you?"

"Strips, sir."

"We'll drag him by his ears to the law!" another man who had come to see what was afoot shouted.

Ingrid was looking at Viggo, intrigued while she kept back the crowd with one hand.

"Very well, Strips, listen to me. Things aren't looking good for you, so pay attention," Viggo whispered a few words in his ear.

"Yes, sir... thank you, sir...." The boy was staring at Viggo, not sure whether Viggo would indeed do what he had told him.

"We'll take him to the guards," Viggo said out loud, looking at the group around them.

"Yeah, to be executed!"

"He must be an example. Teach them a lesson!"

Right then Strips kicked Viggo in the shin, making him cry out. He let go of his arm and the boy ran off like lightning toward the south.

"He's running!"

"Go after him!"

Several people ran after Strips, who dodged people and slipped through the crowd with ease—they would never catch him.

While the onlookers dispersed, Ingrid came over to Viggo.

"What was all that?" she asked him, raising an eyebrow.

Viggo looked around; they were already alone.

"I told him to kick me and that I would let him go. To run south and not get caught or he wouldn't live to tell the tale. It appears to have had an effect on the boy."

"Yeah, I saw. Now will you tell me why you were so magnanimous?"

"Well, I kinda liked the little crook," Viggo shrugged.

"And nothing else?"

"Nothing that needs to be explained right now," Viggo smiled.

"Sure…" Ingrid crossed her arms.

"Keep an eye on your saddle bags and your traveling pack. As we go further in, we'll be the target of more of these city thieves."

"Little thieves like this one?"

"Yup, boys and girls who rob the unwary."

"Kids are thieves in this city?"

"And they're organized. They belong to different thieves' syndicates. They're very well organized, at least they were when I was growing up here. I don't know how things are now, but I doubt they've changed much."

"The authorities should stop children from being used like that," Ingrid said with a look of incomprehension on her face.

"The authorities here are quite lax as to fulfilling their duties, as you'll soon discover," Viggo said with irony. "Let's continue to the fortress. It's time you met with the local authorities; you're going to love them." He made a face.

"I'm dreading it. Will I be upset?"

"Quite," Viggo confirmed as he went for the horses.

"I'm not sure I like this city much."

"Oh no, you're going to love it, you'll see," Viggo said, coming back with their mounts.

They got in the saddle and left the market square.

"Just one warning, my beautiful blonde warrior—don't punch the local authorities, you'd get us in a jam."

Ingrid eyed him, puzzled, but understood the warning.

"I'll try, but I can't promise anything."

Chapter 5

It did not take them long to reach the fortress that served as Magistrate Mustrel's command quarters. It was a building halfway between a fort and a castle, and it looked as if whoever had started it had not had very clear ideas on how to finish it, or perhaps one person had started and another one with different ideas had finished it. Another building rose beside it, a little smaller, also military-looking, which was the city jail. They could see arms reaching out and faces looking through the small barred windows.

They dismounted before the reinforced doors of the building. A dozen soldiers of the city guard were watching the door from the outside. They did not look friendly. Above the doors on the battlement were a dozen more soldiers with bows. They were watchful.

"Rangers on an official mission," Ingrid announced.

The soldiers studied Ingrid and Viggo from head to toe. One of them, a veteran, stepped forward and greeted them with a nod.

"Sergeant Lomen, in charge of keeping the doors," he said. "We're not used to seeing many Rangers around here. I'll need to see your Ranger medallions, nothing personal, simply a precaution."

"It's unusual to ask for such a thing," Ingrid replied, annoyed.

"This is a somewhat dangerous city. Deceit and tricks are everywhere, and we take extraordinary precautions. As I said, it's nothing personal, just what things are like here."

Viggo took out his Ranger medallion and showed it to the Sergeant—only that one, he kept the Specialties medallions hidden. Ingrid was more reluctant, but seeing the Sergeant watching her waiting for her to show hers, she finally took it out.

Lomen looked at the medallions.

"Welcome, Rangers," he said at last.

"We appreciate the welcome," replied Ingrid.

"How can we help the Rangers?"

"We wish to see the city Magistrate," Ingrid said in a serious tone.

"Hmmm… Magistrate Mustrel is a very busy man, I'm not sure he'll have the time…"

"Inform him of our request, Sergeant," Ingrid ordered.

The officer looked her up and down and realized she was determined.

"Very well, I'll inform him of your request. You may wait here," he said and turning, headed to the doors.

"We also need food and water and somewhere to freshen up," Viggo said with a mischievous grin the Sergeant did not see.

"The King's Rangers have a right to that in any fort, castle, fortress, or military camp of any kind," added Ingrid.

Lomen stopped and turned.

"Yes, that is so, they have. Follow me," he gestured toward the battlement. "Open the door!" he shouted.

The great door took a while to open. As it did, Ingrid and Viggo saw another dozen soldiers pushing it.

The Sergeant waved for them to follow him and went into the fortress, Ingrid and Viggo went after him. The building was rectangular with a covered passage that led to a large courtyard. The first floors around the wide courtyard appeared to be barracks for the soldiers. Officers and persons of rank must be housed in the upper levels.

Lomen led them through the courtyard to the back of the building. Several groups of soldiers were listlessly practicing movements of attack and defense with axe and round wooden shield. Two officers of the guard were barking orders, but they were not putting too much interest into it either. Indeed, that way of training was quite different from how the army did it, where the soldiers put forth real effort or ended up in jail. Not to speak of the harsh training the Rangers had to go through and the seriousness they approached it with.

That did not seem to be the case here; in fact, it was more pretending to practice than the real thing. The permissiveness of the officers made Ingrid so angry that she almost stopped to tell them a few things about their lack of discipline and professionalism. Being a soldier and an officer of the guard was a profession that required some basic principles, and she was not seeing them in practice here.

Viggo noticed what Ingrid was thinking and gently pushed her forward so she would keep going and not stop to tell off the officers and soldiers of the city guard. With his other hand he waved her on to follow the Sergeant and smiled at her trying to dissipate her annoyance for what she was witnessing. Luckily, and after a slight hesitancy, Ingrid went on, although it was obvious, by the brightness in her eyes and her frowning, that she was not happy.

They went in through one of the doors that opened onto the courtyard and went up to the third floor. There were several soldiers on guard in the long corridors. The building, being military, was not at all elegant, and it was rather rudimentary. The walls were rock with windows either barred or narrow so as to allow for shooting with bows to defend the position. The doors they went through were made of oak reinforced with steel to resist breaching.

Lomen led them to a room watched by two guards. He knocked and went in. Viggo and Ingrid waited outside until the Sergeant appeared again.

"You may come in," he told them.

They went into the hall. It was a wide room with windows that looked out to the back of the building and let in a lot of light. Four men were sitting behind rustic working desks. A fifth man, the Magistrate, was sitting in a large armchair enjoying the light of the sun as it came in through one of the large windows and bathed his body.

"Magistrate Mustrel, the Rangers that wish to see you, sir," Sergeant Lomen said.

"Come in, please," the Magistrate waved them in from his large armchair. The four men who were working, writing on scrolls, raised their heads to see who had entered and went on writing.

"Magistrate," Ingrid greeted him with military formality.

The man was in his fifties. He was chubby and had dark eyes and an aquiline nose, his blond hair was short, and he was wearing a big necklace over high-quality clothes, the kind nobles used. In fact, if it were not for the necklace that indicated his rank in the city, he would pass for any wealthy nobleman. A Magistrate was acknowledged and respected for the large gold and silver necklace with a square sapphire as the main jewel he always wore around his neck.

"I was dealing with the city's business. As you can see, they don't give me a moment's rest. I already have four scribes and I'm overwhelmed with everything that must be dealt with in the city. I'm going to have to hire a fifth one, and it's not easy to find people trained for this job. Managing a great city is difficult and exhausting," he proclaimed as he continued enjoying the warmth of the sun.

44

"Magistrates have as complex a job as an arduous one," Viggo said before Ingrid could speak. "Especially in this populous and radiant city."

Mustrel looked at Viggo.

"Very true. I always say that, without people like us who spend most of the day managing everything, this city would be chaos and not the commercial power it is. Only Norghania, the capital, is larger and has more trade than us, which is only natural since the Court is there."

"This city is not only radiant, but an example for other Norghanian metropolises to follow that try to emulate us without success," Viggo said flatteringly.

Ingrid looked at Viggo, surprised. She had no idea what he intended with all that flattery; it was unusual coming from him.

"That's what I'm always telling the Count. This city is an example to follow, a beacon in the night that guides the rest of the kingdom's cities. None can rival our city's prosperity."

"Doubtless Duke Pilman Wrotoson appreciates the well-being of his diligent Magistrate," Viggo went on, now appearing to imitate Egil's manner of speaking.

"Unfortunately, he and his sons think I must extract more benefits every season. They don't understand that you can't strangle traders with heavy taxing. Any good magistrate knows you need to keep the city traders happy so that trade prospers. Traders know they must pay their taxes and they do, but I make sure those taxes aren't heavy enough to break them."

"A delicate and difficult task no doubt," Viggo commented.

"You have no idea. Finding a balance that satisfies traders and merchants and at the same time allows the city to grow, and which also pleases the Count and his family, is extremely difficult."

"But a good magistrate finds that balance, which speaks well of his abilities and intelligence," Viggo commented.

"Thanks, I'm glad you appreciate my work. That isn't always the case with visitors. Tell me, what brings you to our beloved city, Rangers? How can I help you?" Mustrel asked.

Ingrid realized then that Viggo had been manipulating the Magistrate to get him in a good mood, which would make their mission easier. She thought it was an intelligent move on Viggo's part. The fact that they were Rangers did not guarantee the full collaboration of magistrates and nobles. Such people could not refuse the King's orders, but they could be uncooperative.

"We're on an official mission. Gondabar is sending us to investigate the strange events of Lake Krystall," Ingrid explained.

There was a moment of silence. The Magistrate eyed his scribes and then Sergeant Lomen.

"I see that rumors have spread... I wasn't expecting them to reach the capital. Or that they would have roused the King's interest.... It's a local matter...." The expression on his face was worried.

"They have," Ingrid assured him.

"There have been some unfortunate incidents... but I can promise they've been investigated already by order of the Duke, since they reflect poorly on his duchy's reputation. His lordship can't have deaths and disappearances scaring the good locals. I can confirm that after the investigations nothing of interest has been found."

"In any case, we need to speak with whoever carried out the investigation," Ingrid said.

"Stirring up such a murky business can only cause more rumors. The Duke won't be happy."

"We're here on an official mission, we have to investigate. These are our orders," Ingrid insisted.

Mustrel did not like Ingrid's reply. He seemed to want to end the matter and leave it well buried and forgotten.

"Have Captain Ingers come," he ordered.

Lomen rushed out to fetch him.

"I'm often surprised to see how the good name of a duchy can be affected by small isolated incidents. The Duke is distraught by this matter, and he will be even more upset once he finds out it's reached the King's Rangers."

"Why should he be? We've come to solve the problem," Ingrid said with a look of incomprehension on her face.

"It's a problem the Duke would rather the King had not heard of..." Mustrel muttered. "It makes him look, let's say... incompetent... for not having been able to deal with the matter."

"His subjects are vanishing and being eaten by some kind of beast. The King should know what's happening, as well as his Rangers. Only then will we be able to do something about it."

"Yes, but it's an ugly business. It would've been better to leave it in the Duke's hands, and mine… as I've already told you, it's been investigated, and nothing relevant has been found," Mustrel explained firmly.

"Unfortunately, people have died. We need to find out why. It could be repeated. It is a matter of importance, and we Rangers have been sent to investigate," Ingrid explained firmly.

"Very well, I won't insist. I see you're very zealous in your duties."

"As any good Ranger would be," Ingrid said.

Captain Ingers came into the room with Sergeant Lomen.

"You called, sir?" he asked Mustrel.

"Yes, please explain to these good Rangers the findings from your investigation at Lake Krystall."

Ingers looked at Ingrid and Viggo.

"I guess you've heard rumors and that's why you're here," he began. "Several people have disappeared in the lake and its surroundings and the locals have begun talking about a monster that eats the unwary. From what they told us, about half a dozen have gone missing, on different days and at different times of the day, but all near the lake. We found traces of dry blood but no bodies. The locals are frightened and speak of a beast that eats people."

"That's what we've heard. What kind of beast?" Viggo asked with interest.

"Well… you see… they're speaking of… a dragon…" the Captain said, clearly uncomfortable.

"Nonsense, there are no dragons," Mustrel replied. "Everyone knows that."

"Well… the locals are peasants and miners. They're not very educated and they're afraid of legends and mythology," the Captain excused them. "If you hear them speak, you'll realize that they do believe it's a dragon or some similar beast."

"That's because they're ignorant illiterates and they believe in witchcraft tales. I'm sure they also believe that witches kidnap babies in their cradles while the parents sleep and sacrifice them to drink their blood," Mustrel commented in a tone of superiority and condescension.

"Yes… they believe that… peasants are very superstitious, sir."

"Bah, it was probably a Troll that's gone back into hiding in his lair. I don't understand the interest," Mustrel said, waving his arms as

47

if the whole matter were nonsense.

"Yes. If that's the case we'll verify it and catch the beast," Ingrid confirmed.

"If it's a mountain Troll you'd better take reinforcements," said Mustrel. "The last thing I want is for something to happen to two Rangers on an official mission. It would be a terrible fiasco and the Duke would have to give explanations, and he's not the kind who likes to give them, least of all official ones."

"We could do with a city guard detail," Ingrid said.

Mustrel thought about it.

"Very well, Captain Ingers, take a detachment and accompany the Rangers. Find that Troll or whatever it is and finish it off. Let's end this matter before there are more ramifications no one is interested in."

"Yes, sir. Very well, sir."

"We appreciate the help the Magistrate offers us," Ingrid said.

"Magistrate Mustrel of the city of Ostangor, loyal servant of the king, always works with his Rangers. You can pass it along."

"We'll do that," Ingrid said.

"Shall we leave at dawn?" asked Captain Ingers.

"At first light," Ingrid confirmed.

"We'll give you lodgings in the guest section," Mustrel said with a wave at Sergeant Lomen so he would take care of things.

"Right away, sir," the Sergeant replied. "Come with me, please," he said to Ingrid and Viggo.

They left the room and headed to the guest rooms. They would leave at dawn for Lake Krystall. If they were lucky, they would find Dergha-Sho-Blaska.

Chapter 6

Egil and Gerd were before the tall, handsome tower waiting in their saddles to be received. The breeze was beginning to grow warm in the southern part of the realm and the sun was shining timidly in an almost clear sky. Spring was on its way, and with it, life was being reborn in Norghana and all Tremia.

"I love this season," Gerd told Egil while he stroked his horse's neck.

"So do I, it soothes the soul. Nothing like witnessing life starting again in nature to feel comforted and cheered," Egil replied, smiling.

"They say in my village that this is the season of life and winter is that of death. I guess because it's farming country."

"There are many that see it that way, not only farmers, my friend. I don't see winter as a season of death, rather as a passage toward a season of regeneration and life."

Gerd nodded. Then he stared at the rocky structure.

"Do you think he'll see us?" Gerd asked with a nod at the tower whose gate remained shut. There was no movement either outside the tall round tower or inside, at least apparently.

"I'm not sure. He's refused all my prior requests, but this time he might agree to see us."

"Have you used any of your contacts?"

"I've rather used all of them at once. If he doesn't see us this time, I don't think he ever will."

Gerd continued staring at the gray rocky tower that seemed to shine as the sun rays touched it. There were windows along the walls forming a round climbing spiral. The tower ended in a pointed roof with a large golden tip over nine feet tall that crowned it.

"The tower that Erudite lives in is truly handsome. It even has a lovely garden surrounding it."

Egil nodded, looking at the building and the large gardens.

"The tower is quite singular and certainly pretty. For a long time it was believed that a powerful Mage of the Dark Arts lived in it. It really was a rumor that Erudite Alvis Dyktig, who's the person actually living here, created and spread so he would be left to study in peace. He also led people to believe that a number of men had died trying to get in to rob him. Soon all the snoops stopped coming near for fear of what might happen to them."

"So, it's not true then?"

Egil shook his head.

"Alvis is a wise man with extensive knowledge of countless subjects, one of the most knowledgeable people in all Tremia, but he's no mage, and least of all in the Dark Arts. He's also never killed any thief."

"Why doesn't he want to see anyone?"

"He doesn't like being disturbed. He lives in this tower with several of his pupils, deep in his studies. He doesn't wish to be disturbed. His studies are everything to him. Everything and the only thing."

"Wow... quite unfriendly."

"It's not that he's unfriendly, he's simply focused on his studies and for him there's nothing else. He has no time for other trivialities and distractions, as he calls them."

"I see, he prefers books to humans."

"That is indeed correct."

"In that case, I'm not sure I'm going to like him much."

"We'll first have to meet..." Egil interrupted himself. The great gate to the tower had just opened. A man appeared and came out into the garden. He looked at them. He was in his sixties, and bald with the exception of a whitish ring that went around the back of his head. He was dressed in a gray robe with white embroidery, and around his neck they could see a gold chain with a medallion with the ancient symbol of knowledge.

"My lord, the honorable Alvis Dyktig, wants you to know that he is very busy and does not wish to receive guests."

"We know that, but we have matters of the utmost urgency to discuss with him," Egil said in a serious tone.

"My lord insists that he does not wish to be disturbed and I, as his First Pupil, must beg you to leave this place and go on your way."

"We know how important the Erudite's studies are, and if there were any other way, we would not have come to disturb him. Unfortunately, we must insist."

"Have you brought the signed order you claim to have?"

Egil took out a rolled parchment out of his right saddlebag.

50

"Here it is."

The man snorted.

"Fine. Follow me. My lord will see you, much to his chagrin."

Egil smiled and turned to Gerd with a relieved look on his face. They dismounted and tethered their horses to one of the trees in the garden. They went into the tower, following the First Pupil who had come out to greet them. If the outside of the tower was singular and beautiful, the inside was the dream of any scholar.

"My goodness..." Egil could not help himself and his jaw fell.

All the walls of the entrance to the tower, even the stairs that led to the upper floors themselves, were lined with books. It was as if they had decided to cover every bit of rock with tomes. They were all placed so you could only see the spines of them. There were hundreds of them just in the hallway alone. Gerd craned his neck to look at the upper levels and saw they were the same, the walls covered with books. He looked up the stairs and saw that all the rock had also been lined with countless books.

"Wait here for a moment," the man told them, indicating an inner room on the ground floor. They went in and found themselves in a room with study tables and chairs. The walls were all books.

"They're not for decoration, are they?" Gerd whispered to Egil.

"What do you think, big guy?"

"That they use those books, because they're placed as if they were on shelves. I guess they have a way of holding them in place that we can't see."

"Irrefutable, my dear giant friend," Egil replied with a grin.

"I bet the cellar's full of more books as well," Gerd said, following the stairs that went underground with his gaze.

"That'll be where the forbidden books are kept," Egil said in a serious tone.

"You're kidding, aren't you?" Gerd asked, his eyes widening.

"Not at all," Egil replied as he started looking through the tomes while they waited to be received.

"Well, that's neat... forbidden books... I'd rather not imagine what they're about," Gerd made a face.

"Better not, you know it doesn't agree with you," Egil smiled at him and patted his huge back.

Gerd snorted. "Not at all," he agreed.

"What I would give to spend some time in this tower..." Egil said longingly.

"Well, now's not the right time... we have to stop the immortal dragon before he destroys Norghana and kills thousands of people..."

Egil sighed.

"Yes, I know... life doesn't always grant you the chance to do what your soul demands. In most cases duty interferes. Today is one of those occasions. My soul will weep for me not being able to grant it its wishes, while honor drives us to continue on the path of duty."

"Yeah, it's like when it's time to seed in my village, the villagers leave everything to go to the fields and seed and plant."

"It's similar, only in this case the need is stronger than the soul's desire. If the need isn't fulfilled, they will die, as well as their own, and their souls know this."

"My lord will see you in the library," the First Pupil told them drily, angrily almost, clearly not appreciating the visit.

Gerd made a gesture to Egil, indicating that the whole tower was a huge library. They followed the Pupil to the third floor. They went by open halls filled with tomes that Egil looked at with longing and sadness for not being able to go near them. Gerd could not stop wondering how they had managed to hold all those books on the rocky walls. He did not see any wood that held them up; it was as if they were fastened to the wall by magic.

They went upstairs to the third floor of the tower, noticing that it only had a single enormous hall that took up the entire width of the tower. The ceiling was high and featured a huge fresco, depicting a clear blue sky with a few white clouds and a large sun in the middle, which seemed to give off a light that fully bathed the hall. Inside it they saw high bookshelves that went up in a circle. They noticed there were a dozen concentric shelves forming a ring with a long corridor that went through them from one side to the other.

"Phew... what a place..." Gerd whistled in awe as he stared around.

"Impressive, isn't it?" Egil said, beaming.

"Please be quiet, my lord is working," the First Pupil chided them.

They followed him in silence and went into the corridor that ran through the round shelves. They were as tall as three men and bursting with books. Leaning on both sides were ladders that allowed one to climb to reach the highest tomes. The enormous sky above their heads gave off golden-blue reflections of the light that entered through the windows and then went down to light the whole space. The place was as beautiful as it was rare. The look on Gerd's face as he stared at the shelves and ceiling said it all.

They arrived at the center of the ringed shelves and found another corridor cut perpendicularly to the one they had been following. A large, round working desk made of oak wood with carved inscriptions was at the epicenter of this singular hall. Sitting at it was a man in his seventies, completely bald, examining an open tome using what looked like a large magnifying glass as he sat in a tall armchair. The armchair was so imposing it looked like a throne.

"My lord Erudite, the visitors," the First Pupil said in an obvious tone of displeasure.

The Erudite did not raise his head or make any attempt to look at the arrivals; he continued examining the book as if it were the most important thing in the world at the moment.

"We are truly grateful to the Erudite for receiving us," Egil said in a humble tone as he gave a small bow.

Gerd bowed too but said nothing.

The Erudite went on with his work.

"I am receiving you because I am bound by this order to do so, not by my wish, so there is nothing to be grateful for," he replied in a reproachful tone.

"We are sorry for the inconvenience. It's something urgent and of the utmost importance, or we would never have dared to disturb you," Egil said, trying to placate the old man's temper.

"Ha! I have heard that a million times, and it is never such. There is nothing so important or urgent that cannot wait."

"I can assure you that in this case the situation is critical and the outcome might be an absolute catastrophe," Egil insisted.

The Erudite continued with his work without bothering to even glance at them. He did not seem ready to give them the slightest attention.

"I have no idea why I had the bad luck of being born in the north of Tremia. A long time ago I sent word to the Court that I do not consider myself Norghanian. I am a scholar and a free-thinking citizen without borders or belongings. The Norghanian kings and their greed are of no interest to me."

"The Erudite is on Norghanian land..." Egil reminded him. "The King has command over this territory..."

"Bah, nonsense. This tower has been no man's land for centuries. The fact that the King of Norghana now considers it a part of his kingdom does not make me a Norghanian."

"But you are of Norghanian ascent, your name and surname are Norghanian..."

"That does not make me a Norghanian. I am a citizen of the world, a free thinker, with the ill fortune that my tower is on the border between the Kingdom of Norghana and the Masig Steppes. I am all for moving it—I am sure the Masig tribes will not annex me."

"The Masig tribes don't take kindly to building on their steppes... they're nomadic tribes ..."

"I know perfectly well what they are and how the Masig live," the Erudite said, upset.

"Of course, no one has more knowledge in all Tremia."

"That is complimenting too far, but you are not that mistaken."

"I have sent you countless letters, seeking your wisdom and advice in serious, complex situations," Egil said.

"And I have ignored them all. Just like thousands of others that come from Norghana and other kingdoms. If I read and replied to all those requests, I would do nothing else. What a waste of time!" he said with agitation.

"I understand, they take time away from your studies."

"From my *important* studies," he clarified. "If I did the same and sent requests to all the sages in Tremia, every time I had a doubt, I would be making them waste their time as well as my own. Apart from being an idiot for not being able to solve my own doubts."

"Some problems are complex for simple minds like ours," Egil said, resorting to flattery.

"Is that so? What is it this time? In one word," the Erudite asked more calmly as he continued with his work.

"Dragon," Egil said dramatically.

Alvis stopped what he was doing and finally turned to look at them.

"Dragon? What else?"

It appeared that the subject interested him since he remained staring at them, waiting for a reply.

"An immortal dragon has resurged," Egil said in the same

54

dramatic tone.

"Resurged?" Alvis asked, raising both thin white eyebrows.

"He has been reincarnated in a fossilized dragon body and has come back to life."

The Erudite looked taken aback; he sat back in his armchair and with his head to one side said to Egil, "Proof?"

"We saw it ourselves; we witnessed it. Seven Ranger Specialists were witness and tried to prevent it."

"You failed?"

"We did, and that's why we're here. We need help to finish off the dragon."

Alvis remained thoughtful as he stared at Egil and Gerd, or rather through them, since he seemed deep in thought. A long moment of uncomfortable silence passed before he spoke.

"This is one of the most singular stories that have reached me in all my existence, which is already long."

"We swear it's true," Egil insisted.

"That is going to be difficult to prove, is it not? Have you any evidence apart from your word, something tangible to show me?"

"We have our word and that of several hundred prisoners the dragon sects had working inside a volcano."

The Erudite cried out in surprise.

"This is becoming both more interesting and incredible. It sounds like one of those stories told around a fire to keep children up at night."

"If you allow me, I could tell you everything that has happened. Only then will it make sense and be believable."

"I doubt very much that any explanation will make this story believable. In any case, I am in a good mood today, and a short break to enjoy a fantastic tale will do me good before I continue my work. Go ahead, delight me with this story."

Egil sighed. He knew the Erudite did not believe him. He would have to tell the man everything that had happened in painstaking detail, or else he would not get the help they needed. Calmly and confidently, Egil told the Erudite the entire story and the sage listened attentively, barely blinking, a neutral look on his face. If what he was hearing seemed to him strange or unbelievable, he did not show it at any moment. He maintained the same look until Egil finished telling him the events.

"It's quite the story, one of the more bizarre I have ever heard or read," Alvis said after reflecting on everything he had heard.

"Not any less true because of it," Egil said, making it clear he stood by everything he had told the Erudite.

"I am sure both you and your friends believe that story. I find it difficult to believe that seven distinguished Rangers, the King's Royal Eagles no less, would invent such a story."

"Then you believe us?" Gerd intervened, cheered by the Erudite's words.

"I have not said that. I said I am convinced that you believe this singular story which for the rest of us humans sounds, to all purposes, incredible. Why you believe it might be explained through different reasons. One might be that you all suffered the effect of a grand and elaborate illusion, which might have been induced by chemical or magical means. I am sure you are familiar with potions that affect the senses, and with the Magic of Illusions. Furthermore, it might even be that you are under the thumb of Domination Magic, even at this very moment and do not know it. It would not be the first or the last time such was the case."

"All of us, at once?" Egil said in a tone that made it sound preposterous.

"It is unlikely, yes. But a lot less unlikely than the story you have brought to me today. When two things are unlikely and there is no other option, the most unlikely turns out to be false nine out of ten times."

"We're aware that it's a story difficult to believe, but you must admit there are hundreds of witnesses and sect followers apart from us. If we've all been victims of a grand illusion, there has to be a tremendously powerful creature or being behind it," Egil said.

"I agree with that."

"Then the difference lies in the fact that we believe it's a dragon and the great Erudite doesn't."

"Absolutely," Alvis said, nodding hard.

"In any case, this powerful creature or being must be stopped. That's why we're here," Egil turned the matter around.

Alvis smiled.

"Very clever. I see what you're trying to do. You want me to help you, overlooking the fact that it's a dragon we are talking about."

"Rather than overlooking it, opening yourself to other

possibilities like a creature or being with a great magical power," Egil replied.

"I see you are intelligent, more than is usual in men that travel armed."

"Thank you. Will the great Erudite help us?" Egil asked, trying not to make the flattery too obvious.

Alvis smiled.

"Fortunately for you—and I am not saying I believe that he has been reincarnated and is now in our world, because it is not so—one of my favorite topics of study has always been dragons. Because of that I will help you. I will share my knowledge with you, and at the same time I will make you see that what you believe you have lived through has not occurred. You have been deceived, or to be more exact, your minds have been deceived and you are convinced of something that has not happened in reality. It is my duty to draw you out of your ignorance and make you see that you have been fooled."

Egil and Gerd looked at one another and doubt appeared in their eyes.

"We appreciate the great Erudite is willing to enlighten us and correct our mistakes," Egil said respectfully.

"Follow me, I will enlighten your world with new knowledge."

"Follow you where?" Gerd asked.

"Where else would it be? To the cellar, the chambers of forbidden knowledge," the Erudite replied.

Gerd swallowed and looked at Egil, who gave him a look that said "I told you so."

Chapter 7

Lasgol called on his skills, one after the other, as he now did during his practice sessions to improve his magic. The difference was that he focused on those that might help him in the situation he was about to enter. He called upon his more physical skills such as *Cat-like Reflexes* or *Improved Agility*, or the ones that provided cover like *Woodland Protection*. Once he had called upon them and checked that they activated correctly, he was ready to act.

He waited for an instant until the leader was standing right between two of his henchmen to whom he was giving instructions. Lasgol nocked a regular arrow in his composite bow, aimed at the leader's torso, and called upon his *Elemental Arrow* skill. There was a green flash that ran through his arm and the arrow—he released and the arrow flew, transforming into an Elemental Earth Arrow in midair. It hit the leader's torso right in the center and there was a burst of dirt, smoke, filth, and a stunning, blinding compound.

The leader cursed and stepped back, half-blinded and stunned. The detonation also caught the two men beside him, who were somewhat affected and put their hands to their eyes to try and wipe them clean to see properly. Lasgol seized the moment and released twice in a row, using the same skill and creating Elemental Air Arrows. Two blasts, followed by two electric charges, left the henchmen unconscious.

Astrid appeared through the bushes on the eastern side of the clearing, fast as lightning, and lunged at one of the bandits. She hit him in the nose and temple, rendering him senseless before he could even realize what had happened.

One of the nearby watchmen heard something and turned toward where his partner should have been. When he did not see him, he went over with a short axe in one hand and a knife in the other. But before he could figure out what was wrong, Astrid appeared on his right and knocked him out with a flying kick to the face.

The third watchman in the east raised his head to see what was going on with his partners. He suspected something and started walking over to their position with a puzzled look on his face, but he had not taken more than two steps when on the third Astrid swept him down with a reaper blow at calf level. The man fell backward. He tried to shout, but three flashing punches left him unconscious.

Lasgol ran at a crouch to the prisoners. The leader was recovering and Lasgol could not allow that.

Ona, take him down, he transmitted to her.

The panther jumped at the man with tremendous power. She knocked him down with the impact and applied her full weight on the man's body.

Hold him down, Lasgol transmitted next.

Ona pressed her body on the man's and bared her fangs in his face. The leader stayed stock still.

"The beast... don't let it... kill me..." he mumbled with eyes filled with terror.

Suddenly three men appeared at a run, shouting and brandishing axes and knives. Lasgol remained calm—he had an arrow nocked ready to be used. He called on his *Multiple Shot* skill. There was a green flash that covered Lasgol's arm and arrow and the arrow flew from the bow, turning into three arrows that hit each bandit in their right shoulder as they raced toward him. The three were knocked down, the arrows deeply embedded in them.

A new threat appeared on the roof of the cabin. An archer was taking position. Before the bandit could aim properly, Lasgol released using his *Fast Shot* skill. He had been practicing this skill a lot lately, and it allowed him to release at more than double the regular speed. The archer received the swift impact in the torso and rolled off the roof. He hit the ground with a hollow sound and was left lying there.

Two more bandits appeared at the top of the steps they were carving down to the hole, and Camu dealt with them. In his camouflaged state he leapt, and as he landed on his four legs, he released a Tail Whiplash. There was a silver flash and the men were hit with Camu's tremendous tail strength. They fell to the ground, winded. Astrid came from the ruins and knocked them out in the blink of an eye.

"Are there any more?" Lasgol asked Astrid as he aimed around the area with an arrow nocked, looking for any bandit who might have slipped away.

"I've taken care of it, there's no one standing," Astrid replied with a nod.

"Good. Let's see what's going on here."

"Those two must know," Astrid said, walking over to the prisoners on the ground, pointing her Assassin's knives at them.

"We haven't done anything wrong!" one of them cried in terror.

"Let us go, please!" the other one pleaded.

"First I want to know what's going on here," Lasgol said, going over to where Ona had the leader of the bandits held between her fangs.

"You'd better want to tell us something, or else I'll tell my panther to rip your throat out," Lasgol said threateningly.

Don't attack, he transmitted to Ona. He did not want the panther to take one of his threats to get information as an order.

"You... have no... right..." the leader muttered.

"Yes I do. We're Rangers," Lasgol said, crouching beside the leader's head.

"You're Rangers? Then you must free us," the light-haired prisoner said.

"We were taken against our will and tortured," the other prisoner with darker hair said.

"We can see that, but we want answers," Astrid told them as she watched them, standing and toying with her knives.

"My name's Umber Ilfensen," the blond prisoner said, "and this is my partner Lars Kender. We're... adventurers..."

"Adventurers? And what adventure has brought you here to this half-ruined building?" Astrid said as she twirled her knife in the air so that it turned several times before she grabbed it again by the hilt nonchalantly.

"A treasure..." Lars admitted at last.

"My, my... so you're treasure hunters," said Lasgol.

"Something like that..." Umber admitted.

"Well, you can't say it was going very well for you," Astrid said ironically.

"Ormag betrayed us," Lars said nodding toward the leader.

"Well, well, so this one's also a treasure hunter," Lasgol commented, staring at Ormag in the ground.

"It appears you didn't choose your business partner carefully," Astrid said.

"We needed help... and he came to us and put his men at our disposal..." said Umber.

"What did you need armed men for?" Lasgol asked.

I know, Camu messaged to him.

Where are you? Lasgol asked, looking for Camu's footprints on the ground.

Inside hole, downstairs.

Lasgol stood up and went to the hole. He nodded at Astrid to take care of things. She nodded back.

"This place was… occupied…" said Lars.

"Occupied? By who?" Astrid asked.

Lasgol went down the steps and found a pretty wide tunnel lit up by torches.

Are you down here?

Yes, in chamber.

"By a sect…" said Umber. "We only wanted them to leave so we could get to the cellar. That's where Count Ilsmarsen's treasure is buried."

"We only wanted him to chase them away from here…" said Lars.

"And what happened?" Astrid asked.

"They killed them," Lasgol said, coming out of the chamber and up the steps. "There are five dead Defenders down there."

"We didn't want to kill anyone!" cried Lars.

"It was them!" Umber said.

"Because you didn't have the guts, you damned wealthy, cowardly brats!" Ormag shouted.

Ona growled and at once Ormag, fueled by fear, recovered his poise and shut up.

"It seems Egil's information was good. There were Defenders here after all. We only arrived too late to question them," Lasgol said thoughtfully.

"Pity," said Astrid ruefully.

"We had nothing to do with their deaths, you can let us go," Lars insisted.

"I wonder what the Defenders were doing here?" Lasgol said, ignoring the request.

"Looking for Count Ilsmaren's treasure?" Astrid ventured.

"It seems to me, more of a coincidence than anything else…"

Egil say coincidences not be, Camu messaged to him.

Yeah, Egil's an enemy of coincidences. There's always a reason behind them, even if it's not immediately apparent.

"I'm going to tie up this nasty character and then we'll hand him over to the authorities at Olstran," Astrid said, indicating Ormag.

Lasgol nodded and continued his questioning.

"What is the treasure?" he asked the two prisoners crouching beside them.

"From what we could find out… gold and jewels… quite a few… we guess…" said Lars.

"The usual for a noble house's treasure… apart from some valuable family relics… we think," Umber explained.

"Relics?" Lasgol asked, raising an eyebrow. This might be interesting.

"There are supposed to be several ancient family relics," said Lars, "believed to be of great worth. A horn of gold and sapphires that belonged to the first Count Ilsmarsen, Ulworf, nicknamed 'the bear ripper.'"

"Nice nickname," Lasgol commented, raising an eyebrow.

"They were a very influential family in their day, in the last century. One of the families that upheld the power of the kingdom of Norghana," Umber explained. "With the passing of time they suffered several betrayals in their struggle for power with the other influential families of the east. The last Count Ilsmarsen, Vendros, is said to have buried a treasure before fleeing when he found himself defeated. It's always been rumored it was in this area, although no one had ever found it until now. We've been after it for a long time. It had never occurred to anyone to search here, the old hunting house where they spent the summers."

"Or, if it did occur to them, they never found anything," Lars added.

"We'd better take a look below," said Astrid.

"But first let's bring all the bandits up here and tie them properly. I don't want any to escape and attack us from behind," said Lasgol.

Astrid nodded and they got to work. It was not long before they had all the bandits tied and locked up in the hunting cabin. They left the two treasure hunters where they were, as they were. They did not give Lasgol and his friends any trouble—they were aware that their lives depended on what Astrid and Lasgol decided.

When they were done tying everyone up, Lasgol addressed Ona.

You keep watch. If anyone tries to escape, stop them and alert us.

Ona growled once.

You don't need to kill them, Lasgol insisted.

Ona growled once again.

Lasgol nodded. He was very pleased that his communication with Ona was so good. Trotter, who was a very intelligent pony, understood what Lasgol transmitted to him very well, and the fact that Ona was now doing so too filled him with pride. He wondered whether the loyal pony would be alright; he had left him at the entrance of the forest, along with Astrid's horse. Nothing should happen to them, since they were far enough from the fighting area, but you never knew. They would soon go and check on them.

"We're going to untie you, and you'd better not do anything foolish if you want to see another dawn," Astrid warned the two adventurers, and her gaze was so stern that she filled the prisoners' souls with fear.

"We won't do anything, we promise," Umber promised at once.

"Remember, we're Rangers. The penalty for going against us or trying to escape our custody is the King's dungeons," Lasgol told them.

"If they survive me, which they wouldn't," Astrid said, showing them her knives.

"We'd never dream of anything like that!" Umber said, agitated.

"We'll do whatever you ask of us, of course we will!" Lars added.

Astrid and Lasgol exchanged looks. These two were not going to try anything, they were terrified.

Lasgol cut their ligatures, and the two adventurers stood up.

"Thank you, you've saved our lives," Umber said gratefully as he stretched his arms.

"We won't forget this," said Lars, rubbing his sore wrists.

"Start guiding us to the treasure," said Lasgol.

The two treasure hunters looked at one another with fear and doubt. The fear was not of death, but of losing their loot.

But they nodded.

I already down, Camu messaged from where he was listening to the conversation at the foot of the steps inside the hole.

"You go first," Astrid said with an acid grin.

Umber and Lars led the way down. Astrid and Lasgol followed, while Ona stayed watching the captured bandits. The steps led them to a hall that looked like an old cellar. The floor and walls were rock and had been built at the same time as the now-ruined building.

On one side, against the wall, were the dead Defenders. Astrid went over to check them. On the opposite side of the hall lit up by torches they could see two holes. The Defenders had been digging. The picks they had been using lay on the floor beside the holes, and a wheelbarrow was on its side a little further in.

No way out, Camu messaged.

Yeah, it looks like a storage cellar, for food supplies most likely, since it's all stone.

"These poor wretches have been killed without any mercy," Astrid said, looking at the wounds on the bodies.

"We had nothing to do with that, Ormag's men assaulted them in the cabin one night and killed them. Then they brought the bodies down here to hide them," Lars explained.

"You did have something to do with it, since you brought this band of thieves and murderers here," Astrid said accusingly.

"All they had to do was scare and throw out those clerics. We tried to talk to them, reason with them, but they refused to leave and would not let us into that cellar. They became aggressive and we had to leave fast," Umber said.

"They're not clerics, and they aren't reasonable either. Of course, they weren't going to leave if they were here doing something for their lord," Lasgol told them.

"We thought they might be searching for the treasure too…" Umber said, "that's why we sought out Ormag and his men, to stop them from getting ahead of us. What happened next was a tragedy."

"There's nothing of interest here," said Astrid, checking the hall, "only these couple of holes in the floor, which I guess is where they were digging to find the buried treasure."

"Yeah, I'm afraid that's another dead end," Lasgol said, letting out a sigh loaded with frustration.

I search, not find anything, Camu messaged as he lay resting on the floor beside the north wall.

Astrid finished searching the hall.

"Any idea where the treasure is?" she asked Umber and Lars.

"If we have to dig out the whole floor it's going to be very cumbersome, it's solid rock…" Lasgol commented.

"Wait a moment, let us study the place," Umber said.

"Go ahead," Astrid said with a doubtful look on her face.

Umber and Lars each picked up a torch and started studying and feeling all the rocks carefully, on the floor, walls, and ceiling. Camu had to move several times so they would not bump into him.

Astrid and Lasgol watched, intrigued.

"From what we found out, the Ilsmarsen had a very peculiar way of hiding their secrets," Umber commented as he went on feeling and inspecting every rock.

"They marked the place with the initials of the first count."

"Ulworf Ilsmarsen?" Lasgol asked.

"U. I.?" Astrid guessed.

"Yes, but no," Lars said, smiling.

"Then what?" Lasgol asked.

"The true mark we're looking for is that of a bear," Lars went on.

"One that's been ripped," Umber added.

"Oh, wow…" Astrid said thoughtfully.

"They marked the treasure with the nickname of the first count?" said Lasgol.

"That's right," Umber corroborated. "And here it is," Lars said, pointing at a stone on the south wall, at mid height and a little to the east.

They all came over to look. Lars and Umber kept the torches high. They could clearly see the area indicated on the wall.

"Is that a ripped bear?" Astrid asked with a look that said it did not look like one at all. "I don't see it either…" Lasgol said, scratching his chin, trying to make sense of the sketch carved on the rock.

Upside down, Camu messaged.

Astrid and Lasgol tried to turn the drawing over in their minds.

"It's belly up," Umber said.

"That's right," Lars confirmed. "If you look at it upside down you can see it."

"With a lot of imagination…" Astrid added.

"It's a mark that usually goes unnoticed. If you look closely, many of the rocks are marked. That's to make it difficult to find the real mark," Lars said.

"They look like the markings left by the digging work," Lasgol said.

Astrid went over to check some other marks and touched them.

"They seem to me like scratches and usual blows."

"That's the best way to hide them," said Umber.

"So, what now?" Lasgol asked.

"Now we break through the wall," said Lars.

"Do you believe the treasure is behind that wall?" Astrid said.

The two treasure hunters nodded.

"Well, then there's work to do," Lasgol said. By now he was intrigued and wanted to know whether or not there was a hidden treasure here and what it had to do with the Defenders.

"Let's break through then," Astrid said.

Chapter 8

Nilsa was returning from the stables. She had sent several messages from Gondabar with riders on the Leader's express request. Nilsa usually preferred aerial means, which were faster, albeit somewhat less safe. Pigeons, crows, and owls were favored by the Rangers and most used, even though every now and then the birds did not arrive at their destination for a variety of reasons.

Hence, when an important message had to be delivered it was done by hand, and Ranger Messengers were used for that. The three he wanted sent were to be delivered by hand and without delay, so, since she was Gondabar's Liaison and in charge of organizing and directing the efforts to find and kill the immortal dragon, Nilsa was busier than she had ever been. She spent the whole day organizing and directing communications, orders, and messages that left the Tower of the Rangers to every corner of the whole realm, and the messages they received that had to be analyzed, categorized, and solved.

The truth was, she was pleased with her position and the trust Gondabar deposited on her. She was aware of the importance of her work and how it was helping the cause. The rest of the Snow Panthers were searching for the dragon, and she had not been able to go with them because of her current job. Not being able to be with them made her sad, since nothing could compare to going on crucial missions for the kingdom with her friends. Luckily, the work she was carrying out filled the void she felt for not being with them.

Besides, she knew her friends were proud of the work she was doing. Egil had already told her that having someone trustworthy receiving all the information and coordinating efforts was going to be essential to finally get the dragon. Ingrid had congratulated her for her post, which she considered a promotion. Gerd had wished her luck. The giant was sad they had to go different ways, but he knew they would soon be together again. Astrid and Lasgol had congratulated her and assured her that she would do a vitally important job. Viggo, as usual, being Viggo, had wished her luck not ending up setting fire to all of Gondabar's messages with him in the midst of them.

Nilsa greeted the two Rangers she passed by who were heading to the stables.

"Rangers," she said with a slight bow in a jovial tone. She recognized them. She had seen them before, although she could not remember their names.

"Royal Eagle," the first one said respectfully.

"Liaison," the second one said, also in a respectful tone.

Nilsa smiled and kept walking. The fact that everyone knew her— well, not everyone, but many—pleased her. Not only was she well known among the Rangers, but also by the Royal Guard, and that, besides pleasing her, made her work easier.

She headed determinedly to a side entrance to the main building of the castle. She had to speak with the King's Master Armorer. Gondabar wanted more steel arrow tips for the Rangers and the last shipment had not arrived as expected. It was a minor matter, not vital, but Nilsa fulfilled all of the Ranger Leader's errands with pleasure, whether they were important or trivial. Ingrid always used to say that no matter was small when it was about fighting. Precariousness in weaponry was something to solve quickly. There were hundreds of small problems, and because of that she was always so busy.

Nilsa arrived at the side gate and found it watched by two Royal Guards. But she did not have to stop and present herself to be let through. Both guards knew her and let her through without any problem. She gained access to the western wing of the main building and started down a long corridor. At the end of it she met two more Royal Guards, who also let her through. Thoran had set guards throughout the Royal Castle. Some people said he was becoming more paranoid by the day, others that he was merely a prudent man. Being a King in Tremia was a dangerous profession after all.

Nilsa went up some stairs that led her to the wing where the King's Master Armorer had his rooms. She went down another long corridor that ended on a landing and continued along yet another corridor. Now she could walk through the castle without impediment. Gondabar had requested a special permit so she would be granted access to practically every corner of the castle, which until now had been forbidden to her. The King had granted it so Nilsa now could go anywhere she wanted with the exception of the King's and his brother's private rooms. This made her feel important too, since only the Royal Guard and the Royal Rangers had such privileges.

She reached the room she was looking for. Two soldiers were on watch duty at the door. This time she did have permission to go in.

"Soldiers," she said with a slight nod.

"Royal Eagle," the one more to the left replied. He was blond, tall, and strong; not as much as one of the members of the Royal Guard but he was close. With a strong jaw and blue eyes, he looked quite rough.

The other soldier looked her up and down.

"What does the Ranger Liaison want?" he asked with a gleam in his eyes and a mischievous smile. He was thinner and not as tall as his partner. He had brown hair and eyes and was quite handsome.

"I need to see the Master Armorer."

"The Master Armorer is very busy," the rough one said, intending to deny her entry, then, as an afterthought, "unless the Royal Eagle really needs to see him for something important."

What my partner means," the other soldier intervened, "is that the Master Armorer has given instructions not to be bothered unless it's something important. I'm sure the Liaison, if she's here, needs something important," he said, smiling, without taking his eyes off Nilsa's.

"Gondabar sends me, it's important," she replied in a serious tone.

"Of course, just as I'd assumed," the brown-haired soldier said, and he smiled charmingly. "Come in, we don't want to make you waste time, although your presence brightens our day," he said sweetly. "Come by whenever you want."

Nilsa understood the veiled invitation and smiled slightly.

"I might have to come back with more errands," she said and went in. She liked being flattered, she used it to her advantage. Most of the soldiers were quite foolish and easy to manipulate. Two smiles, a flutter of her eyelashes, or a slow tossing of her long red mane were enough.

The Master Armorer was working in his study. He was about sixty years old and was built like a true, strong Norghanian. He wore his white hair long and had no beard, so it was obvious he took care of his appearance. He had several assistants, who were making lists and comparing inventories.

"Oh, Liaison… Nilsa. What can I do for you?" he asked, raising a thick eyebrow.

Nilsa handed him Gondabar's written request.

The Master Armorer read it slowly.

"Well, he wants more steel tips. I don't know if Gondabar believes they grow on trees. Arrow tips aren't as easy to make as he seems to think. Why don't the Rangers make their own arrows instead of asking me for them?"

"They do, sir, but right now they're all on missions throughout the kingdom."

"And can you please tell me why they use so many?"

"We're Rangers, sir, arrows are our main weapon. They're essential for us."

"Yeah, yeah…

"Tell Gondabar he'll have his load of arrow tips in three days. It seems the shipment has been misdirected."

"Misdirected?"

"Yes, a convoy with arrow tips and knife blades has vanished on the journey from Olstran to the capital."

"That's weird," Nilsa said, raising an eyebrow.

"Well, yes. It's not the first time a shipload has vanished before, but it's strange. It's probably been stolen."

"Bandits?"

"Bandits, deserters, outlaws and the like. They'll sell it to the highest bidder. It's common. It doesn't happen that much, but it does happen."

"I see."

"If you don't want anything else, I must return to my duties."

"I'll inform Gondabar."

Nilsa left the room and the two soldiers standing there watched her leave. Instead of following the same route she had arrived by, she decided to take a different one through the castle. This way she would see a little more of what was going on there and perhaps notice something or find out any news. Being able to wander around the Royal Castle and access most of the rooms gave her a lot of freedom and ability to act. She could poke her nose into things at will and see whether she heard or saw anything suspicious.

So far, the soldiers and Rangers had been kind to her because of her open personality and the fact that they found her uniquely attractive with her fiery hair and freckles. But since she had been at her new post, they were kind more out of respect and she liked that, it made her feel good about herself. Earning the respect of soldiers and Rangers was no easy thing, even if, as a Royal Eagle, she was already halfway there.

She smiled. It amused her to see how the soldiers and Rangers reacted to her. She was always trying to detect why they treated her so nicely—whether it was because of her character or because they were interested in her beauty, or for being a Royal Eagle, or perhaps because of her new post as Liaison. At first she could not tell, but gradually she was becoming more skilled at identifying the reason. It was a small game she played while she did her duties, which helped her feel less alone and not miss her friends as much.

She went down some stairs and then along another corridor. She took several turns right and, as she had expected, the soldiers she met looked at her but did not stop her. Every now and then she greeted them or asked them something, to exchange some words with them and play this game she had created and which amused her greatly. Besides it was good because she established contacts. She had decided to go back to the tower to continue with her tasks when a female voice hailed her.

"Hey, Freckles, stealing hearts again?"

Nilsa turned and saw Valeria coming toward her.

"Me? No... working..." Nilsa replied. Valeria's greeting had caught her by surprise.

"Don't pretend, I saw you with those soldiers."

"Not at all, I was just greeting them," Nilsa said, waving her hand in denial.

"Well, they were dazzled," Valeria said in a playful tone.

Nilsa shrugged and smiled blushing slightly.

"I'm only being kind."

"That you are, and also very nice."

"Thanks, I try," Nilsa lowered her gaze.

"What have you been doing? I haven't seen you in ages."

"Oh, you know, keeping busy," Nilsa replied, watching Valeria. She had not seen her much all winter. She was always with Princess Heulyn as her personal bodyguard, and on the rare occasions Nilsa had seen her, it had been from a distance.

"Ranger business, huh?" Valeria winked at her and smiled mischievously.

Nilsa giggled.

"You know, Rangers and their secrets," she shrugged.

"I've missed your giggling. It gladdens the heart to hear, and of course greeting you, too.

"Thank you, I'm glad to see your smiling face too." Nilsa was glad to see Valeria, even though she did not trust her. There was too much past history between Valeria and the Panthers, and it was not good. But for some reason she liked the woman despite everything she had done and which Nilsa had neither forgotten or forgiven.

"You're one of the few among your people who are glad to see me."

"Maybe you haven't heard, but I know several soldiers and even members of the Royal Guard who call you the Beautiful Bodyguard."

"Ha! Funny name. I'd rather be called the Precious Bodyguard," she smiled mockingly. "So, I've made an impression among the castle's men." Valeria looked around and passed her hand through her long blonde, wavy hair that she wore loose. Several soldiers nearby could not help but glance in her direction.

"You surely notice how they look at you…" Nilsa said, feeling a little envy seeing the effect Valeria's beauty caused. Not that she was not popular among the Rangers and soldiers, because she was, but Valeria was even more so.

"I see how they look at me, but they're wasting their time," Valeria said, waving at the soldiers and smiling coquettishly.

"It isn't because of Lasgol, is it? You're not still interested in him? He's with Astrid and they're happy," Nilsa became defensive. That might prove disastrous.

"I know. I have no chance with Lasgol," Valeria replied, and her flirtatious smile vanished.

"Thank goodness," Nilsa snorted. The last thing she wanted was another conflict between Valeria and the Panthers, and a manifest interest on Valeria's part in Lasgol would cause it. Astrid would go off like an angry black panther, and that would not be good at all.

"For now," Valeria added naughtily.

"Valeria… you wouldn't be capable…"

"Take it easy, it's not in my immediate plans."

"I don't know whether that puts me fully at ease," Nilsa made a face of disbelief.

"You surely have greater worries other than my love life," Valeria smiled at her.

"Where have you been? I've barely seen you around."

"Princess Heulyn has kept me busy the whole winter. Very busy."

"Why's that? Well... if I may ask..."

"Apart from looking after her safety, I've been ordered to train her."

"Train her in what?"

"In the use of the bow. In Irinel she was taught to use a sword and javelin, she had very good tutors. She was taught from a young age. The truth is, she's surprisingly good with those weapons. But she hadn't mastered the bow and she asked me to teach her. I think that seeing you use it motivated her."

"Wow, that doesn't sound very good. She hates us so much."

"Don't worry, I don't think she's planning on using it against you."

"I wouldn't be so sure."

"Well, you never know with the Princess, that's true," Valeria grinned and made a comical face.

"Funny that the Royal House of Irinel teaches their Royal Princesses to fight. It's not very common, but I think it's great."

"I think it's great too. A strong woman who can defend herself will get farther in life."

"So that's what she's been doing all this time."

"She's also been spending a lot of time with that ambassador of yours who's like a vain eel."

"Ambassador Larsen?"

"Yes, that one," Valeria confirmed with a wave of disgust. "I don't like him, and neither does the Princess. That I can assure you."

"Then why has she been spending so much time with him? She's not one to put up with someone without a reason."

Valeria nodded.

"She's been studying our wonderful kingdom: History and origins, frontiers, culture and main customs, members of the Court, nobles of the East and West, succession to the throne, allies and enemies of the realm... and other things of importance about Norghana."

Nilsa's eyes opened wide.

"She's taking a great interest in our kingdom."

"A great one. The name of the Olafstone family has come up, and of its only member still alive...."

"Egil..." Nilsa had a bad feeling. Why was Princess Heulyn interested in Egil and his family? The answer came to her before finishing the thought—succession to the throne. "Because of the throne..."

Valeria made a face that read as "I'd say so" and shrugged.

"The Princess's interests are her own," she replied.

"Yeah... not sure whether her interests might be good or bad for us..."

"She has no love for you, that I can tell you," Valeria said in a sharp tone, without any hint of joking. "If I were you, I'd stay away from her as far as you can, and then a bit more."

"I see. We guess she hasn't forgiven us."

"Nor will she ever. She's not one to forgive or forget an outrage."

Nilsa sighed deeply.

"Anything else she's been doing? There've been all kinds of rumors during the winter..."

"That, and a couple other things I can't tell you about, for safety reasons."

"Oh, I see."

"I guess the rumors haven't been very flattering."

"The Princess had earned herself a reputation... quite a bad one... with all the service of the palace..."

"And among the soldiers and the Royal Guard as well," Valeria added. "Don't worry, my lady's character is no state secret," Valeria winked at Nilsa ostensibly.

"Her shouting can be heard from the stables," Nilsa said with a horrified look on her face.

Valeria laughed.

"Yes, that's her, the Royal Princess of Irinel, all temper and then more temper."

"Is she the same way with you?" Nilsa asked, suddenly feeling bad for Valeria.

Valeria waved her hand to mean it was not a big deal.

"I'm one of the few fortunate people who receive a special treatment. She doesn't yell at me; she doesn't even raise her voice around me. Mind you, she doesn't repeat her orders or expect any 'buts,' they simply have to be carried out."

"Good. I'm glad of that, otherwise being in her service all day long…"

"Yeah. Others aren't so lucky. In my case it's not so bad. She treats me fairly well, considering what she's like, and I also have quite a bit of freedom of movement, as long as I'm always watching out for her safety."

Nilsa looked around to make sure they were alone and no one could hear her. The only people nearby were the guards Valeria had greeted. She lowered her voice.

"Tell me, what's the relationship between Princess Heulyn and King Thoran like? I always wonder. Well, that's if you can tell me without getting into trouble."

Valeria smiled. She glanced in every direction and, seeing they were alone, she whispered, "The relationship is practically non-existent."

"How come? Don't they get along?" Nilsa was interested; the comment had puzzled her.

"They're both highly temperamental. When they spend more than just a short while in the same room, the walls explode," Valeria whispered.

"But they're engaged, they should have a good relationship."

Valeria let out a guffaw she could not repress.

"Nilsa, you're such a good, innocent person. The fact that they're engaged doesn't mean they get along. In fact, they can't stand one another."

Nilsa made a face.

"Well, that's a shame. They should get along well; they should love one another."

Valeria laughed again.

"Love one another? That's not the case," she said, trying to stop laughing. "In fact, I believe it's the very opposite."

"A union without love isn't a union," Nilsa said sadly.

"This is a political union. It has nothing to do with feelings."

Yeah, that's what we Panthers think."

"How are the Panthers? How's everyone?"

"Fine, busy as usual."

"Anything interesting?" Valeria looked at her inquisitively.

Nilsa was aware that Valeria wanted to know what they were

involved in. But she could not tell her. She did not trust her. Besides, it could prove counterproductive to tell her anything.

"Ranger missions. Protecting the realm. You know…"

"I see you don't want to tell me," Valeria looked at her with a raised eyebrow.

"It's the truth. They are protecting the realm."

"That's not a specific answer," Valeria's look was now distrustful.

"I can't tell you. You know how the Path of the Ranger goes…"

Valeria nodded.

"I understand. I won't insist," she smiled.

"I have to leave you, I have a lot to do."

"Okay, but before you go, I'd like to propose something to you," Valeria looked at her frankly.

Nilsa was surprised.

"What's that?"

"You and I get along fine, in spite of everything that's happened between us."

"Yeah…"

"I want to propose that you and I make an alliance pact."

"Alliance pact? I don't know what you mean," Nilsa frowned. She was not sure of Valeria's intentions. She had already betrayed them once—she could do it again.

"I want the best for my lady and myself. You want the best for the Panthers and yourself. I propose that we help one another. We can both get what we want more easily if we work together."

"I don't need your help. I have the Rangers and Gondabar backing me."

"Yes, but that might change if the Princess becomes the Queen. In fact, I bet what little I have that it will. I could dissuade the Queen, support you and the Panthers."

Nilsa thought about this. If the Princess became Queen, they would be in trouble. She would surely go against them. She would also go against Egil for being in the line of succession to the throne and an eastern noble. Gondabar could not protect him from the Queen. Only the King could, but he would not defend Egil, that much was certain.

"I don't know whether I can trust you."

Valeria nodded twice.

"That's true, you shouldn't. I've already betrayed you once. But now I'm offering my secret collaboration in alliance. I'll do whatever I can for you and you will do the same for me. It's advantageous and it doesn't commit you to anything. If you don't want to do something, don't. There are no strings attached."

Nilsa thought a bit more. She did not risk anything by having Valeria collaborating with them; it might even be an asset, and if she wanted anything they did not agree with, they did not have to do it.

"Okay. But this conversation never took place," Nilsa said with a serious, cold gaze.

"What conversation?" Valeria asked with a questioning gesture of hands.

Nilsa nodded. "See you then," she said, starting to leave.

"See you," Valeria replied with a wink.

As she was leaving Nilsa felt doubtful about whether what she was doing was right. She hoped so, and she hoped that Valeria would not deceive them all again. There was no way of knowing whether that would happen or not. She had granted Valeria the benefit of doubt. She hoped and wished she would not live to regret it.

Chapter 9

The sun was beginning to rise when Viggo returned to the room Lomen had got them in the fortress.

"Where the heck have you been?" Ingrid asked, annoyed with her hands on her hips.

"I went for a walk in the city," Viggo beamed, as if it were the most natural thing to do.

"At night?" Ingrid crossed her arms, her eyes betraying her anger.

"At night is when certain people wander the city, and I wanted to see a couple."

"But you didn't say anything!" she cried, upset.

"I thought if I told you, you might want to come with me."

"Of course, I would've come with you!"

"It was better that I went alone. It's easier for me to blend in with the shadows at night, and I move better in the dark in the city slums. I work better in certain environments... you know that..."

"Even so, you should've told me!"

"Don't be upset, my blonde warrior, you know that it's better if I handle certain matters alone and in my own way."

"And if anything should happen to you?"

"Nothing's going to happen to me in the city I grew up in, I know it well."

"We're on an official mission. You can't deviate whenever you please, to do who knows what that has nothing to do with the mission."

"Don't get angry, I needed to do this. I have unresolved business in the city..."

"Unresolved business?"

"From when I left."

"It's been over seven years, what unresolved business?"

"Things that are written in fire in my gut that I want to solve."

"That's why you didn't want to come back to the city? So those things wouldn't re-surface?"

Viggo nodded. "You insisted. I told you it wasn't necessary... but now that we're here..."

"We have to do things properly. I'll follow the protocol, the path says so."

"That's how we've done it and here we are, in my city. There are some pending matters I have to attend to."

"That doesn't sound good at all. Knowing you, there'll be bloodshed."

Viggo smiled and shrugged.

"Debts must be paid."

"Who do you owe anything to? We might be able to fix the issue before blood runs."

"It's not me who owes anything. I'm owed something."

"Oh… and what's that?"

"It's a long story, horrible and filled with pain, and a secret one. We'd better leave it for some other time."

"I want to know it!" Ingrid demanded, furious because Viggo was not sharing his secrets.

There were two loud knocks on the door.

"Rangers, the Captain's waiting with the horses," a soldier informed them from the other side of the door.

"We're coming," Ingrid replied, raising her voice to be heard outside.

"We'd better hurry," Viggo said, grabbing their things.

"If you think this conversation's over, you couldn't be more wrong. You're going to tell me what's going on and why you're wandering around at night, as my name's Ingrid!"

Viggo smiled and said nothing. He slung his backpack over his shoulder and went out the door.

Ingrid swore under her breath.

"Can he be a greater numskull!" and she followed, ready.

They rode toward the lake, accompanied by fifty soldiers of the city guard with Captain Ingers in command. It was a good detachment of men. They could read between the lines—Magistrate Mustrel was trying to show that he was taking the Rangers' request seriously and wanted to look good in front of the King. On the other hand, the number of soldiers he lent for the investigation was also not too large for their absence to be noticed in the control of the city.

Ingrid, Viggo, and Captain Ingers were leading. The soldiers followed in a double line. The weather was wonderful, and if they had not been on their way to investigate a grotesque incident

79

involving innocent people ripped to pieces by a dragon, they would have even enjoyed the journey. The soldiers' faces were serious; they knew their destination and what had happened there. More than one wished they were not in the expedition, and it showed in their eyes.

For a long while Ingrid and Viggo did not talk. Ingrid was still annoyed with Viggo's night escapade and his refusal to tell her about the unsolved business he had in the city. She could understand he might want to revisit his old life, but she could not accept that he would not tell her the risks of what he was planning. Knowing Viggo, it would not be anything good. He would be getting into one of his messes, and this being his home city, it could end up being a lot more dangerous than usual. Settling old debts was never good. Ingrid feared Viggo might get himself into some mess he would not be able to get out of. Very often the past had tentacles that could grab you in the present and not let go.

"I hope you're luckier than I was," Captain Ingers said. "I spent a week searching for the bodies with help from the locals but we found nothing."

"Can we count on local support?'" Ingrid asked.

Ingers nodded. "I sent a messenger to the village of High Rock. It's the closest to the lake and three of the missing people are from there. Ermos Lostren, the village Chief, will help us with two hunters who already aided us with the tracking."

"That's great, that will help," Ingrid nodded.

"If there's a monster, I'm afraid it's made the bodies disappear."

"Do you believe it could be a dragon?"

"That's what the witnesses at High Rock say, but personally I doubt it. I'm inclined to believe it's a more common beast like an Ogre or a mountain Troll. It might even be a large bear. Every once in a while, one of great size appears that is mistaken for a monster."

"Yeah… that would be the more likely answer. Yet the rumor is that a dragon has been sighted."

The Captain nodded. "The locals insist it's a dragon, but none can give a very detailed description of it."

"But they saw it, didn't they?" Ingrid asked, raising an eyebrow.

"That's the problem. The few witnesses there are only saw a great beast that looked like a dragon out of the corner of their eyes. I couldn't get a witness that saw the beast clearly and could describe it in any believable manner. The thing is, between the fear and the fright of seeing it, they didn't really know what it was they had seen."

"I see. So, no one saw it well enough to give a detailed and believable description."

"That's right. One saw a huge dragon head or what he thought was a dragon. Another one saw a long scaly tail go by, which based on its size had to belong to a dragon. A third one saw some giant claws on colossal scaly legs, and yet another saw the monstrous body of a reptile rising above the lake. If we put all the descriptions together, which is what they've done since they've been talking about it for weeks now, they reach the approximate conclusion that it's either a dragon or some very large beast."

"Ogres and Trolls don't have scales and they don't look reptilian, a bear even less so."

"True. But even so, it's what's more likely. A dragon has never been seen in Norghana, or any other place, and I personally doubt they exist," the officer said, shaking his head.

"You say they've been talking about it for weeks, so I guess the disappearances have taken place at different times, as well as the sightings."

"That's correct. There are no witnesses to the attacks, but the blood trails we found were in different parts of the lake and they seem to have been left on different days. The sightings occurred afterwards, when the neighbors were looking for the missing people."

"Understood. How did you manage with the trails? They're not usually easy to read," Ingrid asked with eyebrows raised, since she doubted the city soldiers had any idea of how to find or read trails.

"We're not very good following trails," the Captain admitted. "I used a couple of local hunters with good reputations. They were in charge of finding them and guessing how old they were—that's how we usually do it. Those of us from the city don't manage well in open terrain, but luckily now I have two Rangers so everything will be simpler."

"It will be," Ingrid promised firmly. "You should've asked for the Rangers' help from the beginning."

Ingers nodded repeatedly.

"I asked Magistrate Mustrel to seek the help of expert Rangers but he refused. Problems in the duchy that might mar its reputation must be solved quickly and without them becoming news…"

"That's not a good policy. No matter how much he might want

81

to hide a tragedy, it will come out sooner or later."

"The Magistrate thought it would be a normal beast and that we'd kill it fast. When that wasn't the case, he didn't want any outside intervention, because of the stain on…"

"Proud men making the wrong decisions," Ingrid commented with a look of disapproval on her face.

"The Magistrate doesn't want to look bad before the Duke, and he doesn't want to look bad before the King. Secrecy and wanting to look good rule over other matters. That's how things work, at least around here."

"That's been made perfectly clear," said Ingrid, shaking her head.

They rode on along a wide road, leaving behind a number of small villages that didn't even appear on the maps. They were mining villages and their inhabitants spent more time at the mines than at their homes. Life in the mines was tough but they earned good money, more than being a farmer or a woodcutter. However, accidents in the mines were usually terrible, while accidents in the fields or the forest did not take so many lives.

As they approached the great lake, Ingrid decided it was time to start a conversation with Viggo, who had been very quiet the whole journey.

"Are you going to tell me what you were doing last night?" she asked, this time in a gentler tone.

Viggo looked at her and smiled.

"You have to understand that I was born and grew up in the streets of Ostangor, in the filthy streets of the poorest slum to be exact. I grew up among filth, mud, a stinky environment, refuse, and rats."

"I understand. But it's nothing you should be ashamed of or keep secret. You've come this far. You got out of those sewers and now you're a Ranger. It's a great success. Very few escape the misery they grew up in and triumph in life."

"I was lucky that my grandfather was a Ranger. Otherwise today I'd be a member of one of the two syndicates that rule the city slums. Or I'd already be dead, at the hands of the city guard or the rival syndicate."

"Fortunately, you were able to get out and nothing like that happened."

Viggo nodded.

"I went in search of some information…" he said at last.

"In the slums?"

He nodded, "Yes."

"What kind of information?"

"For one thing, information about my father. Unlike Lasgol's father, mine was never an exemplary citizen."

"You told us he didn't join the Rangers like your grandfather, that he got drunk and killed a man in a fight at a bar…"

"Yeah, that was good old Valon Kron. He liked to avoid honest work. Instead he'd rather steal, lie, and fight for a few coins. He wasn't what others would consider a role model or someone to imitate. My grandfather, on the other hand, who was a Ranger, was indeed. Blood doesn't always pass down the good qualities between generations. My father preferred to steal, drink, and have fun to serving the King, so he refused the invitation to join the corps when it came."

"I'm sorry. It must've been hard for you to have a father like that, more so if your grandfather was a good person."

"It was, there were many bad days. He had a tendency to get really drunk, come home, and take out all his frustrations on my mother and me. He used to say we had ruined his life, the coward!"

"That's terrible, and detestable on his part."

"He was a bad man. When my grandfather died a couple of years later, he left my mother and abandoned us in the street. He lost the house and everything we had gambling and drinking, so he got rid of us."

"Disgusting! How could he have such little honor?"

"He got what he deserved. He's serving a life sentence in the silver mines for getting drunk and killing a man in a bar fight."

"Sometimes life puts people in their place."

"I think that happens seldom, but this time I believe it has. I've asked and been told he's still alive. I'm surprised, but that seems to be the case. I thought he would've died in the mines already."

"What kind of life did you have when you were left in the streets?"

"You adapt or you die. So I adapted to the streets, the poorest and filthiest. I learned a lot there. It was another kind of training that prepares you for life, a hard life and merciless, but such is life for the least fortunate. I learned to steal, lie, fight, and many other things."

"I'm not sure that's all good. What happened to your mother?

Viggo bowed his head and his eyes became moist.

"Unfortunately my mother couldn't adapt like I did. She got together with an abuser who beat her and one time almost beat her to death. I defended my mother and gave him what he deserved: we fought and I killed him. They issued an order to hang me for what happened. When the invitation to join the Rangers came, I saw an opportunity to run away. Now that I'm a Ranger, they can't hang me for that. Unfortunately, my poor mother didn't make it in the end. She died of fevers in a filthy cellar some time later."

"Oh my…" Ingrid said, shaking her head with a look of dismay.

"Life isn't long for the unfortunate… It was hard, I won't lie to you."

"I'm sorry for everything that happened to you…"

"Don't be. It's made me the man I am today, and I have no complaints."

"Even so, it's a sad story."

"It is. But I want no pity. My life's been worse than others' but I made it, something many don't. I'm not ashamed of where I come from or of what I am. Sewer rats like me know how to survive, and we're almost impossible to kill. I survived in the city sewers and I've managed to come this far. Nothing's going to stop me—I'm much better prepared than most to survive whatever comes. If Dergha-Sho-Blaska achieves his purpose and a time of horror and destruction follows, I'm sure I'll survive. I can't say the same of others."

"No one denies that you have special survival instincts, but let's hope you don't need to use them."

"Let's hope so," Viggo nodded. "But if it's necessary, I'll protect you."

Ingrid looked at Viggo and could not help but nod and smile.

"Thank you."

They arrived at Krystall Lake. The surface looked like glass and reflected the rays of the spring sun. The size of the lake left Ingrid in awe. It was a lot bigger than she had imagined. From the southern shore you could not see the northern side. Surrounding the lake were at least three different forests and two plains with tall grass.

"Wow, you could have a good swim here," Viggo said, joking.

"You don't say, you could have swimming competitions," Ingrid commented.

The Captain indicated a small pier to the west of where they were standing. "To cross it we generally use those boats."

"We'd better follow the trails of the attack along the lake," Ingrid said

"Very well. We'll go to the first location. Ermos Lostren and the hunters are waiting for us there," Ingers said.

The Captain led the detail to the place where the hunters had found the first blood trail. There, half a dozen men were indeed waiting for them.

"Stop! Dismount!" the Captain ordered his men.

Ingrid and Viggo also dismounted and tethered their horses to some nearby trees, then went to speak with the locals.

"Form a perimeter!" the Captain ordered his men, and they formed a circle at once.

"Good morning, we are the King's Rangers," Ingrid told the waiting men.

"We're glad to see you. I am Ermos Lostren, Chief of the village of High Rock. These two are the hunters Endar and Ores. They are both quite skilled and found all the tracks," the Chief said, pointing at two men beside him.

"Thank you for your help," Ingrid said with a nod.

"We wish we could do more," Endar said.

"We haven't been able to locate the beast," said Ores.

"Who are all these others?" Ingrid asked.

"Witnesses who've seen the beast... the dragon..." the Chief explained.

"Good. I want to speak to them first," Ingrid looked at them. They seemed terrified.

"Of course, whatever the Ranger wants," said Ermos.

Ingrid and Viggo questioned the witnesses separately so they would not mix up stories or feelings of what they had been through. The men told them what they had seen and experienced, but unfortunately what they told Viggo and Ingrid was what Ingers had already told them. Horror stories of a beast glimpsed for just a moment and only partially, a creature that resembled a dragon, at least in their imagination, since none had ever seen a dragon before, No matter how much they asked and tried to make sense of what these people had seen, the Rangers did not get any clear answers. They were not exactly witnesses with facts, rather the contrary. Fear

85

and superstitions blurred the witnesses' judgment.

"Thank you all for your cooperation," Ingrid told the men when they finished.

"Can we see the trails now?" Viggo asked.

"Certainly, follow me," Endar led the way for all.

They followed but did not have to walk far.

"It happened here," Endar said, indicating some bushes.

Ingrid and Viggo bent over to check the trail, careful not to alter the place of the attack. There was blood on the ground and on some of the bushes which the scarce rain that had fallen since the attack had not erased yet. They studied the place thoroughly while the rest of the group watched them in silence.

"By the remaining blood and considering the time that's passed, the attack must've been pretty gruesome," commented Ingrid.

"It slew the body, part of it fell here," Viggo indicated more shrubs further back.

"I see it... but there are no tracks of any beast..." Ingrid said, looking puzzled.

"Yeah, it's as if the creature came from out of nowhere and slew whoever it found here."

"Do you know who the victim was?"

"We think it was Pintras Vilfred, a miner who liked to fish in the lake," said Ingers.

"You think?" Ingrid asked, staring at the Captain.

"There's no way of knowing for sure... there are three other blood trails close by," said Ingers. "We can only guess according to what we know about the three missing people," he said.

"Well, that's not much help," Viggo commented.

"We haven't been able to find out more," Ingers said with an apologetic shrug as he looked at the Chief.

"There are no bodies, so it's hard to determine who disappeared where. The attacks occurred in a wide area but close to the village..." Ermos apologized.

"All right. Show us the other two locations," Ingrid asked him.

Ingers nodded and motioned for the two hunters to guide them.

Endar and Ores led them to the next blood trail, which was indeed about five hundred paces following the forest they were in. When they arrived the soldiers again guarded the perimeter while Ingrid and Viggo examined the traces.

86

"Very similar to the other attack," commented Ingrid.

"Yes, lots of blood, but without a trace of the beast or of dragging the body," said Viggo.

"We can't tell what kind of beast it is, or how it got to the victim. Or how it's taken it away," Ingrid said in frustration.

"Only that it killed brutally," said Viggo.

"Are there any other trails that might have escaped Endar and Ores?" Ingers asked.

Ingrid shook her head. "There are no more trails."

"Well... I'd hoped the Rangers could find more traces."

Ingrid glared at him.

"Don't get me wrong, I'm not questioning your abilities, it's simply that I hoped..." the Captain explained.

"You can't find a trail that never existed," Viggo said.

"Exactly," Endar joined in.

"There's no way to know where the beast came from or where it went," said Ores. "I've spent my whole life hunting in these forests and I've never seen anything like this. Every attack leaves traces of coming and going, but not this one."

"But the beast has to have arrived somehow..." the Captain said, looking into the forest and then toward the lake shore.

"Not if the attacker comes from there," Viggo said, pointing at the sky above their heads.

"You also believe that it's a dragon that flew down and killed them?" Ingers said, looking surprised.

"It was a dragon for sure," said one of the witnesses.

"I saw it, all scales and with the eyes of a great reptile," said another.

"It had a huge mouth," said a third.

"It could've been a dragon or a giant eagle. It is said there are giant birds in some remote parts of Tremia," Ingrid commented.

"I'm leaning toward a huge dragon," said Viggo.

"But there's no proof of its existence..." the Captain began.

"Not here," Ingrid shook her head.

"It's a dragon, I don't know why no one believes us," said another witness.

"It's because it's a mythological creature... not easy to believe..." the Chief said, soothingly patting the man on the back.

"Let's go and take a look at the next trail," said Ingrid.

They went on, checking all the trails the hunters showed them. As they went from trail to trail, they headed further north, bordering the great lake. They came to the last place where an attack had occurred. They did not have much hope of finding any clues, but they had to make sure. Being thorough was important when investigating something like this. They could not skip anything or extrapolate what had happened—they had to investigate on site.

So they did, and as they went about their task the sky began to darken and stars appeared in a relatively clear sky. It was not raining and it was not cold, so they could continue investigating.

"Anything?" the Captain asked them after letting them work in peace for a good while.

Ingrid snorted in frustration.

"Nothing. It's just like the other cases, lots of blood but no other trail that might shed light on what happened."

"There are no trails of any beast, which strengthens the hypothesis of a dragon," Viggo insisted.

"Thank goodness someone believes us," said one of the witnesses.

"High time they did," said another.

The soldiers were forming the safety perimeter and were not listening to the conversation. Captain Ingers seemed to prefer it that way. Rumors spread fast among the soldiers.

"From the witnesses' comments?" Ingers asked as he looked at the men in the accompanying group who had last spoken.

"That, and because the attack had to have come from the sky," Viggo said.

"I'm sorry, but I can't accept that. Dragons aren't real," Captain Ingers said firmly.

Viggo opened his mouth to reply when huge jaws clamped down on the captain.

A reptilian creature snatched the Captain away in one bite before taking to the sky.

Chapter 10

"Dragon!" cried Ermos, screaming in terror.

"The beast's attacking us!" Endar yelled as he jumped back, reaching for an arrow.

The Captain's feet were rising in the air while the rest of his body had vanished inside the colossal monster's mouth, of which they could only see the head. The body blended in with the darkness of the night already enveloping them, or perhaps it was hidden by some invisibility spell.

"Everyone, take cover!" Ingrid ordered, waving her arms for everyone to seek cover in the underbrush of the forest. The peasants were so terrified they could not move. With bulging eyes, they watched the monster gobbling up the Captain in the air.

"Hide quickly!" Viggo shouted at them, and when he saw they were not reacting he shoved them forward. If they stayed there staring at the horror with their mouths agape, they were going to end up the same way as the unfortunate Captain.

Ermos shouted again and ran off with his arms raised like a madman. Several of the peasants seemed to react when they saw their Chief flee in terror and screamed as they ran after Ermos to hide among the trees.

"It's... eaten the Captain..." Ores muttered, trying to keep as calm as he possibly could. He nocked an arrow in his hunting bow and lifted his weapon to aim.

Viggo reached for the bow at his back and nocked an arrow, ready to attack the monster that had vanished in the dark sky.

"Don't hide, little dragon, I'm going to give you what for," he muttered, searching the sky, his bow ready to release. "Where are you hiding?"

A couple of large solitary clouds floated in the night sky with such ill fortune that they covered the moon, which meant they did not have much light to see the monster or whatever was above their heads.

"Soldiers, the beast is attacking us!" Ingrid shouted in the direction of the perimeter where the detachment was watching to alert them. The attack had taken place in the blink of an eye and some surely had not even realized.

"Orders, Captain?" came the request of those among the trees.

"Captain Ingers is dead!" Ingrid replied.

There was silence. None of the soldiers said a word, as if they were digesting her words. Suddenly one of the clouds let some moonlight through and a huge head covered in scales with enormous reptilian eyes appeared above them.

Endar and Ores released at the monster. The arrows flew at the dragon's head which, having eaten the Captain, was now coming down for another victim. The hunters released accurately and hit the reptile's head. The arrows buried themselves and seemed to pierce the scales, but they did not manage to stop the attack. The monster ignored them and with its huge maw grabbed another of the soldiers at the perimeter of the forest and ate him in two terrible bites.

The soldiers were screaming, not knowing what to do. They carried spears and axes since they were part of the city guard. They did not carry bows to attack the beast with, as it was already swooping down for another soldier to eat.

"Step back!" Ingrid warned them.

The soldiers ran in fear in every direction, trying to escape the monster. They leaped over the brush and crouched under the branches of the trees in the hopes of putting enough space between them and the murderous beast's maw.

Ingrid and Viggo released at the huge head and their arrows bore into the monster's scales, near one of its eyes. A whistling sound, similar to that of a snake but more powerful, came out if its mouth.

The other cloud moved too, drifting with the night winds, and the moonlight finally reached them. They could see the monster better at last as it attacked from the sky.

"There's the pretty little dragon!" cried Viggo, who could now see it properly.

Ingrid looked at the monster and noticed that although it was coming down from the sky and the head was that of a great reptile with a big snout, it did not resemble the head of a dragon. At least not the one they had seen inside the volcano. A long neck followed the head, long and thick, like the trunk of a century-old tree that went on and on.

"Viggo, what is that monster?" she asked as she released again.

"I have no idea, but that's not our friend Dergha-Sho-Blaska," he replied, releasing in turn.

The monstrous head came down and grabbed one of the three soldiers who, seeing it was upon them, tried to fight it with their spears. The other two were thrown back from the impact of the huge monster's head.

Ingrid aimed her bow and followed the head as it soared over thirty feet up. She realized that the beast's body was long and snakelike, over ninety feet long, and that the end of it was hidden under the lake. She also noticed that all along the rounded body, on what had to be its back, there was a great crest that ran up to its head.

"It's some kind of giant crested snake! It seems to be coming from the lake!"

Viggo watched the body and saw something that puzzled him.

"It's not a snake, it has legs. I see four thick legs with claws."

"Where?" Ingrid was now releasing at the body, which was long and thick, rounded, crested, and covered in scales.

"Follow the part of the body that comes out of the water and goes parallel to the ground," Viggo indicated with the arrow in his hand.

Ingrid did as Viggo told her and managed to see the four legs. These were indeed similar to the dragon's they had seen.

"It's a strange monster!" she cried as she released.

"One third of its body is in the water, another third is on land, and the last third ends in that horrendous head. That's the part it's attacking us with," said Endar, who was releasing, trying to keep his hand steady in spite of his fear.

"It relies on its legs to move but the body is like that of a snake. It can rise to a great height," said Ores, releasing as well and running to hide behind some large bushes.

"Have you ever seen anything like this before?" Ingrid asked them while trying to stop the monster from devouring the soldiers of the city guard, who were no match for it with their spears.

"No, never. There are no monsters like this, at least here," Endar said, leaping over a tree and releasing again at the colossal creature.

"It's clearly a huge, abnormal mixture of dragon and water snake," Viggo said. "I think we can call it 'Dra-co-Sna-ke.' Yup, I like it. We'll call it that."

"That sounds ridiculous. Think about how we're going to kill it

91

instead. In case you haven't noticed, we're not doing very well so far," Ingrid chided.

"Thinking, planning, and such, that's not my thing, I'm better at killing it," he replied and released at its body.

Ingrid watched the long scaly and crested body. Apart from being extremely long it was thick, so although her arrows stuck into the creature, they did not seem to do much harm. She sought another target and saw the legs. In comparison with its body, they were a lot smaller, although also thick. She thought of the weak spot of a giant—it was always its feet. That was where they should attack.

"Soldiers, regroup! Attack the legs one by one!" she ordered. "Everyone, attack the legs!"

The soldiers near the lake ran to do as she said but those in the forest did not follow to help. They remained hidden to avoid being devoured like their companions who had already suffered that horrible fate.

"I think we're working with a bunch of cowards," Viggo told Ingrid.

"Everyone attack the legs, everyone!" Ingrid yelled at the soldiers. "We have to maim it!"

The head was coming down again, and it did so onto the group of soldiers hiding under the forest trees. Somehow the huge snake-dragon saw them and grabbed one of them in its jaws. Then it rose on its long body about thirty feet. The rest of the soldiers, who had been shoved away by the blow of the monster's head which had broken three trees with a terrible sound of splitting wood, were trying to get back up.

Viggo gestured to the hunters.

"Let's follow Ingrid's instructions and release at the front left leg," he said, cold and confident. The monster was fearsome, but Viggo did not care. He was not in the least impressed. For him it was no more than an enemy he had to fight and ultimately kill. A huge, terrifying one, out of a horrible nightmare, but he was not scared of it.

The two hunters nodded. "Okay."

The three released at the leg and the arrows hit it.

"Aren't they too thick?" Endar asked.

"At least they're short, it won't be able to come running," Ores sighed in relief.

"Let's shoot and see if we can maim it," Viggo told them.

"Get on your feet and attack the legs!" Ingrid ordered the soldiers in the forest. Everyone, attack the legs! If you flee I'll hang you from a tree myself, you cowards!"

Her shouts and threats had a positive effect. The soldiers obeyed the order. Those at the lake shore attacked the back left leg while the rest of the survivors in the forest ran through the trees to help them.

"I'll release at the eyes to distract it!" Ingrid warned Viggo and the two hunters.

"Better try and blind it," Viggo told her as he nocked another arrow and prepared to release fast.

The monster swooped down over the group of lagging soldiers running after its legs and caught one of them in its mouth. The man vanished in the huge maw.

"Now we know why there were no traces of the bodies, they were eaten by this gluttonous beast," Viggo commented as he aimed.

"And why there was no trace in the places where it attacked," said Ores.

"It must live in the lake, it's quite deep," Endar commented. "There are stories in our folklore about the monster in that lake, although it was not described like that at all."

"It seems to me that most of the great lakes have stories of monsters," Viggo said. "Just like mountain caves."

"That's true," Endar agreed as he moved to release from another position.

Ingrid shot at the creature's eye but the monster rose with its prey in its mouth to swallow it in the air. Ingrid swore under her breath and tried again. This time she waited for the monster's head to be still for an instant and released. She used an Earth Elemental Arrow. It did not hit the eye by a hair's breadth because the head began to sway, looking for another prey. But the following explosion of blinding earth, smoke, and other elements did reach the huge reptilian eye.

The monster was affected. It tilted its head and shook it hard, trying to get rid of whatever had gotten into its eye while at the same time trying to tear to pieces the men attacking its back leg. The legs ended in tremendous claws and the soldiers were falling fast, either torn by them or crushed against the ground.

Viggo and the two hunters were punishing the front left leg. They had released over a dozen arrows and the leg was bleeding a substance that had to be blood but that was greenish-black instead of red. They had to be wounding it, since the rest of the arrows that had pierced the body had barely drawn blood. This was a good sign. The problem was it could take ages to hurt it enough to cripple it.

The snake-dragon was trying to get rid of the soldiers and the arrows that were hampering both its back legs. It kicked back with one of leg at the soldiers, who had to jump away to avoid being squashed. Then it tried clawing at them. Its movements were slow compared to those of the head, and the men were able to avoid the attack.

Ingrid released anther Elemental Arrow, trying to finish blinding the left eye. The arrow detonated above the eye and the explosion bothered the monster and it shook its head up and down and then sideways to get rid of it.

Viggo reached for his quiver and found it empty. He had released all the arrows he carried against the monster.

"It seems it's time to give a little more love to dear Dra-co-Sna-ke here," he joked and left his bow on the ground. He ran toward the beast at lightning speed.

"What the heck are you doing!" Ingrid cried when she saw what Viggo intended.

"Keep blinding it! You're doing well, but it's still got another eye!" Viggo shouted as he ran at top speed.

Ingrid uttered several curses, but she knew it was useless. She could never reason with Viggo. He was following one of his crazy ideas. It was impossible to make him stop and think in the middle of the fray, so she sighed and calmed down. She sought an Air Arrow in her quiver and nocked it.

"I'm going to change position to try and hit the right eye!" she told the two hunters.

"Should we go with you?" Ores offered.

"No, stay here and shoot from this side!" she ordered them as she ran away through the forest.

Endar and Ores nodded.

"And don't hit Viggo! I'm not sure what he's up to!" she warned them.

"We'll try!" Ores shouted back.

Viggo reached the monster. He ran to its back leg where the

soldiers still standing were wounding it repeatedly with the steel tips of their spears. He noticed they were managing to hurt it. The beast's blood was soaking the ground.

"Keep going! Hit it hard!" he cheered.

The monster tried to crush Viggo with its wounded leg. He jumped to one side nimbly to avoid it.

"I can see you're having a good time here," he said to the soldiers when he finished the movement and stood back up. The monster's claws tried to reach Viggo, but he was too fast for the enormous animal which, although it had tremendous strength, did not move that fast.

The soldiers stared at Viggo in awe. They moved as fast as they could when the beast attacked them, but they were unable to avoid the creature's attacks like Viggo did.

"Keep at it, I'll distract it," Viggo said as he ran and in one great leap jumped onto the first leg the hunters were shooting and which was riddled with arrows. He buried his knives into the creature's flesh and used them to climb.

The soldiers seemed to recover their strength when they saw Viggo's rush and resumed attacking the huge back leg with their spears over and over again. It was like boring into a huge oak, only this one bled if they managed to pierce through the scales.

"Don't release now or we'll hit him!" Endar warned Ores.

"What's that crazy Ranger doing?" Ores said, unable to believe what he was seeing.

"He's climbing up the leg... toward the serpent's body..." Ender was muttering, impressed.

Both hunters watched Viggo as he reached the crested back of the snake-dragon, climbing up the scales using his knives. With a swift push he got onto one of the spikes of the crest and held on to it, carefully making his way along the monster's crest from spike to spike. These were wide but not very tall, not more than three people high. But they were hard as stone. Viggo was looking for a spot to bury his knives in for help as he climbed up the body as if it were a mountain. A mountain that, mind you, moved and thrashed to get rid of its enemies.

"This Ranger is absolutely crazy," Ores muttered, shaking his head while he watched Viggo's acrobatics.

"Absolutely raving mad," Endar agreed, unable to stop watching

Viggo with wide eyes.

It took them a moment to comprehend what they were watching. If the monster already seemed unreal, seeing a Ranger climbing up its crested body was totally unthinkable. They quickly recovered and started shooting at the leg Viggo had climbed.

Ingrid got into a better position to reach the beast's right eye. She was about to release when she saw Viggo climbing along the snake-dragon's body, using the crest like a range of peaks to reach the head. She was absolutely sure that was what he intended to do: reach the monster's head.

"Can he be more reckless!" she cried, astonished. "But what on earth is he doing? Has he lost the little sense he had!" she muttered under her breath with a mixture of fear and frustration. Viggo was unpredictable, foolish and a scatterbrain—only he could have come up with such an idea. The plan to blind it was the best one and the least dangerous. But thinking again, since when had Viggo given a second thought to what was best and safe? Never, or if he did it was purely by accident.

She regained her poise and relaxed. There was nothing she could do now to stop him, so she focused on going along with her plan of blinding the monster before it devoured the fool. The left eye was closed so it could not see much. It was time to target the other one in order to render it useless. She lifted her bow and aimed carefully, following the movements of the monster's head, and released. The Elemental Air Arrow flew to the reptile's eye.

The snake-dragon was distracted and trying to get rid of Viggo, whom it had detected on its back. Viggo's knives did not seem to do much damage, as if the monster had a thick protective layer between its scales and skin the knives could not penetrate. But they allowed Viggo to maintain a better hold when the beast shook itself to try and dislodge him.

Ingrid's arrow hit the monster in the mouth instead of the eye when it thrashed to try and devour Viggo, who was now dangling from his knives from one side to another, trying to avoid the maw that wanted to gobble him up. He had lost his hold on the crest's spikes and was fighting to not fall off and kill himself. There was a loud burst, followed by a discharge.

The snake-dragon emitted some kind of shrill scream and shut its mouth. The arrow had hurt it. It lifted its head with abrupt and sinuous movements in an attempt to avoid more arrows like that one. Viggo was withstanding the thrashing while still attempting to reach the crest to find his hold again and keep climbing up the serpent's body.

Ingrid cheered up. The Air Arrow had hurt it. She reached for another one while Viggo went on burying his knives in the monster's body to climb up it. He tried to not fall to the ground when the serpent thrashed violently, trying to shake him off.

Viggo found himself dangling from his knives after one of these thrashes. He was close to the monster's head, but at the same time at about twenty-five feet from the ground he would surely get killed if he fell.

Ingrid released again without aiming too carefully—she needed the monster to not attack Viggo. The Air Arrow hit it on the head and there was another burst, followed by a discharge. The monster shook its head up and down. This caused Viggo to lose his grip on one of his knives and he was left hanging with one hand from the tremendous height.

Ingrid cried out when she saw him.

The soldiers attacked the leg and the monster screamed again. Both left legs were in bad shape. They were losing that corrupted-looking blood and now the damage was visible in the monster's flesh.

Then the creature's back half came out of the water and like a whip lashed at the last three soldiers left standing and attacking it. It sent them flying. They fell several paces away and did not get back up.

The two hunters continued their attack on the other leg until they ran out of arrows.

"What do we do now?" Ores asked.

"We finish that leg," Endar said.

"It'll most likely kill us," Ores remarked.

Endar indicated Viggo still hanging from one hand.

"If he can do that, we can maim that big leg."

Ores nodded. They both grasped their hunting knives and ran to attack the leg already riddled with arrows.

Ingrid took the last arrow she had left: it was an Earth Elemental arrow.

She knew she would have to hit the eye or else Viggo would not live to tell the tale, so she aimed carefully. The snake-dragon was trying to bite Viggo, but the turning angle was too steep and it did not reach him so it started to shake its head hard to dislodge him. Ingrid was getting nervous—Viggo would not be able to hold on with all that thrashing, and the head was moving too much for her to land a true shot.

Endar and Ores stabbed the leg like crazy, delivering piercing blows with their knives. They were trying their best to help. The monster stopped its thrashing and looked at them. They had caught its attention, and it would now kill them. At that instant, when both hunters were thinking they were already dead, with Viggo hanging from one hand from one of his knives, Ingrid's arrow flew swift and accurate. The beast began to move its head when the Earth Arrow hit the side of the right eye. There was a blinding detonation.

The snake-dragon screamed and squeezed its eye shut. The arrow had been effective.

"Yes!" Ingrid cried triumphantly.

Viggo managed to get a hold on his other knife again and he now hung from both as he tried to climb onto the crest spike closest to the head.

"Move over, it's moving!" Ores warned Endar. Both hunters jumped backward as they saw the wounded leg move.

The colossal snake-dragon turned around as best as it could with two of its legs wounded, moving with heavy, slow, unbalanced movements. It looked like a large ship keeling over against the rocks. It faced the lake and headed to the water.

"It's going in!" Ingrid warned as she ran toward the hunters, who were moving out of its way.

Clumsily and with great difficulty, to avoid capsizing, the monster was about to dive into the water. Viggo had already reached the head and climbed up onto it. There was no crest on top so, with all his strength, he buried both his knives in it.

The snake-dragon gave out a shrill, whistling scream. The head began to come down toward the surface of the water. Viggo saw the movement and was about to jump into the water, but the height was still too great so he went on attacking. The head sought the water fast. Viggo saw they were going to plunge in so he leaped off the head a moment before it broke the surface of the lake. The body of the great monster followed the head and plunged in. Viggo entered the lake with his feet first to one side of the tremendous dive of the monster. A moment later it vanished in the depths of the lake.

Viggo resurfaced, snorting.

"Viggo!" Ingrid cried, running to help him get out of the water. "Are you all right?"

"All right? I feel great!" he said, shaking off the water.

Ingrid was about to scold him, but Viggo got ahead of her and kissed her.

"That's not going to give you a free pass," she threatened him.

"I know, but for the time being it's okay," he smiled. "And how are you two?" he said, looking at Ores and Endar.

"Fine... we're fine," said Endar.

Ores checked himself all over to make sure nothing was missing.

Viggo stretched his arms. "Well, this has been most entertaining. We should do it more often," he told them.

Ores and Endar looked horrified.

"Leave them be, I think they've had enough for quite some time," Ingrid told Viggo.

"It's been a pleasure, Hunters, see you at the next monster hunt," Viggo winked at them as together with Ingrid they headed to see whether there were any surviving soldiers.

Chapter 11

"This has been a horrible disaster!" Magistrate Mustrel cried, looking miserable. He stood up and began to pace in circles in his studio.

"It wasn't a complete success, but at least we managed to wound and drive away the monster," Ingrid replied, standing in the middle of the room. Viggo stood beside her, and a little further back stood the hunters Ores and Endar, Ermos, the village Chief of High Rock, and the four surviving soldiers.

"How am I going to tell Duke Wrotoson what's happened? He's not going to believe me!" Mustrel cried, waving his arms in the air and shaking his head.

"Why wouldn't he believe a story corroborated by all these witnesses here?" Ingrid said, indicating the people with her.

"Because it's about a monster that's never been seen in Norghana before!" Mustrel cried, looking troubled.

"It's a water snake-dragon to be precise," said Viggo. "I call it a Dra-co-Sna-ke, and I want to be acknowledged as the monster's discoverer in the books of history, in tomes of mythical creatures, and in the songs of bards and troubadours. Even more, I want it known that it was me who beat the monster and drove it away."

Ingrid gave him a look that was as much as saying "you can't be serious!"

Then she asked him, annoyed, "Did you beat him on your own?"

"Well, we all fought the monster, but the final blow was mine. Therefore, I deserve recognition."

"A monstrous snake-dragon over ninety feet long, with huge jaws, a thick body like several century-old oaks, and four legs ending in claws?" Mustrel asked, wanting to verify the details before telling anyone. His face showed utter disbelief.

"And a crested back from the head to the tip of the tail," Viggo added. "I climbed up the crest to conquer the abominable beast. Let the poets know."

"I can't even conceive of such a creature."

"Yet that doesn't make its appearance in Lake Krystall any less true," Ingrid insisted.

"You, of the village, do you corroborate this?" Mustrel asked them, pointing his finger at each one.

"A monster like that has never been seen before," Ermos said. "Terrifying. He took the Captain up in one bite and gobbled him up."

"And the rest of the soldiers as well," Ores added.

"It's just like the Rangers have told you. I confirm every word," Endar said.

"We all saw it, we can confirm it," said Ermos.

"Unbelievable! Horrendous!" cried Mustrel.

"It was…" said one of the surviving soldiers, whose arm was broken and in a tightly bandaged splint.

"You confirm it as well then?" the Magistrate asked the soldiers.

"It's just like they've said. Horrible. No matter how many times we stabbed its leg with our spears, we could barely harm it."

"It was a lot more terrifying than they've told you. Horrendous. It was devouring our colleagues like a giant snake would eat small rodents," another solider confirmed.

Mustrel waved his hands to stop them—he had heard enough.

"Very well. I have no choice but to conclude that what you're telling me really happened. I'll inform the Duke."

"You should set a surveillance post at the lake, in case the monster appears again," Ingrid recommended. "We'll inform Gondabar and he'll send Rangers to watch the area, but a permanent post of the Duke's soldiers would be better."

"I'll pass on the recommendation to my lord, it's his decision to make," Mustrel nodded and was silent for a moment. "Do you believe this monster might come back and attack?"

Viggo shrugged, "if it's hungry it might come out again," he said without much conviction.

"We don't know, but since we couldn't kill it, there's the possibility it might appear again," said Ingrid.

"What I don't understand is why such a monster has appeared now when it has never done so before. Why now?" The Magistrate was stroking his chin with his fingers while he tried to reason through the question he asked out loud.

Ingrid and Viggo exchanged looks.

"There's been news of the appearance of a similar monster.

Perhaps the sightings are related. Perhaps not, we'll have to investigate more."

"What strange times we're living in," Mustrel commented.

"They are strange indeed," Ingrid confirmed.

"Sergeant Lomen, have the men withdraw to rest and have their wounds taken care of," Mustrel told the Sergeant, who was standing by the door awaiting orders.

"Right away, sir,"

"You, stay here and tell my assistants everything again. I want to have your testimonies in writing," he told the Hunters and the village Chief of High Rock.

"Whatever the Magistrate needs," Ermos offered with a slight bow.

"We must leave to give our report to Gondabar and the other leaders," said Ingrid.

"Fine, fine, when are you leaving?"

"At dawn."

Mustrel nodded. "You can tell Gondabar, and he may tell the King, that Magistrate Mustrel of the city of Ostangor, loyal servant of Duke Pilman Wrotoson, has collaborated with his Rangers as requested."

"We will, sir," Ingrid promised.

"With a respectful nod, Ingrid and Viggo left the room, leaving the Magistrate and his assistants to the witnesses' depositions.

Once in their rooms, Viggo threw himself on the bed and snorted.

"What an adventure."

"You shouldn't have jumped onto the snake-dragon," Ingrid scolded him. "If you keep doing all that crazy stuff, you'll end up getting killed."

"That wasn't so crazy..." Viggo said defensively. "I'd say somewhat foolish," he said, lying with his hands behind his head.

"No way, that was utterly stupid! You're going to get killed, and I'll have to witness it and suffer!" Ingrid scolded, furious.

"Come on, don't be cross. You know me... sometimes I can't help doing something crazy."

"Don't you realize that if something happens to you it'll be me who'll be left heartbroken? I won't be able to stand the pain." A tear rolled down Ingrid's cheek.

Viggo sat up. He had never seen Ingrid so moved.

"I'm sorry... I..."

"No, you're not, and please use your head before you act."

"I'll try," he promised and tried to hug her. He put his arms around her and tried to kiss her, but she moved her head.

"You're not alone in this. We're a couple. You have to stop thinking only of yourself. You can't walk around as if you were immortal, because you're not, and one day you'll find out. And then what? I'll be left to mourn your death. Me and everyone who loves you."

Viggo was touched by Ingrid's words.

"You're right... I was reckless and didn't think of anyone else... of the consequences if anything had happened to me..."

"I'm telling you because I don't want to lose you during one of your crazy exploits. The pain and suffering you'd bring me would be unbearable."

"I don't want to lose you either..." he admitted, kissing her forehead. "I'll keep it in mind. The last thing I want to do is hurt you, make you suffer. I would never forgive myself."

"If you really care for me, don't."

"I care for you more than anything in this world. You're the most important thing in my life. I won't make you suffer, I promise."

Ingrid was soothed by Viggo's words and by seeing in his eyes that he really meant them.

"Remember, you've promised."

"I will. Don't worry. May I kiss you now? I can't resist those captivating eyes and those intoxicating lips of yours."

Ingrid smiled.

"Kiss me, you rascal."

Viggo kissed her passionately.

It was past midnight when Viggo gently woke Ingrid up.

"What is it? Are we under attack?" she asked, coming out of a deep sleep and reaching for her weapons instinctively.

"No, everything's fine, don't worry."

Ingrid opened her eyes and saw Viggo dressed and armed. She

realized the room was quiet and understood.

"Where are you going?"

"I have a small matter to attend to…"

"You're going out at night again? To the city slums?"

"Yes, there's something I have to take care of…"

"Didn't you promise you wouldn't do any more foolish things?"

Viggo looked up at the ceiling of the room.

"It's not foolish and it's barely dangerous."

"Sure, and I'm buying that," Ingrid folded her arms over her chest.

"But I woke you up to let you know and all," Viggo smiled at her.

"I don't think you fully understand what not doing your kind of foolish things means. Waking me up to tell me that you're going to do them doesn't mean it's all right to go ahead and do them."

"It's a start. I have to go step by step, I can't change overnight," Viggo apologized with a shrug.

Ingrid got up and began to get dressed in her full Ranger gear.

"You didn't even get overnight after promising. It's not morning yet!" Ingrid snapped, pointing out the window.

"Why are you getting dressed…?"

"Because I'm coming with you, why else?"

"No way. You can't come with me. Where I'm going you can't come."

"And you can?"

"I'm a sewer rat of this city, don't forget. That's why I can go where others like you can't."

"If you go, I'm coming."

"Ingrid… don't be stubborn…"

"Viggo… you're not going to persuade me."

Viggo snorted.

"Fine, but do whatever I tell you and keep your distance. If you're seen we'll be in serious trouble."

"Didn't you say this escapade of yours was barely dangerous?"

"I meant for myself, it's not dangerous for me. For you it is."

"Well, I don't care. I'm coming with you."

"You're a charmer, and so terribly hard to please," Viggo said as he gave her a fleeting kiss on the lips and headed to the door.

Chapter 12

Alvis the Erudite rose from his big armchair, and with a sign for them to follow he led Egil and Gerd downstairs. One thing they noticed when Alvis left his throne-looking chair was that he was really a very small man. He gave the impression of being a child who had aged with the passing of the years but who nevertheless had not grown up like normal people did.

The two friends watched him walk down the stairs as they followed him and exchanged a glance. They were both thinking the same thing. He did not appear to be suffering from dwarfism, as was the case with Enduald, Sigrid's brother. He simply seemed to have stopped growing at age twelve. It was curious that the person who was supposed to have the most knowledge in all of northern Tremia could be such a small being.

Egil thought it corroborated the theory of many scholars in Tremia, that the size of the body and that of the mind had nothing to do with each other, something uncultivated people and most Norghanians believed. In Norghana, the size of a person defined in great measure the worth of said person. It was also true that most Norghanians were tall and strong as oaks. They were also brutal and brainless like few others. This was not what Egil thought, but the rest of Tremia did, and not without reason, to be honest.

As they went down underground, what Egil was thinking was that he found it sad and meaningless to have one of the wisest persons in the continent who would not deign to help anyone, more so being a Norghanian himself, whether he liked it or not. He could understand his reluctance—Egil also liked being left in peace to be able to study and experiment. But given how uncommon it was to have a brilliant, sublime mind bursting with knowledge in Norghana, it was a real shame Alvis did not help the people of his own realm. The excuse that in the past the tower had not been part of the kingdom was not valid based on Egil's understanding. The territorial lines on a map should not mark the will to help a people.

Egil was aware that being an Erudite did not necessarily entail being compassionate or altruistic. In this case in particular, it was clear that Alvis was quite selfish and only interested in his own studies and not in the well-being of others. Egil was confident the little wise man could help the Norghanians or anyone else he wanted, and with very little effort on his part. The problem was he did not seem inclined to do it. He had more important things to do than help others. Luckily, they had a Royal Order, otherwise he would not have received them. Alvis might be a surly, self-centered erudite, but he was not so presumptuous as to oppose a royal command. Thoran had no sympathy for those who questioned his orders, least of all for those who refused to carry them out.

Once they arrived at the basement, the Erudite led them to a door with three large locks. Alvis took out a bunch of large keys and skillfully opened the door's three locks one after the other without mixing the keys, which looked hard, since they were all practically identical. They had to be marked somehow, but the distinctions were not obvious.

He opened the door, pushing hard. They moved to help the Erudite, since the door was made of wood reinforced with steel on the inside and weighed a lot. Surprisingly, the little scholar was able to open it without their help.

"Wait here for a moment. I'll go in and light the lamps," said Alvis.

Egil and Gerd waited outside, exchanging intrigued glances for whatever they were going to find inside.

The Erudite reappeared presently.

"You may now come in," he told them with a wave of his arm.

They found themselves in a huge rectangular hall, over twelve feet high and very wide. This threw them off a little. The width of the hall was greater than the base of the tower, or at least that was the impression it gave. Egil stared at the four walls lit by oil lamps carefully placed on top of stone pedestals. Gerd scratched his head, trying to understand how it was possible that the underground floor was larger than the tower itself.

The books the hall contained were placed on wooden shelves against the walls and long metal structures similar to armor racks that rose from floor to ceiling throughout the room, and which seemed to be divided into corridors big enough for two people.

"There are tons of books in here," Gerd said as he gaped at the structures that held them.

"Welcome to the most peculiar and interesting book section of all Tremia," Alvis announced.

"Forbidden books?" Gerd asked in a fearful tone.

"That depends on the eyes of the beholder. Forbidden for some, essential for others," the Erudite replied.

"I bet they're all essential," Egil commented, already looking at the huge shelves in search of interesting tomes.

"That's also my opinion."

"I'd rather think they're essential..." Gerd muttered, more to himself than for Alvis and Egil to hear.

"Very well, follow me to the far end wall," Alvis told them. "That's where my private collection of books about dragons is."

Gerd glanced at Egil with a look that said "where else would it be other than at the far end?"

When they reached the end they saw an enormous wooden shelf that went from wall to wall and from floor to ceiling.

"Here it is, all the books I've found during the course of my life that deal with dragons. Some directly, others indirectly. A few that might be credible, many that are only fables and stories that no one would believe, not to mention those which are pure folklore or essays on northern mythology."

"Which are the ones that might be credible?" Gerd asked, intending to get straight to the point.

"The big guy has a head after all, huh?" Alvis smiled at him in a mischievous way like a naughty, playful child.

"He does indeed," Egil replied, already leafing through books.

"That's uncommon. Such a gigantic, muscular Norghanian like this one seldom has anything up here," Alvis said, pointing his finger at his own forehead.

"Gerd is an exception," Egil said with a proud smile.

"I'm here and I can hear what you're saying," Gerd said, spreading his arms wide, a look of disbelief on his face.

"Here's the deal," Alvis said all of a sudden. "I'll allow you to stay here and look for the information you're looking for in my collection on the condition that you won't disturb me under any circumstance."

"Why don't you give us the information so we can finish sooner and leave?" Gerd asked, unable to believe the Erudite was not going to just give it to them.

"Because that's the easy way and I'm reluctant to take it. Whoever wants something must sacrifice and fight for it. If you are given things in life, you won't learn to obtain them and value them adequately."

"But there are hundreds of books here and we're in a hurry. The Kingdom is in danger, the dragon might attack at any moment," Gerd explained with extreme urgency and arm waving.

"The Kingdom is always in danger. It has always been and will always be. Whether by threat of an external invading force, civil war, a natural cataclysm, the attack of mythological creatures, or any number of other causes. In spite of everything, we're here and we'll keep going, whatever the next threat is."

"This threat is real and dangerous, it could mean the end of the Kingdom," Egil added, trying to persuade the Erudite.

"I understand. But as I have already explained, there will always be threats, and I will not neglect my work for any of them. Today you're here. Others have come before with similar claims, and in a near future others will come still with greater difficulties. I'm not going to waste my precious time every time the kingdom's threatened. That would be incongruous. I'm also not going to make your way easier when it's taken me so much time and effort to get to where I am. You have all the information I have available in here, it's yours to study. How long it takes you is your own business, not mine."

"But..." Gerd started to protest.

"Not a word more. I'm already helping you enough," the Erudite's tone left no doubt.

"We appreciate the Erudite's help. We will continue the search ourselves," said Egil, putting an end to the argument with a resigned look on his face.

"Very well, I don't want you disturbing my assistants either. Since I assume the task will take you days, you'll have to supply your own food and water. I'm sure you'll have no trouble finding both in the nearby woods and fields, since you're Rangers."

Gerd could not believe the Erudite's words and his face showed it.

"What do you mean..."

"Of course, this won't be a problem," Egil said, responding before Gerd could protest.

"Good, I'll get back to my studies. I've already wasted too much time. I'll leave you to start your search. I hope you find what you're looking for." The Erudite left them there, his footsteps fading as he returned upstairs.

Gerd could not stop himself any longer.

"What a fraud, I could strangle him!" he said angrily.

"I understand how you feel, pal," Egil told him, patting his shoulder.

"Let me strangle him once we find what we're looking for."

"No, we can't do that," Egil said, smiling.

"He deserves it. And a good wallop for being such a cretin."

"I'm not saying he doesn't, but it won't be from us."

"I hope one day someone does."

"I have a feeling that someday someone will."

"I hope it's soon."

"It is enough to get angry indeed," said Egil, looking at his giant friend. "Things don't usually affect you so much. You have a big heart. I can barely remember ever seeing you angry."

"I have a good character, but the fact that this vain scholar thinks his time is the most precious thing in the world and that he won't help us when we come to him with a serious problem makes me furious. Besides, the petulant fop doesn't even deign to feed us. It's shameful and it makes me angry. We're not here on holiday. Who does that vain dwarf think he is!"

"And we were lucky that we came asking about one of his favorite subjects, otherwise this interview would've gone even worse."

"Yeah, what a consolation," Gerd was frowning and could not hide his annoyance.

"I'm glad to see you have fire in your heart and that it surfaces every now and then." Egil chuckled.

"If I get angrier it'll explode like a volcano and then he'll have what for," Gerd made a fist.

"Easy, big guy, let's get down to work, that'll make your anger dissipate."

"Yeah, that's true."

"Let's start with the books on the left side. Since there are so many, we'll have to separate those that might contain things of interest so we can go over them in more detail. We'll leave them in the middle of the hall, where there are two study tables, one on each side of the central shelves."

"Okay... but how will I know whether a tome is really interesting or not? What am I looking for?"

Egil looked at the huge collection and scratched his head.

"Let's focus on how to detect a dragon. He's already among us, so anything to do with history and mythology is secondary. I'd love to read everything, but we don't have the time."

"Okay, I'll focus on how to kill a dragon."

"Let's expand on that concept to include how to stop the dragon, force him to leave, freeze him again, put him to sleep, and similar remedies. Not only kill him."

"Oh yeah, good!"

"I'm saying this because I'm afraid we won't find much about killing a dragon. From what we already know, it's practically impossible for men to kill one."

"Right. I'll look for ways to control him or get rid of him one way or another."

"Yes, better. Besides, this dragon calls himself immortal, so I have a suspicion that he's even stronger than a regular dragon. Well, if such a thing exists—I really don't think any dragon is exactly regular."

"That's true. I'll start on the higher shelves since I can reach them more easily, you start with the lower ones."

"That's why I always bring you with me," Egil said, slapping him on the back.

"I thought it was to watch your back."

Egil smiled and shook his head.

"It's because you cover many areas and because I love your company."

"I'm glad, I love all that I learn with you."

"Are you over your anger?"

Gerd thought for a moment.

"I'm completely over it."

"Very good, let's get our hands on those tomes then."

"You know this is going to take weeks, don't you?"

"Yes, but what better place to spend weeks than in this small temple of knowledge?" Egil said, beaming.

"Really, only you could see this situation that way. Viggo is right, you're a bookworm."

"Irrefutable, my dear friend."

Gerd rolled his eyes and started to work. He was going to do everything within his power to finish soon, much sooner.

Chapter 13

Lars and Umber worked on that wall without pause the whole afternoon. They were exhausted, but the thought of finding the treasure seemed to give them renewed strength. Lasgol and Camu went up to the surface and shared watch over the prisoners with Ona while Astrid was in charge of watching the two treasure hunters. Not that they believed Lars and Umber would try anything, but if they did find the treasure and they attempted to escape, it could become a problem. Humans had a tendency to commit unthinkable acts when there was the possibility of getting hold of a good sum of gold.

The two adventurers were working hard and had opened quite a sizable hole in the wall, big enough for a person to get in. Now they were going deeper since they had not reached anything like a chest or trunk or something similar that indicated there was a treasure in there. The hardest part had been the first step: trying to break through the rock wall. It had taken them quite a while, and it had been tough going. Now they were working on a layer of dirt with encrusted stones which, although it was still hard to break, was a lot softer than the first layers in the wall. They were leaving the dirt, stones, and rock on one side of the hole so the debris was not in the way.

"If you don't give it a little more energy we'll be here till nightfall," Astrid said, sitting on the wheelbarrow, watching them.

"We don't have much energy left, to be honest..." Umber protested as he wiped his sweaty forehead. They were perspiring so profusely that the blood on their faces and necks had washed off.

"Water, please," Lars begged, leaning on his pick, exhausted.

"Here you go, and very cool," Astrid threw him the waters-kin that Lasgol had just refilled at the stream.

Both workers drank as if it were the most delicious elixir of a famed alchemist.

"How's it going?" Lasgol asked from the steps.

"No luck so far," Astrid replied.

"Night's beginning to fall and the prisoners are a bit restless."

"Well, there's still work to do here, you'll have to calm them down. I doubt we'll leave before sunrise."

"Okay, I'll see to that. I'm going to take Ona to the cabin to remind them what they can expect if they try to escape or rebel," Lasgol said.

"If you let Ona bite the leader, they'll understand better."

Like that, Camu messaged.

Ona growled once.

"Let's see how they behave first," said Lasgol, who was no friend of gratuitous violence. Unfortunately, very often they had no choice but to make use of it. Some individuals would not see reason unless blows were involved, or as Viggo used to say, until they saw the color of their own blood.

"You two had better find something soon. I'm beginning to think there's nothing buried there. You're in the wrong place," Astrid said with a wave that meant she had little hope they would find anything.

"Treasure is never easy to find," Umber said defensively.

"If it were, it wouldn't be a treasure, but the loot someone had already found and was enjoying," said Lars.

"Yeah... yeah.... Find it, because it's beginning to smell bad in here," Astrid said with a wave to the Defenders' corpses at the far side.

"We're on it," Umber replied, and they both got back to work.

Astrid knew they were exhausted from all their efforts and their bodies had also been punished by the beatings they'd endured, which did not help. But they were both strong young men—they could suffer a little more, even if their strength was giving out.

The hammering on the wall went on at slower intervals, their exhaustion and lack of strength beginning to be noticeable. Astrid looked at the dead Defenders. They all had something in common that caught her attention. Although they looked to be from different regions of Tremia—she could identify Norghanians, Zangrians and Erenalians—they were all young, not over twenty.

"That's curious..." she muttered under her breath.

Her uncle's men had all been older, weathered, with life experience and travels on their backs. They had been with Viggen for a long time, and they had died in the depths of the volcano with him, following his orders. These Defenders, on the other hand, were young, without much experience. There was no doubt they were Defenders—they were dressed and armed the same as the other

Defenders had been, with monk-type robes with the symbols on chest and back and the kind of knife used in Erenal.

Astrid stared at one of them, wondering when her uncle had had the time to recruit and train them. When had he done that? Viggen had been concentrating on reviving Dergha-Sho-Blaska; he had invested all his efforts in providing the immortal dragon with whatever he needed to reincarnate. This being the case, and considering that his most trusted men had been with him, those Astrid had seen gathered at her uncle's home, how had they managed to continue recruiting young men before dying?

She snorted. She did not like this. She was missing something, and it could be significant. She felt like her uncle had defeated her in his last move—he had managed to help the dragon reincarnate and he still seemed to be winning another hand by creating new adepts to his sect who would blindly serve the dragon's designs, whatever they might be. The nervous knot she felt in her stomach told her there was still a lot in play and that the game was not over. What bothered her most was that she seemed to be playing against her dead uncle, who in turn was doing so from the beyond.

"That's impossible... he's dead, the volcano buried him inside it," she told herself in a whisper.

"You were saying?" asked Lars, who was taking a rest.

"Nothing, I was speaking to myself."

"That's never a good sign," Umber said.

"Take it easy. Don't worry about me but about finding that treasure. The voices are telling me there's nothing down there," she said ironically.

The two treasure hunters exchanged looks.

"We'll find it," Lars said as he started digging with renewed energy.

"We know it's here," said Umber, joining his partner.

Astrid remained thoughtful, staring at the unlucky new Defenders. She wondered whether the Visionaries were also still attracting followers and preaching the message of destruction now that their leaders were dead. If they were doing so, there was still someone left in command. This led her to believe that her Uncle Viggen might have had a right hand they knew nothing about and who was continuing his work. That might be. It would explain the existence of the young Defenders.

She turned toward the entrance of the hall and decided she had better explain her doubts to Egil and the rest of the Panthers. She had the feeling that although they had cut off the head of both snakes these were still kicking, and that was not good news. She did not want to jump to conclusions though, they would have to make sure that the Visionaries were also regrouping and attracting members to their sect, and if so, who was directing them. She hoped that was not the case, but it was always prudent to imagine worst-case scenarios. That way you were always alert—that was how you reached old age.

"We found something!" Lars cried suddenly.

"We need light!" Umber cried, his whole body in the hole in the wall.

"Is it the treasure?" Astrid asked.

"Something like that," Lars replied.

Lasgol had heard the cries and came down, followed by Camu, who barely fit through the hole the bandits had dug out.

"What's up? Any luck?"

Astrid pointed her knife at the two treasure hunters, who were carrying dirt out as fast as they could. A heavy gust of air filled with dirt and filth came out of the hole. It was as if a seal that kept something airtight inside had been broken. The two adventurers put scarves over their mouth and nose to protect themselves from the noxious atmosphere on the other side of the wall and then went through carrying torches to light the way.

"There's a second secret chamber!" Umber called.

"Don't touch anything!" Astrid warned.

"Let's see what's on the other side," said Lasgol, looking intrigued as he put his head in the opening.

Astrid followed Lasgol, and they went through the hole Lars and Umber had made. They found themselves in a second hall. It was slightly bigger than the one they had left behind and it was all rock, from the floor to the ceiling and the walls too. But there was no doubt about what type of hall it was. On a large granite table with a huge emblem engraved in gold, there rested a huge closed chest. It was without a doubt a treasure chamber.

"It's the treasure!" Umber cried excitedly.

"It has to be very valuable, look at the size of the chest!" Lars joined in.

Astrid and Lasgol took a look at the rest of the hall. Behind the table where the closed chest lay was an ornamented coffin.

"It looks like the Count decided to be buried along with his treasure," Astrid commented.

"It's a widely extended practice among many powerful lords," Lars explained. "They're buried with their most precious belongings."

"It's said that they keep them from thieves from the side of the night of no return," Umber explained.

"In that case there's not much to worry about. The dead can do very little," Astrid replied.

"On the contrary, the ghosts of the dead can finish off tomb raiders," said Lars.

"I'm not the kind who believes in ghosts," Astrid shook her head.

"Me neither," Lasgol said. "If there's any danger it'll be from the hands of men, not the spirits of the dead."

No can get in, no fit, Camu messaged.

Don't worry, stay in the other hall and see whether your sister needs any help above.

Okay.

One thing though, do you pick up magic of any kind? Lasgol asked him.

There was a moment of silence and then Camu messaged, *Yes, magic.*

Dragon magic?

Drakonian, Camu confirmed.

Well, that's interesting.

Much interesting, but I no can pass.

Lasgol looked at the opening the two adventures had made—it was only wide enough for one person. It would take too long to make it big enough for Camu.

Well, then stay on that side and try to help me if you can.

Difficult, rock walls much thick.

True, I don't like rock walls this thick either, Lasgol transmitted, knowing that, if the thickness was significant and the rock hard, it always interfered with his skills: nothing worse than thick Norghanian rock walls when you wanted to use a skill on something on the other side. Most of the time it was impossible to go through the wall with the skill or it became so distorted that it was useless.

Not me too.

Umber and Lars were staring at the great chest and could barely resist the urgent need to stretch their arms out to open it.

Unconsciously their bodies were leaning toward the table, but they fought the temptation, knowing there could be danger. They were no amateurs. Treasure halls often held hidden dangers, whether from this world or the next.

"Best not to be hasty," Astrid told them while she looked for traps on the floor, walls, and ceiling.

"We won't be hasty. We'd like to stay alive," Umber smiled at her.

"It would be best to withdraw and open the chest with a stick or spear, from a distance," Lars suggested.

"Is that some treasure hunter technique?" Lasgol asked, amused by the idea.

"Something like that," Lars shrugged.

"Don't touch the treasures, be cautious," Umber said, looking as if something bad might happen.

"Move back," Lasgol said.

Both adventurers did so, and Astrid went with them to the other hall. The three went out, leaving Lasgol in front of the table with the treasure. He crouched and concentrated, trying to pick up some magical energy. He did not perceive anything. He then used his *Aura Presence* skill to see if he detected anything, but he did not. Everything seemed dead in there, dead and buried for a long time. The place gave off a smell of dampness, soil, and dirt.

He checked the floor, feeling carefully with his left hand. To see better he called on his *Guiding Light* skill and a spot of light appeared before him. He could now appreciate everything around him. The hall had no doors or windows—it was undoubtedly a tomb. They had brought the Count and his treasure down here and sealed the hall. There was no way to get in or out, other than breaking the rock walls like they had done.

But that did not mean they had not left some physical or magical trap to deal with intruders. Lasgol thought about it—if there was a trap in here it was most likely either close to the chest or in the chest itself. He reached for the bow on his back and nocked an arrow. He withdrew to the opening in the wall and from there he aimed at the slab of rock on the floor right in front of the table. It was large, and there was no way of standing in front of the chest without stepping on the stone. He found this suspicious.

He called on his *Elemental Arrow* skill and released. The arrow flew off and became one of Earth in mid-flight as he had willed it to. It hit the center of the slab and there was a burst, along with the usual blinding and stunning compound, although what Lasgol was after was not to blind or stun but to use the force of the explosion against the rock.

The reaction was immediate. Three metallic spears came down from the ceiling at lightning speed to hit the slab that had acted as a trigger of the trap. Lasgol was glad he was not standing on the spot. The spears would have skewered him from head to toe.

"Wow... skewering trap from above," Astrid commented as she put her head through the hole to see what was going on.

"Yeah, we escaped a good trap," said Lasgol.

"Rather my intelligent boyfriend rid us of one," she replied with a mischievous grin.

"I thought the trap might be there..."

"And you were right. I always knew you were more than just a pretty face," she joked.

"I see that finding a treasure has put you in a good mood."

"And why wouldn't it?" she replied with a smile.

Lasgol nodded, smiling too.

"I'm going to make sure there are no more traps," he told Astrid, and gestured for her to stay back.

"Sure, but be careful, activating traps looks somewhat risky."

Lasgol caught the taunt.

"I'll keep it in mind," he said and called on his *Woodland Protection* skill. A green flash ran through his whole body and a layer of underbrush covered him from head to toe.

"Don't know if I've ever told you this, but with that skill you look quite natural," Astrid joked.

"Yeah sure... not looking very handsome..."

"Oh, don't worry, I see your true beauty under all that underbrush covering you," she said mockingly.

"Thank goodness," Lasgol smiled, shrugging resignedly. He looked like a half-human monster out of a possessed forest. He had been working on improving the protection the skill gave him, and now the layers of underbrush covering him were twice as strong and twice as ugly. But you could not afford to be vain when it was a matter of protecting your own life. Only Viggo would raise objections to underbrush armor. He'd surely refuse it because it would mess with his style. Lasgol smiled—Viggo was like that:

untamable, reckless, and vain. Quite a character.

He nocked another arrow and aimed at the lock on the treasure chest. It was old, the kind no longer used, and that needed a large key to open it. Lasgol suspected that there might be a trap that activated when the lock was touched, so he decided not to run any risks. He released an Air Elemental Arrow at the lock. The arrow hit the lock and there was an explosion accompanied by the sound of thunder, followed by an electrical charge that blew the lock off.

Suddenly the chest opened. A long blade, like that of a large sword, came out from under the table. It moved, slashing from right to left. It would have felled anyone standing in front of the table.

Lasgol snorted in relief.

"It looks like a slash blade trap," Astrid said as she watched from behind Lasgol with her neck craned to see better, a look of slight horror on her face.

"Thank goodness we weren't in its way..." Lasgol commented; he was sure it would have cut them in half. His protection might have held, but he was not too sure. A direct blow with a slashing sword exerting so much force... he was not sure his armor would have born it. He would have to do some tests. The problem was that underneath the protection was his flesh, and if he overdid it the blade would reach it. He would have to be careful.

Everything well? Camu messaged, worried.

Yeah, don't worry, I'm disarming traps.

Treasure have traps? Much interesting.

Not so much...

If have traps sure be treasure.

It seems that way, yeah, we'll see.

"Do you think there'll be more traps, or is it safe to get closer?" Astrid asked with raised eyebrows.

"I couldn't swear on it, but the chest is open now, so we can take a look carefully."

"Let's go look then," Astrid said, then she turned to the two adventurers. "You wait until we call you."

"But... the treasure..." Umber protested.

"We..." Lars joined him.

"Take it easy. If there's a treasure, you'll have your share."

Both treasure hunters looked at one another and nodded amid muffled protests.

119

Lasgol went in first and walked over to the table warily. Astrid followed him, treading lightly. She appeared to hover above the floor, whereas Lasgol did not. When they were closer Lasgol used his bow to touch the chest, the table, and the floor, pressing with one end in case there was anything else waiting to spring.

"There don't seem to be more traps," said Astrid, seeing nothing had happened.

"Let's see what's in that chest," Lasgol said and leaned over carefully to take a look inside. The *Guiding Light* lit up the whole room so he could see well. He looked in for a moment, then he turned to Astrid.

"Are there riches?"

"You'd better take a look," he replied, moving aside so Astrid could look from the same position he had been, which they knew was safe. Astrid looked inside and frowned. She reached for one of her knives and with it in her right hand she took out what was inside the chest.

"A necklace of large pearls... made of silver..." Lasgol said, surprised by the object.

"That's an odd jewel... the pearls are large and silver... too big, and a strange color for a jewel I'd say," Astrid commented as she stared at it hanging from her knife.

"I'm not sure it's a jewel, the hair on the back of my neck just stood up."

"Magic?" Astrid eyed him with concern.

Yes, Drakonian magic, Camu's message reached them.

"That explains it," Lasgol said. "Don't touch it just in case."

"Don't worry, I wasn't going to."

Lasgol went around the table and reached the coffin. He checked it for traps using his bow again to press around the coffin. Then he did the same with the coffin itself. He did not trigger any traps.

"It appears safe, I'm going to open it," he told Astrid.

"Don't be too confident, in case there's one last deadly trap when you open it."

Lasgol nodded. With the help of his knife and from as far away as he could, he forced the cover in several points until it finally moved aside a little with the sound of breaking wood. A terrible smell came from inside, and Lasgol had to put his Ranger's scarf over his mouth and nose. Slowly, and with the tip of his knife, he pushed the cover off until he revealed half a skeleton that must have been the Count.

"It looks like Count Vendros is lying here, the last of the Ilsmarsen," Lasgol said out loud, straightening up and stopping the use of his skills.

Astrid looked toward the opening in the wall.

"You can come in now," she told the treasure hunters.

The two young men entered the hall and looked at everything like two hound dogs sniffing out a suspect. When they saw the empty chest they were so disappointed their faces could not hide it.

"It's empty..." Umber cried with a grimace of rage.

"There was only that strange necklace in the chest?" Umber asked, his emotions caught between surprise and disappointment.

Astrid nodded.

Lars was staring at the necklace, trying to gauge its worth.

"I'd never seen pearls like these, I couldn't even begin to say how much the jewel is worth."

"Don't touch it, it's enchanted," Astrid warned him.

Lars took his hands away and threw his head back at once.

"There's something here!" Umber cried.

They all looked at him. He was searching inside the coffin, around the Count's skeleton.

"What is it?" Lars said, coming to stand beside him.

"Jewels!" Umber showed him his hands. A gold and diamond necklace was hanging from his right hand while in his left hand he had what looked like several gold chains with sapphires as the central jewel.

"Let me see!" Lars knelt beside Umber and they both examined the half dozen jewels they had found.

"It appears there was a hidden treasure after all," Astrid commented.

"It's not as big as we had expected, but we'll get good gold for these jewels," Lars said.

"Well... once we decide how we share the loot, of course," Umber said, looking at Lasgol and Astrid with doubt in his eyes.

"Take it easy, we only want the silver pearl necklace," Lasgol said.

"Really? The rest is for the two of us?" Lars asked in disbelief.

"We're Rangers, we can't keep the treasure. We'd have to hand it over to the authorities," Lasgol said.

"No! It's ours! We found it. It belongs to us!" Umber cried.

"Treasure belongs to whoever finds it," Lars added, nodding.

"Not according to the King's law," Astrid said.

Both men looked at Astrid and Lasgol pleadingly.

"Take the jewels, you've earned them," Lasgol told them.

"Thank you!" Umber rose like lightning and headed to the opening.

"Thanks a million!" Lars followed him as fast.

A moment later the two treasure hunters raced off into the forest as if they were being chased by hungry wolves.

"You'll see when Viggo hears of this," Astrid said, grinning.

"Yeah," Lasgol nodded. "I won't hear the end of it, at least until the summer."

Astrid laughed, "at least!"

Lasgol studied the necklace Astrid still had hanging from the tip of her knife.

"That's an odd jewel." He took out a leather bag, opened it, and Astrid dropped the necklace inside.

"What do we do now?" Astrid asked, uncertain.

"We'll take the prisoners to the authorities and return to the capital. I want Egil and Eicewald to take a look at this discovery."

"Do you think it's important?"

"No idea, it might be. The Defenders were looking for it, on Dergha-Sho-Blaska's order we have to assume. Why or what for, I have no clue."

Astrid nodded.

"Well, let's get going, we have to find out."

Chapter 14

Nilsa arrived at the tower of the Ice Magi. It was a place she did not like to visit very much. In fact, she avoided it whenever she could. If she had no choice but to go, it made her nervous and restless, and she could not shake the feeling off. She was all too aware why this was so; that tower was a place of magic. She no longer felt the hate and distrust she had once felt toward magic, but there was still the remnant of those feelings that caused her to get nervous. She could not help herself, even if she was fully aware of the reason and tried to avoid feeling that way.

She sighed before knocking on the door. She had nothing to worry about. The magic practiced in the Tower and the Magi who lived there were allies. They served the King and Norghana, in a similar way to the Rangers: the former defending the Kingdom with Water Magic and the latter with their bows, axes, and knives. They were very different groups regarding their compositions and way of life, but not so in their goals, which were fundamentally the same.

She nodded repeatedly as she gazed at the large door of the Tower. The Ice Magi had been serving the King of Norghana for generations. They and their magic were well known in the realm. Nilsa had been studying them on her own since she had been at the Shelter trying to obtain her specialty. There were tomes about these Magi, their magic, their history, organization, hierarchy, loyalty, and other interesting aspects in the Royal Library. Since she now had access to practically the whole castle, no one stopped her from consulting those tomes. It was an advantage Nilsa took advantage of. Egil had taught them that there was a lot of knowledge in the tomes, and that if you knew what to look for you could find troves of valuable information. Nilsa agreed with that and put it into practice.

She smiled mischievously. The reason why she studied the Ice Magi was a simple one; she had to study the enemy if she wanted to defeat it. Not that the Ice Magi were her enemies; on the contrary, but they were the closest thing to an enemy a Mage Hunter like her had in Norghana. She spent part of her nights in the Library. A few hours at first, but she was spending more and more time there almost without noticing. It robbed her of hours of sleep, but she knew it gave her a lot of knowledge. Knowledge that would make her a better Mage Hunter and that might save her life someday. At the Shelter she had not been taught anything specific about the Ice Magi. Now that she was out, she realized it was probably because they were allies. It would be frowned upon if they taught the Rangers how to kill their allied Magi.

Nilsa looked up at the rocky wall of the high Tower. She knew that Ice Magi were powerful because of specializing in one type of elemental magic; Water. She wanted to know everything about them and so improve her skills as a Mage Hunter. She continued experimenting and creating her own anti-mage arrows with ever better results. She wished she could test her improvements in a duel with an Ice Mage—not to the death, of course—but she did not think they would accept. Ice Magi, like many other magi, were reserved and extremely evasive, also quite haughty, and they were not prone to helping others. And they would be even less likely to help if they knew the goal was to come up with better ways of killing them.

She could not help but giggle. Not that she wanted to kill any of the Ice Magi, of course not. King Thoran would not be at all happy if she as much as injured one of his Magi. He would send her to the dungeons without a doubt. What she wanted was to improve her arrows and combat tactics against magi, sorcerers, warlocks, and anyone who used magic as a weapon. That was her goal, and since she had lots of initiative, albeit very little free time, she was still trying to get better by herself.

Egil was always encouraging her to try new things and giving her ideas and suggestions. Viggo, on the other hand, messed with her and told her to stop creating anti-mage arrows. According to him the last ones she had created had left him half-deaf in one ear. Nilsa simply ignored his comments and went on with her improvements. She would soon have arrows that not even the most powerful sorcerer would be able to resist. She would manage to make a mage unable to use magic even if they were of the highest level. That was the goal Nilsa was after. A sorcerer or mage who could not use their magic was a dead sorcerer or mage.

She knocked on the door to the Tower of the Magi, which was always shut. She found it weird, since it was a similar tower to that of the Rangers' and their door was always open, albeit guarded. There were no guards at the door of the Magi. They did not need them. No one ever came to the Tower, not soldiers, Rangers, or Royal Guards—no one. They were not needed since no one ever approached the Tower. The only ones who ever did were the poor, unfortunate messengers who had to deliver messages to the Magi and their leader Eicewald, as was Nilsa's case on this particular day.

Thinking about Eicewald and going to see him made Nilsa feel better and she cheered up. The Ice Mage was a friend and fully trustworthy. Besides, he was the Leader of the Ice Magi so she had nothing to fear in that Tower. Well, there was a discordant note there: Mage Maldreck had come back to his post at the King's request, and the Panthers and Eicewald knew he was a treacherous snake. They had better keep their eyes wide open in case the traitor made any suspicious movement.

The door opened slowly and heavily, a creaking noise accompanying the opening movement. A figure appeared at the threshold, dressed in a long white robe, but he was not an Ice Mage, at least not yet. He was about fifteen years old, with light eyes and a long nose. Nilsa could not sense those things, but she knew the boy had the Gift and was capable of doing magic. He must be an Ice Mage apprentice.

Nilsa looked him up and down. He looked harmless, but of course he had magical power. That in itself made him dangerous. It occurred to her then that it would be very useful to have some kind of detector to know whether a person had the Gift or not. As far as she knew there was nothing like that, which was a pity, especially for a Mage Hunter like her. If it could also indicate the grade and level of the mage that would be even better. And if it could do this from over two hundred paces away it would be perfect. She would have to speak to Egil and Lasgol about it. Perhaps even Eicewald might help. It was not anything substantially harmful for the Ice Mage, as long as it was the Panthers who had it, of course.

"Good morning, what can I do for you?" the boy asked in a pleasant and helpful tone. There were dark circles under his eyes and his voice was weak. He looked tired, or rather exhausted. It reminded her of the way she and her friends looked when they were training at the Camp. Very likely he was receiving a tough training at the hands of the King's Ice Magi.

"I've come to see Eicewald, the King's First Mage."

125

The boy nodded.

"I'll ask whether he's available."

"Tell him I bring a message from Gondabar, Leader of the Rangers."

The boy nodded again.

"I'll do that. Wait here," he said and left, shutting the door again. For a moment Nilsa thought the boy would not be able to move the door and was about to reach out to help him.

She waited, and while she did, she took a look around the large courtyard where several groups of soldiers were practicing to their officers' orders. What a difference between the life of a soldier and that of a Ranger. A soldier's life involved practicing every day and doing some other tasks, especially as escorts of supplies loads, or people, or cleaning and supplies in general. As a rule, their life was quiet and not too hard and they could be found calmly resting in their barracks most of the time, with the exception of an armed conflict—then their life became truly difficult, risking death in the battlefield. A Ranger's life was busier. They were always out on missions, here and there. And when there was an armed conflict, they fought as well.

Nilsa smiled; she would rather be a Ranger a thousand times more than a soldier. Even if their lives were more difficult than the soldiers,' who had a much smaller daily load of work and ran less risks. She did not underestimate them, because a kingdom without soldiers was prey to a more powerful one, so they were essential, but she preferred the Rangers who, even though they were not essential—other kingdoms did not have them—did give Norghana a great advantage. Or so she thought.

The door opened again with a slow creaking noise. The young man appeared again but he did not invite her in, although Nilsa was not surprised—no one was welcome there who was not another Ice Mage. Behind the boy was Eicewald, who smiled at her.

"Nilsa, what a lovely surprise."

"Eicewald, I'm glad to see you," she replied, smiling too.

The leader of the Ice Magi came out of the Tower and gave her a hug. Then he motioned Nilsa to follow him.

"Let's walk. It's a beautiful day, and I want to enjoy it a little."

"You spend too much time locked up in that tower," Nilsa said as they walked past the soldiers practicing their offensive and defensive moves over and over.

"I dare say that's so. Come and fetch me more often, it's good for me to come out and be in the sun a little."

"You Ice Magi are so pale I wouldn't be sure the sun is good for you," Nilsa teased him, giggling.

Eicewald smiled.

"Although you may not think so, it is good for us. The sun is always good."

They went on walking and enjoying the sun's rays.

"I have a message from Gondabar for you, to deliver by hand," Nilsa told him, handing him the rolled and sealed message.

"Then it must be something important," Eicewald commented as he took it and stopped to read it.

Nilsa watched the Mage read the message carefully. When he finished, he looked up at the sky for a long moment.

"Bad news?" Nilsa asked, although she knew she should not. But she could not help herself.

"No, it's not bad news, don't worry."

"Thank goodness," she snorted.

"It's about Dergha-Sho-Blaska."

"Oh…"

"I have to admit that I'm still having trouble accepting that a dragon has been reincarnated in our day. I've been thinking and trying to make sense all winter of what you told me in confidence about what happened and what you discovered, and even so I'm still having trouble accepting it," the Mage said, shaking his head.

"I swear it's true. I witnessed it. I was there. We all witnessed it, it's not our imagination, and we weren't under the effects of any magic or volcano fumes or anything of the sort. It happened. You have to believe us," Nilsa insisted, remembering that, when they had told him, Eicewald had had reservations to accept the facts.

"I know, and I believe you. It's cost me, but I've reached the conclusion that it has to be true. It's funny, if anyone else had told me, no matter whether it was an illustrious mage, king of a powerful realm, wise man, or spotless erudite, I most likely wouldn't have believed them. Yes, I definitely wouldn't have, the story is unthinkable. But you, I believe. I've lived a few adventures with all of you and, knowing you as I do, I know you're telling the truth, no matter how unlikely it sounds."

"Besides, these things tend to happen to us," Nilsa shrugged and made a face that meant "what bad luck."

Eicewald let out a small guffaw.

"That's very true. The messes you find yourselves involved in ought to be in the books of the History of Norghana, in the Royal Library," he said, glancing at the main building of the castle, "so they're never forgotten."

"I'm afraid they'd end up in the section of Norghanian fairy tales and fables."

The Mage smiled.

"Most likely. But, no matter how wild this mess we're immersed in is, it's roused my curiosity."

"In what sense?"

"In the sense that I want to collaborate in the solution of the dragon problem. If you think about it, it's something quite fascinating."

Nilsa looked horrified.

"Quite fascinating?"

"Okay, terrifying too," Eicewald nodded. "But for a Mage like me, having a mythological creature with power at hand's reach is a chance that doesn't occur in the course of a thousand lives."

"A chance that can take your life away," Nilsa said warningly, wagging her finger.

"I understand the danger we're all facing. Even so, it's a unique opportunity. According to the studies of several erudites regarding the matter, dragons vanished from Tremia about five or six thousand years ago."

"And that's those who believed dragons even existed once upon a time."

"Exactly, since the great majority of scholars believe they never existed, that they're only mythological creatures that belong in fables."

"Well, when we finally find Dergha-Sho-Blaska they're going to have the shock of their lives. One that will be very short, since he'll incinerate them."

"Let's hope we can prevent that so it never happens. The more I think about it, the more thrilled I am at the possibility of seeing and studying that creature. It must be awesome. A being that existed in ancient times and became extinct and has returned to Tremia."

"It is. Although I'd call it monstrous."

"I can imagine. Are we sure he wants to do evil? Couldn't we have him as an ally and study him?"

"I'm afraid he wouldn't let himself be studied, and as for having him as an ally, I don't think so. I think he wants to destroy this world."

"But that's what his acolytes proclaim. Are you sure the dragon has expressed it like that?"

"Oh yeah, he's left it pretty clear. He wants to rule over all of Tremia, and to do that he'll raze any who oppose him."

"A pity, it doesn't sound promising, no."

"Don't look for any alliance or friendly solution with the dragon and his followers. That won't work, and you'll come to a bad end," Nilsa said.

"Thanks for the warning," Eicewald smiled.

"I say the same to everyone. Only thinking about Dergha-Sho-Blaska gives me the willies."

"I understand."

"What does our leader want from you?" Nilsa asked at last. She could barely keep still with curiosity.

"Gondabar requires my help. He wants me to help him with the Pearls and the Portals… he wants me to study them. They trouble him. That's an entryway that might be used against us. Being something that has to do with magic and power, he wants me to help in its study. Apparently Enduald and Galdason aren't getting very far."

"Will you be able to?" Nilsa asked hopefully.

Eicewald sighed deeply.

"I hope to be of help somehow, but my knowledge about portals is scarce. There's very little written about them and little is known about magical doors between different locations. Furthermore, most of what I've read is pure theory that scholars think might work or the fantasy of very imaginative minds, since a portal has never been found."

"Until now."

"Yes, until now, when you and your friends found them. Not even in my wildest dreams as an explorer and scholarly mage could I have thought that the White Pearl at the Shelter could generate a Portal to another Pearl at another location in Tremia."

"These are real, and very much so. I've crossed them and they take you from one Pearl to another. I have no idea how they work, but when you use them, you lose consciousness and wake up so sore that you can't get up off the ground, I swear."

"Fascinating. I can't wait to study them," Eicewald's eyes shone with expectation. Then his face became somber. "The problem is my duty to King Thoran…"

"He doesn't allow you to focus on the study of the dragon and the portals," Nilsa guessed sadly.

"Exactly. The King keeps me very busy. We've just recruited young apprentices to train them to become Ice Magi, and that involves a tremendous amount of work."

"Yeah, I've met one, the boy who opened the door, right?"

"Yes, that's young Yodrik. He has potential, I hope he makes progress. He's going to need a lot of training and attention."

"Can't the other Ice Magi take care of him and free you from that workload?" Nilsa said, looking at the Tower.

"It's my responsibility. Besides, I wouldn't want Maldreck to take him on as his pupil. I'm sure he'd pervert his young soul. I must stay close and make sure he's taught properly."

"Argh, Maldreck!" Nilsa made a face of disgust and waved her hand in annoyance. "Is he making trouble for you?"

"Not yet. He's behaving, doing what I tell him to and appearing helpful."

"Don't trust him, he's a treacherous snake."

"I know, and I don't trust him. But you know the saying: keep your friends close and your enemies closer."

"If Viggo were saying that he'd change the end for 'and your enemies dead,'" Nilsa smiled.

"Typical of Viggo, yes," Eicewald smiled. "Unfortunately, I can't kill him, and don't think the thought hasn't crossed my mind, but I'm not a murderer."

"Oh, you wouldn't have to do it. Viggo would be delighted to."

"I have no doubt. But the King would demand an investigation. Ice Magi are very valuable assets for the crown, and at the same time very scarce."

"Yeah, it wouldn't do."

"Have Lasgol and Camu returned yet? I'll need to speak with them about the Portals. We haven't discussed in depth what they discovered about how they work."

Nilsa shook her head.

"No, they're still on the mission, I've had no news."

Eicewald nodded.

"They've been away on missions more than they've been here, so we haven't been able to talk much about the subject. It's a pity, too many duties."

"The main mission is to find Dergha-Sho-Blaska. They're all devoted to that goal."

"It's logical. He's the more obvious danger. We'll have to wait for their return to find out more about the Portals."

"Let's hope they don't take too long."

"You know, I miss teaching them," Eicewald admitted with a kind gaze.

"I'm sure they miss learning from you. From what they commented, they loved your lessons. Besides, I'm sure they'll need everything you've taught them."

Eicewald shook his head and waved his hand dismissively.

"For now they can get by with the basic principles I've taught them. They can improve their magical skills on their own, without my help."

Nilsa smiled.

"Just imagining those two practicing with one another makes me smile, it must be worth watching."

"A real spectacle," Eicewald chuckled.

"I have to continue my tasks," Nilsa said, indicating the Tower of the Rangers.

"I'll come with you. I'll speak to Gondabar and see how I can help in any case."

The two walked over to the Tower, chatting about less troubling things. Nilsa knew it was a way of clearing their minds for a while and stop thinking that, at any moment, Dergha-Sho-Blaska would appear in the sky above their head and attack the castle. At least she was with Eicewald, although she had the clear feeling that the great Ice Mage would not be able to do anything against the immortal dragon. They would both die, incinerated or torn in pieces.

Chapter 15

They went out in the streets of the city by the fortress gate like the Rangers they were. The soldiers on watch duty greeted them respectfully and let them through without any trouble. Viggo wanted to use back windows and roofs to leave without being seen, but Ingrid did not see the need. They were Rangers and could come and go as they pleased. No one would say anything. Viggo argued that leaving by the roofs without being seen was a lot more fun and elegant.

Once in the city streets Viggo led her to the south, through the deserted main streets where the honest citizens were resting to get up early and face another day of work. At that ungodly hour all the honest people would be sleeping, with the exception of those who had to work at night in order for everything to be ready for dawn, but they were the minority.

Ingrid followed Viggo, who was walking with marked speed and stealth as if he were on a mission, which worried her. The streets they were passing through were deserted, except for a few locals who had drunk too much and were wandering about, talking to themselves or looking for a fight.

But, Viggo soon left the good areas of the city and entered others which, based on their neglected, poor look, were not so good. He navigated the web of narrow streets and alleys without stopping to get his bearings or hesitate for a moment, as if he'd lived there his whole life and knew every corner and intersection, square and alley. Here they started to see ill-looking places and their customers, who did not look promising at all.

Viggo moved like a shadow and left behind taverns, inns, and other joints and the people who frequented them. In the blink of an eye they had already left them behind. They also began to see night characters who looked a lot more suspicious and did not seem to be doing anything good. They were leaning against walls or at the corners of dark streets, as if passing the time. Ingrid watched everything around her and knew they were thieves, troublemakers, criminals, people without scruples and, as such, capable of anything for a few coins. So, her hand was resting on the pommel of her knife—if any of those men approached her, they'd find it in their neck.

The area where Viggo had just gone into looked most depressing. It looked like a dunghill with half-collapsed huts and houses. Ingrid was not happy at all to be there, but since she had insisted on coming with Viggo, she could not very well back out now simply because the area was horrible and dangerous.

As if he had read her thoughts, Viggo led her down even grimier streets that looked even more noxious and dangerous. There were shadows running here and there in the distance, and Ingrid guessed they were criminals who did not want to be seen. There could be nothing else there but rats, cockroaches, and vermin.

Viggo's raised fist indicated her to stop. Viggo squatted. Ingrid could barely see him since the dark of night, the total absence of light and the narrowness and filth of the alley they were in, did not let her see anything. She noticed Viggo doing something on the ground. She squatted beside him and watched him. She was able to glimpse some dirty bars in the middle of the narrow alley forming a forged 4x4 square and Viggo's gloved hands on them.

Viggo lifted what must have been a barred grate in the alley floor, which instead of being fixed on the cobbles had been loosened and disguised to appear to be still in place although it was not really, or so Ingrid guessed. Viggo put the grate to one side and looked at her, motioning to go down. Ingrid looked surprised and Viggo shrugged. He started to go down the hole he had revealed when he removed the grate.

Ingrid snorted. She took a moment and followed him. She went down the hole to what she guessed was some kind of sewer system. She felt Viggo beside her as he reached out and pulled the grate back in place. She knew from the sound of metal dragged on stone, since she could not see a thing.

"Wait a little for your eyes to get used to the darkness," Viggo whispered in her ear.

Ingrid waited, although she did not have much hope that her eyes could see anything. They were underground and there was no light in there. She started feeling around—there was space for about three people and the walls were rock. A repugnant fluid flowed on her right, so she stepped aside to avoid it.

133

"What is this place?" she whispered.

"The sewers. The southeastern section of the old sewers to be precise."

"Why are we here?"

"I wanted a romantic stroll with you," Viggo joked.

Ingrid was about to reply but Viggo interrupted her with a kiss, then started along the sewer.

Ingrid followed him in spite of herself. The stench was terrible and the walls and floor were covered in horrible slime.

They reached an intersection of the sewer and Viggo stopped. He looked ahead, left and right, then he took out his knife and tapped on something metallic with the flat of the blade. He tapped five times, slowly, following a pattern that did not sound random but learned.

All of a sudden from the left side they heard a reply. Three taps, also in a pattern that sounded like a signal. An instant later they heard the same from the right side. Viggo listened without moving.

Ingrid was about to ask him what was going on when Viggo began to move. He crossed the intersection in a straight line and went further into the sewer. She followed. As she passed the sewer's crossing she looked left and right, trying to catch a glimpse of whoever had replied to Viggo's signal, but she saw no one. It was as if the gloom of the sewers prevented her from seeing who was inside them. She did not stop to try and find out what was going on and followed Viggo so she would not lose him down there.

Viggo took several left turns following the main channel, one with a bigger fetid flow than the ones they were leaving on the sides. Rats appeared and vanished everywhere. They were considerably large with long tails. The Rangers could hear them scurrying about shrieking and then vanish. Everything was so dark that Ingrid could only glimpse them for a moment and they were gone the next, although she knew they were not far. She could feel them. She thought that if she tripped in the slime and fell on her face in this channel of refuse, the rats would jump on her.

The further they went into that underground world, dark and putrid, the less Ingrid liked it, and she already had a feeling about what she was going to find out. They arrived at another channels' crossing and Viggo repeated his signal with his knife. He received the same two replies. He went on toward the depths of the sewers.

Suddenly, after turning left they saw light at the end of the tunnel they were in. Viggo signaled for Ingrid to follow. They came to the origin of the light. To the left a tunnel opened into a well-lit hall. Viggo put his index finger to his lips and then nodded at her to look.

Ingrid put her head out to look inside. It was a rectangular hall and it was filled with filth and garbage, although the pestilent fluid of the sewers did not reach here. There were many rats, but this did not surprise Ingrid. What did surprise her was what she saw in the middle. A dozen children between eight and twelve years old, grimy, dressed in rags, and looking starved, were sitting around a fire. They were warming themselves and talking.

She saw piles of dirty clothes, ragged blankets, and other broken utensils, old and filthy around the fire in a circle, a bit further back from where the children were sitting. Ingrid realized they were really the beds where those kids slept, and all the shaggy rubbish mounds were their belongings.

Several of the young kids were sharpening their long penknives, and by the looks of them and the expressions on their faces, Ingrid guessed they were criminals and not poor children getting by in that miserable world. They were likely both, which meant they had been forced into that life by their circumstances.

Viggo motioned Ingrid to keep going. She wanted to ask him about what she was seeing, but Viggo kept indicating her to keep silent and follow him. They went along the sewers until they reached another point of light. They approached and Viggo signaled to her to look inside.

Ingrid saw a similar scene. Inside this filthy, dark, and stinky hall there were about fifteen kids between eight and fourteen years old standing around two fires. Several of the older ones were teaching the younger children to fight with penknives. They made them repeat attack moves, delivering cuts and slashes. When they did it wrong, they received merciless blows in the head or kicks in the butt or shin. Then the older children barked instructions for doing it right.

The looks of the older ones was a mixture between looking like the children they still were and back alley bullies. They were dangerous—their tough life had made them hard, bad. Ingrid could almost read it in their eyes. What was clear were their actions, and the way they treated the younger ones said a lot about them and the type of life they themselves had lived through.

One of them, who looked like the oldest of all, was teaching four younger kids to rob a bag of gold. One of them acted as the victim with a pouch inside a ragged jacket. Another tried to take it from behind without him noticing while a third one distracted the victim. They were all following the older one's instructions. When one of them did something wrong the guilty party received a punch in the stomach or a sharp rap on the head, along with much shouting. Not even the "victim" escaped punishment.

Ingrid did not like what she was witnessing at all. The living conditions of these kids, many of them still children, were extremely harsh. They lived in utter poverty, surrounded by grime, rats, stench, and an unhealthy environment. Many would die down there simply from filth and illnesses. And to make things worse, they were being prepared for a life of crime in the streets that would not end up well in most cases.

Viggo continued moving and went further still into the sewers. More lit up areas appeared, which Ingrid guessed were inhabited by other crews of kids like the ones she had already seen. Considering the number of areas and that the conditions were still so horrendous down here, Ingrid wondered how all those youngsters could live there.

At long last Viggo stopped before a round opening, high in the wall, where a person could crawl through and from which came a lot of light.

"This place is horrible," Ingrid whispered to Viggo.

"It is. That's why I didn't want you to come."

"I understand, but I'd rather see it and understand it."

"This was my home. I grew up here, like the kids you've seen. Nothing has changed much since I left."

"I never thought that when you spoke about being a sewer rat you were being literal."

Viggo muffled a small guffaw.

"I did mean it literally, as you've been able to see for yourself in this cozy place that I used to call home."

"Every day you surprise me more, but this... this I had never imagined," Ingrid admitted, thinking about this underground world of rats, filth, illness, and pestilent smells.

"I hope it's in a positive way," he smiled.

Ingrid pulled up her Ranger scarf above her mouth and nose to protect herself from the fetid aroma that came from all directions and which she could no longer stand.

"Very positive," she assured him, and there was not the slightest irony in her tone.

"I knew that once you visited my domains, you'd fall at my feet in surrender."

Ingrid saw two huge rats cross before her feet and climb up onto some debris and nodded.

"I will fall, but it'll be due to the unbearable stench and filth in here."

"Oh, the perfumes of the sewer have a very special aroma that not everyone appreciates at once. It takes time to get used to their special fragrance. I swear that   with time you get to even find it charming.

"I doubt that, it's making me gag."

"Won't it be because of the wonderful company we have today?" Viggo approached the two rats and squatted before them, offering them something he carried in his Ranger's belt. It was a piece of some food and the rats took it from his hand.

"Wow, I'd never expected to see that either. Eating from your hand?"

"Yes, if you know how to interact with them and offer them some food, they do. They're charming creatures. Not loved and guilty of many ills that aren't their fault. In fact, they're very smart and playful. When I lived here, they kept me company."

"I don't know how you could live here... this place is... horrible," Ingrid trailed off, looking around and feeling awful for Viggo.

"It's not so bad. Besides, when food was scarce, which was often, particularly in the beginning when I still didn't know how to defend myself in the lower parts of the city, here there was always something to put in your mouth if you weren't squeamish."

"It wouldn't be what I'm thinking!" Ingrid cried with a look of horror in her face.

Viggo shrugged.

"You do what you have to do in order to survive, especially when you've spent days without eating," and he eyed the two rats he was feeding. "I'm not ashamed, and I'd do it again if necessary. If you're squeamish down here you die fast. You do what you must do to survive."

"I'm so sorry…"

"Don't pity me. This place, living here, has made me who I am. I managed to get out and become a Ranger. Many of those you've seen today in these tunnels never manage to leave them. They'll die here or above ground trying to make a better living."

"Were you taught to fight and steal down here?"

"That's right, and many other things as well. I was one that learned fast. I soon rose up the ladder."

"Rise up the ladder? How? I don't understand."

"The groups you've seen and others all along the sewers are organized. Every crew you've seen has a leader and every leader is responsible before one of the ten leaders of the syndicate, in this case of the Crazy Crow Syndicate to which I belonged. Strips, the kid we found stealing in the market and I let escape, belongs to the Red Fox Syndicate, which works pretty much the same but is located in the western sewers. The territories and domains of both syndicates are well defined down here. Above ground as well, but there you compete for the prey, and there are usually conflicts and casualties."

"Among the members of both syndicates?"

"That's right. There are also settlings of accounts, and now and then, a large fight in which dozens of members of both parties take part."

"All that sounds terrible. How many of these kids die?"

"Quite a few. The life expectancy down here is very low. If hunger doesn't kill you, sickness, frays, or the city guard—when it catches you—kill your wish to get out of here."

"Your wish to get out of here? I don't follow…"

"Despair. There comes a moment when it's so strong that it drives you to commit acts you shouldn't. You risk too much, or you don't even care whether you're caught or killed. You end up in a dark place."

"What you're telling me is horrible…"

"That's life in the poorer areas of the cities. I'm sure that what happens here also   happens in other large metropolis."

"Perhaps, I don't know. All I know is that this has touched me deeply and it makes you think. Many are only small kids. They deserve a chance."

"Being here offers them a chance, even if you don't think so. You can survive if you're tough or smart. In the world above ground, children without means don't survive, they disappear. I survived here, but above ground I wouldn't have. I would've been caught stealing, starving to death, and they would've cut off my hand or hanged me."

"I see. You say you rose up the ladder?"

"That's right. The crews teach you certain skills. The lowest, the ones we saw when we came in, teach you the basics: stealing, robbing, fighting, surviving, etc. If you're good you go onto crews of a higher level, where you learn more advanced techniques of the slums."

"I'm not sure I want to know what techniques those are..."

"Some of those you saw I already had when we first met at the Camp. As a rule, the higher you rise, the better you learn how to kill a rival or assassinate someone by order, or how to rob from highly guarded properties and other related skills."

"Yeah... that explains a lot..."

"The syndicate is a world in itself. Many don't survive it. Others even excel and rise in hierarchy."

"Are they all youngsters, or are there adults among the members? Everyone we've seen was less than fourteen or fifteen years old."

"As a rule, the age range in both syndicates is between eight and seventeen. From eighteen on, those who reach that age either fight for leadership or go above ground and join other criminal gangs. They already have a good chance of being useful in those gangs."

"Then both syndicates in this city recruit children for criminal activities?"

"That's right. Very often the kids themselves seek out the syndicates, knowing that they won't survive otherwise. There's a lot of poverty and broken families in the big cities."

"I haven't seen girls, does the syndicate reject them?"

"They are accepted, the syndicate makes no distinction. If you can steal and kill, they don't care. And you have seen them, but they dress and cut their hair like the boys. Many times you can't tell them apart in this underworld."

"Just to think what the life of a ten-year-old girl might be in this environment with these people makes my heart cringe."

"It's not as bad as it seems. Remember that you can make it through, you can survive and seek a better life one day. I did it. Others do it too."

"Even so..."

"The options are worse above ground."

"That's what I find hard to understand. They ought to have a chance. The poor and hopeless have none. There are too many poor to help them all. The King should do something about it."

"Not this King."

"Maybe the next one."

"Maybe, but I doubt it, unless it's a wise-guy king we already know…"

"We'll tell him everything we've seen. You'll tell him your story, let him know what goes on here and in other cities of the kingdom. If necessary we'll bring him here. Egil will help all these lost boys and girls, he'll rescue them from the claws of the syndicates and other criminal organizations of the slums."

"First he has to become King, and that doesn't look like it will be the case. Let me remind you that soon we'll have a Druid Queen and the Crown will be stronger."

"Having a new Queen to strengthen the throne isn't good for Egil's interests, I admit. But she's not the Queen yet, many things might still happen."

"Many, agreed, but she will most likely be the Queen."

"In any case, we'll tell Egil everything. He might find a way to help all these unfortunate children."

Viggo climbed up into the opening to see what was going on.

"Can I look?" Ingrid said, curious. There was only room for one, so she could not watch with him.

"Climb up and look, but stay silent."

Ingrid got into the round opening, like a channel, and looked at the huge hall it opened on to. The opening was about the height of two bodies above a wide hall and she could see over fifty youngsters around what looked like an iron throne above a huge pile of grime. A dozen fires lit the space up and warmed it, and around the fires there were groups of young people. They were syndicate crews. On the throne was a young man who looked to be in his mid twenties. He was wearing some kind of iron crown and behind his back there was a large banner with a crazy-looking crow on a white background.

The people there were between eighteen and twenty-two years old. These had to be the members of the syndicate who had survived their teens. They were the oldest, those who would soon follow other paths in the above-ground gangs. The place looked to Ingrid like the throne hall of a kingdom of grime and darkness. How could they live there? It seemed incredible. But they did. She could see youngsters eating around the fires, and they had barrels, some with beer and others with water to drink from. Ingrid preferred not to know what it was they were eating, but they were roasting it on the fire, and the smell of food roasting mingled with the stench of the sewers produced a most disgusting smell.

She looked again and, among the piles of filth around the fires, she glimpsed what looked like beds made of shreds of clothes and dirty wool. She also saw piles of utensils forming large mounds near the fire, as if they were each group's loot. The "king" had a great mound of all kind of objects under his feet, forming the mountain on which his throne rested. Some of the objects at his feet were silver and gold. They looked like knives, plates, and goblets they had stolen. There were also two large chests, one on each side of the throne, and they were open. Several of the objects inside the chests gleamed when the reflections of the flames reached them. Ingrid realized they were jewels.

Ingrid blinked hard. The king of the sewers had jewels and gold in his chests, and he showed them to his henchmen. But if he had two chests full of gold and valuable jewels, why did he stay in this world of filth? He could surely live in a better place, both him and all those in his grimy throne hall. It did not make much sense, unless he continued to live here to control his empire closely, living with his own. Perhaps it was safer for him to be here than above in a beautiful villa where he might be attacked by the rival syndicate. Yes, that had to be it, otherwise it did not make much sense.

Two youngsters, about twenty years old, rose from one of the fires, leaving their fellow crew members and approaching the leader. After getting on one knee, they offered him two leather bags. The syndicate leader took the first bag and poured its contents out at his feet, then he examined what he had been brought. He kept the gold coins and put them in one of the chests. He also kept some silver objects, then he did the same with the second bag. He returned what he did not want to the two youngsters, who took it back to their crew.

Ingrid was beginning to understand the way this underground kingdom worked. The crews obtained the loot which they brought to their chieftain, and he kept whatever he liked, that which was most valuable. She wondered whether they had quotas to fulfill, surely they must. A third young man from another crew came forward to hand the bag to the leader, who poured the contents on the floor. After checking what he had brought the king began to yell at the young man—he did not look happy with the loot. He did not keep anything. He stood up and took out a long knife, almost a short sword, with a jeweled pommel and put it to the young man's neck. Then he whispered something in his ear. The young man fell to his knees, begging for his life. Ingrid thought he was going to be killed. The leader kicked the boy in the face, making him roll down the mountain of filth until he stopped, unconscious, at the foot of it. No one moved to help him, not even his own crew members.

This was a world of horror.

Ingrid went back to Viggo.

"What did you think?"

"Horrible."

"It is," Viggo nodded as he got into the opening.

"What are you going to do now?"

"Now I'm going to have a friendly chat with an old friend."

"Don't you dare go down there," Ingrid warned him harshly.

"Don't worry. You stay here."

"No way!"

"If they see you, we'll have to fight against all of them. Not a good strategy."

"And won't you have to fight them all anyway?"

"No. I'm still one of them. They have to let me through."

Ingrid was about to retort, but Viggo slid down the wall into the hall.

"Viggo!" she cried in frustration.

Several children saw Viggo slide down the wall and took out their penknives. They pointed at him, whispering.

Viggo raised both arms, indicating he did not want any trouble.

"Who are you?" the leader of the nearest crew asked him, pointing his finger at him from where he stood by the fire.

"Don't you recognize one of your own?" Viggo replied.

"Show the mark," one of the older boys said from another nearby crew. He was about twenty, with red hair and freckles.

Viggo nonchalantly stepped up to an oil lamp and showed them his forearm.

The leader rose from his throne and pointed at Viggo.

"Check the mark."

Four kids between seventeen and eighteen years old, armed with penknives, went over to him quickly and checked it.

"He has the mark of the Crazy Crow."

"Well, well, an old member," said the leader.

"Once a member, always family," Viggo said as if it were a mantra.

"Family is for life, long or short as it might be," the leader replied also, as if he were reading from a book of psalms.

The kids moved away and let Viggo through as he walked to the center and stood before the leader and his throne.

"Who are you?" the leader asked Viggo, pointing his long knife with the jeweled pommel.

"Have you forgotten your old mate?"

"What mate?"

"One you betrayed."

A tense murmur rose from the hundred young throats in the hall.

"Take off your hood," the leader said aggressively, "I want to see your face."

Viggo pushed back his hood slowly, letting everyone study his face.

"Do you remember me now, Klaus?"

"Viggo!" Klaus cried, looking surprised.

"I see you do."

"It can't be, you're dead."

"I was nearly killed but not quite. It was a good ambush, that I have to admit."

"What are you doing here?" the leader's tone sounded worried and annoyed.

"I've come to challenge you," Viggo said, taking out his knives.

All those present stood up and took out their knives.

"I don't know how you're still alive, but I can promise you one thing."

"And what's that?" Viggo asked, completely unfazed, as if he was not in any kind of danger.

"You're not getting out of here alive!"

Chapter 16

The tension in the hall could be cut with a knife. The youngsters started murmuring death threats and several began to approach Viggo, who watched without flinching. About twenty formed a circle around Viggo, showing their weapons, their faces menacing and their eyes seeking blood.

"I see I still can't trust you. Is this how you greet an old friend?"

"I don't know what you're talking about, you're no friend of mine." The tone was frankly hostile.

"You can deny we were once friends, Klaus. But I can tell the truth. We grew up together in these sewers. I knew you well. I know who you were, and considering how little people change with time, I can guess how you got the position of Crow leader."

"I earned it by right."

"You earned it with treachery and tricks, like you got everything else back then," Viggo replied.

The group of youngsters kept coming closer. They were young but not inexperienced, since they were lowlife criminals and knew how to use their knives. They were closing in on him, moving slowly and gradually, like in a death dance where the dead one was about to be executed.

"Shut his filthy mouth. He's no one's friend," Klaus ordered.

"You lie like you've always done. You do know me and we were friends. Just like Dirty Lex knows me," Viggo said, pointing his knife at one of those present of a similar age to him who was watching Viggo from a distance beside one of the fires. He seemed to be the leader of a crew. "Fast Sean also knows me," Viggo went on, indicating another older boy beside another fire, also looking like the leader of a crew. "Not to speak of Nimble Fingers Mike, whom I taught everything he knows," he said, nodding to a third boy with tussled blond hair a couple of years younger than Viggo.

The youngsters surrounding Viggo stopped hesitantly. He knew several crew leaders and had mentioned them by name and alias. That puzzled them.

"I know you," said a thin boy with short blond hair and blue eyes.

He was in his early twenties and looked tough.

Viggo turned to him.

"I see you're still alive, Sharp Knife Brendan."

"There hasn't been anyone capable of finishing me off."

"I won't be the one to try. You earned your nickname, and I guess you haven't lost your touch," Viggo raised both hands in a pacifying gesture. This was no time for bravado.

"No, I haven't," Brendan said as he reached for a curved knife and started sharpening it with a water stone.

"I told you to shut his mouth forever!" Klaus ordered.

Ingrid was following everything from within the opening. Her chest was about to burst with the tension of seeing Viggo surrounded down there. She did not know how he was keeping his cool. The opening was too narrow for her to shoot and help Viggo. If things went south, and it seemed as if they might, she could only jump down there like Viggo had done and join him in the fray. The problem was the sheer number of syndicate members. They were all well-armed, and she had the feeling they knew how to use their knives no matter how young they were. They were weathered by the life they led. They were criminals, trained since childhood to steal and kill. Ingrid knew that she and Viggo could not deal with all of them. There were too many—they would die. And what was worse, and she found hard to accept, they would die killing street urchins who had never had a chance of being anything other than the criminals they now were.

"I'm a Crazy Crow just like you. I have a right to be in these sewers. And I have a right to challenge you," Viggo said, pointing his finger at Klaus.

"You're not one of us and have no rights to anything!"

"I'm not? What do you say, Lex, Sean, Mike, Brendan?" Viggo asked, jabbing his finger at each of them.

The rest of the youngsters waited expectantly. They were wondering whether to follow the order or not. Ingrid knew that Viggo did not have much time. The moment one of them attacked he would be in big trouble.

"He's one of us," Mike said. "He taught me what I know. He was my comrade for many years. If he's still alive, he's still one of our own. Once you're in you never leave the syndicate."

"Thanks, Mike, you were always honest and true," Viggo bowed slightly in recognition.

"He's a Crazy Crow," said Sean. "One we were told was dead. He seems to be alive, so he's one of us. Once you're a Crazy Crow you're a Crazy Crow forever. That's what the syndicate rules say."

"As you can see, the ambush Klaus set up for me didn't turn out as he'd expected," Viggo said, spreading his arms open and exposing his body.

"Don't accuse me of anything unless you can prove it!"

"I don't need to prove it. I know you betrayed me, that you sent me to my death in order to clear the path to the throne you now occupy. I know it, and the rest of the crew leaders know it. You can deny it all you want, but that's the truth," Viggo said with assurance. "That's why I'm here today. I want to pay the debt that was left pending. I'm going to kill you and take away that throne that doesn't belong to you."

"In your dreams! Kill him!"

The youngsters began to move toward Viggo with their knives in their hands.

"I have a right to challenge you as a Crazy Crow!" Viggo cried in a firm tone filled with authority.

"Kill him, I said! Kill him and make him shut up!" Klaus shouted furiously, standing in front of his throne.

The first boys were reaching Viggo, who had not taken out his knives. The situation was getting increasingly complicated in the blink of an eye. Even so, Viggo kept his cool as if nothing could affect him, as if he had a right to be there and do what he was doing. He knew that if he initiated the confrontation, he would not be able to stop the bloody events that would follow. So, he decided not to. He did not want any bloodshed, not of those kids,' only Klaus's. Treachery had to be paid for, and today Klaus would pay for what he had done, one way or another.

"Stop! He has a right to challenge the leader!" Mike said.

"No he doesn't! Do as I say!" Klaus cried.

"He's one of us, he does have a right," Sean said.

"They're our rules, and we follow them. We all know them!" said Brendan.

"I'm a Crazy Crow, and it's my right to challenge the leader. I'm challenging you, Crow Leader," Viggo insisted, pointing his finger at Klaus.

They all turned to look at Klaus. Ingrid was afraid he would order his boys to kill Viggo again. The younger ones seemed anxious to please their leader, to show their worth and kill the stranger. The older ones though looked disgusted. They did not seem to agree with what their leader was doing. If what Viggo said was true and he had a right to challenge the leader, and so it seemed from what a number of the older ones had said, the leader would have to fight Viggo. That was not a relief at all since it put Viggo at risk once again, but at least he would not have to fight half the syndicate.

Klaus was glaring at Viggo with eyes half closed.

"If you want to die, I won't stop you! I accept your challenge as Leader of the Crows."

Viggo smiled. He had achieved his purpose.

"I'm glad you're not changing the rules to suit your own convenience, that wouldn't be very nice."

"The rules of the Syndicate are the ones we live by and die for. I always respect them, I don't alter them. You've been acknowledged as a Crow and as such you have a right to challenge me," Klaus cried, covering his previous denial.

"You're even more twisted than you were back in the day."

"I'm the Crow Leader! I'm the law in the sewers!"

"And as a Crow, I challenge you, Klaus," Viggo said coldly.

Klaus took out a long knife and showed it to Viggo.

"I'm going to take your guts out! Move away, he's mine!"

The Crows moved back at once, leaving Viggo in the middle of the hall.

Ingrid breathed out in relief. Things had come close to being disastrous. Now, Viggo had to fight the leader. He looked tough and clever. He would be dangerous. Viggo would have to be wary.

Viggo took out one of his knives and showed it to Klaus.

The challenge was completed.

As Klaus came down from his mountain to where Viggo was waiting, a chanting started among the Crows.

"Challenge to the Leader, fight for the Crow Throne!"

The Crows made a large circle around Viggo and Klaus, who had come down from his throne and was standing three paces from Viggo.

"Challenge to the Leader, fight for the Throne!" the chanting continued, all the voices joining together and growing stronger.

"It'll be like the old times. Only now I'll defeat you and avenge your betrayal against me," Viggo said with a lethal glare.

"I've defeated you many times and will do so again," Klaus replied.

"That was years ago. Things change. They change a lot," Viggo replied with a dangerous smile.

"You always believed yourself to be better than you actually were. Today you're going to pay for your arrogance with your life," Klaus showed him his other long knife with a bejeweled pommel.

"It's me who's going to make you swallow yours, and I'll make you pay for what you tried to do and couldn't accomplish."

They both began to move, facing one another in a circle, showing their weapons, measuring one another.

"I'll have to finish what I started, and I'll do so gladly. I never should've let you get out alive."

"I'll agree with you on that."

The chanting rose louder. No one cheered either of the contenders, they only chanted the same two sentences as if they were a dogma.

Klaus launched his attack suddenly, without warning, leaping forward and delivering a cut at Viggo's face. The attack was so fleeting that it would have caught many unaware. Not Viggo though. He threw his head back faster than the attack and the blade brushed in front of his face without grazing him.

"Times change, Klaus. Your games won't work on me now."

"I'll kill you all the same!" Klaus lunged twice, at Viggo's stomach and neck.

Viggo avoided the thrusts easily without using his own knives, simply by shifting his weight. He seemed able to anticipate his rival's movements, and the Crows stared in awe at what was going on.

Ingrid watched closely, a little worried. She knew that Viggo was in fact reacting to the attacks at tremendous speed and was measuring distance and risk before moving and before the attack ended.

"Your attacks seem a little slow," Viggo said to his rival with a triumphant smile.

Klaus did not appreciate the mocking and delivered several quick repeated thrusts at Viggo's body, seeking his heart. Viggo took half a step to the left, and as Klaus was correcting the direction of his attack to catch him Viggo made two more swift, measured movements around Klaus. The knife stroke hit nothing but air. They were always two fingers away from Viggo's torso but fell short.

"I'm going to kill you!" Klaus yelled, enraged, and lunged forward to attack like a madman, slashing and thrusting and cutting with all his strength as fast as he could.

Viggo had to raise his arms at the furious attacks and started to block them with his Ranger knives, deflecting Klaus's with amazing speed and coordination. But he was only defending himself, not counter-attacking. He seemed not to want to fight, only to infuriate the leader of the syndicate by ridiculing him in front of everyone. It looked like Klaus was losing his mind from the rage he was feeling because of being made a fool in his own lair.

With every failed attack Klaus grew more enraged. He let loose two bursts of irate and uncontrolled attacks driven by the frustration he felt for Viggo responding with sliding away from his reach, like a dancer doing a dance around a bonfire and avoiding the flames that tried to reach him.

Klaus went on delivering attacks and trying to reach Viggo. He quickly changed his strategy, seeing he could not even graze him. Klaus started making feint movements, leaving his guard open so Viggo would attack and then catch him with a counter-attack. Unfortunately for the leader of the syndicate, Viggo did not fall for his tricks. He saw them and ignored them. He would not take the bait. Instead, he smiled, amused, as if this were no more than a game to him.

Klaus's frustration at not being able to hurt Viggo reached its limit.

"Fight, you bastard!" he yelled, enraged.

"I can defeat you without even trying, so why make the effort," Viggo smiled.

Klaus took this as the worst of insults. He was being laughed at, in front of all his people. It was a terrible humiliation. He was being ridiculed, being made a fool.

Unable to bear it any longer, he renewed his attacks without control, charging like a raging bull. After a failed knife thrust by Klaus, Viggo tripped him and, unbalanced as he already was from his own impulse, he fell down.

The chanting stopped when they saw the leader of the Crows humiliated on the ground. His face was so red with rage that it seemed like it was going to explode.

"Is this the great Leader of the Crows? Incapable of delivering the slightest cut to his rival?"

"Kill him! Don't let him live to tell!" Klaus ordered his people from the ground.

But none of the Crows moved. Not even the younger ones.

"They're not going to intervene. I challenged you and you accepted. No one's going to intervene. It's against the rules. They know it. They respect the Rule. Not like their cowardly, treacherous leader."

"A thousand gold coins to whoever kills him!" Klaus offered, pointing at one of his chests.

The money offered did have an effect. The younger ones began to exchange glances—it was a fortune. More than they would ever get. It would enable them to live a normal life forever, far from all this. A couple started toward Viggo, squinting with the look of one seeking blood.

"Everyone, stop!" Mike cried. "Nobody intervenes in the fight!"

"We'll gut anyone who interferes!" Sean threatened.

"It's forbidden to intervene in a challenge!" shouted another crew leader.

The young ones stopped, thought again, and withdrew.

No one intervened.

Viggo smiled.

"I see the rules…" he started to say, when Klaus threw a handful of moldy, filthy dirt at his face from the ground.

Viggo raised his arm to cover his face. Part of the dirt could not reach him, but the part that did unfortunately went into his eyes and suddenly Viggo could not see.

Klaus got up like a crouched tiger and lunged at his prey. Viggo could not see and the leader's knives sought his stomach.

Ingrid's heart skipped a beat. He was going to get killed!

Viggo jumped backward with the same speed Klaus had lunged with to kill. The leader's two slashes brushed his stomach.

"Die!" Klaus yelled and threw two knives at Viggo's heart.

Unable to see and trying to recover, Viggo took a tremendous leap backward from pure instinct. But he tripped on something behind his back and started to fall.

Ingrid could stand it no longer. She put her head through the opening and was about to go down to intervene.

"Now you're mine!" Klaus yelled as he jumped on his prey.

Viggo threw himself to one side as he was falling, in an evasive action. Then he rolled to the left twice more like a balled-up porcupine escaping from a predator.

Klaus launched several attacks trying to reach Viggo, but he only managed to graze his right shoulder.

Viggo somersaulted forward twice, and as he did so he reached for his Ranger belt.

"Stop!" Klaus cried out and chasing Viggo as he delivered frantic thrusts that did not reach his target. Viggo would not stop moving defensively, thereby not presenting a static target.

As if he were obeying Klaus's last order, Viggo suddenly stood still, crouched. Klaus was at his back.

"It's your death!" Klaus yelled and stabbed Viggo in the back.

With a lightning move, Viggo turned around and deflected the knife in Klaus's right hand, as he sought Viggo's back, with his left knife. Klaus's eyes opened wide when he saw that Viggo's face and eyes were wet.

He had wiped his eyes clean!

Klaus tried to stop his advance on Viggo but it was too late. The inertia of his own attack drove him upon him. The Crow Leader delivered another knife stroke with his left hand.

Viggo moved at a crouch to let the stroke pass him by brushing his ribs, and with a movement Klaus did not even see, he stabbed him in the heart. Viggo's knife went in, pierced the heart, and came out so fast that only a few of those present were able to see it.

Klaus took two steps forward, looked down at his chest with eyes wide open, and fell to his knees. He dropped his two knives, gave out a muffled cry of rage, fell to one side, and died.

Chapter 17

Viggo stood up.

Ingrid, half her body already into the hall, quickly backed up as best as she could so no one saw her. Everyone had their eyes on what was happening in the fight so no one noticed her presence.

Two of the crew leaders went over to Klaus to check that he was dead. They bent over him and stated the fact.

"The Crow Leader is dead!" the first one proclaimed.

"Let the new Crow Leader rule!" cried the second, pointing at Viggo.

Everyone in the hall began to repeat the proclamation at the top of their voices.

"Viggo is the new Crow Leader!" Sean cried.

The cheers continued.

"Viggo, new Crow Leader!"

"He's the winner! To the throne!" they called.

"Put him on the throne!" they went on shouting at the top of their voices.

Viggo spread his arms wide with his knives in his hands. He turned slowly so everyone could see him well.

Ingrid was watching carefully, knowing full well that Viggo was enjoying his success. She shook her head and sighed. That was Viggo. You either loved him or hated him. She could understand that he had wanted revenge for a betrayal in his past, even if she did not approve. The risk he had taken to avenge himself had been too high. Viggo would not see it that way, she had no doubt about it, but if she did not manage to make him see the unnecessary risks he took, sooner or later they would find themselves in trouble they would not know how to get out of. She was not angry at Viggo, although she should have been. She was concerned for his inability to see the dangers he took and the dangerous situations he got into without being really aware of them, or at least not as aware as he should be.

Viggo climbed up to the throne slowly so that they would all see him. He stood at the top and looked at the two chests. He put his weapons away and knelt beside the chests, staring at their contents.

He put his hands in one of the chests and then in the other. He smiled from ear to ear. In one hand he was holding gold and in the other jewels. He threw them at the youngsters at the foot of the pile of grime.

The cheering stopped. They were all puzzled, not knowing what to do.

"Take it, it's yours!" Viggo cried.

No one dared. They were looking at one another; they seemed to think it was some kind of test or trick and that if they took it, they would pay for it with blood.

"Come on, take it! You've earned it!" Viggo said, throwing them more handfuls of gold and jewels.

This time one of the youngest bent down, unable to hold back, and took a gold coin. With fearful eyes he looked at those around him in case someone might attack him for what he had done. The crew leaders and the older boys were staring at Viggo as if they were waiting for an order to punish the perpetrator.

The order did not come.

Viggo threw several more handfuls of coins and valuable objects at the feet of the Crows.

"Take them, they're yours! It's your reward for the work you've done!" he shouted and continued putting his hands in the chests and throwing the contents to them by the handful.

Ingrid was watching, spellbound. If there was one thing she would never have expected of Viggo, it was that he would be throwing away riches. On the contrary, she was almost certain that Viggo had planned to take those two chests away with him. She had thought that the whole challenge to Klaus had been to take his place and keep his treasure. What she was witnessing made no sense. It would surely stop soon. Viggo was not going to squander all those riches.

But Viggo did not stop throwing away the contents of the two chests to the Crows. They all vied to get something. There was pushing and shoving but no fights so far. Everyone, younger and older, was filling their pockets with the treasure Klaus had accumulated in his rule as the leader of the syndicate. Many stared at Viggo as if he had lost his mind. This was the last thing they had expected.

Ingrid looked on, unable to believe what she was seeing while

Viggo threw away the riches as if he were some mythological being who had come to this world of filth   and darkness to spread riches among the unfortunate that populated it. As if that gesture could bring light and hope to the dingy sewers.

"Take it! Enjoy it! It's yours!" Viggo was saying as he went on emptying the chests with both hands.

To everyone's surprise and Ingrid's stupefaction, Viggo practically emptied the two chests, throwing the contents to the Crows, who did not understand what was happening but were not going to let the opportunity pass of grabbing a bit of the treasure. With Viggo's last handfuls, greed made its appearance and several fights ensued.

"No fighting or I'll stop sharing!" Viggo threatened, and the fights stopped at once.

Viggo handed out the last of the treasure, leaving a small amount.

"Always remember that it was Viggo Kron who gave out Klaus's treasure!" he shouted.

"Hail, Viggo Kron!" cried one of the youngsters, and he was soon joined by a dozen.

"Hail, Viggo, Leader of the Crazy Crows!" cried another, and at once the crowd joined in.

"Hail, Viggo, our new Leader!" they all cried, raising their arms and chanting songs of praise for Viggo.

The cheering and singing went on, and with every moment that passed Viggo's satisfied smile grew wider and wider.

Ingrid was watching everything that was happening closely. Viggo was standing before the throne above the mountain of rags and objects. He seemed to be enjoying his triumph like never before. Ingrid began to worry. Was Viggo going to stay on as the leader of the Crazy Crows? He certainly looked happy. He was smiling proudly, enjoying the victory and the adoration and praise the Crows shouted in their songs and chants. Ingrid wished Viggo would remember who he was and the important mission they were on. Unfortunately, at that moment Viggo seemed to have gone back in time, savoring the glory he had once dreamed of and had finally achieved today.

"Come on, come to your senses, don't let power blind you…" Ingrid muttered under her breath.

But Viggo remained standing before the throne for a long time, letting the Crows praise him and show their respect to him. With every chant and cry of his name, Viggo puffed up more. Without a doubt he was enjoying this moment like few others before. He was enjoying being acknowledged and also the power he held in the syndicate.

Many of the Crows were mimicking a bird in flight with their arms spread out and pointing a finger at Viggo. Ingrid guessed it was some sign of recognition or respect. They flapped their arms like wings and then pointed at Viggo and cheered. This made her nervous. If Viggo barely needed any encouragement for his own deeds to go to his head, all this had put him at the top of a mountain and it was going to be impossible to bring him down.

After a moment, Viggo began to make the same gesture back. He flapped his arms as if he were flying and then pointed at the Crows. The more Ingrid saw, the more restless she became.

Viggo started making a different sign. He was asking for silence with his hands. The Crows stopped their singing and chanting gradually and the hall became silent.

"I appreciate the honor and I can assure you that I would like to stay and lead you, but I must go on my way. There are other matters of great importance I have to take care of."

The cries of annoyance and the questions about the future came up again among the Crows.

"What are we going to do then?"

"Who will lead us?"

Viggo nodded repeatedly.

"As a Crow by right, I'll choose among all of you the one I think will be best to lead you."

They were all silent at that.

"I know a number of you from the old days, and from among you I'll choose the one I consider best suited for the post."

No one said anything, hanging on Viggo's words.

"Dirty Lex, Fast Sean, Nimble Fingers Mike, and Sharp Knife Brendan, come over," Viggo called.

The four crew leaders exchanged glances. There was a tense moment of hesitation and then the four started up the mound toward Viggo and the throne behind him.

When the four were standing before Viggo, he spoke.

"You are the ones I know best from everyone present. I see other familiar faces but I never had much to do with them, so it'll be one of you that I'll chose to take my place."

"I'm the one who most deserves it," said Lex. "I was already second-in-command."

"I'm the best prepared," Brendan offered. "I'm the one who gives more grief to our rivals."

"I'm the one who can do more for the Crows," Sean said, pointing his finger to his head.

Viggo looked at them up and down. They were all more or less his same age, and in their eyes, it was clear they had lived through a lot and endured difficult circumstances for their age.

"The three of you are prepared to lead the Crazy Crows, I have no doubt about that. Lex is like the late Klaus and would take the Crows down a similar road. He would be the traditionalist option."

"It hasn't been that bad for us, and I'd be a great Crow Leader," Lex nodded.

"Brendan prefers using his knives to speak. He'd surely make the syndicate grow, shedding lots of blood no doubt."

"Only the strong and the best with knives survive in the slums," Brendan replied and tapped the two long knives he carried on his sides.

"Sean is cunning and his style is that of someone who makes the best of situations without shedding too much blood."

"Cunning and speed are the best weapons to triumph, I'd be the best Crow Leader," Sean said, staring at his rivals.

Viggo was thoughtful.

"Why haven't you said anything, Mike?" he asked the fourth crew leader he had called.

Mike sighed.

"I don't want the position. I don't wish to be Crow Leader."

"That's odd. Don't you want the power?"

"I don't want the responsibility," said Mike as he waved his arm at the people in the hall. "You have to feed them all, the whole year round. It's a lot of mouths to feed and the times aren't always good up there in the city," he indicated the roof with a worried look.

"That's true. Many mouths and bad times," Viggo agreed. "Because of that, you're also the best person to lead the Crazy Crows."

"I don't follow you," Mike said, looking puzzled.

"Precisely because you don't want the job, because you worry about the fate of the Crows is why you'll be a great leader."

"I don't think so…"

"I've decided. Mike will be your next Crow Leader," Viggo announced.

"He's not the best choice," Brendan protested.

"He doesn't even want the job," Lex complained.

"I've decided, and my decision is definitive," said Viggo.

"It's a mistake," said Sean.

"No, it's not," Viggo assured them. "It's my decision, and it's the right one."

The three crew leaders expressed their disagreement.

"And I want you to understand this well. If anything should happen to Mike, if you go against him, I'll come back, as I have today, and I'll kill you. One by one, or all three at once, I don't care which. What I can promise you is that you will die."

The threat sank in for the three rivals.

"I won't go against him," said Sean.

"And what if it isn't us that kill him?" Lex asked.

"I'll think you did anyway and I'll hold you responsible, so you'd better protect him well," Viggo warned them seriously.

"On top of it all we have to protect him?" Brendan said, annoyed.

"If you don't want me to appear in your nightmares and cut your throat, you'd better," Viggo said menacingly.

The three crew leaders were quiet and looked at one another.

"Mike is the Crow Leader, we'll protect him," Sean said firmly. Lex and Brendan joined him, nodding.

"Then it's decided," said Viggo. "I give you the new Crow Leader," he said to all the rest, and taking Mike's wrist, he raised his arm.

Everyone began to cheer.

"Mike, new Crow Leader!"

"Good luck and strength for Mike!"

"Hail the Crazy Crows and their new Leader Mike!"

Sean, Lex, and Brendan came down from the throne mound to take their places with their crews. Mike and Viggo remained by the throne.

"Mike, take your throne," Viggo said with a wink.

"What a favor you've done for me…" Mike protested.

"It's best for everyone," Viggo assured him.

"Not for me," Mike replied.

"You don't see it now, but you will someday. This is the best decision for everyone, including you."

"If you say so."

"I'm certain."

"You've done it because I was always following you everywhere, asking questions. It's revenge, right?"

Viggo gave a small guffaw.

"That's right. You didn't think I put up with you and educated you for nothing, did you?"

"Apparently not," the ghost of a smile appeared on Mike's face.

"Besides, the decisions are now yours. You won't die because of anyone else's decision."

"But for my own."

"There's a big difference," Viggo said.

Mike was thoughtful for a moment.

"True, there is," he nodded and seemed more convinced.

"Sit in your throne."

Mike nodded and sat on the throne slowly. Once he was sitting all the Crows clapped their hands and cheered his name. The ovation echoed on the walls.

"Will you stay for a while?" Mike asked Viggo in the midst of the din.

Viggo shook his head.

"Duty awaits."

"Pity, I would've liked you to stick around for a while."

"I can't, but I might ask you to do me a favor in the future."

"Whatever you need. You've put me here," Mike replied, grabbing the arms of the throne. "You only need to let me know what it is."

"Thanks. It's always good to have friends in high places."

Mike laughed out loud.

"At the highest of the lowest," he said, glancing around.

Viggo laughed too.

"I couldn't have said it any better."

"Good luck on your way, Crow," Mike wished him as Viggo started down the mound.

"Good luck on yours, Crow Leader," Viggo replied as he left the hall amid chanting and cheering of the Crows for the new leader.

Viggo returned to where Ingrid was hiding, watching.

"You can come down now," he said from the tunnel.

Ingrid came to the opening and dropped into the tunnel.

"Are you done with your business?" she asked in a tone that implied she was not in the least happy with his actions.

"Yeah, everything's done," Viggo said nonchalantly, as if he had come out for a walk on a warm summer evening.

"Do you think what you've done in there is normal?" Ingrid did not want to be angry with Viggo, but she was upset and she was becoming more annoyed as she spoke.

Viggo shrugged.

"Well... a little normal. I had to improvise a bit, true, but everything went perfectly well. There was nothing to worry about."

"Perfectly well? You come to a lair filled with dangerous lowlife criminals and they all jumped on you and nearly killed you!"

"I had the situation under control. I was never in any serious danger. I'm one of them. I wasn't in as much danger as it might appear from the outside."

"You have to be kidding me! I almost had to go down there and help you!"

"That would've been a serious problem indeed. Thank goodness you didn't."

Ingrid let out a loud snort, venting her annoyance which helped her calm down a little. She did not want to scold Viggo, but she wanted him to realize the dangers he got into because clearly, he was not aware. But getting upset and shouting was not going to work, so she would try reaching him in a quieter way—if she managed to cool off of course.

"We'll talk about it, but now's not the time. But don't think you're getting off so easily. We'll talk extensively about what happened here."

"But I didn't do anything..." Viggo insisted, unable to see what problem Ingrid had with him and what he had done.

Ingrid rolled her eyes.

"Shut up, you're stressing me out. Let's get out of here. I don't like this place at all."

"Fine. Follow me," Viggo said, and as they retraced their steps through the sewer tunnels, he went throwing kisses left and right: "Bye, home sweet home."

"Gods of the Ice, give me patience!" Ingrid cried, following him.

Chapter 18

Egil and Gerd had been cloistered in the underground floor of Alvis the Erudite's Tower of Knowledge for two weeks. Two long and arduous weeks, during which they had not stopped working without any assistance. Even so, the two friends had worked unspeakably hard to obtain what Egil considered relevant information.

Alvis the Erudite had not appeared once in all that time to help them, as he had told them. Gerd could not believe Alvis could be such a mean human being. It was one thing that he did not want to help because, according to him, he had better and more important things to do, but he had not even deigned to peek in to see whether they were still alive, him, or any of his assistants.

Egil spent half his time searching among the tomes on the bookshelf and the other in the middle of the hall, working at one of the tables. He wrote down in his little notebooks everything he found that might be relevant or important. As well as information he would like to peruse in the future when they had more time.

They slept down there, among the books. For days Gerd had been having nightmares where he was chased by flying tomes with bleeding maws that tried to bury their fangs, sharp as stilettos, in his flesh. He fled but the books were faster and they always ended up catching him and biting him all over. He would wake up in a sweat and with the feeling of having been devoured in a sea of torment. A feeling he detested and that repeated itself every morning. He could hardly wait for the moment when they would leave that basement. The idea of setting fire to that basement and letting it all burn right to the top had crossed his mind several times.

The only pleasant moment for the giant was when he went out for something to hunt and fill their water-skins in the nearby stream every morning. They had run out of their own food some time ago, but Gerd was happy for an excuse to leave that library-dungeon and breathe in the fresh air—that was a true relief. Besides, it gave him the vigor he needed to go back.

Egil, on the other hand, had not left the basement once since the

Erudite had left them there to their fate. Gerd insisted that he come out of the Tower and tried to make his friend come out to breathe fresh air and stretch his legs; Gerd knew it would be good for him. Egil replied he would, in a moment, but then he never found the time to do so. There was always another tome to read, some new information to find or a possible clue to follow.

For Gerd the days spent there had been intense and frustrating. Trying to get valid information from the books was a slow and maddening process. They had to read great amounts of text and try to reach valid conclusions. It was not easy and it took too long. There were tomes written in languages Gerd did not even know. But what made everything more maddening was that most of the books did not have relevant information, which is what they needed.

Egil did not let his dismay show, if he felt it—Gerd was beginning to doubt he did—and continued working tirelessly. For Egil every book that came to his hands was a small treasure, and he tried to extract all the information he could. When he finished one, he went on to another one at once. His determination and consistency were remarkable.

There were days when Gerd had to remind his friend to eat and drink. Others when he made Egil go to bed and rest a little, although most of the days Egil collapsed from sheer exhaustion with a tome in his hands.

Luckily, that torture was about to end. Gerd expected they would finish with the last tomes they had not gone through yet that same day. They were already at the right end of the large bookshelf. On the lower corner there was barely nothing left to finish.

"Let's finish the job, we're almost there," Egil said cheerfully.

"Yes, please. I'm dying to get out of here."

They both worked as fast as they could, going through the remaining tomes. No matter how much Gerd felt like cheating and skipping every other tome, he did not. He took a deep breath, calmed down, and read each book to see whether he could find anything interesting in its pages. He did not want them to miss any crucial information on his account—he would never forgive himself.

At last Gerd shut the book he was reading, the last one they had left to check, and finished the study.

"We're done, at last," he said with a loud snort.

"Nothing in that one?" Egil asked from the table.

Gerd shook his head.

Egil closed the tome he had in his hands.

"Nothing interesting in this one either."

"Have we finished then?" Gerd's face betrayed his eagerness for the answer to be an unequivocal "yes."

"Yes, we've finished," Egil confirmed, nodding.

"Yay! At last!" Gerd raised his arms above his head as if he had just won the battle that would change the course of the war.

"I must admit it's been very interesting and intense," Egil said as he gathered his things.

"It's been real torture," Gerd replied as he returned the last tomes back to their places in the huge bookshelf against the wall.

Egil smiled.

"Thanks for your help, I couldn't have done it without you."

Gerd turned toward him and smiled back.

"Yes you could've, it just would've taken you a little longer."

"I think my mind and my body would've collapsed trying to understand all the information in these books."

"Your mind can cope with this entire collection of books and a lot more," Gerd replied with conviction.

"Well, my body would've failed me. In any case, I'm glad to the bottom of my heart that you were here to help me."

"The pleasure was all mine," Gerd teased, pretending it had been a torture.

Egil laughed at the joke.

They finished picking everything up to leave it all as they had found it.

"You think we have what we came here to find?" Gerd asked, raising one eyebrow.

Egil eyed his friend before answering.

"I believe we've found something that will be of great help. I also think that now we have a better understanding of what we're up against."

"Well, we do understand the problem a little better," Gerd commented with an unsure look on his face.

"We'd better go up to speak to Alvis the Erudite," said Egil once he had picked up everything.

Gerd already had a foot outside the basement, and he turned to look at his friend.

"Do we have to talk to him…?"

Egil nodded.

"Yes, I need to confirm some assumptions and calculations I've made."

"Well then he'd better answer our questions or I'll get really angry," Gerd made a nasty face.

"Easy, big guy. We'll try to get his help. Let's not lose our cool."

"I'm not sure I'll be able to contain myself after the way he's treated us."

"You can't blame someone for ignoring the needs of others."

"Yes you can, if those needs are important and urgent and have been explained to him."

"He doesn't see it that way."

"In any case, he should have treated us better. He didn't even give us water. You don't do that, even to the enemy."

"Yes, you do it to the enemy," Egil replied.

"You know what I mean…"

"Yes I do, and I understand you."

"Well, he'd better be well-behaved, or before I leave, I'll give him a parting gift," the giant said, making a fist.

"Don't say that, you're good…"

"Don't let that deceive you. Sometimes even I get angry."

"I see," Egil said in a somewhat surprised tone.

They left the basement, and before shutting the door Egil threw one last glance inside.

"You might not believe me, but I'll miss this a little."

Gerd snorted loud.

"I believe you, and I won't miss it at all."

Egil smiled and closed the door. They went upstairs and wandered around until they met with one of Alvis' pupils and asked for an audience. The First Pupil appeared at once and gave them the same cold answer.

"My Master is very busy and can't be disturbed," he told them in a tone that implied they should be going.

Gerd frowned and looked him straight in the eye.

"Tell Alvis that he either sees us right now or I'll start setting fire to all his books, one by one," Gerd threatened as he grabbed one of the books lining the wall with his big hand and held it up high.

"You wouldn't dare…" The assistant was staring at Gerd with his

164

eyes popping out of his head.

"Where's there an oil lamp I can use?" Gerd replied, looking around for one. "Oh, I see two over there," he pointed and made as if to go and fetch them.

"No, wait, I'll go and inform my master."

"Well go ahead, we're in a hurry," Gerd urged him.

Once the assistant had left, Egil put his hand on Gerd's shoulder.

"That was a good performance. And it worked well, you looked very intimidating."

"What do you mean 'a performance'? I was speaking in earnest," Gerd said.

Egil stared at him, surprised.

"Were you really going to burn books? That's the greatest atrocity a man could commit."

"I think there are worse things," Gerd replied. "And no, I wasn't going to burn any books, I just wanted to scare him," Gerd smiled.

"Well, you certainly did."

"Sometimes, in circumstances like these, it's easier to scare with the mind rather than with the size of one's muscles," Gerd said. "He wouldn't even have flinched if I had threatened him with a good beating,"

"Just in case I don't tell you enough, every day I'm more and more proud of being your friend," Egil admitted with a big smile.

"Thanks, my friend," Gerd replied, slapping Egil's back so he had to step forward from the blow.

The First Pupil came back and told them the Erudite would see them. They accompanied him to Alvis' table where he was sitting in his armchair.

"Master, the visitors," said the Pupil.

Alvis lifted his gaze from one of the books he had, open, on his desk.

"Very well. Leave us," he said with a wave of his hand.

"Thank you for seeing us again," Egil said in greeting.

"I had no choice. I've heard you've threatened with burning my books. Such a crime! A barbarity like no other!" he cried out, alarmed.

"It was me," Gerd admitted. "But I won't unless I'm forced to."

"What is it you want? I've already given you access to all the information I have about dragons. What more do you want?" he said angrily.

"I need to make sure the information I've gathered is correct. I had to deduce many things in a short time. I'm not sure it was all right," Egil explained and showed him the notebooks he had been filling with valuable notes and information.

"That's not my problem. If your minds aren't capable of reaching correct conclusions with the information presented, that speaks poorly of you and is truly sad."

"It'll be even sadder to see how this entire tower burns from the inside out," Gerd threatened with a vicious look on his face.

The Erudite glared at Gerd, trying to gauge whether he would be capable of following through on his threat or not.

"All right, but make it brief. Only important and relevant information. Don't make me waste time on nonsense."

"Of course, Erudite," said Egil.

"Well, what information do you need to discuss with me?"

"First, I need to verify the dates in which all this has happened. From what I could gather from these tomes, there are remains of dragons that indicate they arrived in Tremia before anyone else. The date has been established at about six thousand years based on a partial skeleton found in the Nocean deserts: 'the backbone of the sky' they called it."

"That's correct, the skeleton is the backbone of a great dragon, a part of it, no matter how much some scholars might deny it and want to indicate that no trace of any dragon has ever been found. The date, though, is incorrect," Alvis corrected.

"Some tomes mention they might have arrived ten thousand years ago," Egil looked at Alvis, awaiting confirmation or denial.

"That is correct. I personally lean toward the theory that they arrived in Tremia about ten thousand years ago and ruled over the continent at will. There are other remains: the jaws of the great terror, which was found east, which indicate as much."

"But no one's been able to establish with assurance that the jaws belonged to a dragon. There are those who maintain it was from another creature, even older," Egil argued.

"It was a dragon, what kind is still to be determined, but a dragon nevertheless. Just like with the skeleton found, they've tried to make it look like they aren't real dragon remains," the Erudite said.

"Is it known where they came from?" Egil asked. "Why they

came to Tremia?"

"Those questions don't have an answer we can give. They would only be speculations without much base. Nothing's been discovered to indicate where they came from or the reason why."

Egil nodded.

"It's a pity we don't know the answers."

"Not everything has an answer," the Erudite replied in a contemplative tone.

"True. The next thing I'd like to establish is the time they ruled over Tremia. There are multiple versions about how long it was. There are those who speak of three thousand years, others of six thousand—there are even those who claim they ruled until the arrival of Man three to four thousand years ago. There's no way to come to agreement on this point."

"That's because no one knows when or why the dragons disappeared," the Erudite said with a frustrated wave of his arms.

"What can be established is that they vanished before the arrival of Man, because they don't coincide."

"No, men and dragons didn't co-exist."

"But there is record of some tribes that saw dragons, we saw evidence in the desert through their archaic paintings in caves," said Egil.

Alvis nodded thoughtfully.

"Some men saw dragons three thousand years ago, maybe even two thousand years, but those dragons were the last of their kind that hadn't yet left Tremia or were ending their journey. While there were dragons on Tremia there weren't any humans," Alvis sentenced.

Egil checked his notes in one of his notebooks.

"Then something happened to the dragons five or six thousand years ago that made them leave Tremia, and it wasn't men who forced them to leave."

"That's right. About that time the dragons vanished from Tremia. The reason is unknown, although there are several theories. It's the belief that they suffered from some illness that made them leave, or an event that made it impossible for them to continue living in Tremia, or a civil fight for power broke out among them which nearly annihilated them. Although there are no bodies, or remains of all those dead dragons, or at least we haven't found them yet. There are also those who believe that more powerful enemies arrived that drove them out. And no, it wasn't men, because it's well known that there's nothing man can do against the power of a dragon."

"That theory is interesting—I mean the arrival of more powerful enemies that might have defeated them," Egil said, eyes filled with interest.

"Evidence hasn't been found, although I haven't delved deeply into that theory."

"Why don't you believe in it?" Egil asked, raising an eyebrow.

Alvis was thoughtful.

"It's not the most viable of the theories. In my opinion, dragons are too powerful for any other species to surpass them. I lean toward the theory that some catastrophic event occurred or that they fell prey to some terrible illness that forced them to leave in search of a better place to live."

Gerd was nodding without realizing. He believed nothing could overpower a dragon and that the Erudite's theory was more likely.

Egil continued going over his notes. He seemed to find that something did not fit, or that there was something he wanted to discuss with the Erudite.

"It might be like that... yet, in several tomes there's mention of weapons that can kill dragons. According to the texts they were used to actually kill dragons," he said.

"It is mentioned, indeed. That is correct. 'Neil's dragon-killer' is one of them, supposedly a gold sword capable of piercing a dragon's scales. There's also 'Rogdon's golden spear,' a spear old King Gontel Dungers of Rogdon was supposed to posses, also with the power to kill dragons. According to Rogdonian history, her famous mounted lancers were created to serve King Gontel. The weapon vanished a few hundred years ago, after the King's death, without a trace. It is said that his son, Bernar, hid it, jealous of his father's fame, and he is also said to have almost ended the corps of Royal Lancers. Apparently, father and son didn't see eye to eye."

"It's hard to live in the shadow of a great king," Egil commented.

"It is, and more so if he doesn't fulfill the expectations the kingdom has about the new king," the Erudite agreed.

"Are there any other weapons?" Gerd asked with interest.

"There are several more. Like 'Sansen's Knife,' which you can supposedly use to take out a dragon's heart and then eat it to obtain its power."

Gerd's eyes opened wide and he made a face.

"A little disgusting…" he commented.

"'Gim's Double Death' is a two-headed war axe supposed to be capable of cutting through a dragon's neck as if you were felling a tree. Gim's legend is interesting, since he lived in the Frozen Territories to the north, in our realm."

"Was Gim a Norghanian?" Gerd asked, greatly interested.

"It is not known whether he was Norghanian or a Wild One of the Ice. Legend tells that an ice dragon kidnapped Ursula, Gim's wife, and he went searching for her. When he found the dragon's lair, he fought the creature to rescue his wife."

"Did he win?" Gerd asked, fascinated with the story.

Alvis shook his head.

"The dragon won. He left him for dead and took Ursula into his lair. Some shepherds found Gim half dead and took him away. When Gim recovered from his terrible wounds, he went in search of the best armorer in the north to make him an axe capable of killing the dragon. He found a dwarf who was a famed armorer, Ripdis Ulken, rejected by his own people for his short height but who was said to be able to create bewitched weapons. He made the Double Death for Gim, promising the weapon was capable of cutting through the neck of a dragon. Gim went back to the dragon's lair and challenged him. They fought and Gim severed the dragon's head, killing him. He rescued his wife, Ursula, and returned home to live a prosperous life."

"What happened to the axe?" Gerd asked.

"It disappeared in the North," the Erudite replied. "No one's ever seen it again."

"Like all the other weapons," Egil added. "They've all vanished."

"Indeed, such are legends, you can never be sure whether they're true or the invention of an exalted imagination," said Alvis.

"Are there any other weapons?" Gerd asked.

"Those are the most well-known. Then there's 'Aodh's bow.' It's a bow of fire, a weapon supposed to kill dragons, and 'Antior's beam,' a javelin that pierces any shield, or protection, including dragon scales. A true shot of the javelin to the heart of the dragon would kill him."

"I like that javelin already," said Gerd.

Egil was silent, writing down in one of his notebooks all the notes he was taking of the Erudite's explanations.

"We could defeat the dragon with one of those weapons," he commented.

Alvis tilted his head to one side.

"Remember, they might only be myths."

"So was the dragon..." Gerd said, "and now it's a reality."

"We need to understand everything that's happened and see how to use it to our advantage," said Egil thoughtfully.

"Understanding the past is often the key to solving the future," Alvis told them, nodding.

"On that we agree. That's why we've been studying the past history of dragons. Only thus will we understand their future and ours," Egil said as he wrote something down in his notebook.

"There won't be a future for us in a world of dragons," Alvis sentenced.

"Luckily there's only one," said Gerd. "If we manage to kill him or throw him out somehow, we'll have a future."

"That's what you should focus on indeed. I've already devoted too much time to you. You must go on your way," Alvis told them, pointing at the exit with his finger.

Egil heaved a deep sigh.

"Fine, we'll leave."

"I wish you luck. May the studies you've made be of help," the Erudite said.

"Let's hope so," Egil said, taking his leave.

"We'll be back," Gerd said in a threatening tone.

Alvis's eyes opened wide.

"I certainly hope not," were his parting words.

Egil and Gerd left the Tower. They had to get back to Norghania and speak with the rest of their comrades and with Gondabar. They were a little closer to knowing how to defeat the dragon, and that gave them hope.

Chapter 19

On that particular morning, Nilsa was coming back from the pigeon coop after sending messages on Gondabar's orders. In her hand she had the five messages received about the search for the dragon. They were from Rangers assigned to check the North and West of the realm. Something strange was going on. The five were informing of suspicious activity in different places.

Nilsa snorted, troubled. In the last few days the sightings of large reptilian-looking monsters had multiplied. If at first she usually received news of one sighting every two or three weeks, now it was five or six throughout the realm.

"Something's wrong..." she muttered under her breath as she went down the stairs feeling thoughtful.

"Everything well, Liaison?" a Ranger, who crossed with her and had apparently heard her, asked.

"Yes, don't worry. Everything's fine, Oswald," Nilsa replied as she continued her way down. This time she was not jumping steps or exercising her reflexes, she was not in the mood. Her concern was growing with every message that came of a new sighting. Some were even of attacks with casualties, which left Nilsa very upset. In others there were no attacks, they just mentioned people who had glimpsed a monster in the distance.

Thanks to the Rangers who had traveled throughout the kingdom asking the local authorities of villages, towns, and cities to inform them at once if there was any attack or an unknown large monster was seen, the warnings came promptly to the capital. What Nilsa found unusual was that there were so many now.

She headed to her post to organize the tasks of the Rangers she was sending out to investigate, at least to do a first check. If they found anything serious, they were to give warning and she would decide whether she sent out any of the Panthers. She wished it was not Dergha-Sho-Blaska, since she still had not received news from her friends, which meant they were busy.

The Rangers on watch duty outside Gondabar's room greeted her, and she went in to start working without wasting a moment. She went into the room where Gondabar's assistants had set up a desk for her. They had set it in their midst as if they wanted to protect her, which she found endearing. She spent a lot of time working there. The assistants respected her for her position as Liaison, she had no doubts about that. They were very nice to her and, more importantly, they helped her with anything they could.

The moment she sat at her desk one of the assistants rose and came over to her.

"Gondabar wants to see you," he told her.

She rose at once to go to his study.

"No, not here, at the Castle."

Nilsa stared at the assistant, surprised.

"At the Castle? Where in the Castle?"

"He's waiting for you at the throne antechamber."

Nilsa stiffened.

"Is anything wrong? Do you know anything?" she asked, uneasy.

The assistants shrugged.

"Two Royal Guards came and asked to speak with our lord. Then Gondabar left with them. He left instructions for you to join him there," another of the assistants said.

"Has it been long?"

"No, a very short while ago. You've only missed them by a little," the first one told her.

"I'll be off." She waved at them as she went out and leaped down the stairs and out of the Tower. Several Rangers had to step back to avoid being run over by Nilsa's impetus.

She had no idea what might be happening, but if Gondabar had asked her to join him in the throne antechamber it had to be something important. She was hoping it was not very serious, simply because the Panthers were away and they would not be able to intervene. She began to get nervous. She felt it in her stomach and how it was rising up to her chest. She stopped for an instant to calm down. She breathed through her nose and filled her lungs; she held her breath as long as she could and then let it out. She did this five times and it worked. She felt calmer. She no longer fell prey to her nerves, if she felt she was beginning to lose control, she stopped and did several exercises she knew helped her until she regained control. A Mage Hunter who gave in to her nerves was a dead Mage Hunter—she always repeated this to herself.

She headed to the antechamber, walking along the corridors at an easy, quiet pace. She went up some stairs and through three more corridors with several landings within the main building of the Castle. No one stopped her. The guards watched her with slight unease as she approached, since as a rule the corridors were quite deserted, but when they recognized her unmistakable long red hair and her Ranger Specialist attire, they let her through.

She cheered up and started to run to get to Gondabar faster. She ran as if chased by two dragons. Several guards looked at her sternly because she was running and one even cleared his throat in a clearly censoring manner, so Nilsa had to slow down.

She finally arrived at the door of the antechamber and stopped. She smoothed out her clothes so as to be more presentable and entered, pretending she had arrived walking, although her heartbeat and heavy breathing betrayed her, but she pretended to the several Royal Guards posted there.

Gondabar was standing in the middle of the room. He was accompanied by First Ranger Raner. He motioned her to come over and Nilsa hurried to join them.

"You're just in time," Gondabar told her.

"I came as quickly as I could."

"Yes, I see, try to calm your breathing," Raner advised her.

"What's going on, sir?" Nilsa asked, looking at Gondabar and then at Raner.

"I have no idea. King Thoran requested my presence and that of the First Ranger," said Gondabar. "I wasn't told the reason, only that it was urgent and important."

"Oh, but then it's not necessary for me to come too…" Nilsa felt out of place, attending a royal interview with the Leader of the Rangers and the First Ranger.

"You're coming in with us, we may need your insight," Gondabar explained.

"You think it's about the dragon?"

"It might be. Perhaps it's made an appearance, here or in some other kingdom, and the King is now aware of the situation. That's why I want you with us. It'll be easier to explain with you present, and you may also want to add important details."

Nilsa nodded, "Of course, sir."

"Credibility is crucial in this matter, more so—imperative I'd

173

say," Raner added.

The double doors that permitted access to the throne hall opened up. Two Royal Guards appeared at them. An officer was following. He came into the antechamber.

"His Majesty King Thoran awaits you," he said solemnly.

Gondabar nodded and started walking. Raner followed at once. Nilsa hesitated, and Gondabar motioned her discretely to follow them. She reacted and followed them in.

They entered the throne hall and went along the aisle to the throne. Nilsa had been there a number of times and knew the place well, but even so it always impressed her, how magnificent and forceful the room was. The fact that it was full of Royal Guard soldiers posted by the columns and walls contributed to make the hall an awe-inspiring place.

Gondabar walked slowly. Lately he was doing everything slowly. Any physical effort was hard for him. Nilsa could see that he was growing more and more tired, the pressure and excessive workload he was carrying were too much for him. The leader of the Rangers realized his frail state but never ceased to fulfill his duties, which worried Nilsa. She feared he might faint if he did not take things more calmly. She was helping all she could and knew that Raner was doing the same. Perhaps between the two of them they could take some of the work off his shoulders so he might recover somewhat.

As they went by the Royal Guards posted on both sides, Nilsa began to feel nervous. She could see the throne at the end and King Thoran sitting in it. She also saw his brother, Duke Orten, on the King's right. The looks on both their faces was stern, but that was not uncommon. They always had that look, so you could never know whether the situation was more serious than usual or not.

They reached the throne and Gondabar stopped at a respectful distance. Raner stopped at his right, one step back, and Nilsa stopped two steps behind both.

"Your Majesty, always at your service," Gondabar saluted the King with a deep bow.

Nilsa, watching him, thought he might fall on his face, and she nearly stepped forward to stop him.

"Gondabar, I am glad to see you," King Thoran said in a dry tone but not altogether unpleasant.

"You don't look too well, old Ranger," Duke Orten addressed

Gondabar with his usual lack of finesse.

"Age is unforgiving, my lord. But I feel fine, in spite of my looks, I'm only a little tired."

"I don't know, Raner looks great," Orten replied. "He looks fresh, vital, sharp as a dagger."

"Thank you, my lord Duke," Raner said with a small bow.

"I am sure that with a little rest our old Ranger Leader will be good as new," Thoran said coldly, as if he were ordering Gondabar to rest and get well.

"I will rest at once and recover. I am sorry to appear before Your Majesty looking poorly," Gondabar apologized, bowing his head.

"You should. You must keep up appearances. You must come to the throne looking your best and perfectly fit," Orten said disdainfully. "We're not here to contemplate decrepitude or illness."

Nilsa felt enraged. Gondabar was exhausted from working day and night for the kingdom, he did not deserve to be treated that way—on the contrary, he deserved a medal and to be thanked for all his good work.

"Absolutely. Please, once more I apologize for my poorly appearance," said Gondabar.

"Who's the young Ranger accompanying you? She looks familiar," Thoran asked.

Gondabar turned to Nilsa.

"It's Nilsa Blom, Ranger Specialist, one of you Royal Eagles."

"Your Majesty," Nilsa bowed, trying to keep her nerves under control.

"That explains it. I knew I recognized you," Thoran said. "How are my Royal Eagles?"

"Very well, Your Majesty. On missions to protect the realm."

"I am glad to hear that. I will likely need you. I have a couple of matters I want solved... delicate matters."

"As Your Majesty commands," Nilsa bowed her head, showing respect while she wondered what new missions the King would involve them in. They had no time for other missions: they had to find and destroy the dragon.

"You should lend them to me," Orten said to his brother.

"To send them on one of your conflict-inducing missions? No, no way. I already have enough headaches as it is."

"They don't always end in conflict," Orten said defensively,

175

crossing his arms.

"Erenal almost declared war on us because of one of your master plans. No, I will not lend you my Royal Eagles. Besides, you're capable of sending them on a suicide mission, and they're too valuable."

Orten waved his hand to indicate he did not agree.

Nilsa snorted. They had already been on a couple of missions that Orten had managed to land them in, and they did indeed lead to conflict.

"The Rangers are always at the service of the realm," Gondabar said in a conciliatory tone.

"You'll be wondering why I have summoned you," Thoran went on without waiting for an answer. "It's for an important reason. A reason of great joy for the kingdom."

Nilsa was surprised. A reason for joy? This could not have anything to do with the dragon.

At that moment the eastern door opened and a retinue came through. It was led by Princess Heulyn of Irinel. It was her without a doubt. Nilsa watched her advance. Her red mane of curly hair fell down her shoulders and back. Her face was beautiful and delicate, with porcelain white skin spattered with red freckles. Yet her beauty vanished in the haughty, arrogant look on her face. Valeria was on one side of her and Ambassador Larsen on the other, and they were followed by a dozen Irinel soldiers, the Princess's guard.

"Princess Heulyn, you're just in time," Thoran greeted her.

"Your Majesty, are you announcing it?" Heulyn asked.

"Yes, indeed. To the leaders of the Rangers first before making it public, so they may prepare."

"Go ahead then, continue," the Princess said as she went to stand on King Thoran's left with all her retinue. She did not even look at Orten on the other side. The Duke did look at her, and his eyes shone with a gleam very much like hatred. They did not seem to have a good relationship, something that surprised no one given their characters. The retinue saluted King Thoran respectfully.

Thoran continued his announcement.

"The time has come for the Royal Wedding to be celebrated. I will marry Princess Heulyn of Irinel. The kingdoms of Norghana and Irinel will be thus joined and there will be an alliance which will strengthen the positions of both kingdoms among the military and economic powers of Tremia."

Nilsa had already guessed what was going to happen, and she swallowed hard. This could not be good for them. The Princess hated them and she was going to become Queen. She had already tried to have them hanged; now that she was going to be Queen she might succeed. She saw Valeria glance at her out of the corner of her eye and she remembered the pact they had agreed on. Perhaps, if Valeria kept her word, it would not happen. But it was not the time to worry about that possibility. She focused on what was being announced, since it was going to change the future of Norghana and maybe even of all Tremia.

"This is fantastic news, Your Majesty, it will fill the realm with joy," Gondabar said gladly.

"Great news which will strengthen the Kingdom and the Crown," Raner said in turn.

King Thoran nodded, but on his face, they could appreciate a dichotomy. His twisted smile seemed to show distaste while his eyes shone with a gleam of triumph. Nilsa saw the gesture and interpreted it. The King achieved an important triumph in gaining an alliance with Irinel. It strengthened him and placed him as one of the main sovereigns in Tremia. On the other hand, he was obliged to marry Princess Heulyn, which clearly was something he really did not want to do. Perhaps Nilsa was wrong in her reading of the situation and the King's look, but she was almost sure she was not.

"Indeed it is," Thoran nodded.

"Norghana will once again be a feared military power in Tremia," Orten said. "No one will dare challenge it once we have Irinel's support. Our kingdom will flourish, we'll improve our army, and all the kingdoms in the continent will tremble before our power."

"Yes, brother, that will happen, but let us not get ahead of ourselves. The first thing we must make sure of is the Royal marriage. This is a historic moment for Norghana and it will be one of the most important events of the decade."

"Possibly the century," Ambassador Larsen said in his honeyed tone as he bowed to the King.

"My first idea was to have a small wedding, with only the Royal Families of Norghana and Irinel, but my future wife demands a Royal Wedding with all the honors due and in the style of the royal weddings of old," said Thoran, glancing at Heulyn. "And of course, she shall have it. This wedding will be one all the kingdoms of Tremia will remember."

The Princess, future Queen, nodded, staring at King Thoran. The gesture made it appear as if they had arrived at some kind of agreement rather than being fully pleased. Thoran, on his part, did not look particularly happy with this wedding, his smile was not very sincere.

"It'll be a wedding everyone will envy," Orten added.

Thoran nodded.

"The announcement to our beloved kingdom and the rest of the kingdoms will be made this evening. The invitations for the Royal Wedding will be sent off tomorrow," the King looked pointedly at the Ambassador.

"Everything's ready, Your Majesty. The announcement and the invitations have been validated by the Queen and your humble servant."

"That pleases me," Thoran said.

"All the principal kingdoms of Tremia have been invited: allies, neutrals, and enemies," Orten added. "We'll see who they send to the Wedding. Once we see whether the Royal Houses come or only their ambassadors are sent, we'll know who's beside us and who isn't, as well as who wants to be, now that we are once again a great kingdom."

"The cowards who do not come to the Wedding will go onto my list of enemies," Orten said angrily.

Nilsa guessed that list would have infinite names on it, many crossed out, since he would have already killed them. If the Royal Houses came to the Wedding or sent ambassadors, the event was going to be huge, and a problem, not only because of its size but for the political frictions that might come up if half of Tremia's rulers and representatives gathered in the Royal Palace. Nilsa felt a cold sweat on her forehead.

"Ambassador Larsen and the other ambassadors of the realm will work to make sure the right people come to the Wedding," the King ordered.

"Of course, Your Majesty, we will put all our efforts into having all the Royal Houses come to the Wedding," said Larsen. "The representatives they send must be in accordance with the importance of the event."

"It had better be that way. We will not tolerate any slight," Orten barked.

"Whoever does not come to my wedding will pay dearly. Just give it time," said Princess Heulyn suddenly.

Nilsa watched the Princess, and her haughty mien and lethal glare made it clear she was speaking in earnest, seriously.

"I'm sure the Royal Houses of the Kingdoms of Rogdon, Erenal, the City States of the East and some of the minor kingdoms, besides the Kingdom of Irinel of course, will come," Thoran said. "The Nocean Empire will send Ambassadors, the Emperor never goes anywhere there might be danger. Zangria will send some of their generals, the cretins!"

"We'll try to have all the kingdoms and some of the minor nations," Ambassador Larsen added.

"Don't bring the stinky Masig," Orten told him.

"As you wish, my Lord Duke," Larsen said.

"The wild Masig of the Steppes and the Usik of the unfathomable forests are picturesque. We could have some as entertainment," said Thoran.

"That would be good to entertain the guests."

"Also some Wild Ones or Semi-Giants of the Frozen Continent," Thoran added. "We could exhibit them in cages."

"I like the idea," said Princess Heulyn. "The more exotic the wedding, the more it will be talked about."

"You heard the Queen. We will have a grand, exotic wedding," said Thoran.

Nilsa could not believe her ears. Not only was the wedding going to be a tremendous diplomatic headache, but it was going to exhibit people in cages like animals to amuse the guests. She felt so horrified that her stomach turned on her. How could they be so cruel and ruthless? She expected that from Thoran and Orten, since she already knew them. But not from the Princess; she had expected more of the future Queen but she was beginning to see that Heulyn was not that different from Thoran or his brother. As the saying went, birds of a feather flock together.

"What does Your Majesty need of the Rangers?" Gondabar asked.

"As you see, it will be a glorious event, but at the same time it will be dangerous. We are going to open the doors of our castle to retinues of other Royal Houses and nations. That in itself is problematic, since spies and even assassins will come with them."

"That's for sure," Orten added.

"I want my Rangers to protect the guests and deal with any spies or assassins. I want a wedding without incident. Everything must go perfectly. And we must avoid any bloodshed."

"Any bloodshed during a wedding is considered a bad omen," Larsen commented.

"I don't think so," said Princess Heulyn, "but I don't want any scandal at my wedding. I want it to be remembered as an amazing ceremony, something to envy. There can't be any confrontations or deaths, and if there are, it must be done secretly and without creating a diplomatic incident that might stain the wedding."

"The last thing we want is to start a war with this wedding," Thoran said firmly.

"It will be according to Your Majesty's wishes. We'll prepare everything," Gondabar said in a helpful tone. "It's an honor to have been chosen for such an important task."

"We'll be in charge of the safety of the guests. Nothing will happen to them. There won't be any incidents. We'll stop any possible betrayals and have the guilty leaders arrested," Raner promised.

"That's promising too much. There will be many guests, and among them will be traitors or people with unfriendly intentions," Orten warned.

"You're right, brother. There are some people who do not want this wedding to take place, and they are not only from foreign courts. There are also some right here, in the West."

"There are some in Irinel as well," said Princess Heulyn. "Not everyone in my kingdom looks on this wedding with kind eyes."

Nilsa was surprised to hear that. Who would want to stop the wedding in Irinel if it had been the Princess's own parents, the King and Queen of Irinel, who had organized everything in the first place? She glanced at Valeria to see whether her expression revealed anything. It did not. She was serious, alert and quiet. She was performing her role of loyal bodyguard. Nilsa would have to speak to her and ask her about the Princess's enemies in Irinel.

"Very true. We're going to invite our enemies into our home. It is a risk that does not please me at all."

"Our friends will be here too," Heulyn noted.

Thoran nodded, but his face showed annoyance.

"I know the saying, yes, but I prefer my enemies dead, not closer."

"That's the best strategy, without a doubt," Orten said.

"I will not take any risks. I want the generals of the three armies with their forces camped around the city. Let all see our military power."

"I'll take charge of that, brother, consider it done. They'll tremble as they come into the capital and see the armies."

"And I want all the Rangers back and protecting the ceremony," said Thoran, pointing his finger at Gondabar and Raner. "All of them. Nothing can happen during the wedding that might mar it or cause a military conflict. We must make sure."

"So it will be done, Your Majesty," Gondabar said.

"We will protect the guests and prevent any attempt at treason," Raner promised the King.

Nilsa was frozen. That meant they would have to stop the search for the dragon and all their efforts would have been in vain. Worse than that, if all the Rangers were assigned to the ceremony the kingdom would be unprotected, not only from Dergha-Sho-Blaska but from any other danger that might come up. Nilsa swallowed. What she was witnessing was the beginning of a coming nightmare.

"Go now and organize everything. The wedding will be in five weeks."

Gondabar, Raner, and Nilsa left the throne hall.

Nilsa had the feeling this wedding was going to bring many, and bloody, problems. Problems they certainly did not need right now.

Chapter 20

It was evening and Ingrid and Viggo were resting beside a small bonfire. They were near the capital, and if everything went as planned, they would arrive the following day. They were not expecting any setbacks, being so close to the city, so they would enjoy a peaceful night by the fire and reach Norghania in the evening of the following day. A little peace and quiet would be good for them for a change.

"You look even more beautiful in the light of the moon and the stars, my blonde warrior," Viggo complimented her in a sweet tone.

"If you think you're going to get off so easily, you're dead wrong," Ingrid replied as she heated some soup in a metal pan over the fire.

"I guess you're not very happy with what happened in my beloved sewers of Ostangor."

"You guess correctly," Ingrid said drily.

"I figured," Viggo nodded as he also began to heat his own dinner: vegetable broth, dried beef, strong sheep cheese, and a slice of berry pie. Except for the broth they were heating up the rest of their dinner was tough, albeit tasty. It was not exquisite by all means, but this way they would not have to stop to hunt, which usually took quite some time.

"I need you to get a sense of the danger and the true risk behind critical situations through your thick head. It's as if you're incapable of measuring them."

"I do measure them, I'm not blind. I'm serious when I say I wasn't in as much danger as you think I was."

"Things might've gone awry. If the young Crows had lunged at you following Klaus's orders, you'd be dead, and most likely me too, because I would've run to help you."

"They could have attacked me and that would have gone wrong, yeah. But they didn't, just as I calculated they wouldn't. I was within my right to challenge Klaus. It was a calculated risk."

"You had a right? After all these years? When almost no-one knew you now? To simply come in and challenge the leader? That's calculating very low."

Viggo was thoughtful.

"Perhaps I did calculate the risk as too low, yeah…" he had to admit.

"Do you mean that, or are you saying it to keep me happy?" Ingrid did not trust Viggo to really admit his miscalculation.

"I mean it. They could've attacked and things would've gotten ugly, that's true," he said, looking down at the fire.

"Wow, this is progress. I can't believe it," Ingrid said, raising her arms.

"Look, I might be a little crazy, but I can appreciate reality when I keep my eyes open, or have them opened for me," Viggo said and winked at Ingrid.

"Well, the fact that you're willing to admit that means a lot."

"But in general things were pretty under control, except for a couple of dodgy moments."

"I don't want us to argue. We'll have to agree that there was more danger than you had guessed and less than what I felt," Ingrid said in a conciliatory tone.

"Well… okay… yeah, we can agree on that, fine."

"Promise me that next time you'll calculate the risk as higher."

"I'll try," Viggo smiled, trying to get away with it.

"Promise," Ingrid insisted, who was having none of that.

"Okay fine… promise," he said and offered her his hand.

Ingrid looked him in the eye and took his hand.

You can't break a promise."

"I won't," Viggo said seriously.

Ingrid relaxed and heaved a sigh. She hoped she had achieved even a small change in the right direction for Viggo. She would have to wait and see how he progressed. She wished with all her heart for a change to happen.

They had their dinner in peace and enjoyed one another's company. The following day they would enter the capital of the realm and report at the Tower of the Rangers. They would have to explain everything that had happened to their comrades and to Gondabar. They would also find out what new information their friends had gathered. They would likely find themselves involved in new and complicated situations. But that would be tomorrow—tonight they could rest and enjoy a pleasant spring night in beautiful Norghana, in the best company possible.

"How did you know the correct tapping to go through the tunnels? It's been years since you were in the city, they must have changed since the last time you were there," Ingrid said suddenly.

Viggo smiled.

"You can't stop thinking things over, can you?"

"You know I don't like loose ends."

"I met a couple of Crows on the first night I went into the slums and made them sing."

"You made them sing?"

"Tell me what I wanted to know. Since they're Crows, I thought the word choice was appropriate," Viggo smiled.

"Better if I don't ask how you did it, right?"

"Let's say that I used a technique similar to that used by Egil with Ginger and Fred."

"You don't have animals like Ginger and Fred..." Ingrid said, tilting her head to look at Viggo through the flames.

"I have my knives and a dozen poisons and toxic elements in my Assassin Ranger's belt."

"Oh... I can imagine."

"The good thing about having intelligent friends with initiative is that if you pay attention, you can learn a lot," Viggo said with a bitter grin.

"Aren't you always messing with Egil, saying he's a bookworm and a wise guy and other nonsense?"

"I am. But that doesn't mean I don't appreciate how intelligent and resourceful he is. To be honest, I think he's a phenomenon, someone exceptional, not just because of his mind but for his character. But don't tell him, I don't want it going to his head. That's why I tease him, so he stays grounded."

"I guessed as much, but I wanted to hear it from you," Ingrid said, smiling at him.

Viggo let out a small guffaw.

"Well, there, I've said it."

They continued talking and then Viggo got up to get the water-skin hanging from his saddle. When he came back, he sat beside Ingrid and offered it to her. She smiled and drank.

"We'd better sit together," Viggo said, putting his arm around her waist, holding her delicately but tightly.

"Yes, much better," she nodded.

Viggo kissed her cheek tenderly.

"Don't think I don't see that you're trying to make me change for my own good, to be a better person, to improve. I know, and I'm grateful."

"You're welcome. I do it so we both don't end up in pieces in some corner of Tremia."

"That's a very good cause," Viggo laughed.

Ingrid laughed too and it felt good to do so; she did not laugh much, and the few occasions when she did, like now, made her feel good. Viggo always made her feel well, even despite the spats, but then afterwards she felt good again.

"I can't believe you gave away all that treasure. I would never have expected it of you," she admitted in a surprised tone.

"You thought you knew me so well and that I had no more surprises in me, huh?" Viggo asked mischievously.

"Well, not that well, but I do have to admit that I was very surprised. It was totally unexpected."

"You thought I was going to keep the treasure, didn't you?"

"To be absolutely honest, I did."

Viggo smiled from ear to ear.

"You're so skeptical."

"Don't say that, you know I'm not."

"The truth is that for a moment I did think about keeping it all, for more than a moment. In fact, it might have been several moments. I could've if I'd wanted to."

"I don't have a doubt. But why didn't you?"

Viggo smiled and looked up at the moon appearing between two large clouds.

"That treasure is the hard work of the Crows. They've risked dying for it and it belongs to them by right, they've earned it."

Ingrid did not agree.

"They're criminals. You can't talk about them as if they worked honestly for it."

"They're criminals and that gold is stained with blood and dishonor, yes. But it's their own neck they've risked to get it. The treasure is theirs by merit."

"Funny way of seeing things. Those treasures belong to those they were stolen from. You should've given it to the authorities to be returned to their legitimate owners."

Viggo laughed out loud heartily.

"Ingrid…"

"Why are you laughing?"

"Because you're so strict and honest that sometimes you make me laugh. Those treasures would never reach their legitimate owners if they were delivered to the authorities. They would vanish."

"Corruption in the city guard?"

"In this city, as in every other one. You should be slower to trust. I'm sorry to say that most people aren't like you: honest and with a sense of honor. They're mostly the exact opposite, and if they're in any position of power, whether the city guard in one city or another, they're even more corrupt, believe me."

"I believe you… in spite of myself, but I still think there are honest people in positions of power. There have to be."

"That's wishful thinking. But since it's wrong to generalize, let's say there are dishonest people in public positions and one can't be too quick to trust."

Ingrid sighed.

"If I come across them, they'll stop being in any position."

"Oh, I know that. It's one of the things I like the most about you, your unwavering honesty and principles, even if you're so often disappointed."

"Without honesty and principles, we're nothing."

"That reminds me that there was nothing that bugged me more, when I was an active part of the Crazy Crows, than having to hand over my loot to the crew leader so that he in turn would give it to the Leader. I always thought it was unfair. They gave us the crumbs and the crew leaders, and especially the Leader, took all the loot. It made my stomach turn, that's why I gave it away."

"It's a command hierarchical structure," Ingrid reasoned.

"Rather it's a pyramid put together so that those in the lower range continue being poor and those above enrich themselves."

"That's true," Ingrid nodded.

"I left some funds for Mike so he can go on leading the syndicate."

"You've lost a chance to be rich, something you've always wanted. Or at least that's what you're always saying."

Viggo nodded.

"I already have you, who is the greatest treasure of all," he said flatteringly and kissed her cheek.

Ingrid blushed and turned her head to look him in the eyes.

"Don't give me flattery and tell me the truth."

"I would've liked to keep the treasure, but that would've meant staying with the Crazy Crows for a while and leading them. They weren't going to just let me leave with it the moment I took possession of the throne. They're no fools, much the opposite. If I'd tried to take the chest, they wouldn't have taken it kindly. One challenges the leader to take his place and lead the syndicate, not to take their gold."

"Deep down you would've liked to lead them, isn't that right?" Ingrid could tell what the answer was.

Viggo smiled and took a deep breath and then let the air out in a long breath. Then he nodded repeatedly.

"I would've loved it," he admitted.

"I knew it!" Ingrid cried.

"I would've been the king of the sewers of the city. Of course, I would've loved it. It was what I wanted to be before I had the opportunity to join the Rangers, or what I wanted if I didn't manage to do so. I never fully believed I'd be accepted, not with the father I had and being a sewer rat like I was."

"But they took you in without looking at your past."

"Yeah, something that I still find hard to believe. But if they hadn't, I would've become leader. It's the dream of all Crows. And under my leadership we would've annexed the Red Fox Syndicate, either the easy or the hard way, and then we would've ruled over the whole city slums and the black market. From there I would've achieved ruling the city from the shadows."

"Grimy and pestilent shadows," Ingrid noted.

"Yeah, from where we'd rule the whole city. A beautiful dream, don't you think?"

"Not a very legal dream, to be truthful."

"Anyway, it's a glorious dream. Especially for the young sewer rats like we were. A pity it couldn't come true."

"You had a chance. You could've sat in that throne, not steal treasures, and fulfill your dream."

Viggo nodded with a melancholic look in his eyes.

"Unfortunately, it's a dream that couldn't come true, since I would've lost what I love most. I would've lost you. And I'd never let that happen, I'd die before that."

Ingrid turned to face Viggo. She wanted to see whether he was joking or he meant it. She could see in his eyes that he was absolutely serious.

"You're giving up that dream because of me?"

"That, and any other."

Ingrid kissed him passionately, and Viggo kissed her back.

"Why do you believe they're incompatible?" Ingrid asked him after a moment. "Your dream and being with me?"

"I don't really see you as queen of the sewers," he smiled.

"It's not so much the sewer that turns me off, it's the crime."

"Yeah, I know. It's not a lifestyle you'd approve of."

"It's not an honest lifestyle."

"True. That's why I decided not to stay. Besides, we have bigger problems to solve. It's not very useful to be king of the city if a giant dragon attacks it and razes it to its foundations."

Ingrid nodded.

"Something we know can happen at any moment if we don't stop it somehow."

"Riches are no good if you're dead."

"I fully agree with you on that."

"You can't have everything in life. You have to choose. I've already chosen and I'm happy with my choice," Viggo said, looking into Ingrid's blue eyes.

"Does that mean you're no longer seeking riches and a position?"

Viggo bowed his head.

"Who said that? What you choose is one thing, but if along the way opportunities appear to obtain more things…"

"I guessed as much. Make sure you don't deviate from the right path in order to obtain them," Ingrid said, wagging her finger in warning.

"I will always follow the right path."

"Sure, but just in case I'll make sure to show you."

"I expected nothing less," Viggo said, beaming.

Chapter 21

Astrid and Lasgol were crossing the capital of the Kingdom and walking up toward the Royal Castle along the main avenue of the metropolis. The city was crowded. There was no room for one more soul in the streets. The people came and went from one side to the other as if they were late for something, which was not usual—the Norghanians only hurried if there was a battle. As they went along, they could clearly appreciate the incessant activity in the streets around them. If the city was already a busy place as a rule, now it was chaotic.

They had heard the news of the Royal Wedding a couple of days before on their way back to the capital. It had not really surprised them. They knew the Princess had demanded to be married in spring, since she refused to hold the event during the winter. The event was being announced in all the cities, towns, and villages of the realm by Royal Decree. In a few days everyone in Norghana would know about the Grand Wedding. The Royal Messengers and nobles had made sure the news spread throughout the Kingdom.

Lasgol thought perhaps the Princess of Irinel would back out, or rather he wished she would. No matter how little he liked the young woman, and the truth was that she was obnoxious and dangerous, marrying Thoran seemed to him a disproportionate punishment. He saw it as a life sentence of heavy labor in the mines, perhaps even worse. He did not wish it upon anyone. That was why, hearing the news that the wedding would be in a few weeks, had made him uneasy and a bit disappointed.

Astrid, on the other hand, did not seem to feel any pity for the fate Princess Heulyn was going to suffer. She was just as aware as Lasgol of the severe emotional punishment she would undergo in becoming Thoran's wife, but she did not feel bad for the Princess. According to Astrid, Heulyn more than deserved whatever was coming to her. She could have rejected Thoran, escaped, or simply never arrived in Norghana. But she had done nothing of the sort. Heulyn had consciously decided to marry Thoran, she must have her reasons, and because of that, Astrid did not feel the least bit sorry for her.

Lasgol believed that Heulyn's parents were forcing her into this convenient marriage, since that was what this wedding was—an alliance between royal houses through a loveless marriage. And because of this, he felt bad for the Princess. What he could not understand was why she had not opposed it, seeing that she had at first, until the Panthers had captured her in the Druid's Forest and taken her back to her parents. He had always believed the Princess would oppose the wedding and escape to some remote place. But that was not what had happened, and this had him puzzled.

"The city is buzzing like a bee hive," Astrid commented beside him.

"You don't say. Everyone's preparing for the Grand Wedding," Lasgol said, stroking Trotter's neck. There were so many people coming and going everywhere that their horses were nervous.

Several people suddenly crossed the street in both directions in front of them and Trotter nickered in alarm.

Easy boy, Lasgol transmitted to the pony.

"All this excitement is contagious," said Astrid. "The people are thrilled with the Royal Wedding." She pointed at several groups of women, who were laughing out loud about the great event.

"Look, they're decorating the city," Lasgol indicated a group of soldiers hanging Norghanian flags and other decorations with the Kingdom's colors.

"There are more over there," said Astrid, pointing more to the west where another group of soldiers were putting up more wedding decorations.

"It's going to be a real spectacle," Lasgol commented as he watched a busy group of merchants arguing with the city guard about where to put their market stalls.

After crossing the city and taking in all the commotion surrounding the event, they finally arrived at the castle. They were let in after identifying themselves and went to the stables to leave Trotter and the white spotted mare Astrid was riding with the stable boys to look after them.

They dismounted at the stables and looked at the castle. If out in the city there was bustling, in here there was even more. The soldiers were decorating the whole Royal Castle. They could see them working on the walls and battlements, putting up flags, banners, decorations, and shields, both Norghanian, and from the Kingdom of Irinel. There was a group of people in the courtyard, about fifty men and women, and Astrid and Lasgol realized they were tailors and dressmakers working on long wooden tables, cutting and sewing the great decorations that would hang throughout the fortress and surroundings.

They could also see over a hundred soldiers in front of the barracks doing formation and parade exercises. The officers indicated the formation to execute and then they made them parade back and forth. Once the exercise finished they repeated it. A second regiment appeared from the farthest barracks and took the place of those that had been rehearsing the steps and formations. A moment later they began rehearsing. They could see that these soldiers had never paraded because they could not keep the pace and were performing poorly. The officers' shouts could probably be heard all the way in the Frozen Continent.

Instead of taking a rest, the first regiment that had finished the parade exercises followed two officers to one of the warehouses beside the barracks. The soldiers went inside and came back out carrying swords, axes, and shields. It looked as if they were going to practice combat, but they did not. The soldiers sat on the ground before the warehouse and some boys brought them pails with water, bars of soap, grease, wax, and rags. They were not going to practice, what they did was start cleaning the weapons. They were going to polish them till they shone for the parades.

Astrid and Lasgol watched it all. Their faces betrayed their surprise at seeing something unexpected.

"They're really making an effort," Astrid commented as she watched another group of soldiers with supplies coming through the main gate.

"Yeah, they're really working hard on their tasks," Lasgol said, watching the soldiers working, following the officers' directions. He noticed that a dozen stalls had been raised at the far end, beyond the barracks, with crafts: carpenters, farriers, and others, all working in preparation for the Royal Wedding.

"It appears our King wants to get married in style," Astrid said with a bitter smile.

"It would seem so. I've never seen so many people working like that, not in the city or here," Lasgol replied as he realized that more stalls had been raised between the buildings to help with the preparations.

Without missing a detail of what was going on, they headed to the Tower of the Rangers, watching with interest all the jobs the soldiers and the craftsmen were doing.

"I'm afraid they're going to sweat it out," Astrid said with a mischievous look on her face.

"It looks that way indeed. They look nervous, the officers do nothing but bark orders." Lasgol could see by their faces that the workers and soldiers were not happy and seemed to be working under duress.

"The King probably wants everything ready and to his taste right away," said Astrid. "Well, seeing the fast pace I'd say he wanted it done yesterday!"

"It wouldn't surprise me. Kings are prone to demanding impossibilities from their subjects…"

"You mean bad kings, like Thoran," Astrid winked at him.

Lasgol's eyes opened wide, and he made a sign to Astrid to be careful about what she said. He looked around to see if anyone had heard her.

"Kings bear a burden we don't understand," he said.

Astrid smiled.

"You're a terrible liar. You haven't learned anything in all this time," she whispered in his ear. "And I know you think the same."

Lasgol shrugged—he was not a very good actor.

"Rangers," he pointed ahead where several comrades were chatting.

All of a sudden a running figure came out of the open door of the Tower. The figure covered the distance between the Tower and Astrid and Lasgol in a sigh. She lunged at them like a tiger.

"I'm so happy you're back!" Nilsa cried, hugging them so hard that Astrid and Lasgol struggled to keep their balance.

"Nilsa… what a welcome surprise," Lasgol said, laughing.

"For a moment there I nearly took out my knives… I thought you were attacking us," Astrid said, also laughing.

"Forgive me, but I saw you from one of the windows and I couldn't resist myself. I'm so happy to have you back!"

"The happiness is all ours," Lasgol assured her, hugging her back.

"You're all right, aren't you?" Nilsa asked, concerned.

"We're perfect, don't worry," Astrid assured her, hugging her too.

"You two have no idea how happy I am to see you. And Ona and Camu?"

"They're fine, don't worry," Lasgol said. "We've left them in the Forest of the Green Ogre."

"Oh good, yeah. The castle is bursting with people, as you've already seen, and the bustle of people is constant day and night. They've brought craftsmen from all over the realm, and they're working without pause on the wedding preparations. You do know about the wedding, don't you?"

"Yeah, we heard," Lasgol said with a smile.

"It's going to be the kind of wedding that makes history," Astrid commented as she watched the commotion around and inside the castle, soldiers and craftsmen constantly coming and going.

"It has to be!" Nilsa cried, nodding hard.

"I guess it's what the Princess wants, a Royal Wedding in style," said Astrid.

"It's also what King Thoran wants," Nilsa added.

"Really?" Astrid and Lasgol looked at one another, surprised.

"Yeah, it's not only the Princess who wants the grand wedding, King Thoran too," Nilsa looked around to check that they were far enough from curious ears. They were. "He wants to impress, not only his allies but his enemies too, especially those. He's given the order that everything must be spectacular."

"Political games?" Lasgol asked, feeling that the wedding would be used to show Norghana's economic and military power.

"Yup, he wants to show off the power of the new Norghana, due to the alliance with Irinel."

"Military power as well?" Astrid raised an eyebrow.

"The three armies have been summoned. The generals are gathering them and they'll arrive in a week," Nilsa explained.

"Wow, he does mean to impress," Astrid commented.

"The Invincibles of the Ice will be here too," Nilsa said.

"Yeah, I'd already guessed they would be present, they're Norghana's elite infantry. The King will want to show them off," Astrid commented.

Lasgol frowned.

"How many guests?" he asked Nilsa.

"Lots. All the significant nations and kingdoms of the continent.

We still don't know the exact number because we're still receiving replies from those coming about the size of the retinues accompanying them."

"Well, then it's obvious Thoran wants to show his new power to everyone," Astrid said.

"When are the guests arriving?" Lasgol asked.

"They'll start arriving in a few days. We keep getting confirmations every day," Nilsa told them. "I thought many would say no, but it's the other way around. Almost everyone's coming."

"I guess it must be because everyone wants to make sure of the alliance and that Thoran's Norghana is back to being the mighty Norghana of old," said Astrid.

"Mmmm… there'll be lots of spies among the visitors…" said Lasgol.

"Yes, that's something the King and his brother have already considered, the presence of spies and assassins. We're expecting some trouble…" Nilsa said.

"This is going to get very interesting," Astrid smiled and her eyes shone.

"That's what I'm afraid of," Nilsa made a horrified face.

"Let's not get ahead of ourselves, maybe nothing will happen. The wedding guests will know how to behave, and with them whatever spies they bring along with the other members of their retinues," Lasgol said, trying to make light of it.

"I highly doubt it. Besides, how do you expect Thoran and Orten to behave?" Astrid asked. "And the future Queen? I wouldn't be so sure."

Lasgol thought it might be too much to ask for.

"Have any of our friends arrived yet?" he asked.

"No, you're the first. I guess they'll start arriving soon. The news of the Wedding will make everyone hurry once they've finished," Nilsa said.

"Yes, that's for sure. Let's hope they're all right," Lasgol said with some concern.

"Yeah, I hope so too. Waiting for news here, unable to join in the missions, has been quite frustrating," Nilsa admitted, wrinkling her nose.

"They will be I'm sure," Astrid said. "And you're doing essential work here."

Nilsa nodded, but her face showed she felt a little unsure.

"You should know that we won't be able to leave the castle for now," she warned them seriously.

"We won't? And why's that?" Lasgol asked, surprised.

"The King wants all Rangers present during the wedding. He has charged Gondabar with the safety of the guests."

"Ufff…. what a mission…" Astrid shook her hand as she gave a low whistle.

"A mission that's going to be most complicated," Lasgol murmured as he watched the main building of the Royal Castle.

"First Ranger Raner will inform you of what's been planned out for each one of us. Most of the Rangers have been summoned."

"That's not good for us. We won't be able to continue hunting the dragon," Lasgol said in a tone of annoyance.

"We'll see what we can do. Once Egil returns we'll have to think of something," Astrid commented.

"It's not going to be simple. The order comes directly from the King to Gondabar and Raner. I was present."

"That's a serious problem…" Lasgol was thoughtful. "But surely Egil will find a way around it. We'll talk about it."

"They might make us help with the decorations or the banquets," Astrid commented humorously while she watched soldiers and craftsmen working frantically.

"I don't think so. I'm afraid it'll be a lot more serious and potentially dangerous," said Nilsa.

"Really? That sounds interesting. Do tell," Astrid said.

"I think it's possible that they'll have us escorting foreign dignitaries," Nilsa said.

"And the danger?" Lasgol asked with a frown.

"That other dignitaries might want to kill them," Nilsa shrugged.

"I believe we're going to have fun at this wedding," Astrid smiled cheerfully.

"And I think exactly the opposite," Lasgol said gloomily.

"What's important is that no one dies and that there are no serious political problems," Nilsa said hopefully.

Astrid grinned naughtily.

"That *definitely* won't happen."

Lasgol looked at Nilsa and knew that was precisely what was going to happen.

Chapter 22

Ingrid and Viggo were trying to reach the Royal Castle of Norghania. They were trying to cross the city as fast as possible but their mounts were struggling to advance through the crowded streets, and they were not the only ones with similar problems. Soldiers, merchants, craftsmen, everyone was having trouble. It had been almost impossible to get through the city for a few days already.

The streets were packed from the first light of day until dusk. In addition, there were not only Norghanians who filled the streets, and public establishments within the city, there were also more and more foreigners from near and distant lands, come to witness the Grand Royal Wedding.

The foreign monarchs and their retinues had not arrived yet. They would come only a few days before the ceremony, some even the day before the celebration. But part of their retinues arrived before, to have everything ready for the arrival of their lords and ladies and make sure everything was to their taste. Also, for a matter of safety, and especially to spy on their rivals. Political games were being played in Norghania, games that would affect the immediate future, and even the not-so-near future, of the entire continent of Tremia.

"Look, Rogdonians," Ingrid indicated to Viggo, pointing at a group of tanned men with brown hair, brown eyes, their height and build somewhat smaller than the Norghanians. They were all dressed in blue and silver, the colors of their kingdom.

"I see them. They don't look like much to be honest," Viggo said with an air of superiority as he spurred his horse on so it would open a way through the crowded main avenue.

"Well, Rogdon is a civilized and advanced kingdom with a good reputation. Her armies are feared, in particular her magnificent cavalry."

"Bah, the cavalry can't do anything against superior archers like us. I'd knock all their lancers off their horses without ruffling my hair."

"That's nonsense. To begin with, they carry a large shield and full armor, even a helmet with a visor. Where would you hit them when they charged at you?"

Viggo wrinkled his nose.

"In the neck. That's always a weak spot."

"Yeah, sure, and do you expect me to believe that you'd always be able to hit the necks of a bunch of lancers on their impressive war chargers?"

"Where I put my eye…"

Ingrid rolled her eyes.

"Let's hope we never have to fight against the Kingdom of Rogdon."

"We'd destroy them. Especially if the Rangers fought."

"I'm not so sure… luckily we're at peace with Rogdon, and even if we went to war, the Rangers don't usually go with the invading armies, as a rule."

They went on toward the castle, navigating their mounts through the sea of people.

"Look, Zangrians. The ugly ones are already here," Viggo said as he nodded in the direction of half a dozen Zangrians wearing yellow and black. They were unmistakable: short, strong of arm and shoulder, ugly, hairy, and dirty, both in their speech and manners.

"Near that fountain there's a group of Noceans," said Ingrid, looking in that direction. They could see two clear groups: one of brown-skinned men, thin and lean with long curly black hair, and another of tall men, strong and muscular with shaven heads and ebony skin.

"Those worry me more than the Rogdonians," Viggo said.

"Really?" Ingrid was surprised.

"Yeah, they look dangerous."

"And the Rogdonians don't?"

"The Rogdonians are square of mind and jaw, and straighter than rods, they're not dangerous."

"Oh, duly noted."

"That's the way. I like it when you listen and heed me," Viggo smiled.

"I always listen to you—as for heeding you, almost never."

"That's why we get along so well, my bellicose blondie," Viggo threw her a kiss.

Ingrid sighed, but she could not help the ghost of a smile that appeared on her face.

"I think we're seeing people of different kingdoms arriving in the city for the Grand Wedding."

"I find it amusing. We can see what they look like, see whether they're a danger, bet what kingdom will be the next to enter a war and lose. That sort of thing…" Viggo said cheerfully.

Ingrid waved a hand; she did not think it was so amusing. They continued up the main street. Little by little they managed to make way for their horses and move forward, not without quite a bit of pushing to make passersby move out of their way. The carts were worse; they got stuck among the people and Viggo and Ingrid had to go around them, which made their advance more difficult.

They reached the castle and found the walls decorated with all kinds of Norghanian flags, ensigns, and hangings. They were taken over by a great number of Norghanian soldiers. In front of the gate and the drawing bridge, about a hundred soldiers were guarding the way, forming a sort of welcoming committee. Several officers and scribes stood beside a table covered with a cloth of vibrant Norghanian colors. Norghanian flags and banners flapped in the breeze next to the soldiers and table.

Ingrid and Viggo reported to the officers, and as soon as the soldiers realized they were Rangers they were admitted at once. The hundred soldiers split in two with a rehearsed movement, creating a corridor they moved through to reach the drawing bridge. After crossing it, another group of soldiers stopped them. They identified themselves again before the officers in command, and at last they were permitted to go into the Royal Castle.

"Security has been doubled," Ingrid commented.

"Are you surprised?" Viggo asked. He was not. "Things are going to get interesting around here."

"I'm not sure I like your definition of 'interesting.'"

Viggo smiled.

They dismounted at the stables to hand over their horses to the stable boys. They had some trouble getting the boys' attention; they were all busy and none came to help the Rangers. At last, they managed to catch the attention of one.

"Sorry, we're up to our eyebrows in work," he apologized.

"Don't worry, but please look after our mounts," Ingrid told him.

"It's not going to be possible… we don't have any more room for more horses," the boy told them apologetically. He indicated the stalls with three or four horses or mules where there used to be only one.

In case you haven't noticed, we're Ranger Specialists," Ingrid said in a dry tone.

"I know, forgive me, but we're overwhelmed. People haven't stopped coming, important people," the boy said.

"We Rangers have priority, you know that," Viggo winked at him and gave him a coin unobtrusively.

"Sir, that's not necessary... I'll look after your horses with pleasure. You're Rangers, and Specialists no less, the problem is that there's no room." The boy did not accept the coin Viggo was offering him.

"In that case, move out someone else's horses and make room," Viggo told him, winking again and offering him two coins instead of one.

"But sir... that... I can't..."

"Don't tell me ours aren't more important than some of the horses you already have here," Ingrid said, pointing at several horses.

"Yes, of course... but I'm not anyone to..." the poor stable boy did not know what to do to get out of the spot he was in.

"I'm not leaving here without making sure my horse is well tended," Ingrid said, crossing her arms.

"If you go away for a short while I'll find space for our horses," Viggo told the boy, and he smiled roguishly.

The Royal Stable Master saw them arguing with the boy and came over.

"Ranger Specialists," he greeted them with a nod.

"Perhaps you can help us," said Ingrid sternly. "We've just come back from an official mission. We have to go and report and our horses must be looked after."

"I understand, of course," The Stable Master looked at the boy, "take the Rangers' horses to one of the stables in the center."

"In the center?" Ingrid asked, frowning.

"Because of the massive influx of people, we've been forced to use all the stables in the city. Now we manage them all, on the King's orders."

"And how are you going to feed and look after all of them?" Viggo asked, raising an eyebrow.

"All the stables in the city have been commissioned by the King. They're all working now to accommodate the mounts of the guests who have come for the Grand Wedding. The King has also taken over all the city's barns and nearby counties. There'll be no lack of food for the horses."

"And for the hungry travelers?" Viggo asked, rubbing his stomach.

"The same has happened with the inns and taverns. They're all under Royal supervision and must serve the wedding assistants. Foreign guests have priority. They're also bringing hundreds of large carts with all kinds of food and drink that are being stored in several huge warehouses outside the city, guarded by soldiers. No one will go hungry; everything has been well-organized."

"Ah, that's much better," Viggo said, satisfied.

"And what if we need our horses urgently?" Ingrid, who was not so convinced, asked.

"You'll be given fresh mounts at once," the Stable Master assured her.

"Well, that sounds good."

"It's not my place to say, but I don't think you'll be needing them for the next few weeks."

"We won't? Why?" Ingrid asked, perplexed.

"You see... a lot of Rangers are arriving, but to stay."

"For the wedding?"

"Yes, that's one of the reasons why the stables are so full. The Rangers and soldiers arriving have orders to remain here."

Ingrid and Viggo looked at one another.

"That's news for us," Ingrid replied, not liking this.

The Stable Master shrugged.

"That's what I've heard. Forgive me. I have to return to my tasks, which seem to multiply all by themselves."

"Of course, go on," Ingrid said with a wave.

"I apologize for the inconvenience, although I'm sure there will be more. The important guests haven't arrived yet."

"Yeah, I assume when they finally do this it will be madness for everyone," Ingrid commented.

"That's how Grand Royal Weddings are. One like this hasn't been seen in a very long time. Let's hope we survive it," the Stable Master said. Then, after saluting them, he left.

The stable boy reached out for Ingrid and Viggo's horses' reins.

"May you have a good return," he said and left.

They made their way toward the Tower of the Rangers but stopped unconsciously to watch all the activity in the castle. The orders, hammer blows, shrieks, blows, creaks, and innumerable other sounds reached them at once.

Viggo whistled at the sight of all the hustle and bustle.

"It looks like there's going to be the kind of party I like," he beamed, opening his eyes wide.

"There are hundreds of people just working outside the main building of the castle. What's all this? We seem to be going to war," Ingrid commented, watching the people who came and went busily here and there.

"To a most entertaining war, with food, drink, singing, and lots of partying!" Viggo proclaimed, raising his arms when a cart loaded with barrels of beer, followed by another loaded with meat cuts passed beside them. Viggo made as if to go after them.

"Stop right there! Don't even think about it!" Ingrid told him.

"Come with me, it'll be fun," Viggo promised.

Ingrid was trying to stop Viggo and go to the castle to report when someone coming out of the Tower of the Rangers saw them.

"Ingrid! Viggo!" Astrid called, raising her hand.

Ingrid turned and saw her friend.

Astrid!" she waved.

Viggo stopped attempting to follow the beer cart and went over to greet Astrid, who was running toward them.

"What a joy it is to see you!" Astrid said, and she hugged Ingrid first and then Viggo. The hugs were strong, honest, and long.

"The joy is all ours!" Ingrid said with a big smile.

"Are you still as sharp as a knife and lethal as poison?" Viggo asked Astrid, winking like a rascal.

Astrid moved swiftly, and in her hands there appeared one of her knives and a wooden container.

"You want to find out?" she asked with a challenging gaze.

Viggo raised his hands.

"I see you're still in top shape," he beamed.

"Always," Astrid beamed back.

"Where are the others? Is everything all right?" Ingrid asked, looking toward the Tower of the Rangers to see if she could spot them.

Astrid nodded.

"Everything's fine. Well, as fine as it can be in the midst of this Royal Wedding madness," she said, waving toward the center of the courtyard where the activity did not stop for a moment. "Lasgol has gone to see Camu and Ona, he'll be back at dusk. Nilsa is going here and there nonstop, all day and into the night."

"Well, that's normal for her," Ingrid said.

"Yeah, but now it's five times more than what she's used to," Astrid made a horrified face.

"That I have to see," Viggo said with a smile.

"You won't even see her, she goes in a flash from one place to another," Astrid replied.

"Gerd? and Egil? are they back yet? Any news from them?" Ingrid asked.

Astrid shook her head.

"They haven't arrived yet, but they're on their way. They've sent news that they'll be here soon."

"Great, I wonder what they've found. I hope it's something significant that can help us find Dergha-Sho-Blaska."

"How did you fare?" Astrid asked them.

"We met several creatures. One was colossal—it might have been the dragon but it turned out to be a snake-dragon, not Dergha-Sho-Blaska."

"It was lots of fun, I had to climb up its back and it almost ate me," Viggo smiled. "I played with it a little and then I made it flee. I call it 'Dra-co-Sna-ke.' I need to tell the court bards. My heroic performance deserves an ode, or at least an epic song."

"Don't listen to him. There he goes with his delusions of grandeur," Ingrid snorted hard. "It was a lot more complicated than that, and you didn't make the monster flee on your own."

"I practically did. The others didn't help much."

"Don't pay any attention to him, I'll explain later," Ingrid told Astrid.

"Okay. We've also found something that might be worth investigating," Astrid told them.

"Good, we need leads," Ingrid nodded.

"Is it true that we won't be allowed out on missions?" Viggo asked. "Because we won't be able to do much or hunt the dragon down if that's the case."

"I'm afraid so. The King wants all the Rangers here to protect visitors during the wedding," Astrid said.

"Isn't that a bit excessive? He already has the Royal Guard," Ingrid said.

"If anything happens to the foreign dignitaries during the wedding, it would start a war, and that wouldn't be good for him. Besides, it's also for his own protection. He's worried that some rival kingdom might strike against him during the wedding."

"Well, we know he sees threats everywhere," Viggo said. "He's pretty paranoid."

"He does have some reason… this is going to turn into a wasps' nest very soon," Ingrid said, making a face.

"Let's hope no one stirs it," said Astrid, watching the soldiers.

"I'm afraid there are many chances of that happening," Viggo said.

"Don't be a bird of ill omen…" Ingrid chided.

"I'm realistic, my dear blondie, and you know that," Viggo replied, winking at her.

Astrid smiled.

"You have to go and report to Gondabar."

"Yes, let's go," Ingrid nodded, and the three headed to the Tower.

Soon the dignitaries would arrive and the wasps' nest would be complete and filled to the brim.

Chapter 23

Egil and Gerd were riding at a good pace and would reach the gates of the capital by late afternoon. They had sent a pigeon from a nearby city informing the Rangers that they would arrive in a few days. They were anxious to see their friends. And not just to see them but also find out what had happened in their absence.

Their horses were galloping, crossing the forests and clearings of the south part of the kingdom. The terrain was a lot kinder in this part of Norghana, and with spring in all her splendor around them, the landscape became a delight to the senses. Both Gerd and Egil loved spring and those southern lands of the realm.

After bordering a beech wood, Gerd raised his hand to stop. "Watch out," he said.

Egil pulled at his horse's reins and stopped too.

"What's the matter?"

Gerd dismounted and went to examine the back leg of his horse.

Egil dismounted as well and went to see what the problem was.

"It looks as if the horseshoe is about to come off," Gerd told Egil, showing it to him.

Egil bent over to examine it.

"What's the matter?" he whispered to the giant.

"There are two men watching our advance up on the hill, to the north, among the oaks," Gerd nodded, unobtrusively indicating the direction.

Egil acted as if he were checking Gerd's horse's shoe and squinted to see what his friend indicated.

"Yes, there are. What a good eye you have, big guy," he whispered back while he continued pretending.

"A farmer's eye," Gerd smiled, not letting go of his horse's back leg and keeping up the pretense.

"I'd say you have the eye of a skilled Ranger."

"What shall we do? I don't know if it's us they're watching or waiting for. But they're waiting for someone."

Egil glanced at them for a moment, looking between Gerd and his horse which hid him from view. There were two men with hooded cloaks. The Rangers could barely distinguish anything else about them at that distance.

"Did you know the Noceans have invented an instrument that allows you to see things in the distance? They say it lets you see things far away as if they were close."

"No, I didn't know."

"I think it would be a valuable acquisition for cases like this. And in general, for Rangers, since we're always squinting to try and see beyond our range."

"One of those would be good right now. How does it work?"

"Through lenses placed inside a cylinder-shaped tube."

"Oh… I can't even imagine it."

"Remind me that I have to get myself one. It annoys me when I can't see what's in front of my eyes and it escapes me."

"Are you saying that metaphorically or literally?" Gerd asked him. Egil smiled.

"Both, my dear good friend."

"Irrefutable," Gerd replied, and they both laughed.

"Maybe it's us they're waiting for. We'd better make sure if that's it. Let's go past them but stay out of shooting range and we'll head east."

"But the capital is north…"

"Exactly. If they follow us, we'll know it's us they're looking for."

They got back on their horses and put their plan into action. While they rode, they both prepared unobtrusively for battle, just in case. Their bows were ready to be used, and so were the arrows. If things went awry, they'd both release from the saddle in the blink of an eye.

The two observers now appeared riding out of the forest where they had been waiting.

"Come on, the chase begins," said Egil.

"Let's go," Gerd said, and they spurred on their horses.

They galloped as fast as their horses would go. Maybe they would be able to lose them without much effort. Or perhaps they were not chasing Gerd and Egil after all.

They looked back and saw the pursuers galloping after them.

"There they are again!" Gerd said. The breeze and the speed they were riding at ruffled his hair.

"Then there's no doubt, they're after us!" Egil cried as he held onto his reins before taking a glance.

"Good or bad intentions?"

"Prepare for bad intentions. If they're good we lose nothing!" Egil said with a wink.

"Okay! How do you want to handle this?"

"We separate and move to surround them!" Egil said.

"Okay, I'll turn north and you go south!" Gerd said.

Egil nodded.

They galloped faster, and when they reached a small shoulder on the road and passed it Gerd gave the signal on the way down. They went in opposite directions as fast as their horses could go, as if Dergha-Sho-Blaska himself were after them.

Their pursuers seemed to hesitate for a moment. They looked at both riders and then decided to go after Egil.

Egil noticed he was their target and went as fast as his horse allowed. He saw a forest up ahead and decided to go around it to begin their maneuver to surround their pursuers. Gerd had already noticed they were not after him and was already getting into position.

The pursuers were not bad riders and, although they could not manage to get close, did not lose too much distance with Egil. He was riding a good horse with strong stamina and was holding up well. After the years of training and experience gained through missions, Egil had become a great rider. The fact that he came from a noble family and had been taught to ride when he was young, besides being quite short, also helped. By the time he entered the forest he had already increased the distance with his pursuers and, if he chose to, could lose them entirely. The thing is, he did not want to. He wanted to know who those men were and why they were after him.

The wind changed and started blowing from his back. This helped him even more. His horse now seemed to fly on the breeze that pushed him. Egil widened the circle he was tracing, and in the distance, saw Gerd, who was completing the movement and was coming to intercept him, or rather intercept the pursuers.

Egil started slowing his horse down: not too much so it would not raise suspicion but enough to make them believe they were catching up with him. A moment later he slowed down even more so the pursuers would think they already had him. He finished the maneuver. They had returned to the point where he and Gerd had initially separated.

With a strong pull, Egil stopped his mount abruptly and faced his pursuers. He reached for his bow and nocked an arrow with a swift Ranger movement.

The two pursuers, caught by surprise by the maneuver, pulled at the reins of their horses to stop them. What they had not seen was that Gerd was already at their backs, galloping toward them with his bow ready and riding like a horse master.

"Surrender or die!" Egil shouted threateningly.

"Surrender now!" Gerd shouted behind them.

The two pursuers looked back and saw Gerd riding toward them, ready to release and kill them.

The two pursuers did not take much time to think.

"We surrender!" cried one with blond hair and a weathered face who seemed to be in his mid-thirties.

"Don't shoot!" cried the other one, who was dark and had light eyes and was a little younger.

They raised their arms and did not move. Gerd reached them and stopped his mount, all the time aiming at them. Egil moved his horse forward until he reached the two men, also aiming his bow.

"Silence! We speak and you listen!"

They both nodded and said nothing.

"Dismount," Egil ordered in a dry tone, indicating with his bow where he wanted them to stand.

The two men dismounted and stood where Egil had told them, and then he dismounted nimbly as well. Gerd did so too, although more clumsily because of his size. They had the two men between them. Gerd walked around them until he stood beside Egil. It was always safer for archers to stand on the same side and not on opposite sides.

"Drop your weapons," Egil ordered.

Both men dropped a knife and a short axe on the ground.

"Are you with the Defenders or the Visionaries?" Egil asked.

The blond one opened his eyes wide and looked at his comrade. He had a look on his face that made it clear he did not know who Egil meant.

"Answer, are you with the Defenders or the Visionaries?" Gerd asked more sternly.

"We... don't..." the blond one shook his head.

"We don't know who those are..." said the darker one.

Egil and Gerd exchanged glances. They both knew the members of either sect never denied what they were so either these two belonged to a different organization or Egil and Gerd were mistaken.

"Who are you? Explain yourselves," Egil ordered as he continued aiming his bow at them.

"My lord, we're messengers of the Western League," the blond one said.

Egil watched him with interest.

"Admitting that you're messengers from an outcast organization pursued by the King of Norghana isn't a good strategy," Egil told them.

"The League sends us to inform you, my Lord. We're faithful servants of the West."

"Do you know who I am?"

"Of course, my Lord, you're the King of the West," the blond one said.

"The true King of Norghana," the other man added.

"I'm just a Ranger Specialist."

"You're Egil Olafstone."

"The Western League wants to contact you."

Egil scratched his chin.

"How do I know that's true?" he asked with his head to one side.

The dark-skinned man with light eyes took out a rolled parchment.

"We were instructed to deliver this message by hand only to you."

"Don't trust them," Gerd warned Egil.

"How long have you been waiting for me?" Egil asked without reaching for the message.

"Ten days, Sire."

"How did you know I would come this way?"

"The League followed you when you left the capital," said the blond one.

"And this was the most likely return path," said the dark-skinned one.

"I see, only you didn't know when I'd be coming back," Egil said, lowering his bow.

"No, Sire. We had to wait since we were instructed to deliver this message to you," the dark one still had his arm outstretched, offering the message to Egil.

Gerd reached out to take it.

"I'll hand it to him," he said, looking hard at the two men in case they were thinking of trying anything.

Egil slung his bow over his back and took the message. He studied the seal—he recognized it. Finally, he broke it and read. When he finished he remained thoughtful, gazing at the horizon. The breeze ruffled his hair and caressed his face.

"What's the matter?" Gerd whispered, standing between Egil and the two messengers.

"Bad news."

"The dragon? The King?"

"Extreme discord within the league," Egil whispered back so the messengers could not hear.

"Oh well, that's not so serious, is it?"

"I'm afraid it is."

"Why?"

"Because it forces me to act."

"Well, we're always acting," Gerd said, making light of the fact.

"No, it forces me to act as King of the West."

Gerd stared at him with wide eyes.

"That's not good... Thoran..."

"Exactly."

Gerd understood.

"What are we going to do with these two?"

"They need to leave."

"Okay. Mount," Gerd ordered the two messengers, who obeyed at once.

"Inform the Western league that I have received the message and will make contact from the capital," Egil told them.

"Very well, Sire. We will," the blond man said.

"It's an honor," the dark-skinned messenger said, saluting with a respectful bow.

A moment later they were riding to the northwest.

"So, we have new problems," Gerd commented.

"That's what it looks like."

"Well, we already had enough..." Gerd waved his raised arms like a windmill.

"I have to admit that this arrives at a very inopportune moment," Egil nodded.

"Don't worry, we'll fix it."

"This time I do worry."

Gerd looked at him, puzzled. He had not expected that answer. Egil always radiated optimism, even during the biggest messes. The fact that he was obviously worried troubled the giant.

"Let's get back to the capital. There's much to prepare and do," Egil said.

As they were riding back to the capital, Gerd had the feeling that everything had just become a lot more complicated. He tried to remain cheerful. Whatever it was, they would fix it. But Egil's worried expression did not let Gerd relax during the rest of their journey—on the contrary, it troubled him even more.

Chapter 24

With the arrival of Gerd and Egil at the Royal Castle, the Snow Panthers were together again after spending some time apart. This filled them all with joy and provided a bit of peace. Nilsa had reserved the same large room they always shared. The other Rangers were already calling it "The Eagles' Nest" and no-one dared go in. They were undisturbed. For a while now they had been treated with great respect, which the Panthers really appreciated. Still, they never forgot they were all Rangers and therefore comrades.

The Tower of the Rangers was as crowded as the whole city since, following the King's orders, Gondabar had summoned all the Rangers who were not in key posts watching the Shelter, the Camp, the mountain passes to the north, and the borders. As it was impossible to have all the Rangers in the Tower—two large barracks and a canteen had been built behind the Royal Castle, outside the walls on the plain on the north side. Most of the Rangers rested and slept there. Only those who had been assigned to the Tower did so inside the castle.

Nilsa had intercepted Egil and Gerd at their arrival and had led them to the room after giving them many hugs; she was happy to see them safe and sound.

"I'm so happy to be back in this room with all of you," Gerd said, beaming as he stowed his things in the chest at the foot of his bed.

Egil was hugging his friends amid smiles and laughter.

"It's an indescribable pleasure to be back. I've missed you in such a way that I can't express with just mere words."

"We've missed the two of you a lot," Lasgol said as he hugged Egil hard and then went on to hug Gerd.

"You're just in time, things are moving fast with the Wedding," Astrid told them, hugging them tight.

"More than fast, I'd say. This is going to be a nightmare," Ingrid said, coming over and hugging them affectionately.

"Nothing like a Royal Wedding to liven things up at the Court," Nilsa was smiling eagerly, making her freckles dance around her face.

Viggo muttered something unintelligible, then went on to say,

"I'm not at all happy to see you, the room is already crowded and we barely have space to move. Besides, now I'll have to listen to the endless explanations of the know-it-all that no one understands.

"And on top of that we can't sleep with the giant's snores, that are like thunder in a winter storm," Viggo complained.

"We're happy to see you too," Egil replied. "Gerd, why don't you give him a bear hug to show him how much we appreciate his company?"

"That's a fantastic idea!" Gerd cried and went to hug Viggo.

"Don't you dare put your paws on me, you brainless semi-giant!" Viggo protested as he attempted to escape Gerd's hug, but everyone knew he did not really intend to avoid him. He let himself be caught and Gerd lifted him off the ground.

"Oh, how I was looking forward to giving you one of these hugs," Gerd was twirling, delighted.

"Put me down, I'm telling you, put me down!"

The Panthers laughed, and for a moment they were once again just a group of close friends enjoying a moment of happiness. Being apart was tough for all of them, and when they met again, the shows of affection were invaluable. They all felt happy and enjoyed that moment they knew would not last.

"You have to tell me everything that's happened," Egil told them when at last the laughter and the expressions of love stopped.

"Yes, what did we miss?" Gerd wanted to know.

"There's not going to be much time for that," Nilsa told them. "Gondabar has asked that you report to him as soon as you arrive."

"That's okay, then tell us, as quickly and summarized as you can," Egil said.

Their friends told them what had happened as fast and with as much detail as they could. Egil and Gerd listened carefully. When they finished, Egil remained thoughtful, sifting it all in his head.

"Interesting... very interesting," he was muttering as he walked along the aisle formed by the room's beds.

"What have you found out?" Ingrid asked.

Egil was about to answer when there was a knock on the door.

"What's the matter?" Nilsa asked, going to the door. She opened it to see who it was.

"Gondabar requests the Royal Eagles," she was informed by a Ranger.

"All of us?" Nilsa turned to Gerd and Egil with a puzzled look on her face.

"Yes, all of you, now," the Ranger told them.

"Okay, we'll come right away," Nilsa replied, closing the door.

"You think something's happened?" Astrid asked, wondering.

"Maybe. Although it might only be that he wants to hear Egil's and Gerd' news and he'd rather have us present all together," Ingrid said, already preparing to go and see the Leader of the Rangers.

"He'll surely want something else besides listening to these two," Viggo said ominously from the bed he was lying on.

"We'd better go and find out," Lasgol suggested.

"Indeed, that will be the best," Egil agreed.

The group left the room and headed to Gondabar's study upstairs. As they went up, the other Rangers moved aside to let them through and nodded in respectful greeting.

They went into the Leader's study and greeted Gondabar and Raner who were waiting for them.

"Welcome, Royal Eagles," Gondabar greeted them. "I see you're all together and, apparently, well."

"We are, sir," Ingrid replied.

"Egil, Gerd, everything all right?" Raner asked.

"Yes, sir. We haven't suffered any mentionable altercations," Egil replied.

"I've summoned you because I was told about Egil and Gerd's arrival to the castle," Gondabar explained. "I thought it would be good to listen to the progress they've made before it's impossible for me to see them due to my duties in preparing for the wedding. I'm finding it increasingly difficult to find time to see anyone."

"The duties resulting from the wedding are many, important and urgent," Raner commented.

"We're at our Leader's disposal," Egil said.

"What I would like to be clear about, before it's impossible for me to find time, is whether the investigations you've done with the great Erudite Alvis have been fruitful," Gondabar said.

"They have, he's revealed some important information," Egil replied, nodding repeatedly.

"I'm glad, it wasn't easy to get him to agree to help us. I had to go to the King in person to sign a Royal Order to make him comply. Luckily, Thoran didn't ask for too many details about the matter."

"The King still isn't aware of the danger, is he? I mean of the existence of Dergha-Sho-Blaska," Egil said, and by his look it was obvious that he hoped it was still so.

"He's not aware. He hasn't been informed yet. After weighing the matter carefully, both the other leaders of the Rangers and myself thought it would be better not to present this matter to the King, at least until we have reliable and indisputable evidence," Gondabar explained.

"His Majesty isn't going to believe the story of the terrible dragon that's going to destroy the kingdom," Viggo commented in an ironic tone.

"The King already has many state problems, plus the Royal Wedding, on his mind. Presenting him with a new one as serious and unbelievable is reckless..." Gondabar said.

"He's not going to believe it until he sees it with his own eyes," said Viggo.

"Neither His Majesty, nor his brother the Duke I'm afraid. They're not men open to such possibilities. The Leaders of the Rangers are already having trouble believing it, but we've given you the benefit of the doubt because of who you are. Unfortunately, King Thoran and his brother Orten wouldn't. That's why they haven't been informed of what's going on or the searches we, the Rangers, are carrying out," Gondabar admitted.

"When the dragon reveals himself and the problem is undeniable, then the Leaders of the Rangers, and all of us, will be in real trouble for not having warned the King of something we already knew was going to happen. Of an imminent terrible danger for the whole kingdom," Ingrid said in a tone that made it clear she did not agree with the decision of not informing Thoran yet.

"The King will be informed when the time is right, not before," Gondabar insisted.

"This has been decided," Raner added. "Besides, with the wedding, His Majesty isn't open to discuss anything that doesn't have to do with the great event."

"Well, in that case, we must accept that this is the most prudent course and that we may very well have to explain in the future why we decided to take it," Egil concluded. "It's certainly the least dangerous option, since the King would likely forbid us from continuing the investigation at all."

Gondabar nodded.

"That's right. Let's focus on the progress we've made so far. Astrid and Lasgol found an interesting object of power. Eicewald has it now and is studying it. He has confirmed it has magic of Drakonian origin. We are hoping he can reveal what it is for, and thus inform us what Dergha-Sho-Blaska is up to."

"They also found out that the sects are still active, in spite of having lost their leaders," Raner said.

"That's right, and their members are now younger," Astrid commented, "which leads us to think they must be recent recruits. It also means that someone is recruiting them, and we don't believe it's Dergha-Sho-Blaska himself."

"New leaders?" Egil asked.

"That's what we think, yes," Astrid said with a nod.

"That's not good news," Gerd said, wrinkling his nose.

"No, it's not," Gondabar commented. "Ingrid and Viggo have another piece of news   that isn't encouraging either."

"We've encountered colossal monsters that have never been seen in Tremia before," Ingrid said.

"Monsters difficult to kill and with an appetite for humans," Viggo added.

"How monstrous were they?" Egil asked, interested.

"The last one was a snake-dragon almost as big as Dergha-Sho-Blaska himself. The difference was that this creature was a sea reptile with legs and no wings."

"But with equally large jaws," Viggo noted.

"All reptiles?" Egil asked, tilting his head.

"Reptilian, rather, since we couldn't classify them as any of the reptiles we know," Ingrid explained.

"Huge beasts that looked reptilian," said Viggo.

"Do they feed on humans?" Gerd asked with a horrified look on his face.

"It would seem that way. They attack distracted humans and devour them."

"Yeah, but those monsters aren't dragons... I don't see the relation," Raner commented.

Ingrid and Viggo looked at Egil, waiting for his opinion on the matter.

Egil nodded.

"They're not dragons, but they are monstrous reptiles that have never been seen before. I'm afraid it's no coincidence that they've appeared just now when the dragon has returned. There must be a relation between those monsters and Dergha-Sho-Blaska."

"We're also hearing about more and more incidents, and sightings," Nilsa commented. "They've multiplied. They all tell the same story, monsters and beasts that look like snakes and dragons attacking defenseless farmers or forest workers."

"That makes me think that the return of the dragon might be waking up and attracting other creatures," said Egil thoughtfully. "Beings somehow related to the dragon without being one."

"Yet no dragon has been sighted," Gondabar commented. "All those creatures, whatever they might be, did not fly."

"That's right," Nilsa confirmed.

"That means no-one has yet seen Dergha-Sho-Blaska since he vanished," Egil said.

"Why is he still hiding if he's so powerful?" Raner asked. "He should've attacked already."

"Has there been any news of attacks in foreign kingdoms?" Egil looked at Gondabar.

"Not that we know of, but I highly doubt they would've told us if such a thing had happened," the leader replied. "The problems of other nations are usually kept secret as long as possible."

"A dragon attacking a kingdom can't be hidden. Rumors would fly all over Tremia faster than a hawk does," said Egil.

"Summing up, we have more monstrous activity while the dragon remains hidden. Perhaps he's hiding somewhere far away," said Raner.

"I'm afraid it's the other way round," Egil replied. "We're seeing more activity because the dragon is here in our kingdom."

There was a moment of silence. The Panthers looked at one another. Raner and Gondabar exchanged glances.

"If that's so, we have to find it and kill it," Gondabar said, and by his tired and troubled look he seemed to have aged a hundred years.

"That's our priority," Egil assured him.

"Tell me, Egil, what's the most critical piece of information that can help us that you discovered with Alvis?" Gondabar asked him, seeking some good news amid the bad ones already mentioned.

Egil was thoughtful for a moment.

"After having studied the Erudite's tomes as much as humanly possible, since we didn't have the necessary time to study them in depth, there are two things we think are important."

"Which are …?" Raner leaned forward to hear Egil's reply.

"The first important thing we've found out is the chronology of the dragons in Tremia, and I believe it can help us."

"The chronology? How does that help us? We're dealing with the problem now. The past is in the past," Raner said, not convinced by the idea.

Egil smiled slightly.

"The past helps us understand the present and face the future," Egil recited as if it were a dogma.

"That's very true, Egil," Gondabar agreed. "Continue, please. Tell us about the dragons' past so we might understand the present."

"After speaking with the Erudite Alvis, we lean toward the theory that the dragons arrived in Tremia ten thousand years ago. Some remains dating from that time, like 'The Jaws of the Great Terror' that were found in the east of the continent indicate so. The jaws belonged to a powerful dragon of colossal size; the type is unknown, but it was a dragon. As it was larger than the 'Backbone of the Sky' found in the Nocean deserts, it establishes that there are different types of dragons. Besides, we ourselves have seen cave paintings in the deserts which establish that different types of dragons flew over Tremia at different times in the past."

"Very interesting," Gondabar commented. "This invalidates the theory that dragons are pure myth and never existed."

"Those are our thoughts too," Egil said, nodding.

"Not to mention that we've seen a giant one coming out of a volcano," Viggo added acidly.

"If that's so, where did they come from? And why? Or did they originate here, in Tremia?" Raner asked, still wearing the look of disbelief.

"That's the part of the mystery about dragons that we haven't been able to determine," Egil said with a shrug. "There are many things we still don't know, and speculating without evidence is complicated. We also don't know how humans came to Tremia or whether they originated here. Something tells me that both mysteries might be related."

"Which leads us to their disappearance…" Gondabar

commented, leaning back in his armchair, looking pensive.

"We know it was before the beginning of the era of men. That means the dragons left Tremia or became extinct before the arrival of men in the continent, about three or four thousand years ago. There are records of some tribes who saw the last dragons, like we ourselves saw in the deserts, in cave paintings," argued Egil. "From this we guess that dragons ruled in Tremia for about five thousand years. Something happened with the dragons about five thousand years ago that forced them to leave the continent."

"If not the ancient men, who forced them to leave then?" Raner asked, frowning.

Egil sighed deeply.

"That's a very good question. The reason is unknown. There are several theories about this. It's believed they might have suffered some illness that made them leave, or an event that made it impossible for them to remain in Tremia, or some civil strife for power among them that nearly annihilated them. The thing is that there are no remains of all those dead dragons, or at least they haven't been found yet. There are also those who believe that more powerful enemies forced them to flee."

"Enemies more powerful than dragons, which are indestructible? What enemies?" Gondabar asked.

"We don't know. That's also a theory, although Alvis doesn't share it. In his opinion the dragons were too powerful to be defeated by any other species. The Erudite thinks it's more likely that there was a catastrophic event or that they became sick with some terrible illness that made them leave in search of a better place to live."

"I agree with the Erudite. If the dragons were as powerful as we suppose, I doubt another species even more powerful appeared and defeated them," Raner commented.

"True. Besides, if that species defeated the dragons, who defeated them? Since no traces of *that* species have ever been found."

"Perhaps humans?" Gerd asked, not very convinced.

"If that were the case we'd know. It would be recorded in the tomes of History, painted in the caves, transmitted from parents to children in traditional folklore," said Gondabar. "That's not the case, so we have to assume it wasn't the humans."

"Whatever it was that finished off the dragons, it happened five thousand years ago. We do know that," said Egil. "The three theories about their disappearance point to an event of nature, an illness, internal fighting, or the appearance of an enemy that destroyed them."

"I also lean, like Alvis, toward illness or perhaps a natural catastrophe," Gondabar said, returning from his thoughts.

"In any case, we know thanks to this that they can be defeated, that they can die," Egil said with a gleam of triumph in his eyes.

"True, that is good news," Raner cheered up.

"Hmmm, and how do we defeat them?" Gondabar asked.

"Here's where another theory comes into play, and this is on record," said Egil. "I'm referring to legendary weapons that can kill a dragon."

"Those weapons are made up to create fables where the heroes vanquish the dragons," Raner said. "They don't exist."

"That's what Gerd and I thought too," said Egil, glancing at his friend. "But some might have that capacity. Alvis wasn't sure, but he didn't entirely dismiss the fact that some were in fact weapons designed to kill dragons."

Gondabar sighed.

"Enchanted weapons do exist; we know that much. Weapons that bestow on their carriers more strength, skill, and even the ability to terrorize their victims—that is documented in tomes, and there are some warlocks and even kings who possess them. But, weapons with the power to kill a dragon have always been treated as a figment of the imagination."

"Perhaps because there was no dragon to kill," Viggo commented, raising both eyebrows.

"That's right. There's no record because there aren't any of dragons either," Egil explained. "But I think it's an area of research we should delve into. We know that the dragons disappeared—who can swear it wasn't because other beings wielded those weapons and killed them?"

Lasgol and Astrid exchanged glances. Here was a possibility of finding a way out of the problem they were up against.

"That would help us end the dragon problem," Ingrid said, encouraged.

"If they really exist and if they can really pierce through the scales of a dragon, which are harder than diamond," Viggo said incredulously.

"And that can pierce through their magical defenses," Nilsa added. "Dragons, just like magi, have power and therefore must have some defensive magic."

"We must assume so, yes," Egil nodded.

"The tomes we've consulted stated that these weapons were capable of killing dragons, piercing through all their defenses," Gerd said. "Not only that, they attested to the existence of the weapons. They were not guesses; the tomes discussed these weapons as fact."

They all started commenting and expressing their opinions out loud. All except Gondabar, who raised his arms.

"A moment please. Be quiet."

The Panthers and Raner stopped talking and looked at Gondabar, who once again looked over a hundred years old.

"Please, sir," Raner said.

Gondabar nodded.

"Before we decide whether these weapons exist and if they have the power they allegedly have, I'd like to know what they are," he said and motioned for Egil to continue explaining.

Egil opened one of his notebooks and started leafing through until he got to the page he was looking for. He began to read.

"The weapons are 'Neil's Dragon Killer,' a gold sword with the capacity to pierce dragon scales. We also have 'Rogdon's Golden Spear,' a spear an ancient king of Rogdon, Gontel Dungers, possessed and which also has the power to kill dragons. There's also 'Sansen's Knife' which you can use to presumably tear out the heart of a dragon to then eat it and obtain its power. We also have 'Gim's Double Death,' a two-headed war axe supposed to be able to fell a dragon's neck. Then there's 'Aodh's Bow' which is a bow of fire, a weapon supposed to be capable of killing dragons, and 'Antior's Beam,' a javelin that pierces through any shield or protection, including the scales of a dragon."

"I see you've done an excellent job of gathering information," Gondabar commented, looking pleasantly surprised.

"We did everything we could with the time we had," Egil apologized, and his gesture showed that he would have liked to have a lot more time.

"Then, if I understand correctly, if we could get our hands on one of those weapons, we could kill the dragon," said Raner.

"We might, although there are many aspects of them that we

don't know," Egil said warily.

"Aspects?" Gondabar said.

"I believe these weapons are all magical," Egil said. "They have to be, to be capable of killing a dragon."

"If they can even do that," Viggo intervened.

"Correct. But we start from that supposition, which might not be true in all cases," Egil went on. "Some of the weapons I mentioned might not possess the power they claim to have, or it might also be the case that all of them can kill dragons, but I doubt it. It's more likely that only one really has the power to kill dragons and that most are inventions based on the story of the real weapon."

"That would be more than likely, yes," Gondabar nodded.

"We only need one of them to be real," said Raner. "If we find it, we can kill the dragon."

Egil made a face.

"Here's where other aspects might come into play. From what we know, weapons with power, just like objects of power, usually have certain requirements for their use."

"And limitations," Nilsa added, "as is the case with any mage's magic."

"It will have both," Lasgol said.

"I'm not sure I understand you. What would be the problem if we find the one that's real?" Gondabar shifted in his chair uneasily.

Egil looked at Lasgol and prompted him to explain.

Lasgol nodded.

"The weapon might have requirements as to who can wield it. Most likely it would have to be a mage with enough power to master it. It might also have limitations as to how it might be used against the dragon. It's not going to be as easy as facing the dragon and killing it. The world of magic always has a cost and some limitations. We must understand them when we find the weapon, before we face the dragon, or we won't survive."

"Whether it's a knife, sword, axe, spear, or bow, you wield it. You use it seeking the heart of the enemy and you kill him," said Raner.

"Well said, I couldn't have put it better," Viggo said, pleased.

"That's not the case..." Egil said.

"We're talking about a weapon with power we have to use to kill a creature of power. It's a lot more complex than that," Lasgol corrected.

221

"The problem is, we don't know what the requirements and limitations are yet," Astrid said.

Lasgol shook his head.

"We first need to find the weapon, or weapons," Ingrid said.

Gondabar looked more tired—the conversation was draining him of energy, and yet he wanted to go on with it.

"This is an important revelation. We need to find the weapon, or weapons," the Leader of the Rangers said. "We must be prepared to kill the dragon when he reveals himself. We'll have an advantage we can't afford to waste. If we manage to obtain the weapon without the dragon's knowledge, we can catch him by surprise. He'll come, thinking he's invincible, that we can do nothing against him. That'll be his weak point. We'll kill him in the midst of his arrogance."

"So it must be," Raner joined him.

"What should we do to find the weapons and be ready for when the dragon appears?" Ingrid asked, looking from Egil to Gondabar.

Gondabar sighed.

"The King's orders are going to complicate things—they interfere with our search for this weapon. All Rangers have been commanded to stay here at the castle, for the ceremony."

"Does it have to be everyone?" Astrid asked.

"All except those we need actively watching the borders of the kingdom, the Shelter and the Camp," Raner explained.

"Some of us should go in search of the weapon," Ingrid said.

Gondabar threw his head back.

"Let me think about it."

"If we don't act now, we won't have the option of killing the dragon later," said Astrid.

The Leader of the Rangers raised his hand and asked for silence. The Panthers waited while he meditated on what to do.

"I believe that trying to find the dragon wherever he's hiding is going to have little success, as we've already learned," he began to explain. "Furthermore, if we find him, we don't know whether we can kill him. It's likely we won't be able to. That's why I think the best thing is to get ourselves a weapon that can kill him. This is essentially a matter of magical quality. Therefore I believe the right people to look for this weapon are Lasgol and Eicewald. The Mage still has some freedom of movement. As for Lasgol, we can cover for his absence saying he's on a critical mission for the kingdom. I don't think it would be necessary to specify any more for now. In any case, the King might want all his Royal Eagles at any given moment, so we must take that into consideration."

"I can bring our owl, Milton, and communicate through him," Lasgol suggested, looking at Nilsa to make sure she had him in the Tower. Nilsa nodded, indicating that Milton was home. "If the King needs me, I can come back at once."

"I think that's a good idea," Gondabar said, who seemed to be turning the matter over in his head.

"We'll try to cover for your absence as best as we can," said Raner. "If the rest of the Royal Eagles are here, I don't think there'll be any trouble."

"Then it's decided, that's what we'll do," said Gondabar. "I don't like the deceit, least of all used against our King, but the situation is critical and I have a bad feeling. I've been feeling it in my bones for weeks. Something terrible is going to happen. Everything points to the arrival of the dragon. We have to be ready for when this happens."

"And what will we do, sir?" Ingrid asked.

"You'll stay in the castle and follow the orders I give you," Gondabar said, "or by default, Raner."

"We'll do that, sir," Ingrid promised.

"Go now. Raner and I will finalize the details of the plan and the possible countermeasures," Gondabar told them.

The Panthers departed the study, leaving the leaders discussing strategies to follow. As they went down the stairs, Astrid looked at Lasgol with eyes filled with concern. Lasgol suddenly felt the weight of the responsibility he had been shouldered with. He had to find the weapon to stop the dragon or the kingdom would be destroyed.

Chapter 25

The next morning Lasgol and Egil headed to the Tower of the Ice Magi to speak with Eicewald. As they were crossing the courtyard, they noticed the arrival of a group of Rangers. They seemed to be heading to their Tower. Most likely they had just arrived at the capital and were going to receive their orders.

Lasgol stopped as he recognized them. Egil did too and stopped as well.

"Those four over there are Nature Specialists who trained with us at the Shelter," said Lasgol.

"Yes, and if my eyes aren't mistaken, and I don't think they are, it's Elina, Frida, Sugesen, and Gonars. And you're right, they graduated with us at the Shelter," Egil said.

"Specialists, over here!" Lasgol waved at them.

The four comrades turned and seemed to recognize Lasgol and Egil. They came quickly, smiling.

"Lasgol, Egil, what a surprise!" Gonars greeted them. He was just like they remembered him, a little more mature but with the same intense eyes.

"It is a surprise indeed! It's been ages since we've seen each other," Lasgol replied.

"You look exactly the same!" Elina said. Lasgol studied her. She still wore her long light-chestnut hair tied in two long tails on both sides, Norghanian style. Her face was not beautiful but her brown eyes shone with a special light, that of a bright mind.

"I'd even say more handsome," Frida smiled. Lasgol looked at her next: she had not changed either. She was short and pretty as always, with a face with slanted eyes and a nose like a mouses. Her copper hair was still not too long. Lasgol remembered she always spoke with a calm, gentle voice which transmitted peace.

"Particularly Egil, he seems to have grown at least a hand since the last time we met," Sugesen said, jokingly.

"And you are all more handsome and tall, indeed," Egil said, smiling.

"Can we greet and hug the famous Royal Eagles, or do we have to keep up appearances?" Gonars asked, looking around as he watched all the soldiers going here and there following the officers' orders.

"Maybe fame has gone to their heads and they want nothing to do with old acquaintances they studied and trained with," commented Sugesen ironically.

"I don't think so, am I right?" Elina said, raising both eyebrows.

"It would be a shame if they'd become all aloof…" Frida said.

"Of course, you can greet and hug us. We're still the same as when we were together in the Shelter," Lasgol said, spreading his arms wide.

"The same, just with a few more experiences on our backs," Egil commented. "Nothing is as comforting as seeing old friends again." He smiled and opened his arms to them.

They exchanged hugs and affectionate, well-intended words.

"How have you been? How have the years treated you?" Lasgol asked, all of a sudden feeling like he was rejoining friends lost a long time ago. He felt a strange mix of melancholy and joy at seeing them again.

"Not as well as the Panthers," Gonars smiled. "You're the most famous Rangers of the realm."

"I'd say of History! It's as if we were standing before legends," Frida said, giggling.

"No legends!" Lasgol waved the comment away.

"Let's say we've found ourselves involved in interesting events that we had to get out of as best as we could," smiled Egil.

"They say all kinds of things about you," Elina said. "Some are quite crazy, like that you've made a pact with a forest goddess who protects you and grants you powers."

Lasgol and Egil laughed out loud.

"That would be nice! Very, very nice," Lasgol said.

"Unfortunately, that's not true. We only have this and this," Egil said, pointing at his head and then his heart.

"Better that way. I admit I've been worried with all the rumors about you," Frida smiled.

"I've spent most of my time in the forests on the border with Zangria," said Gonars. "They needed a good Forest Trapper to catch spies and prevent any possible incursion by the Zangrian army. I believe I've set so many traps on the border these years that now the forests are impassable," he smiled proudly.

"We've been in that area a couple of times," Lasgol said. "I think I might have encountered some of your traps."

"Well, being you, I'm sure you saw them and avoided them."

"By a hair's breadth, but yes," smiled Lasgol. "The truth is that we chose less frequented passes, more to the west. You must've been wandering the eastern forests."

"That's right, avoid them if you can," Gonars advised them, "I won't be responsible for what you step on."

They all smiled.

"I've been sent to the north, in the frozen forests before entering frozen territory, watching for the presence and movements of the Wild Ones of the Ice and other tribes of the Frozen Continent," Sugesen told them.

"It must have been tough, even for a Forest Survivor like you," said Lasgol.

"Yeah, winters are terrible up there. This change of scenery will be good for me."

"He's protesting for no reason. See how good he looks! And that in spite of spending half a year frozen alive," Frida said, and they all laughed.

"Have you detected any significant movement of the peoples of the Frozen Continent?" Egil asked with interest.

Sugesen shook his head.

"That's why I've been sent here. I've been relieved by an even greater beginner Specialist sent up there to cover my post."

"What doesn't make much sense is to make me come, a Healer Guard," said Frida with a shrug. "They have the King's surgeons, apart from healers of great reputation here in the capital."

"Then what could I say? I'm an Expert Herbalist," Elina commented. "Why am I needed at the castle?"

"I'm afraid the reason is that situations might happen in which you might be needed to heal someone or identify a little-known poison," Egil speculated.

The four newly arrived Specialists looked at them in surprise.

"Are they afraid there'll be trouble during the wedding?" Gonars asked, looking worried.

"It could happen, yes," Egil confirmed.

"Wow, that's not good," Frida said sadly.

"I thought they had brought us to fill holes in the parades," Elina said.

"I'd already suspected that something might happen. It's not normal for all of us to be summoned at once to the castle," commented Sugesen.

"Most likely nothing will happen," Lasgol said, trying to calm them down, "it's a simple precaution. Besides, you're not wrong. The King wants to show off his strength so he wants all his soldiers and Rangers in the parades to impress his rivals."

"Well, in any case, the Royal Eagles will take over if anything goes wrong," Gonars said, winking and smiling with irony.

"It's good to know we have old friends with us who no doubt will come to our aid," Egil winked back.

They all laughed and remained chatting a little while longer, remembering past times at the Shelter and their adventures since their paths had parted until reuniting now, a few years later.

Lasgol felt the camaraderie of his colleagues, the respect and affection they felt for each other, and his heart filled with joy. Nothing like remembering the good times, funny anecdotes, and laughing peacefully to forget for an instant all the problems, all the pressure, and feel good.

They took their leave with the intention of meeting later on if their duties allowed it.

By the time they arrived at the Tower of the Ice Magi, Eicewald was already waiting for them. The door was opened by the young apprentice who led them into the hallway. The first thing that made Lasgol's jaw hang open was that the whole interior of the Tower was snow white. The walls, the floor, the ceilings, even the furniture— everything was white.

Lasgol saw an Ice Mage walk by with his white hair and robes, and he could hardly see him since he blended into the environment. That had to be done on purpose. In the middle of the white hallway Eicewald was waiting. He looked well, radiating power here in his Tower.

"How are you? Forgive me for not having been able to be with you more often, but King Thoran has me so busy with the preparations for this wedding I've barely had time to breathe."

"We're great, and we perfectly understand how busy you are," Egil said and greeted him with a nod. "In any case, I've just come back," he smiled.

"Then you must tell me everything," Eicewald said. "I've had occasion to speak with Lasgol, although not as much as I would've liked to."

"Enough," Lasgol replied, also smiling.

"I wish these were other times and I could continue training you and Camu. I miss it."

"And we miss our teacher," said Lasgol gratefully. He missed the lessons too and he knew Camu did as well.

"The duties to the Kingdom can sometimes be a bane," the Mage commented.

"But no less unavoidable," Egil said mischievously.

Eicewald laughed.

"Please, come with me to the guest study where we welcome visitors to the Tower," the leader of the Ice Magi waved them forward.

Lasgol and Egil nodded and followed him.

Eicewald led them to a door on the right of the hallway. Like everything else there, the door was white and had no handle or lock. The Mage placed the palm of his hand on the door and uttered a word of power. Lasgol felt the magic summoned and saw the hand shining with a white flash. The door opened without a sound.

The room was spacious, and the fact that it was completely white made it look bigger. There were four large armchairs on a white bear-fur rug in front of a fireplace where a strange fire was burning. It was bluish, the color of ice. It had to be decoration, since it was spring and the weather was wonderful. Then they remembered they were in the Tower of the Ice Magi so it was likely always cold here. Indeed, the fireplace was not for decoration.

On the wall to the right there was a large armory, only it had no swords, spears, or bows on it but ice magi staves, made of ice of different lengths and with strange white gems at their tips. Lasgol could feel power radiating from them. On the left wall there was a bookshelf with arcane tomes. The light filtered through some long, narrow windows in the nearest wall.

"Let's sit and chat quietly," the Mage told them.

Lasgol and Egil sat down while they looked around the room.

"Are we even allowed to be here?" Lasgol asked. "I thought only other Ice Magi could enter your Tower."

"You are allowed as my guests, but only to this room. The rest of the Tower is forbidden to those who don't possess the Gift and follow the path of the Element of Water," Eicewald explained.

"Is it safe to speak here? There are things we'd rather not be known, and there's one Ice Mage we know we can't trust..." Egil said quietly.

"I'll deal with that," Eicewald started to cast a spell in the middle of the room, standing on the bear rug and moving his staff in circles as he uttered strange words.

Lasgol and Egil watched carefully—Lasgol to learn and Egil to try and understand what Eicewald was doing.

Once he had finished casting his spell, a sphere formed around the three of them, engulfing the chairs they were sitting in. It looked like it was made of thick ice, but it shone with a strange gray hue that indicated there was something else.

"This sphere will prevent Maldreck or any other Ice Mage from hearing us."

"Impressive," Egil said, touching it with his hand. "It's not cold."

"It's a protective sphere. I've modified it to prevent any sound from leaving it."

"Good thinking," Egil congratulated him.

"I'd like to be able to conjure up something like that," Lasgol admitted with a little envy he could not hide.

"You'll soon be able to, don't give up," Eicewald said encouragingly.

"Don't you worry, I'm going to try," Lasgol said.

Eicewald nodded and smiled.

"I have no doubt."

"How's your research on the pearl necklace we brought you?" Lasgol asked restlessly.

"It's going quite well. I've been able to find out that it's not a necklace."

"It isn't?" Lasgol looked at him, surprised.

"No, this necklace only serves to disguise the Silver Pearls. The key is in each of the twelve pearls that make it."

"Then the necklace is just a ruse?" Egil said.

"Yes, in order to make the Pearls pass for a harmless, exotic necklace that a noble woman with lots of gold can wear," Eicewald explained.

"That's why we found it as part of a treasure," Lasgol guessed. "Its owner thought it was very valuable."

"What's important are the Pearls. They're similar to the Great Pearl we found in the Druid Forest and which I hid in order to continue studying it without Maldreck and the other Ice Magi's interference."

"Could they feel its power?" Lasgol asked.

"Yes, indeed. Drakonian Power. All of them," Eicewald told them. "I still don't know their purpose, but each one of these Pearls is filled with immense power."

"Then the necklace isn't safe here," said Lasgol.

Eicewald nodded.

"I know. I have to move it to a safe place like I did with the Great Pearl."

"What we do know or can guess from the events is that Dergha-Sho-Blaska seems to be searching for them. At least the pearls in the necklace, since his servants were looking for it," said Egil.

"What we have to find out is why," Lasgol said.

"Hmmm, they have nothing to do with any specific end," Eicewald commented. "Power is power. In any case, we must prevent Dergha-Sho-Blaska from recovering the Pearls," said Eicewald. "I'll hide them, but the dragon might be able to feel them. They radiate power, and he might detect them from afar."

"How are you going to prevent that?" Egil asked.

"The source of power inside the pearls is so manifest that I've had to hide them in two special boxes. They're objects of power with the ability of masking sources that radiate power. The Silver Pearl of the Druid's Forest is in one, and the Silver Pearl necklace is in the other."

"Excellent idea. It can't have been easy to find those boxes," Egil said.

"We, Magi have some artifacts that come in handy every now and then," Eicewald said and smiled.

"Will you hide the necklace Pearls with the other Pearl?" Lasgol asked.

"I think it'll be better to keep them separate, hide them in two different places. If the dragon finds one of the two boxes, at least he might not find the other."

"I agree," Egil said, nodding. "You should never put all your eggs in one basket."

"Where will you hide it?" Lasgol asked.

"I still don't know. I need to think about it."

"Very well, when you decide we'd like to know," said Lasgol.

"Of course, I'll let you know," Eicewald promised.

"Good, that way we'll be able to guard them," said Egil.

"Very well, and now, Egil, tell me everything that's happened in your search for information please," the Mage asked him.

Egil told Eicewald everything he had found out, as well as what Gondabar and Raner had decided. He did it calmly, in a way that the Mage might understand everything that was at stake. Once he finished Eicewald remained thoughtful.

"It's going to be difficult to help you in this search. The King... isn't going to let me leave for a few days...." Eicewald leaned back in his armchair and was thoughtful again.

"Perhaps the help you can provide is identifying which of the weapons is really the one we need to find," said Lasgol. "That would shorten the search time, and if it's the right one we'll have done it. Searching for all of them, one by one, will take us a very long time, several seasons."

"Yes, I see what you mean, Lasgol, but it's risky. If I'm wrong, we'll be lost when Dergha-Sho-Blaska appears."

"We have no choice. At least for now, while the wedding is on course," Egil said.

"With more time we could search for all of them and then discover which was 'the one.' But since we don't have time, we will have to focus on one of them," Lasgol insisted.

"I understand," said Eicewald.

"If we had to choose between having a weapon now or several weapons later on, we'd most likely choose the second option," Egil went on, "since we don't know which one is the real one that can kill the dragon. But, having one now, if we find the correct one, might save us from destruction if Dergha-Sho-Blaska appears all of a sudden."

"He might not appear," Eicewald said. "He might remain hidden, recovering for a long time. We are speaking of a being thousands-of-years-old who has lived several existences. He won't be in a hurry. It's not in his nature. Haste is something that belongs to humans, not to millenary creatures."

"True, but on the other hand, we have a Royal Wedding, with the presence of several monarchs and royal envois from the most powerful kingdoms of Tremia," Egil replied. "If there was a moment to make an appearance and cause a massacre of great impact in the whole continent, it's this one."

"Besides, we believe he's here, in Norghana," Lasgol added.

Eicewald was still thinking about everything they had told him.

"Very well. Leave me all the information you have about the weapons which supposedly can kill dragons and I'll study it. I'll tell you which one in my opinion we should search for first."

"Wonderful," said Egil.

"I won't be able to guarantee it's the weapon we need," Eicewald warned them.

"We know, and we'll take that into consideration," Lasgol said.

Eicewald sighed deep.

"I hope I am not wrong."

Lasgol and Egil looked at one another. They were expecting too much of the Mage and they both knew it. To be right with such limited information as they had was going to require a lot of good luck, something that was never good.

Chapter 26

The following morning, the Rangers were summoned to gather in front of the Tower. All the Rangers, both those inside the Castle and the ones hosted outside. The Royal Guard and the soldiers who were on duty inside the castle moved back to leave space for the Rangers.

"D'you have any idea what's going on?" Gerd asked while he was putting on his boots, sitting on his cot.

"We've been called to line up," said Ingrid, who was ready to leave already, "no idea why."

"It must be a simulation drill for when the big shots arrive," Viggo commented, still lying in his bed as if it had nothing to do with him.

"We'd better get down there and line up right away and find out what's going on," Lasgol said as he finished getting dressed.

Astrid winked at him.

"You go first so I can see that nice body of yours in movement," she said mischievously.

Lasgol chuckled and played along with her, "I'll be delighted to."

The door opened suddenly and Nilsa appeared in front of them, panting.

"It's not a drill, something's actually happening," she said.

"You heard Nilsa, Viggo. Get moving!" Ingrid told him.

"One can't even take a breather around here," Viggo protested, getting to his feet.

"Nothing like a little morning intrigue for the body and mind to start working," Egil said with a smile.

"Let's hope it's positive intrigue," said Gerd.

"Yes, let's hope so," Egil agreed, smiling.

They left the room. The lower area of the Tower was swarming with people. Luckily, the Rangers knew how to move and soon they were distributed before the Tower to line up, facing the access gate to the castle. The Panthers moved to the front line and stood there by rank. Because they were the Royal Eagles, they had to line up first. Only the Royal Rangers or the leaders would line up in front of them.

They waited a while and then saw Raner appear with the Royal

Rangers, coming out of the castle's main building. They headed toward them at a fast, firm pace and stood in front of the Royal Eagles. A moment later, Gondabar came out of the Tower and stood in front of them all. He walked with a pace that was neither fast nor firm, which worried the Panthers, who could not help but notice.

For a long moment, silence took over the courtyard of the Royal Castle. The Rangers were lined up and stood motionless, creating a large square in front of the Tower. The soldiers watched silently.

The grille rose. From outside came a retinue of riders while the horns of the soldiers on duty at the walls announced their entrance. The retinue was small, only a dozen riders. Leading it was an old man. All the Rangers recognized him at once: it was Dolbarar, the Camp leader. He was followed by Ivana, Haakon, Esben, and Sylvia, the four Master Rangers, leaders of their respective specialties.

"Ode of the Homecoming," Raner ordered.

The Rangers obeyed at once and started singing the Rangers' Homecoming Ode. The men and women of the Corps sang at the top of their voices, giving thanks for gathering together again safe and sound. Lasgol watched the Leaders of the Camp while they sang the old Ranger Ode. They had not sung it in a long time, nor had he heard it either, and it filled him with joy. Beside him Astrid was singing at the top of her voice too, with a feminine tone that had something lethal about it. All the Panthers were singing, and Lasgol looked at his friends one by one as they also looked at one another in turn. The moment became special, one that had not taken place in a long time.

The Leaders of the Camp looked good, even Dolbarar, although in his case the weight of his years could not be hidden and was manifest. Esben continued looking like a large mountain bear, with thick brown hair and a bushy beard the same color which covered his face except for his big brown eyes, which shone bright above a flat nose. Then there was Ivana with her cold Nordic beauty whose years never showed—she still looked like she was in her thirties. Her long blonde hair was tied in a low ponytail as always and her gray eyes shone true. Haakon had the same dark look and gloomy aura Lasgol had never liked. He watched Haakon closely; he was still thin and wiry and his skin stood out, dark for a Norghanian, and he still wore his head shaven. He had small eyes above a beak-like nose. And last came Sylvia, who had taken over Nature and who Lasgol barely knew but who gave him a good feeling.

They arrived before Gondabar and stopped their mounts. The Leader of the Rangers welcomed them with a smile and arms wide open.

"Welcome all!" he greeted them.

The Leaders of the Camp greeted Gondabar, showing their respect by nodding from their saddles.

"Ode to the Leaders," ordered Raner.

The Rangers changed their tune and sang the respectful ode that lauded the work of their Leaders, mentioning their praiseworthy devotion, their invaluable efforts, and the honor they brought to the Corps. This time Lasgol could not help becoming emotional as they paid tribute to the Leaders who had trained and guided them. He felt truly honored to belong to the Rangers and to have had the privilege of learning from all of them, even from Haakon.

Dolbarar and his Master Rangers waited for the singing to end. When Raner ordered to maintain the position in silence, the leaders of the Camp dismounted.

"I'm happy from the bottom of my heart to see my lord and leader," Dolbarar said to Gondabar, coming over to him and hugging him tight.

"The feeling is mutual," Gondabar told him, appearing touched by the meeting.

Ivana, Haakon, Sylvia, and Esben greeted Gondabar respectfully once he finished greeting Dolbarar.

"I see the Master Rangers are looking great, time doesn't pass for you. I find you rejuvenated and I am glad it is so," Gondabar said in greeting.

"We keep in shape to face the dangers of the Path," said Haakon.

"An exceptional archer must maintain body and mind in a perfectly calm state," Ivana said.

"Sylvia's revitalizing potions are to blame," Esben said, smiling.

"That's not true. You spend your days busy amid nature's wildlife and that's what keeps you so fit," Sylvia replied.

"The Path teaches us to always be in top physical condition, since we never know what the future holds," Dolbarar said.

"You'll have to share your secrets with me. I don't feel very fit," Gondabar admitted.

"That's because of the life you live, locked up in the castle in that unhealthy tower," said Dolbarar, pointing at the Tower behind them.

Gondabar smiled and looked back at the Tower.

"You're probably right."

Gondabar went on with the welcome. He dedicated kind words to the five leaders while they in turn returned the greetings respectfully, feeling honored. During the greetings the Rangers maintained their formation, watching and following the indications of First Ranger Raner.

The castle soldiers were watching the event, unaware of its significance or repercussion. For them it was a Ranger thing they did not understand. The officers had told their men not to interfere or disturb them, and that was what the soldiers were doing. They watched in silence, having abandoned the tasks they had been doing.

Finally, after the leaders had greeted Raner and the Royal Rangers, they withdrew inside the Tower where their accommodations had been prepared.

The Rangers made a corridor of honor to the door of the Tower and then maintained the position while Gondabar accompanied the newly arrived.

"Now I understand why I was told to urgently vacate several guest rooms in the Tower," Nilsa murmured.

"Yeah, this explains it," Gerd nodded. "I'm glad to see them all doing well."

"It's a joy indeed," Ingrid nodded. "Especially seeing Dolbarar looking so well."

"A lot better than Gondabar," Nilsa commented.

"Isn't that Luca in the retinue with them?" Lasgol said as he tried to make sure he had recognized him.

"Yes it is," Astrid said, nodding.

"He looks well. He's always been handsome, but now he's more manly, isn't he?" Viggo said, looking for trouble.

Lasgol felt a small sting of jealousy in his stomach, but he pushed it down to make it go away. That had happened a long time ago in the Camp.

Ingrid noticed Viggo's intention and elbowed him in the ribs.

"Don't start…"

"Me? Never," Viggo looked innocent, as if he had never so much as broken a plate, as he always did when he was guilty.

"I'll try to find out where he's lodged," Nilsa said, "I'm looking forward to hearing what he's been doing all this time."

"If he's coming with them, he must be serving at the Camp," Gerd ventured.

"Rangers, break formation!" Raner ordered, ending the welcome of honor.

As fast as they had gathered to line up, the Rangers vanished, returning to their different tasks.

That evening, under the cover of moonlight, Lasgol was getting ready in the room they shared in the Tower. He took his traveling bag and weapons and shut his trunk where he kept his scant belongings.

"I have to go," he told his friends.

"Good luck!" Gerd wished him, coming over and giving him a strong hug.

"Take good care of yourself and don't trust anyone, especially not mages," Nilsa told him as she hugged him too.

"I will, don't worry."

"Better to shoot first and ask questions later," Viggo advised him.

"Not sure that's a good policy," Lasgol smiled and hugged Viggo.

"If you follow it, you'll live a lot longer, believe me."

"Don't listen to him. Use your head, you have good judgment," Ingrid said. "Stand firm in the face of any danger."

"Thanks, Ingrid, I will."

"Everything ready?" Egil asked him.

Lasgol nodded.

"I have Milton here," he indicated the cage Nilsa had brought him.

"The crosspatch's bitten me three times," Viggo protested.

Milton seemed to know Viggo was referring to him and clicked his beak menacingly.

"That's because you're always mean to him," Nilsa told him. "He's never bitten me."

"He has it in for me."

"There must be a reason," Ingrid said, crossing her arms.

"We'll cover for you during your absence," Egil told Lasgol.

"Go for that knife you can use to tear out the dragon's heart. I like that one myself," Viggo said. "Besides, in the end it'll surely be me who has to kill the beast and save the day. It's always me…"

"The bow would be better," Ingrid said. "It's a lot safer to be able to kill him from a distance. And no, it won't be you who kills him," she turned to Viggo, annoyed, "it'll be me with that bow and a true shot to the heart."

"Or the double-headed axe," Gerd joined in the suggestions. "I think it's easier to cut his neck with a great axe. The knife or an arrow from that bow… I'm not sure they'd be capable of piercing a dragon's scales. Better a couple of axe blows with two hands to the neck with all your strength," Gerd made the motion with his arms.

"That's a brutal approach, Gerd. The javelin is an intermediate option, a better one I'd say. You don't need to get close enough for the dragon to kill you, and you wouldn't have to throw it from too far and miss, or not make it penetrate enough," said Nilsa.

Lasgol listened to all their suggestions, looking at each one, and they all sounded so valid he did not know what to do.

"You're not helping much…" he complained.

"You'll find the right weapon," Astrid assured him. "I know it. If anyone can do it it's you. Follow your instincts," she told him and put her hand on his chest and stomach. "These will tell you which weapon you need to find."

Lasgol sighed deeply.

"I hope I can find the weapon that'll kill the dragon. Wish me luck."

"You don't need it, my friend. You'll find the way." You'll see," Egil told him. "Pay attention and be alert, there will be critical information that'll help you decide."

"I hope I choose correctly… and, well, find the weapon."

"We wish you courage and honor," Ingrid told him, putting her hand on his shoulder. "We trust you."

Lasgol took leave of his friends and left the room. Astrid went with him to the stables. He had asked Trotter to be brought to him in advance and a stable boy had him all ready to go.

"Promise me you'll be careful," Astrid said, and there was pleading in her eyes.

"I will, don't worry," he said with a brief smile.

"I am worried. You're going on a difficult mission. I wish I could come with you, be at your side."

"You're always with me. You travel here," Lasgol replied, taking her hand and placing it over his heart.

Astrid shivered.

"Lasgol... you know what I mean..."

"I won't be alone. I have Camu and Ona coming with me."

Astrid sighed.

"That eases my mind, but even so, be careful."

"You know I will be."

"I can't lose you. I couldn't go on without you," Astrid said with moist eyes.

"Nothing will happen to me. Be at peace. I have to find that weapon, for the good of all of us," he told her and embraced her tenderly.

"I love you, never forget that."

"And I love you, Astrid. Now and forever."

They kissed with a passion born of the great love they felt.

"I'll be waiting for you," Astrid said while Lasgol mounted Trotter.

"I'll come back with the weapon," Lasgol promised and rode away.

Chapter 27

Lasgol arrived at the Forest of the Green Ogre and dismounted. That place filled him with good memories, and knowing that Ona and Camu were there and he was going to see them in a moment filled his heart with joy. He led Trotter through the trees to the heart of the forest, where he hoped his two friends would be waiting by the blue pond.

But, when he and Trotter arrived at the spot where they had the set up the tent they used to take cover during bad weather, he could not see them anywhere. Lasgol used his *Hawk's Eye* skill but could not find them.

Can you see them? he transmitted to Trotter, who snorted and then shook his neck for one side to the other.

I'd better call them. You rest, there's water from the pond and fresh grass all around.

Trotter snorted again and went to the water to drink.

Lasgol concentrated and used his *Animal Communication* skill, only he amplified its reach since his friends were not close by or he would have seen them.

Camu, Ona, where are you? He transmitted.

There was a moment of silence. Lasgol started to worry.

Lasgol, you come! he suddenly received Camu's message, along with a feeling of great joy.

Lasgol looked in every direction but did not see them.

Show yourselves, I can't see you.

All of a sudden, Camu came out of some trees to the north, behind the pond, followed by Ona. Camu called on his Drakonian Flight skill as he ran and rose in a leap as if he were about to dive into the water head first. Instead of that, the impressive silver wings appeared on his back and Camu flew over the pond.

Trotter saw Camu flying toward him over the pond and ran away, frightened.

Easy, Trotter, Lasgol transmitted, but the pony took refuge among the trees of the forest.

Camu finished crossing over the pond and with decent skill

descended beside Lasgol. The landing was not perfect and Camu slowed down too fast, but it was a lot better than the landings he usually executed.

Ona was running, following the pond with her feline speed provided by her strong back legs.

Come for a hug! Lasgol transmitted to Camu.

Me want hug!

Lasgol put his arms around Camu's neck and hugged him tight.

I've missed you.

Me miss you.

The two friends remained hugging for a long moment. Then they moved away and Lasgol studied Camu physically. He looked okay.

Everything all right here?

Much well, Camu messaged, nodding.

What have you been doing?

Practice magic. Improve power.

Lasgol felt a pang of envy, because although he also practiced every day, he could not do it for a long time because of his duties and because, most of the time, he was surrounded by his friends the Panthers. He loved them dearly, but they were not the best company when you needed to concentrate and do magical exercises, or any other kind of exercise for that matter. Lasgol always had to slip away and find a quiet place where he could practice in peace.

You have to show me all you've improved.

I show, Camu messaged, along with a feeling of pride.

Right then Ona arrived at a run and without stopping leapt and pounced on Lasgol, making him fall backward.

Ona, I'm so happy to see you! he transmitted.

Ona licked his face with her long, rough tongue.

Lasgol laughed with joy while he rolled and tumbled on the damp grass, hugging the snow panther.

Camu wanted to join in the celebration and started doing his happy dance, flexing his four legs and wagging his long tail.

Seeing him Lasgol, laughed again, still hugging Ona, who was licking his whole head now.

Lasgol ended up with a sore stomach from laughing so much and his face and hair as if a cow had licked them.

He spent most of the afternoon explaining to Camu and Ona, as best he could, the situation regarding the Royal Wedding and their

241

search for the weapon to finish off the dragon.

I want be wedding.

Ona chirped once. She also wanted to attend the event.

What's the matter with you two? No way, you can't be there.

I want see Royal Wedding.

Ona chirped again.

A snow panther and a Drakonian can't go to a Royal Wedding, Lasgol said adamantly.

Why not?

Because… because… because you can't.

Not be reason.

Because you'd scare the guests, the King and the Royal Princess, everyone.

I very handsome. Ona too. Not scare.

Lasgol slapped his forehead in frustration, not for the last time.

People get scared when they see panthers and creatures of the Frozen Continent. And when they get scared anything can happen. I've told you a thousand times.

We invisible camouflage.

You can't keep Ona camouflaged all the time.

Yes can. I improve much.

I don't think you've improved that much.

Yes much.

Lasgol did not want to argue, and since he knew that stubborn Camu would not give up, he did not insist.

You have to come with me to search for the weapon, so I'm sorry, but you'll miss the wedding.

Oh…

Ona chirped twice.

Duty comes first and then pleasure, Lasgol transmitted to them.

Okay, but next wedding we go.

We'll see, he transmitted to end the discussion.

They spent the rest of the afternoon with an exhibition of power by Camu, who had really improved quite a lot. Mainly in his flight, which is what he devoted most of his time on. Now his takes off were smooth, although rising high and then dropping was still difficult. In spite of some bad maneuver, it was clear that he had mastered the art of flight pretty well and was able to do so with ease.

Lasgol was happy for Camu. All the effort and falls he had taken were beginning to bear fruit. He also showed Lasgol how much he had improved his Magic Tail Whiplash, Frozen Claw Slash, Ice Breath, and other skills. Lasgol was impressed by the fact that Camu was using his recently acquired skills as if they had been part of his magical arsenal for a while.

I'm pleasantly surprised at your improvements, Lasgol had to admit.

I much good with my skills.

Very good with my skills, Lasgol tried correcting his grammar, although he was sure he would not succeed.

That.

At nightfall they received a visit from a figure who came over to the small fire Lasgol had built in front of the tent where the three friends were resting.

"Good and starry evening," the new arrival greeted them.

"Good evening, Eicewald," Lasgol greeted in turn.

Eicewald! I happy! Camu messaged.

Ona chirped once in greeting and wagged her thick tail happily.

"I see you're enjoying this spring evening."

"We are," Lasgol nodded. "I wasn't expecting you so soon."

"Urgent decisions require even a mage to hurry, and you know we're not quickest people in the world."

"Then you've decided? Which weapon should we look for?" Lasgol asked eagerly, since the decision had been weighing on him and not letting him sleep at night.

"I want to do one more test with Camu and decide based on that."

Test me? Camu stared at Eicewald with his bulging eyes.

"Yes, after all, you are Drakonian. If anything can kill a dragon, you might know what it is or at least recognize or feel it."

"We lose nothing by presenting the options to Camu," said Lasgol, who thought it was a good idea, albeit complicated that Camu could know what weapon was good for killing the dragon.

Okay, I try.

Very well. I've brought an object you're already familiar with," said the Mage and took out the Learning Crystal. He put it on the ground.

Lasgol smiled, "Yeah, it is."

Lesson?

"No, it's not for a lesson. What I've done is put the knowledge we have of those weapons in the Learning Crystal so we can visualize them and even perceive their power. But I must say that it's simply an approximation, nothing more. They're not the real weapons of course."

"But it might help us," Lasgol said, nodding, eager to try and see.

"I hope Camu is the one that holds the key to perceiving or identifying which of them it could be," Eicewald said.

I ready.

"Good. I'll activate it." The Mage placed his hands over the object and started to cast a spell. A mist formed over the Crystal and gradually a weapon started taking shape in the middle of it. A beautiful, long gold sword appeared with inscriptions all along its blade.

"That's 'Neils' Dragon-Killer,' capable of piercing the hard scales of a dragon," said Eicewald. "Concentrate, Camu, feel it. Try to discern whether this really can or can't do that. Or whatever impression you do get. Any feeling might be a clue."

I concentrate, I try.

The next image was that of King Gontel Dungers' "Rogdon's Golden Spear." Lasgol studied the beautiful weapon, a grand spear the color of gold, of the style used by Rogdonian lancers. It looked so real that he could almost touch it with his fingers. He felt the urge to wield it and put it through a wild beast.

Camu looked very focused. He was not even blinking. He was trying to detect the power of the weapon being shown to him. Eicewald left up the image of the weapon for a good while so Camu could study it properly.

"Sansen's Knife" followed, which just as the previous weapons was made of gold. It looked deadly sharp and radiated death. Lasgol felt it was a lethal weapon, with which you could disembowel any beast.

Then came "Gim's Double Death." The two-headed war axe was so imposing that Lasgol felt like he could truly use it to kill a dragon. What he was doubtful about was whether he would have the strength or the skill to wield it, since it had to weigh a ton.

The next image showed "Aodh's Bow." Lasgol felt that he could use this weapon. The bow looked light, and he wondered whether it was indeed made of gold. It couldn't be... but of course, they were looking at a magical bow. Perhaps it was made of gold after all.

At last, "Antior's Beam" appeared—a golden javelin that looked lightweight and easy to throw. Lasgol felt it would be true. With a strong arm it could be launched far and pierce through a monster.

More, Camu said.

Eicewald nodded. He cast a spell and showed all the weapons to Camu over again, a second time and a third time.

Camu blinked at last, and Eicewald stopped the images, which vanished.

"What do you think, Camu?" Eicewald asked him.

Not know. All good.

"Have any of them made you feel like it could be the chosen one?" the mage asked him.

Can't choose. All look good weapons.

"Well, that's a shame," Lasgol said ruefully.

"Please try, Camu. If you had to choose, which one would you pick?" Eicewald said.

Camu was thoughtful, with his eyes shut.

Sword, axe, and spear be more impressive, he said, opening his eyes.

"Only impressive, nothing else?" Eicewald asked.

Nothing else.

"Hmmm, I don't know whether that's enough," said Lasgol.

"No, I don't think it's enough. I thought that maybe we'd get more out of this, but I can see we're not going to," Eicewald sighed deeply.

"Then which one do I choose?" Lasgol said.

"I think that now that we've arrived at this point, we have no choice but to simplify," Eicewald said. "I know one of the weapons. I've studied it and searched for it previously. I don't know the others, and I'd guess that finding them would be very difficult and take time we don't have."

"You mean Aodh's Bow, don't you?"

"That's right. I see you remember."

"I remember you mentioned it when you went to Irinel after returning from the realm of the Turquoise Queen."

"Indeed. I told Thoran and Orten that I was going to Irinel in search of the Bow, and that's where we met again."

Lasgol nodded.

"I'd completely forgotten about the Bow until Egil mentioned it the other day. I never asked you about what happened with your search for that reason."

"I couldn't find the Bow in Irinel. The person who had it, Riagain, is an important nobleman in Irinel, cousin of King Maoilriain who was predecessor of the current king, Kendryk. Riagain took it out of the kingdom secretly."

"He was afraid it might be stolen?"

Eicewald shook his head.

"It would seem that tensions between Riagain and Kendryk have grown in the last few years. Riagain is in line for the throne now held by Kendryk. From what I was able to find out, fearing for his life, Riagain left Irinel and, before doing so, sent his most precious possessions ahead of him."

"I see we're not the only kingdom to have succession issues."

"Practically all kingdoms have them, one way or another. There's always more than one contender for the throne."

Lasgol nodded.

"Where did he go for shelter?"

"That's the problem. He took refuge in the Kingdom of Moontian."

"The Kingdom of Moontian?" Lasgol did not know the name. He was surprised—he knew all the main kingdoms of Tremia.

"It's a recently created kingdom. It's south of the Kingdom of Irinel, to the east. Until a few years ago it was only a tribal kingdom. They lived in cities hollowed out of the rock of their great mountain range. In the last fifteen years it's grown quickly and is becoming an important kingdom. It has had issues with Irinel to the north."

"And that's why Riagain's chosen that place for refuge."

"Exactly. He has the support of the Moontian nobles, whom he knows and to whom he has promised to return the disputed lands if he reaches power in Irinel."

"Tremia, her kingdoms and her disputes, never cease to surprise me."

"You and everyone else," Eicewald grinned.

"Do you think he'll get the crown of Irinel?"

"No, I don't think so, at least not for the time being, least of all when Irinel and Norghana have become allies through this wedding. Moontian is a small kingdom. It doesn't wield enough strength yet."

"Who rules Moontian?"

"Queen Niria. I don't know much about her. She's said to be intelligent and beautiful."

"A Queen. Interesting."

"Yes, it is. I wanted to go down to Moontian, but I was denied entry at the border."

"And you believe Riagain has the Bow with him, in Moontian?"

"He should have it. From what is known, he's a skilled archer and uses the bow often. He considers it his most precious belonging. I don't think he'll have gotten rid of the weapon. I think he still has it."

"In that case, I'll pay him a visit."

"That will take you too long. It's far from here. You'd have to go to Erenal and take a ship there to Moontian."

"I have another plan to make the journey faster."

"Your plan wouldn't be flying on Camu, would it?" Eicewald joked.

Lasgol weigh much.

"No, that's not my plan, but you're not that far off."

"I hope your plan works out. In any case, when you arrive in Moontian it won't be easy for you to get the Bow. Riagain has soldiers loyal to his cause with him."

"That's not good. If they're loyal to the cause of his succession to the throne, they'll put up quite the fight."

"That's what I'm afraid of," Eicewald said.

"All right. We'll leave at dawn."

"I wish you the best of luck."

"Before I leave, where did you hide the Silver Pearl? You said you'd hide it here, but where?"

I know.

Eicewald smiled.

"Camu can tell you."

In pond.

Lasgol was perplexed.

"It wouldn't be inside the pond?"

"Exactly there. At the bottom of the pond to be precise."

Lasgol's eyes widened.

"That's a good place to hide it."

"That's what I thought. Now I must get back to the Royal Castle. Tomorrow I have a busy day serving the King."

"I also wish you good luck," Lasgol said, grinning.

Eicewald said goodbye and left.

Lasgol was left with a funny feeling in his chest. He was not at all clear that Aodh's Bow was the right weapon. It was the only one they had any clue how to find, but that did not make it the true weapon. He snorted and tried to relax. His troubles were beginning to weigh on him.

Chapter 28

It was well into the night when a Ranger on duty went to the Panthers' room. He knocked on the door urgently with his fist.

Astrid jumped to her feet with her knives in her hands and a lethal look in her eyes.

Ingrid got up an instant later and signaled for Astrid to wait.

"Who is it?" Nilsa asked, hurrying to the door while the rest of the Panthers got up.

"Ranger on duty," the caller replied.

"What the heck's going on? We're sleeping!" Viggo protested loudly, still in his bed with one eye open and the other one shut.

Nilsa opened the door.

"The First Ranger wants you in front of the Tower," the Ranger on duty told them.

"Very well. We'll be there at once," Nilsa said, closing the door and turning to her friends with a puzzled look on her face.

"It seems something's up," Ingrid said.

"Let's go out and see what it is," Astrid suggested. "I hope it doesn't have anything to do with Lasgol and the search for the weapon."

"I don't know what it'll be about, but this is certainly no time for games," Viggo muttered, annoyed, as he got up.

"I don't think it'll be a game if Raner wants us," Gerd told him.

"Let's hurry and find out," said Ingrid, who was all ready.

Viggo made a face but said nothing more and got dressed.

They came outside the Tower and found the First Ranger and his Royal Rangers forming and looking toward the great gate of the outer wall.

"Royal Eagles, line up on this side," Raner ordered, indicating his right.

They nodded and lined up as told. It was raining lightly, and although it was warm rain, by Norghanian standards, it got them wet all the same.

All of a sudden, the main gate opened and a retinue formed by a dozen riders entered the castle grounds.

"We have visitors," Nilsa whispered.

"Important ones I'd assume," Astrid whispered back.

The retinue arrived before Raner. They were all wearing hooded cloaks which hid their faces. The light outside the Tower was poor and gave the figures an air of mystery.

"Can anyone please tell me why we're lining up in the rain, at night?" Viggo asked his friends in a whisper.

"Because the First Ranger has ordered it," Ingrid snapped at him.

"Well, he could order us to go to the tavern for some beer instead."

"Shut up, you numbskull, he's going to hear you."

"Nilsa, do you know who they are and why we're waiting?" Gerd asked.

Nilsa shrugged. "No idea."

"If we're here, and the Royal Rangers are here, it's because it's someone important," said Egil, "and they belong to the Rangers..."

"Oh..." said Gerd, understanding who Egil meant.

Gondabar came out of the Tower escorted by two of his assistants. The leader of the Rangers was walking slowly, dragging his feet. Under the rain he looked even worse than usual. He reached the front of the retinue, which dismounted at a signal of their leader.

"You don't look well, Gondabar, Annika should take a thorough look at you," the leader said to him. It was a woman.

"I'm glad you're still as straightforward as usual, Mother Specialist," Gondabar replied with a big smile.

"Forgive me, but you know I'm no friend of formalities," Sigrid said, uncovering her head.

Annika pushed her hood back and dismounted.

"You're going to keep me busy, my old friend," she said, coming over to him and examining him with eyes expert in finding out what might be wrong with the body.

"I'm afraid I will, a lot indeed," Gondabar admitted with a sad smile.

"I don't think you look so bad," Ivar said. "I bet you can still use a bow."

Gondabar let out a small laugh.

"I wish I could, but no. That's a thing of the past."

Engla pushed back her hood, and when he recognized her Gondabar smiled.

"And how's the Elder Specialist of Expertise?"

"Quite better than my Leader," she replied.

Gondabar nodded several times. Then he opened his arms.

"Give me a hug, Leaders of the Shelter, Parents of Specialists."

Sigrid was the first to hug him fondly. Then, one by one, the Elder Specialists hugged him, showing Gondabar the love and respect they felt for him. The Leader of the Rangers could not help feeling touched and honored. His face, wet from the rain, could not hide the tears that filled his eyes.

"We've brought someone else in case Annika's ministering isn't enough," Sigrid told him, and with her arm she indicated another figure in the retinue who approached Gondabar. She pushed her hood back and the leader recognized her at once.

"Healer Edwina, it's been such a long time and such a joy to see you."

"The joy is all mine," Edwina replied, taking a bow.

"No formalities. It's a pleasure to have a Healer among us," Gondabar said.

"Maybe she can improve your health," Sigrid said.

"I'll do everything I can," Edwina promised.

"I'm sure that between the ministering of Annika and Edwina, I'll end up like a young lad and be able to hold a bow once again!"

"I don't think their powers are that good." Sigrid smiled.

Gondabar smiled too.

"You should've arrived in the morning so that we could've given you all the welcome you deserve," Gondabar told them.

"No welcomes or formalities," Sigrid shook her head. "It's better that our arrival goes unnoticed."

"There being so much movement in the realm and in the city, it's the most prudent," said Raner.

Yes, that's why I didn't warn you of the hour of our arrival, or the route we would take. We've had surprises in the past. It's safer to make the journey incognito."

"The Mother Specialist is wise beyond her years," Gondabar complimented her.

"I'm not so sure. It'll be better to continue this conversation inside before we're drenched to the bone."

"Of course," Gondabar waved them inside the Tower.

Sigrid turned to one of the riders.

"Molak, take care of the horses."

"Right away," the rider replied, pushing back his hood to salute the Mother Specialist respectfully.

Viggo stared at him with eyes wide.

"What's Captain Fantastic doing with the Elder Specialists?"

"I guess making sure nothing happens to them," Nilsa said.

"That's all I needed, now I'll have to put up with him."

"Molak is a great Specialist. He's not a burden you have to put up with," Ingrid told him.

"Yeah, that's what *you* say…" Viggo stared, annoyed as Molak led away the horses.

Gondabar and the Elder Specialists entered the Tower. A moment later Raner ordered them to break formation.

"Go back to your rest," he ordered and left with the Royal Rangers heading toward the main building of the castle.

The following day the first royal retinue was due to arrive. It was none other than the retinue from the Kingdom of Irinel. Unlike the rest of the royal retinues, this one had permission to reach the Royal Castle with all its members and attendants. King Thoran was thus showing his future father- and mother-in-law that he trusted them and opened the gates of his kingdom to them. The rest of the retinues would have to be much smaller in number, at least once they arrived in the city.

To represent the union of the two kingdoms in a symbolic manner and to welcome his new family with due honor, King Thoran organized a grand parade to welcome the King and Queen of Irinel. It was prepared during three days, in which the capital prepared day and night. It looked as if they were on the war path: the three Norghanian armies took their places around the capital. The Thunder Army-"the ones who clear the way, the ones who pull down walls, the ones who take fortresses"-were lined up to the south. They were unmistakable in their vivid red uniforms with white diagonal stripes, the unmistakable Norghanian shield in the middle of their chest: the majestic Snow-White Eagle with spread wings, the ensign bird of the realm, a shining albino white. The Snow Army was lined up to the east, with their white uniforms and flags. The Blizzard Army, the light-moving force, that used breastplates with horizontal traces of red and white, were to the west. The Invincibles of the Ice, the best heavy infantry of the continent, were lined up in the castle's courtyard.

The retinue of the Kingdom of Irinel was made up of the Royal Family, accompanied by their attendants and an escort of over a thousand soldiers. They were all wearing their best attire. When they arrived at the city's southern gate, the Thunder Army was waiting in close formation. At an order of their leader, General Olagson, the army split in two with military efficiency, leaving a long corridor for the Royal Retinue of Irinel to enter through the southern wall gate. As they advanced, half the soldiers of Irinel led the way with the Royal Family in the middle and the other half of the soldiers behind them. The Norghanian soldiers saluted them with respect, and from the walls the welcome trumpets announced their arrival.

The retinue entered the city and found it swarming with people. There was not room for a pin in the streets of Norghania. Half the kingdom was there to witness the arrival of the Royal House of Irinel. The city was decked with the colors of the kingdoms of Norghana and Irinel. They were everywhere. The red and white predominated amid the sea of people present, as well as in houses and the castle. But among them were also the green and white of Irinel. The colors honoring the Royal Family of Irinel were present in flags, and banners placed along the main avenue where the retinue had to pass through.

The King, Queen, and Prince of Irinel waved at the crowd as they went up the main avenue that was cordoned off by Norghanian soldiers to stop anyone from reaching their retinue. There was too much at stake and King Thoran did not want any incidents. His soldiers were watching the city streets and guaranteeing the good behavior of the citizens; they expected there to be hidden spies and assassins from other kingdoms among them. Beside the soldiers, Norghanian flags and banners had been placed on one side of the avenue and those of Irinel on the other.

Additionally, there were Rangers in the crowd all along the parade every few paces, following the course of the retinue. They were also posted with their bows ready on the roofs and other elevated positions on top of houses on both sides of the main avenue. They were aware that there might be dangerous elements present from other kingdoms. They had orders to keep their eyes open and prevent any attempt against the Royal Family of Irinel. If anyone broke through the safety cordon of the soldiers to reach the retinue, the Rangers would bring them down.

Thoran did not want anything bad to happen during the wedding, and so he had his whole army in the streets of the capital and surroundings, and that included the Rangers placed strategically all along the way. Raner and Gondabar had taken charge of establishing the positions and the action plan. The Rangers were ready for anything and had orders to shoot to kill if anyone tried anything suspicious against the Royal Family.

The public applauded and cheered the retinue. The sound the thousands of attendants made in the crowd could be heard leagues away. The Royal Family waved to the crowd from their beautiful coursers, looking pleased at the grand reception while the trumpets sounded loudly, heralding their arrival.

The soldiers of Irinel accompanying the King and Queen marched as if they were returning triumphant from a conquest. They were unmistakable with their red hair of different shades, lighter or more auburn; pale faces speckled with freckles; thin and wiry build, and lively eyes. They were wearing half chain mail with visor-less helmets. In their right hands and on their backs, they carried javelins. On their left arm they carried a tear-shaped shield of steel. The uniforms and shields were painted green and white and were emblazoned with the six-headed white flower. If anyone tried to get near the King and Queen, the soldiers would throw their javelins at whoever dared to do it.

The Royal Eagles had received the order to wait for the retinue at the castle, beside Gondabar, Raner, and the Royal Rangers. They would have preferred to escort the retinue of Irinel or be posted at strategic points along the main avenue in case anyone tried anything, but those were not their orders. Gondabar wanted the Royal Eagles with him for the reception at the Royal Castle.

Egil was watching everything with great interest. King Thoran, his brother Orten, and Princess Heulyn were awaiting the arrival of the retinue in the courtyard. With them were Ambassador Larsen and Ellingsen, the new Commander of the Royal Guard who was leading the Royal Guard behind King Thoran. The new Commander had been appointed recently. Thoran had relieved his two predecessors during two of his tantrums for not meeting his high expectations, which were numerous. Egil was interested to know how long Ellingsen would last in the position. He did not foresee a promising future for him. If the man maintained his job during the wedding it would be a triumph.

Thoran and Orten were each wearing Norghanian dress armor, gold for the King and silver for his brother. They both carried a spider-handled long sword and long knives at their waist, weapons of good quality decorated with jewels to match their status. Red and white capes fell from their shoulders to the ground. King Thoran was wearing the crown of King of Norghana. Princess Heulyn was wearing an elegant green dress with a white fur stole. Her fiery hair fell down her back, and on her head, she wore a silver tiara.

Forming a wide U, the Invincibles of the Ice enveloped them all. The fearsome elite infantry of Norghana was entirely dressed in white, from head to foot. The coat of chain mail was hidden under white chest-plates, cloaks, and their shield. On their heads they wore white winged helmets, and even the handles of their swords were white.

A little further away, the nobles of King Thoran were waiting for the guests, wearing their best gowns. The noblemen were clad in expensive materials and furs in the Norghanian style and armed with long swords, while the ladies wore long dresses made from expensive fabrics, decorating their necks and hands with gems that shone in the sunlight.

By the look of loathing on Princess Heulyn's face every time she looked at the Royal Eagles, Egil guessed she was not at all happy with them being at her family's reception. He could see her hatred toward them in her eyes.

The Royal Retinue went on along the avenue amid the joyful cheers and applause of the Norghanians, who had not witnessed such a positive event in a very long time. War, death, and destruction were what they had known recently, and a turn of events as propitious as this one had everyone happy. The illusion of a strong, peaceful Norghana was something everyone looked forward to. The wedding could obtain such a sought-after goal; at least, this was what the people yearned for.

The Rangers who were on either side of the avenue moved with the retinue as best they could. They walked through the crowds as if they were crossing a thick forest, full of trees and impassable underbrush. Those on the roofs and balconies made sure no one tried anything from above. They jumped from roof to roof, following the retinue. A sniper might give them trouble, but they had searched the roofs and higher floors along the avenue from the first light of the morning. They had needed to clear any elevated position to prevent trouble, which had not been easy since the homeowners wanted to watch the parade from the comfort of their widows and balconies. With the help of the soldiers the Rangers had cleared them out in order to be able to control the passing of the retinue.

All of a sudden, several Norghanian soldiers forming the protective cordon were pushed down to the cobblestones near where the Royal Family was passing by at that moment. At once, the Rangers posted on the roofs aimed their bows to the spot. The Irinel soldiers reacted at once to protect their monarchs. Some raised their javelins, ready to throw against whoever was endangering their King and Queen, and others raised their shields to block any possible attack.

Several people fell on the ground from the pushing and shoving of the crowd, who wanted to see the monarchs of Irinel up close as they passed by where they were. There was a small tumult between Norghanian soldiers, Irinelian soldiers, and the people who were being pushed toward the street and falling on the ground on top of one another. The Rangers missed no detail and were about to shoot, but it was not necessary, there was no attack. It was only the consequence of the massive affluence of people and their eagerness to see royalty on parade as they arrived in the city.

There were more falls and clashes on both sides of the avenue as the retinue approached the castle and the soldiers of Irinel were forced to form a defensive rectangle around the King, Queen, and Prince with their shields while the retinue kept going. The monarchs smiled and waved at the crowd without paying attention to the clashes and tumults their presence caused.

At last, the Royal Retinue of Irinel arrived at the castle, leaving the crowds behind. The Norghanian soldiers were lined up at the entrance and above the battlements. They stood firm and saluted as they let the retinue into the castle where King Thoran and Princess Heulyn were waiting for them.

As they entered the great courtyard, the soldiers of Irinel at the head of the retinue moved to one side, forming a compact square to free up space for their monarchs. Those coming behind did the same on the other side. The King and Queen of Irinel rode forward until they were right before Thoran, Orten, and Heulyn.

"Your Majesties and Royal Prince of Irinel, welcome to Norghania," Thoran greeted them with a slight bow of the head.

"We are happy to be here and appreciate the reception given to us," King Kendryk spoke in Norghanian with an eastern accent. In his impressive full suit of heavily plated armor of bright green over a white hauberk, he looked astounding, not only because of his armor, but for his height and physical appearance. He had long blond hair that was beginning to show the first white of the passing of time. Looking at his face, it was clearly kinder than a Norghanian's, with a fine nose and the brown eyes of the East. At fifty years of age, he looked powerfully fit.

"I hope the reception has matched what was expected by the monarchs of Irinel," said Thoran.

"It has. It's been a remarkable reception and an honor we accept gratefully," King Kendryk replied.

"We trust the journey has been pleasant," Duke Orten said with a fake kindness   that was strange to hear from him.

"It was. We had favorable winds and the sea was calm, so the ships had a good sailing."

"Daughter, we are happy to find you well," Queen Gwyneth addressed the Princess. The Queen was wearing a dress made of fine fabrics of Irinel in various shades of green with embroidered white flowers. Mother and daughter resembled each other. The Queen wore her long, beautiful hair the color of fire in loose loops that fell down her shoulders and back. Her face was beautiful, delicate and with very white skin, almost discolored. Reddish freckles decorated her nose and cheeks. She must be in her mid-forties and still looked young.

"And I am happy to see my parents and my brother in such good health," the Princess replied, bowing lightly.

Prince Kylian, who was behind his parents, returned the bow. He was dressed in the colors of the realm and wore a heavy, elaborate set of armor with the shield of Irinel over his heart.

After their Majesties, came two elderly men who stood by the king. One wore dress armor of good quality and a green cloak that fell from his shoulders. It was Reagan, First General of the Armies of Irinel. Next to him was the Royal counselor, Kacey.

Egil saw someone in the retinue who caught his attention. It was none other than the Druid Aidan. With him were three other Druids, with their characteristic tattoos and dress of the Druids. Egil wondered what they were doing here. It was understandable, up to a point, that Aidan had come since he acted as intermediary with his people, but why bring other Druids to the Royal Wedding? That intrigued him.

For a while the formal greetings and praises continued between the two Royal Houses. Thoran also introduced several of the important nobles of the court to the monarchs of Irinel. Everyone seemed to be enjoying the welcome, honors, and salutations, all except Orten, whose face showed he did not want to be there an instant longer. Heulyn noticed and threw him several disdainful glares.

At last, the reception was over and the monarchs of both kingdoms went into the castle itself.

Egil watched how they withdrew inside amid the applause of the Norghanian nobles and the cheers of the soldiers lined up there, and he had the feeling that this wedding was going to become very interesting very quickly.

Chapter 29

Two days after the arrival of the Royal Retinue of Irinel, the retinues of the allied kingdoms, or those who had maintained good relations with the Kingdom of Norghana up until now started to arrive. Gondabar entrusted Raner with the assignment of the protection details.

The first to be called to be assigned her post was Ingrid.

Ingrid presented herself before the First Ranger.

"You'll be assigned with the protection of the Kingdom of Rogdon's retinue. They're about to arrive. Meet them outside the city, introduce yourself, and escort them here."

Yes, sir. Are the monarchs of Rogdon in the retinue, sir?"

"I'm afraid not," Raner said, and by his tone Ingrid guessed that something was not right.

"King Solin and Queen Eleuna have excused themselves and refused to attend the wedding."

"The Prince of Rogdon then?"

Raner shook his head.

"No, they're not sending Gerart, which is understandable since he's still quite young and has no experience in political affairs. They're sending Drocus, First General of the Army of Rogdon, Ambassador Albust, and some nobles of the kingdom," Raner explained.

"Oh, I see," Ingrid tried to hide how surprised she was that they would not be attending the event.

"I must warn you that the situation has become complicated and that you'll have to be tactful."

"I don't understand, sir..."

"You see, King Thoran has taken the King and Queen of Rogdon's refusal to attend the wedding as a personal insult. He's furious; I had to bear the brunt of his rage about it. His brother Orten has taken it even worse. He's going even further, talking about going to war against Rogdon for such an insult."

"We can't go to war... we have a peace agreement signed with Rogdon, isn't that right?

"We do, yes indeed, hence the problem. Being allies, they should have attended the wedding. Thoran was expecting it. They're the most powerful kingdom in the west, and although the relationship with our kingdom has always been tense, we've been at peace for a long time. King Thoran wanted to show King Kendryk that he counts on powerful allies. The blue and silver kingdom with her mounted lancers is an important seat of power, both military and economic."

"And they refused to come…" Ingrid could indeed see the conflict and the repercussions it might bring.

"And that makes the King look bad in front of his father-in-law. It makes it seem like King Solin doesn't respect him. The fact that he's sending his best general might be interpreted as a warning to Norghana that Rogdon is ready for war, if it should come to that."

"This is quite an uncomfortable situation," Ingrid agreed.

"Which has made the King and his brother furious. Therefore, it's important that things being as they are, nothing happens to the General and the Ambassador of Rogdon."

"I'll take care of it, sir. Nothing will happen to them."

"Right now, I think even the King himself might cause an undesirable situation…"

"I understand, sir. You don't need to say anything else," Ingrid stopped him. She knew how uncomfortable it was for Gondabar and Raner to explain the tantrums of both the King and his brother.

"I trust your discretion in this matter."

"You can count on my full discretion, sir," Ingrid said.

"Good, I trust you."

"I'll fulfill my mission," Ingrid promised, and she left.

In the afternoon the First Ranger summoned Egil.

"Sir, how can I serve the Kingdom?" Egil asked when he presented himself.

"I've summoned you to assign you to the protection of one of the royal retinues   already near the city."

"What retinue is that, sir?" Egil asked, intrigued.

"The Kingdom of Erenal's."

"Oh, it'll be an honor to protect them."

"I've been told you know their language—that'll be an advantage."

"'Know' is saying a lot, sir, let's say I understand it a little. I'm learning. Languages fascinate me, sir."

"It's still an advantage."

"Thank you, sir, I'll use it if the occasion presents itself, although I'd assume some ambassador or interpreter who speaks Norghanian will be in the retinue."

"True, the thing is, King Dasleo is personally attending."

Egil's eyes opened wide, he hadn't been expecting that.

"Curious, we don't have an alliance with King Dasleo..." Egil commented. The presence of the King of Erenal seemed suspicious in his opinion, to say the least.

"No, we don't, which makes his presence at the wedding so important. King Thoran is thrilled he's coming. The Kingdom of Erenal is important. It is well known as an economical power and widely appreciated for its arts and research into technological advances. After being refused by several important people, the King and the Court have gladly received this piece of good news."

"Does it have anything to do with the fact that the Zangrians aren't sending their king?" Egil suggested.

"That might be the reason indeed. Perhaps King Dasleo wants to seize the opportunity to establish alliances with the other kingdoms in the absence of the Zangrian monarch."

"That would be an intelligent strategy."

"But a dangerous one. The Zangrian spies will be on the alert."

"Then I'd better be as well."

"That's what I wanted to emphasize. This mission is important. Nothing can happen to King Dasleo, no matter what the monarch's intentions in coming to the wedding are. He must return to Erenal without a scratch and feel happy with the visit. It's also possible that he might seek an alliance with Norghana to go against Zangria."

"Yes, sir, that had crossed my mind," Egil nodded.

"King Thoran hopes the attendance of King Dasleo might be fruitful. Because of the Zangrians' attendance at the wedding as well, we need to be extra careful. They could even come to fighting..."

"I'll be careful, sir. I'll protect King Dasleo."

"Very well, good luck!"

"Thank you, sir."

The last two days before the ceremony were those chosen for the arrival of two of the most conflictive and dangerous retinues. The first one to arrive was that of the Kingdom of Zangria, which waited at the gates of the capital until they were allowed to enter the city.

Raner summoned Viggo.

"You are assigned to protect the retinue of the King of Zangria," the First Ranger informed him.

"Protect? Wouldn't it be better to eliminate them?" Viggo suggested nonchalantly.

Raner made a face.

"I've heard talk about you and that tongue of yours that shouldn't run so loose," he told Viggo.

"It's natural, I'm the best Ranger Assassin in the kingdom. And the most famous too, apart from being one of King Thoran's Royal Eagles, which are already famous throughout the realm."

"I am the best Ranger Assassin of the realm, not you," Raner replied without acrimony, firmly as if it was an absolute truth.

"That's debatable," Viggo said in his usual acid tone.

"No, it isn't since I'm the First Ranger, which makes me the best among all the Rangers. That includes the Assassins, which is my own Specialization."

"Well, if the First Ranger says so…"

"I say so."

Viggo shrugged.

"We'll have to leave it as a matter of opinion."

"Opinions are useless. What counts are facts. You are ordered to protect the Zangrian envoys. Will you follow the order?"

"I always follow orders, even if I don't like them. I'm a Ranger after all."

"Very well. Nothing can happen to the delegation they are sending, is that clear?"

"Crystal clear, sir. What do I do if the opposite happens?"

"The opposite? What do you mean?"

"If I catch them colluding or trying to kill a rival…"

Raner stroked his chin.

"True, that might happen."

"Knowing the Zangrians, rather than a possibility it's a certainty."
The First Ranger was thoughtful.

"Your mission is one of vigilance and protection. If you discover anything suspicious, come and tell Gondabar or myself at once."

"And I'm to do nothing?"

"Not without our authorization."

"Don't my leaders trust my good judgment?"

"It's not a matter of trust. It's a matter of political repercussions. Nothing can happen to the Zangrian envoys, nor can we antagonize them with our actions. A war could start because of an unwished-for intervention."

"Oh, I see…" Viggo smiled. "Even if they try something, it may be that the King doesn't want us to punish the envoys," he turned the matter around.

"Something like that. We need to understand what they're up to and how to act without causing a political conflict."

"So, I can't kill them in the castle."

"No, you can't."

"Wound, maim?"

Raner shook his head. "Only protect and report. You can't touch them."

"Well, that's great…"

"Don't touch a hair of their heads, understood?"

"Understood," Viggo resigned himself and snorted disappointedly.

"As to who is the best Assassin in Norghana, I'll take the challenge. We'll resume the debate after the Royal Wedding."

Viggo smiled. He nodded at the First Ranger and left.

The last retinue to arrive was that of the Nocean Ambassador. He arrived at the gates of the city with five hundred elite Nocean soldiers. The Nocean soldiers were denied entrance to the city and had to camp outside, together with the camps of the other nations that had settled on the plain south of the city. The camps of the different kingdoms and nations attending the ceremony formed their own enclaves, and   the activity and vigilance were continuous.

The Norghanian soldiers of the three armies had been forbidden from going anywhere near those enclaves. The Norghanian generals made sure it was so. If a spark should start in a casual confrontation, they could have a fire on their hands that would be difficult to control. The generals were under orders to show the might of Norghana but not to use it even if they were subjected to instigation and provocation.

The hatred between the soldiers of the different kingdoms was well known. They all wanted to prove they were stronger and better warriors than the rest, which might start a conflict which could escalate into a war if they were not careful. So far, the soldiers and warriors of the different kingdoms and nations at the enclaves were behaving and there had not been any conflict other than small skirmishes and fist fights that had not escalated. The question was whether things would continue the same or get worse with the arrival of the Zangrians and Noceans.

The First Ranger summoned Astrid.

"Sir," Astrid said with a nod.

"The last of the retinues has just arrived, the Nocean envoys. You are assigned to protect them," Raner told her.

"Sir, I'll take care of it."

"Stay alert. The Noceans are probably the most feared, and not without reason. They have many enemies among the attendants, since their Emperor, Malotas, is constantly seeking to expand his Empire outside the deserts of Tremia that are already his."

"The Nocean Empire controls the whole south of the continent, but I understand he hasn't ventured into the kingdoms of the north, west, or east."

"Not so far. The internal wars in the Empire have kept the Emperor very busy. But there are rumors that Emperor Malotas wants the west… and he'll most likely want to expand into the north if he manages to conquer Rogdon."

"I wasn't aware of those intentions."

"It's what we think we know about the Emperor's ambitions. Therefore, we must remain vigilant."

"Don't worry, sir, I'll keep my eyes wide open."

"The Noceans might try something to destabilize the west or north. The King has indicated that we must be very careful with their spies and assassins. They'll already be among us."

"Will they try anything during the wedding?"

"Maybe. But if they do, I doubt it'll be a direct attack. They'll try to blame another kingdom. They're cunning, very cunning."

"They won't fool me, sir."

"With this particular retinue I'm more concerned about them starting something, rather than other kingdoms doing anything against them."

"I see... rather than protect them, I'll be in charge of watching them."

"That's right, and preventing them from creating chaos or incidents. Of all the retinues, this one worries me the most."

"I'll take care of it, Sir," Astrid promised.

"I've heard good things about all the Royal Eagles, but for this mission I need someone who can spy, and not only an assassin. That's why I've chosen you."

"Thank you, I won't fail."

"They might not try anything, and they might only be here to gather information for the emperor. In any case, don't take your eyes off them."

"I won't, sir."

Astrid left, and with her ended the assignments for the Panthers. Now they had to prevent anything from happening during the wedding, which was not going to be an easy task.

Chapter 30

Egil arrived on horseback in the vicinity of the entrance to the Cave of Scorched Hill around midnight. He dismounted and tethered his horse, hidden in a nearby forest. He waited a moment to check whether there was any danger around, but he could see nothing.

Then he saw three riders arrive who went straight into the large cave on horseback. The moon was shining quite clearly, and although there was no light at the entrance of the cave, Egil was able to recognize the riders.

He decided to act. He needed answers, so there was nothing else to do but go into the cave and get them. It was not going to be easy and he feared there would be conflict. Even so, only he could resolve the situation—he knew that and was determined to do so. If the worse came to pass, at least he would have tried. Remaining a mere spectator knowing that things were getting complicated and might explode was not his style.

He knew it was not a good idea to come alone. He could have brought Gerd as a bodyguard or even the whole group. But that would have been a problem. He would not get the true answers, along with the intentions that went with them if the Royal Eagles were present. He would only get real answers if he went by himself.

He did not think twice and carefully approached the cave. Although he could not see anything inside, Egil was sure there were armed men watching the entrance. He was not wrong. As soon as he was close enough a voice asked from the darkness, "Who approaches?"

"A Norghanian seeking shelter," Egil recited.

"Only the Sons of the West receive shelter in this place," the voice replied.

"I am a Norghanian and a Son of the West," Egil said, following the manner of identification of the Western league.

"Do you come alone?"

"Yes, I do."

"Come in," said the voice.

Egil went in slowly, and soon he was able to see figures armed with bows in the gloom.

At the far end of the cave, he glimpsed a light and three other figures beside it.

"Go toward the light," another voice said.

Egil did as he was told and went toward the light. When he arrived, he saw it was the entrance to another cavern. The three men guarding it saluted Egil with a nod and waved him in.

"They're waiting for you," one of them said.

"Go ahead, Sire," the other one said courteously.

Egil relaxed somewhat. Everything seemed to be going well. There was no reason why that should not be the case, but the news he had received was not good and he was worried. There might be unexpected betrayals.

Egil recognized the figures waiting around a small fire that lit the cave up. On one side of the fire were Dukes Erikson and Svensen. On the other side were the Counts: Count Malason, the oldest son of the late Count Bjorn, Axel, and Harald. There were also several minor Western nobles a little further back talking amongst themselves and a couple more people he did not know.

"It's a pleasure to see so many friendly faces of the West," Egil greeted them all with a smile.

"Welcome, my lord, King of the West," Duke Eriksen replied.

"The happiness is all ours, Sire," said Duke Svensen.

"The Western League has been anxiously awaiting the King's visit," said Count Malason.

"It's good to find you all in good health. Without you the Western cause and the future of Norghana would be in serious danger," Egil replied, looking at all those present.

"The King mustn't worry about us. If one of us should fall, our children, our heirs would replace us. They're ready for the task. We've spent years teaching them what the honor of the West is," Erikson said, pointing at Count Bjorn's eldest son.

"I'm glad to hear it. The blood of the West is what will save Norghana," Egil said seriously.

"That's a great truth," Svensen said.

Egil smiled and opened his arms so they could greet him with a hug. He was no friend of formalities, least of all among old friends. He hugged them all one by one, the Dukes and the Counts. He also greeted the minor nobles and looked kindly at those he did not know.

"It's been a long time since we've all gathered together," Egil said.

"Since our defeat to the East we've had to take extreme precautions. We've been watched night and day for a long time. It seems they're beginning to relax their vigilance a little. They have other, more important matters in their hands," Duke Erikson commented.

"Bad times prevent good encounters," Duke Svensen said. "Let's hope the times improve soon."

Egil realized that if all the Western League nobles were gathered here it was because something was afoot. He could guess what it was.

"You received our message," Count Malason said.

"Indeed, that's why I'm here. I'm glad to see you all and find you well. But, from what the message said, this isn't a courtesy meeting, am I wrong?"

"The King of the West is rarely wrong," Erikson said.

"Let's get down to business then. What's the matter?" Egil asked straightforwardly. He needed answers.

The Dukes and Counts exchanged glances. At last Svensen spoke.

"There are disagreements in the midst of the league, important disagreements."

"Division is a more appropriate term," said Erikson.

"Disagreements, division, and urgency," Count Malason specified.

"That doesn't sound very good," Egil commented, frowning. "What's the reason for the disagreements that are causing the division in the midst of the League?"

"Everyone here wants to expel Thoran, Orten, and his eastern allies and regain the throne for the West," Erikson explained.

Egil nodded.

"That's the goal, and we'll reach it one day."

"And here is where the arguments begin," said Svensen. "We want to throw them out now. There's a great opportunity and we must seize it."

"The Royal Wedding..." Egil guessed.

"It's time to take action. We can finish with Thoran and his fake rule in one fell sweep if we act at the wedding," Svensen stated with conviction.

"An attempt on the King's life during the wedding is too risky," Egil said firmly. "If we fail and he survives, it'll cause a second civil war. The cost in lives and economy of the first one was too high and we'll be paying for years. Now it would be even worse. Furthermore, with the alliance with Irinel, it would destroy us. None of us here would survive."

"We know that if the agreed alliance with Irinel takes place through the Royal Wedding, our possibilities will be reduced to practically zero," said Erikson.

"That's why we have to act now. We have to prevent the alliance," Svensen said.

"It's not the opportunity we're waiting for. During the wedding it'll be almost impossible to attack the King. He'll be well protected, precisely because he fears an attack," Egil insisted.

"We're tired of waiting for a perfect opportunity," the new Count Bjorn commented.

"While we keep waiting for the opportunity you're talking about, the East is growing stronger every day. With the reinforcement of Irinel, it'll be very difficult to dethrone Thoran," said Count Axel.

"Without forgetting that if an offspring is born of this marriage, he or she will inherit the crown and our possibilities of recovering it will practically vanish. It's one thing to bring down the impostor who has occupied the throne, and a very different one when it's the child born to succeed the father's throne," Erikson explained.

Egil saw what they wanted him to feel. He also knew the implications of the alliance with Irinel and what a new heir to the throne would mean.

"We have an advantage," said Svensen. "We're not the only ones who don't look kindly on this wedding."

"All the kingdoms present at the wedding, with the exception of Norghana and Irinel, don't want this alliance to happen because it strengthens the two kingdoms."

"There are even dissenting voices in Irinel speaking against the wedding. They want the Druid Princess back," said Svensen.

"The Druids?" Egil asked.

"That's right. They call her the Druid Princess, and they want her back," Svensen told him.

"But she doesn't want to go back, for whatever reason," Egil said.

"In any case, it presents us with an opportunity," said Erikson.

"You want to kidnap Princess Heulyn and give her back to the Druids?"

"It's a possibility," said Erikson.

"We could also kill her and blame King Thoran for his incompetence," said Erikson. "The Royal Family of Irinel might even declare war on him."

"We're not going to kill the Princess of Irinel," Egil was adamant. He was shaking his head hard. "It's not only very risky, but we can't assure that Irinel would abandon the alliance plan. The pain of a father for the loss of a child might be our doom. It might even have the opposite effect of what you want."

"Then we'll kill Thoran and that'll be the end of the problem. There won't be a wedding or an alliance," Svensen concluded.

"That's the most direct way," Count Bjorn joined in.

"You really intend to kill Thoran before the wedding?" Egil asked, unable to believe what he was hearing.

"During the wedding," said Svensen.

"That's not going to work. Security is very high. He has the whole army and   the Rangers protecting him. Apart from the fact that he's paranoid."

"That's the right moment. The suspicions won't fall on us," said Bjorn. "They'll fall on one of the legations of the attending kingdoms. We won't even be in the King's mind as a possible danger."

Egil continued shaking his head. He did not see how they could pull it off.

"It's already prepared," Svensen said all of a sudden.

Egil looked him straight in the eye.

"Without my consent or approval?" He had been expecting that move, he had guessed it from the moment he received the letter.

"It has to be now. We won't have another chance like this one. Everyone's looking at the foreign legations. No one's looking our way," Axel insisted.

"We can take back the throne without a civil war. We kill Thoran at his own wedding and the blame falls on a foreign kingdom. It's perfect," Svensen said.

"War will be declared on whoever receives the blame for the regicide," Egil said. "It's nowhere near perfect. We won't have a civil war but a war against another kingdom, which might be even worse."

"We can choose who to blame: Zangria, Erenal, Rogdon, the Noceans, practically all of them have reasons to want Thoran dead and a weak Norghana," said Svensen.

"It's too complex. There are too many things that could go wrong. You're not taking into account all the factors. If they discover the plan, if they catch the assassin and he or she talks, the blame will fall on us. Thoran and Orten will make anyone they catch talk, that's a fact. Their means of torture are very efficient."

"But we'll be rid of Thoran and the whole alliance with Irinel. We can regain the throne," Svensen replied.

"You are the King of the West, our King. Let us act and give you back the throne that you and your family deserve," Bjorn said.

Egil noticed that Malason had not said anything and that Erikson had said little. Were they against the regicide plan? He would have to find out.

"Let me think about it. It's a very serious matter with consequences that could be terrible for us."

"We thought you'd already have an idea how to carry it out, that you would've planned it yourself," Erikson said.

The Duke's plea sounded to Egil like begging. He wanted to see whether he had another plan.

"I have thought about it. I also see the possibility. But the plan is too risky."

"There's no worthy victory without risk," Svensen said.

"A Norghanian proverb which isn't all that accurate," Egil replied.

"We need you to give the order to proceed," Svensen said.

"Who's in favor and who's against the plan?" Egil asked.

"Those who are for it are..." Svensen began to say, "Bjorn, Axel, plus them," he indicated three other minor nobles.

Egil nodded.

"I see. Duke Erikson?"

The Duke snorted.

"I'm undecided. I can see the chance and I want to take it, like them. I also see the high risk and the great possibilities of failure..."

"I understand. I see the division and the urgency," Egil commented and was thoughtful.

"We want your approval, you're our King," Svensen asked him. "We don't want to break the League."

"Count Malason, Duke Erikson, Duke Svensen," he addressed them in turn, looking them straight in the eye. "You are the ones who created the Western League together with my father. It belongs to you."

"And you," noted Erikson.

"This alliance exists thanks to you," said Egil, "in an unfair and bloody manner I've simply inherited it."

"Without you there's no future for the West," said Erikson.

"Without an Olafstone to be precise. I'm the last one of my line, nothing else," Egil pointed out.

"You're a lot more than that," Malason said. "Thanks to your wit and intelligence, we've survived and we're still here."

"We need you to lead us and recover the throne for the West," Svensen said.

"You need a king, not me specifically," said Egil.

"You're the heir to the throne. As long as you live, only you must be king," said Malason.

"And what if I abdicate? What if I don't want to be King? Or if anything happened to me?" Egil said, wanting to find out what the League would do in any of those cases.

The nobles looked at one another in shock.

"In that case, we'd have to search among your lineage..." said Erikson.

"I have no family left," said Egil. "Would one of you take command?" he asked. He was genuinely curious to know which of them would step up. It would have to be either Erikson or Svensen.

The three nobles looked at each other again.

"Count Berge married your father's sister, Alisa Olafstone," Duke Erikson started to say.

Egil nodded.

"That's correct, but the Counts of Berge died in a fire in their castle. They and their descendants," Egil explained.

"That's not entirely correct. His son Lars survived," Svensen said.

"He survived?" Egil was surprised. "I thought that no one in my family had survived that fire."

"I survived," a voice said at the far end of the cave.

All gazes went to the bottom of the cave. Among the minor nobles was a young man, not over sixteen, blond, tall, and very strong for his age with a square jaw. He stepped forward.

"Are you Lars?" Egil asked.

The youth took another step forward, revealing himself.

"Greetings, cousin. Yes, I am Lars Berge."

Egil studied his features. He did not look like the Olafstones, but of course he was a Berge. He tried to see something of his aunt in Lars. He thought that perhaps the eyes, deep gray, and the sad look resembled his aunt's.

"Greetings, cousin. I'm glad to see you alive. The last time I saw you, you must've been about five years old. You've changed a lot."

"You're just as I remember you," Lars smiled.

"Why wasn't I informed that he was still alive?" Egil asked.

"That's how your father wanted it," said Erikson. "He suspected that the fire hadn't been accidental but intentional. Count Berge was a strong promoter of the West."

"Yes, my family believed the East was behind the fire." Egil remembered the conversations with his father and brothers. They had all cried out for vengeance but no evidence was found, and his father had needed to set aside his intentions of revenge.

"Who's kept him hidden all these years?"

"I have kept him hidden and raised him since the death of his parents," said Svensen, "at your father's request."

Egil understood his father's gamble. If the East had known there was still a descendant left, they would've murdered him. All of a sudden Egil saw what was going on perfectly clearly, the reason why they had told him about Lars' existence.

"I see you have a new candidate for the crown. That's why you've brought him here today and revealed him to me."

"You're our candidate for the crown because you're the legitimate King," Count Malason protested.

Egil felt his mind racing, thinking through all the possible moves in that game.

"But if I don't comply with what the League wishes, I could be replaced."

"That wouldn't be desirable," said Svensen.

"You're still the heir to the crown. You simply have to reach out and take it," said Axel.

Egil looked at his cousin.

"And if I don't reach out, you already have someone in my place who will."

"We hope it won't be that way," said Bjorn.

"But it might be if I don't act as the League wishes me to," Egil said.

"No one wishes that. We all want to see you as King of Norghana," Count Malason assured him.

The warning was clear. The gamble was a good one. They were tired of his prudence. They were tired of waiting for him to act. They though the time had come, that they had a manifest opportunity, and they wanted to grab it. The worse thing of all was that they were wrong. But if he did not give them what they wanted, they would replace him with Lars. It would be one way or the other. The situation was as severe as Egil had anticipated, if not more so.

"I must think about it. I'll return to the capital and send you word of my decision."

"We'll be anxiously awaiting your reply," said Duke Svensen.

"We trust the King's good judgment," Malason said supportively.

"For the West, for the throne!" Erikson cheered.

"For the West, for the throne!" the rest of the nobles cheered in unison.

Chapter 31

Nilsa was walking along the lengthy corridor watched by the Royal Guard. She was on a liaison task between legations, which meant gathering information about whatever might be happening. The rest of her colleagues had been assigned to the protection of the legations and she was in charge of managing communications and the flow of information toward Raner and Gondabar. The legations had been reluctant to have a Ranger assigned to each of them but King Thoran had been inflexible on this. The legations had been forced to accept it for their own safety. The foreign dignitaries saw it as an intromission, covert spying, and formal complaints had been sent to the King. But Thoran had not yielded.

The situation inside the castle was curious and tense. The legations of each kingdom had specific areas assigned to them, and although they were not forbidden to wander about, they were all aware it was not advisable. The soldiers of the Norghanian Guard watched the other areas of the castle, but not the areas where the legations were lodged. Every kingdom had their own soldiers and personal bodyguards watching their chambers and protecting their leaders, along with the real imposition of a Ranger.

Nilsa was fascinated by all of this: the organization of the areas, the number of guards that each legation was allowed to bring into the castle, the rooms, the demanded comforts, etc. The thousand and one arrangements she had had to make had driven her crazy, and at the same time fascinated her. Not even in her wildest dreams would she have thought that a Royal Wedding could entail so many problems to solve. Luckily, she had only had to deal with a part of them. King Thoran had provided that his quartermasters, servants, butlers, managers, cooks, and others responsible for all the castle jobs would be strengthened with an infinitude of assistants in order to be able to fulfill all the wedding requirements.

Nilsa turned right at the next corner and could not help a smile. If she ever got married, she was going to have a wedding as big as this only to enjoy not having to do the thousand and one errands she had been doing. And well, to get married, of course. She walked faster, smiling. None of the Royal Guards stopped her now, they only greeted her as she went by. The guards were tense, Nilsa noticed. They used to be friendly and compliment her all the time, but now they were stern and stiff as spears. The officers had warned them with shouts that anyone who failed In their duties would be hanged at the castle gate.

She greeted the last Norghanian guard as she went by before arriving at the area assigned to the Kingdom of Rogdon. When she arrived at an antechamber, she met four Rogdonian guards. They were wearing blue and silver and cuirasses and helmets and carrying spears and shields. The truth was that their armor and spears shone as if they spent the whole night polishing them. Nilsa liked the Rogdonians. They were polite, a little cold and quite formal, but they were nice to her.

"Liaison Nilsa Blom," she reported, although they already knew her.

"Reason for your presence here?" an officer, who was a little further back, asked her. He spoke Norghanian with a Rogdonian accent. If the guards' weapons and armor shone, the officer's armor, all metal, dazzled her. He was not carrying a spear but had a long sword at his waist. His name was Gustav, and Nilsa thought he was some Rogdonian nobleman serving in the army.

"I have a communication for Ranger Ingrid, assigned to this legation."

Gustav turned around. A moment later he reappeared with Ingrid. They reached Nilsa and the officer went back inside, leaving the two Rangers on their own. Nilsa and Ingrid turned their backs to the other Rogdonian guards and moved a little ways away to talk without being heard.

"How's everything going?" Nilsa whispered.

"Everything's all right. No suspicious movement so far," Ingrid replied. "First General Drocus, Ambassador Albust, and the nobles accompanying them are resting."

"Have they made any contact?" Nilsa asked.

"Not that I've seen. But I've been informed that Ambassador Albust is having a meeting at the Royal Library before the Gala Dinner this evening."

"Do you know who he's meeting with?"

"No, not yet. But I'm going with him, so I'll find out then."

"Very well. Tell me at the dinner."

Ingrid nodded.

"Don't worry, I will."

"What are they like?" Nilsa asked, out of personal curiosity.

"I like them. They're efficient and military-minded, even the ambassador and the two nobles who've come with him, not just General Drocus," Ingrid admitted.

"If you like them that means a lot," Nilsa smiled. "I'm going to continue my rounds."

"You do that."

"Be careful, you never know…"

"I will be, don't worry."

Nilsa followed the corridors and stairs of the castle, which she now knew like the back of her hand, and went quickly to see how Egil was doing with the Kingdom of Erenal. She arrived at the area of the castle assigned to King Dasleo and stopped before half a dozen Erenal soldiers who were blocking the anteroom where the King and his nobles were lodged.

The soldiers stopped her. There was a noble with them; Nilsa had no doubt of his nobility because of his stance and the luxurious clothes he wore, some kind of toga, as well as the bejeweled weapons he carried.

Nilsa stopped and asked to see Egil.

The soldiers passed on her request to the nobleman, and after a moment he sent for Egil.

"Any news?" she asked him.

"Quite a few in fact."

"Really? What's up?" Nilsa was suddenly uneasy.

"King Dasleo has had two meetings: one with our dear King Thoran and one with the Ambassador sent by the Confederation of Free Cities of the East."

"Wow, he hasn't wasted any time."

"This is an auspicious occasion to speak face to face with monarchs and representatives of other kingdoms and obtain agreements which otherwise would be a much more complicated to reach."

"Do you know what they talked about? What agreements they're negotiating?"

"Unfortunately, I wasn't allowed to attend. I had to wait outside.

I saw Viggo accompanying the Zangrian legation and Sugesen, who is with the legation of the Confederation of Free Cities of the East."

"Did they say anything?"

"There's a lot of movement and they might be planning something," Egil replied.

"They also informed you of their movements?"

Egil nodded.

"It would seem that both the Zangrians and the Confederation are establishing different contacts."

"I'll have to go and speak to them at once."

"Viggo whispered to me that the general the Zangrians sent must be very well-known and with a bloodthirsty reputation. He's defeated Erenal in several battles. He's been talking to a couple of suspicious characters in his chamber. Viggo couldn't hear what they were saying but he says they 'stink' of spies.

"He also said he's dying for the Zangrians to try something, especially against us."

"Why is that idiot always looking for trouble? As if we didn't have enough to deal with already."

"There are things that can't be changed in some people's natures, they're what define them," Egil apologized with a smile.

"I hope he's wrong. Being him, if they try anything against King Thoran or his brother Orten, the moron is capable of doing nothing and letting it happen to see their reactions."

Egil waved his hand, indicating it would not surprise him either if that happened.

"Viggo has his own loyalties..."

Nilsa snorted.

"I hope nothing happens. What's even worse is the fact that I can't share this information with either Gondabar or Raner so Viggo's not caught if he screws up."

"Better that it stays between us," Egil agreed.

"With Lasgol and Gerd being so sensible, why has Viggo turned out like this?" Nilsa protested, even if she knew it was in vain.

"Sugesen has told me that he feels the Confederation is here to try and reach commercial agreements. I agree with him. The Confederation is no friend to alliances, but it is indeed of commerce."

"They are an alliance of commercial city states, after all," Nilsa commented.

"King Dasleo of Erenal, together with our monarch King Thoran, will have dealt mainly with the Zangrian problem."

"Do you think they will reach any kind of agreement?" Nilsa asked, interested. All this fascinated her.

"I'm practically sure they will with the Cities of the East. Erenal has the sea and needs trade with the eastern coast. As for our monarch, it's hard to predict how that meeting might have gone. Erenal is an advanced kingdom and a growing power, a rival for Norghana. On the other hand, the two kingdoms have a common enemy: Zangria, which isn't such an advanced or illustrious kingdom but is indeed bellicose and with an important army, which is a threat for both."

"In that case, Norghana and Erenal will surely join in alliance against Zangria."

Egil looked unsure about that.

"It'll depend on the ego of both monarchs. Remember, they're competing for the glory of being the most powerful kingdom in Tremia. That's usually a pretty big obstacle for reaching any political agreements."

"Oh, well, then we'll have to wait and see what happens."

"It would seem so, yes. What I can guarantee is that we're going to see increasingly suspicious moves. Everyone's plotting, and everyone's here with the intention of obtaining advantages for their kingdoms."

"That doesn't sound good at all," Nilsa said with a troubled look on her face.

"That's what politics are about, and the ambitions of kings. Not all of them can reach the highest peak," Egil said with a shrug.

"I'll go on with my rounds."

"Who are you going to see now?"

"First, I'm going to see Gonars. The kingdom he's been assigned to is a lesser one, but it seems to be growing fast and strong."

Egil nodded.

"The Kingdom of Moontian is gaining strength and her perspectives are good."

"The curious thing about this kingdom is that it has no King but a Queen: Queen Niria. They say she's young and very beautiful, like her mountainous realm. They also say that its inhabitants have violet-hued skin. Doesn't it sound incredible?" Nilsa was speaking excitedly.

"I find it fascinating. One day I want to go and see it," Egil smiled.

"Next, I'll go and see Frida. She's been assigned to two minor nations. I don't think they'll cause any trouble. Then I'll go and see Elina, who's been assigned to the tribal representatives. I'm not expecting trouble there either. And then I'll go and see Viggo."

"I see you're leaving Astrid and the Noceans for the end," Egil said, raising an eyebrow.

"Ah, because I do expect trouble there. It is said that their Ambassador has brought a Curses Warlock, and I don't have my bow and arrows with me."

"You can't shoot at someone from a legation just because he's a warlock."

"I bet he'll try something," Nilsa said, who was growing angry just considering the possibility.

"Let Astrid deal with it," Egil advised her.

"I'm the Mage Hunter."

"But now you're acting as Information Liaison for the Royal Wedding. Don't get involved. Do your job, we need you. You're our contact."

"You're right. I need to do my job and keep you informed and coordinated."

"That's right," Egil smiled.

"I'm off! See you later."

As she had expected, neither Gonars, Frida, or Elina informed of anything suspicious. Having to protect small kingdoms and tribal representatives had that advantage. Anyway, Nilsa had reminded them that nothing was to happen to them, because if anything did happen the King would get into a rage. The three Rangers had assured her that they had everything under control and not to worry. Nilsa was not all easy. Sometimes the greatest trouble came from the most insignificant places.

Viggo's visit was short because Zotomer, the Zangrian General, wanted to visit the city to stretch his legs. What Viggo had confirmed, as she had already suspected, was that if anyone was going to make an attempt against Thoran and Orten, he would not exert himself to stop it. Nilsa had gotten furious and almost yelled at him. Luckily the Zangrian guards had appeared and she had been forced to swallow the scolding she was about to give him.

After the brief encounter with Viggo she went to see Astrid. She did nothing but race all over the castle, since the guests' quarters had been strategically located as far as possible from one another.

When she arrived at the area reserved for the Noceans, she found five soldiers guarding the entrance. They had dark skin and black eyes, and they wore a long blue tunic over black baggy pants. They also wore a cuirass with a golden engraving of the sun, the Nocean emblem. Covering their long, curly hair they each wore the Nocean helmet, round and crowned with a sharp spike. They all carried a spear in one hand and a small round metal shield in the other with a sharp spike in the middle.

"Liaison Nilsa. I need to speak to Ranger Astrid," she told them. She was not sure they would be able to understand her. There was no doubt that these soldiers were from the distant south, from the deserts. They would most likely not speak the unified language of the north.

One of the soldiers turned and said something in Nocean to some huge bodyguards who stood at the entrance of their lord's antechamber. These Noceans were enormous, as big and strong, if not more, than one of King Thoran's Norghanian Royal Guards. They wore their heads shaven and their skin was so dark that, beside them, the soldiers in front of Nilsa looked discolored. They wore their arms uncovered, revealing powerful muscles. On their forearms, which were also chunky, they wore wide gold bracelets. They were dressed in a red sleeveless vest with a cuirass on top. The pants were also red and very baggy. Hanging from their waists they each carried a huge scimitar, longer than a long sword.

Nilsa swallowed when one of them came over to her and looked her up and down.

"She is coming," he told her and then left.

As he moved away Nilsa noticed that the man's back was as broad as Gerd's but even more muscular. He must have tremendous strength. If she ever had to fight those mountains of muscle of the deserts, she was going to shoot first. She was certain that if they got close to her at all they would break her in two with one blow.

281

Astrid appeared a moment later and they moved aside to be able to talk unheard.

"What thugs the Noceans have…"

"Impressive, huh?"

"They're almost three times my width."

"Don't worry, they're slow and clumsy," Astrid winked at her.

"I hope so… any news?"

"Quite a few. The Nocean Ambassador Hamal has been meeting with different characters since he arrived in the city."

"Characters? What do you mean by that?"

"Well, he hasn't met with anyone from the legations. He hasn't even asked for an audience with King Thoran or the King of Irinel. He and his warlock have gone down to the city. They did not even want me to accompany them and I was told to turn back as soon as we were outside the castle.

"But you didn't."

"Absolutely not. I followed them, of course."

"I guessed as much. What did they do?"

"They've met with several dark characters at an entertainment house, most likely spies. I couldn't hear what they were saying, but the conversations seemed serious."

"Did they see you?"

"No. Here." Unobtrusively, Astrid handed Nilsa a note. "The premises and the description of the spies. Give it to Raner."

"I will," Nilsa put the note away, also unobtrusively. "What can you tell me about the warlock?"

Yeah, Himnomec. He looks dangerous. He goes everywhere with the Ambassador. He never speaks and carries two curved knives with jewels that look ceremonial."

"Don't you find it strange that he doesn't meet with the other legations? They're all doing it."

Astrid shrugged.

"Well, the Noceans don't tend to make alliances, rather to break them, from what Egil has told me. Their Emperor, Malotas, must live for conquest. He wants to dominate all of Tremia. With this premise, I doubt any kingdom would want to negotiate anything with them."

"They might try something against Norghana or Irinel…"

"They might, yeah. I don't think they're interested in their impending union."

"I'll inform Raner."

"Good."

Nilsa went down the corridor at a fast pace. Political intrigues fascinated her, but at the same time they made her very nervous. Anything might happen, and no matter what it was, it would not be good.

Chapter 32

Nilsa was terribly nervous. She was rubbing her hands behind her back so no one would notice. The Grand Gala Dinner was taking place before the wedding ceremony the following day. They were at the Grand Hall for special events adjacent to the Throne Room. She was at her post, standing beside one of the columns. She had a member of the Royal Guard on either side. In front of her was the long table of honor where King Thoran and his betrothed were dining.

She snorted. She needed to calm down. The problem was that seeing the great table filled with such important guests before her was becoming unbearable. She could see the backs and heads of the important guests, and the animated conversation thundered in her ears. She was trying not to listen to chatter that was none of her business, but it was hard, she found everything interesting.

At the center of the table were Thoran and Heulyn, presiding over the meal. On Thoran's right sat his brother Orten and several important members of the nobility, such as Count Volgren and Duke Invernsen and their companions. At the end of the table on the right were Eicewald and Gondabar. The fact that the Leader of the Ice Magi and the Leader of the Rangers were at the King's table indicated the high standing they had at Court. It also showed other kingdoms and nations that Norghana had Ice Magi and Rangers in her service, which the others did not, and everyone was aware of their lethal power.

On the left side of the table sat the guests of honor of the Kingdom of Irinel: King Kendryk, Queen Gwyneth, and Heulyn's brother, Prince Kylian. Also sitting beside them were Reagan, First General of the Irinel armies, and Counselor Kacey.

A line of Royal Guards stood behind all the guests at the table, shoulder to shoulder, preventing anyone who might try to access or attack the two Royal Families and members of their courts who were sitting at the table of honor from the back. The Commander of the Guard, Ellingsen, was in the middle, right behind the chair where King Thoran sat. No one could reach the King without first passing through the Commander.

Between the Royal Guards and the guests there were three people: Nilsa, right behind Gondabar, on his request, the Druid Aidan, behind Counselor Kacey of Irinel, and Valeria, right behind Princess Heulyn. Nilsa and Valeria had exchanged several glances. Nilsa had asked Valeria about the Druid with a nod, and Valeria had replied with a gesture that she need not worry, that everything was all right. Nilsa trusted Valeria, at least in this kind of situation, where Valeria was charged with looking after the Princess' safety. In other, different circumstances Nilsa would not trust her. It was a funny feeling to be there between two Royal Guards; it made her even more nervous.

Two round tables had been placed at both ends of the table of honor, slightly separated from each other. At the right, there were members of the King's Court and important nobles. Nilsa noticed that although most of them were from the East, there were a couple of noblemen from the West. It must be some kind of maneuver by Thoran to keep the West happy, making it appear as if he took them into consideration. At the other table were the leaders of the Rangers. Nilsa could see the Elder Specialists with Sigrid at their head, and the Master Rangers with Dolbarar. They seemed to be enjoying the dinner, which pleased Nilsa, who had always seen them too busy and concerned with one thing or another. She could also see Molak and Luca in the shadows, watching over the Rangers. She smiled at them and they returned the greeting unobtrusively, although their smiles for Nilsa were broad.

The fact that the table of the Leaders of the Rangers was a little separated to one side indicated that the King did not consider them of the utmost importance, but the fact that they were there at all, as guests, was revealing. The same thing happened with the other table of nobles, with the guests from the West, but they were there, and that was remarkable in itself.

Placed close and perpendicularly to the table of honor, other tables had been set for the other guests, the really important ones. Each table was assigned to a legation so they were separated. Nilsa knew that it was not only for comfort, but also for security and to avoid possible altercations. It was not a good idea to sit rival nations together and serve them wine and beer.

The servants were working without pause, bringing delicious

dishes with food to the tables, along with different types of beverages. All the guests had a large glass for the Norghanian beer and a silver goblet for wine. The glasses at the table of honor were from a magnificent royal set. Nilsa watched trays of food pass between the tables as if on wings: all kinds of roasts, from pheasant to wild boar, and all kinds of big game, as well as dishes with vegetables, aromatic sauces with herbs, and other delicacies to bring out the flavors.

The legation of the Kingdom of Rogdon was sitting at a table more to the right. Dressed in blue and silver, they showed their polite, cold character. Drocus, First General of the Rogdonian army, Ambassador Albust, and some nobles of the kingdom were dining peacefully. Nilsa saw Ingrid standing on guard near the table at the opposite end to the King and that relaxed her a little.

The legation of Erenal, with King Dasleo at the head, was at the next table. Egil was watching not only the Erenal table but everything that went on around him. He did so as unobtrusively as he could, but he missed nothing. The King of Erenal was accompanied by officers of the army, besides a couple trusted nobles. General Augustus, Commander in Chief of a hundred men of the infantry army, and General Militius, strategist and counselor to the King, were clearly identifiable as soldiers because they wore armor over their togas, just like King Dasleo, who wore plated armor that looked silver over a long toga.

The table where the Zangrians sat was the noisiest. They seemed to be protesting about everything and constantly asking for more food and drink. Nilsa thought they were rude; in fact, they honored their reputation for being wayward and undisciplined. Viggo was watching them with a smile on his face. It amused him to see how unruly they were and the noise they were raising. They were worse than the Norghanians when they got drunk, and that was saying a lot.

The Nocean table was the absolute opposite. They were polite and thanked the waiters and butlers for the food and drink they were being served. They were quiet and their manners were exquisite. Nilsa was surprised. She had thought they would be more like the Zangrians, but she had been completely mistaken. She could not stop staring at the Warlock Himnomec as he enjoyed the food beside Ambassador Hamal both throwing glances at King Thoran. Astrid was watching the Noceans closely. If they tried anything she would take care of it.

The next table was that of the legation of the Confederation of the Free Cities of the East. Their envoi, named Cordilio, was tall and thin with white hair, and he represented the six City-States of the Eastern Coast. He was a kind man and very experienced in commercial treaties and commercial maritime routes. Sugesen had told her this; he was standing watching near the head of the table, where there were several nobles of different races with a variety of appearances. They must come from the different city-states and were there to make sure the treaties that the representative made were acceptable for each city. From what Nilsa had been able to find out, the relationship between the Confederation and Norghana was barely existent, but not so with Irinel. According to rumors, Irinel and the Confederation did not have good relations because of commercial problems.

At the end of the great hall at three other tables, parallel to the table of honor, were the legations of the minor nations and the tribes. Nilsa saw Frida, Elina, and Gonars near them.

The kingdom assigned to Gonars was that of Moontian, one which little by little was growing in strength and which would soon become a power according to Ambassador Larsen. The interesting thing about this kingdom was that it was not ruled by a king but a queen. Queen Niria. She was said to be young and beautiful like her kingdom. According to what Gondabar had told Nilsa, two large gold mines had been discovered in the kingdom, the largest on all Tremia it was rumored, and thanks to them they were growing in power, both economically and militarily. The military consisted of mercenaries, bought with the gold. The kingdom was in the east, below the Kingdom of Irinel, and it was beginning to conquer territories Irinel considered her own. She suspected problems would emerge because of this, similar to the struggle between Zangria and Erenal. King Thoran had been on the verge of not inviting them for the rivalry they maintained with the Kingdom of Irinel, but in the end he had had no choice but to do so by request of the Confederation. The fact that this new kingdom had the support of the Confederation was not good for Irinel, and this in turn posed a problem for Thoran.

Once more, Nilsa marveled at how complex and twisted relations between all the kingdoms and nations of Tremia were. They were supposedly all very civilized, but   in reality, they would jump at each other's throats at the slightest provocation. Now they were all dining in harmony, but at the same time they were all plotting against one another. Nilsa would love to see the invisible threads of different colors that went from one table to the other, indicating who was plotting with who, and against whom. Most likely the whole room would fill with lines in all directions. This looked like a wasps' nest, and if anyone should stir it… she became nervous again.

She looked around the great hall and saw Raner and the Royal Rangers strategically positioned throughout the hall, that made her feel better. No fool would try anything here. The Royal Rangers would riddle them with their arrows or the Royal Guard would cut them up with their swords. Besides, Raner was pacing behind the table of honor up to the two round tables, making sure everything was all right. She snorted and relaxed. Nothing was going to happen. The dinner and the guests could not be more watched and safe than in that room.

The servants kept working without pause. The trays came and went from the guest tables to the kitchen, carried by countless waiters. The Norghanian cuisine dominated, as it could be no other way, being famous for its roast meats. But dishes from Irinel had been included to the delight of the guests of honor. And there were Nocean wines and some dishes from other kingdoms. Thoran wanted everyone to be happy, and it seemed he was managing it.

King Thoran stood and started to speak.

"This evening, I wish to thank you…" he began in a voice loud enough to be heard above the many conversations going on at the different tables.

"Silence! The King's speaking!" Orten shouted.

The conversation at the other tables stopped at once. Everyone turned to see what was happening.

"Continue, my brother," Orten said to Thoran.

The King nodded to his brother.

"This evening I wish to thank you all for being here and for having accepted the invitation to our Royal Wedding. It is a special honor to have the King of Erenal here in person."

King Dasleo stood and made a gesture of appreciation.

"It is my honor to attend such an important event," he said in a courteous tone.

Thoran returned the respectful greeting.

"I also wish to thank Ambassador Albust for his presence, although I would have preferred that King Solin had deigned to come," he said and was unable to hide the rage behind his comment.

The Ambassador bowed respectfully.

"His Majesty the King sends you his best wishes. Rogdon supports this magnificent union," he said in a polite voice without entering any argument.

Thoran did not seem at all convinced, but he went on with the greetings.

"The representative of the Confederation of Free Cities of the East has transmitted the appreciation and good will of the commercial City-States. I value their treaties greatly," Thoran greeted Cordilio.

"The City-States wish a long and prosperous life to the King and his bride, and for the commercial relations between our nations to prosper, bringing riches to all," Cordilio replied with a deep bow.

"Yes! Riches!" cried Orten, who had clearly been enjoying the beer too much. He drank without pause from a large glass that looked more like a jug based on its size. It was something common in Norghana. The Norghanians liked their beer in a large glass if possible.

Thoran now addressed the Nocean table.

"It pleases me to see that Emperor Malotas takes us into consideration and has sent an important representation to the wedding."

The Nocean Ambassador stood and bowed his head.

"Our Emperor sends his best wishes to the king of Norghana and his future wife, Princess Heulyn of Irinel. He wishes them a prosperous life and that the alliance between the kingdoms of Norghana and Irinel may be long and strong."

"Yeah, sure…" Orten muttered under his breath.

Thoran looked at him and put his hand on Orten's shoulder so he would stay quiet.

"Send the Emperor our best wishes. May his empire prosper beyond his dreams."

Orten choked on the beer he was drinking when he heard his brother.

Nilsa had never seen Thoran remotely as courteous, so the words did not seem to fit coming out of the King's mouth. On the other hand, she realized that the King and Queen of Irinel would be scrutinizing every detail of the proceedings. Nilsa assumed Thoran's words were because of that. He still had not married the Princess. There was still no firm alliance with Irinel. He had to behave, at least until after the wedding. Then things would be different.

Thoran continued greeting and thanking the guests from other minor kingdoms, nations, and the tribes. He made sure to stress his appreciation for the presence of the young kingdom of Moontian.

"Your kingdom is young but no less worthy, and I am pleased you have come. Queen Niria is a mystery to all of us," he said, opening his arms and waving them to enfold the whole room. "I would like to meet her. It is a pity she has not come."

"Queen Niria begs to be excused. She feels she is not at the level of such grand kingdoms and monarchs. She feels she must improve her political arts before she can talk and deal about important matters with such powerful figures."

Nilsa found the Ambassador's words interesting. The Queen was smart. She did not feel in a state to attend and was flattering the power of the other monarchs, trying to appear weak, when economically she was anything but. Nilsa was also curious about that woman, about her plans and future intentions. Something told her they would soon hear talk of Queen Niria of the Kingdom of Moontian. She also found the legation very exotic with their violet skin and bright violet eyes.

"I like that she shows respect for the powerful kingdoms," Thoran said and smiled, glancing at King Kendryk of Irinel, who smiled in turn and nodded.

Orten was laughing while he called for more beer.

At last, the King addressed the table consisting of the Zangria legation. Nilsa feared what the King might say.

"I see that General Zotomer and his companions are enjoying the dinner this evening. I wonder whether they will enjoy the wedding tomorrow when the Kingdoms of Norghana and Irinel join forces. Perhaps it will upset their stomachs."

General Zotomer looked as if he had been slapped, and everyone at his table became tense. But Zotomer rose slowly, arranged his Zangrian uniform, and replied in a temperate voice.

"The Kingdom of Zangria has accepted the King of Norghana's invitation. No doubt an invitation made in good will. I do not think this delicious meal will upset our stomachs tomorrow. There is no reason for it. The Kingdom of Zangria will continue being the war power it is, quite superior to other kingdoms present here today. We appreciate the efforts they make to try and equal our status, but we are not afraid that they will achieve it in the near future."

Thoran suddenly turned red. Nilsa had noted that the General had ignored him in front of everyone. Ignored him and Irinel and, by extension, Erenal. King Kendryk stood up, and in his face was a look similar to Thoran's.

"Let me skewer him like a pig," Orten said to his brother, and he said it louder than expected so he was clearly heard.

Everyone at the Zangrian table rose and reached for their weapons. The Royal Guard prepared to intervene. The Royal Rangers nocked arrows in their bows, ready to release.

Nilsa looked at Raner, who also had his hand on his bow. She stiffened and quickly armed hers in case she had to defend Gondabar or the King, which was her mission. She looked at the Zangrian table and saw Viggo regarding it nonchalantly. He was smiling. His hands were at his back, but Nilsa realized he was already holding his knives in them. Egil was also armed beside King Dasleo. This was not good; things had become terribly tense. One more stir and the wasps' nest would explode.

Thoran looked at Orten.

"Easy, brother," he said and squeezed his brother's shoulder hard so he would not say anything else.

His look of insulted monarch changed all of a sudden.

"I think General Zotomer has misinterpreted my words. I do not wish any ill on the legation or the Kingdom of Zangria," said Thoran.

Orten wriggled and tried to say something, but Thoran squeezed harder.

Seeing he could not speak, Orten searched for more beer. They had not brought his yet, so he grabbed the one they had just brought for the King and drank it all in one gulp.

"I am glad to hear that, Your Majesty. I apologize for the misunderstanding. My knowledge is in the battlefield. I am afraid I am not a good diplomat, as you have witnessed," Zotomer apologized insincerely.

"There is no need to apologize. Misunderstandings happen. Let us continue with the celebration."

"Let us," the General said and saluted Thoran with a nod.

Nilsa could see that the King was making a tremendous effort to control himself, something uncommon for him. He did not want an altercation there now; later on, General Zotomer would pay, of this she had no doubt. She could see King Kendryk and King Dasleo, both looking irked.

"Now, allow me to make a toast," said Thoran, rising again. "I raise my cup of wine to my future wife, who will reign in Norghana, and to the Royal Family of Irinel."

Everyone raised their goblets to toast.

"And for an unbreakable alliance between Norghana and Irinel," Thoran added.

He was about to drink when his brother Orten collapsed face down on the table.

"What...?" the King muttered.

Raner appeared like lightning and took the goblet from the King's hand.

"Don't drink, Your Majesty," he said. "No one drink!" he shouted.

Nilsa realized then what had happened.

Orten had been poisoned!

Chapter 33

The chaos that followed the discovery of Orten's poisoning was absolute. King Thoran was screaming, beside himself.

"Orten, brother!" he was shaking his brother hard, trying to reanimate him. "Wake up!"

The Duke was unconscious, as if he had been hit on the head. His brother's shaking and shouting were not helping him regain consciousness.

"Don't eat or drink anything!" Heulyn was shouting to her family.

King Kendryk was standing with his hand on his sword.

Queen Gwyneth had put her hands to her head and seemed unable to believe what was happening.

Prince Kylian left his cup on the table and pushed his plate away. Then he reached for his sword. Reagan, First General of the Armies of Irinel, and Counselor Kacey were also on their feet, staring at Orten.

The Royal Guard surrounded the entire table, preventing anyone from reaching it or the guests from leaving it. The Royal Rangers took their positions behind and on the sides, ready to release at anyone who tried anything.

The guests of the other legations at the other tables also stood up. Bodyguards and soldiers brought out their weapons to protect their noble lords and kings, around whom they had formed in clusters. In the center of each was the king, ambassador, or lord their men were charged to protect.

After the initial confusion and seeing that there was no other attack on any of the legations, the groups started to try to move toward an exit. But these were shut and guarded by Thoran's soldiers. The guests did not want to move too fast, since that would provoke the Royal Guard or Rangers to attack them thinking they were responsible. The guests also were not sure if any other legation might attack them, so they were moving in circles without advancing much in any direction. Beside each group that had huddled together was the Ranger responsible for their protection.

Nilsa had remained within the protective circle formed by the

293

Royal Guard at the table of honor. She looked at Valeria, who was watching the proceedings, bow in hand, and gave her a questioning look as to whether she had seen anything. Nilsa answered by signing that she had not. But what she had noticed was that the Druid Aidan had moved and was now closer to the Princess and Valeria.

"Call the King's surgeons!" Ellingsen ordered, already beside Thoran and helping keep the Duke alive.

"Orten! Hold on, brother!" Thoran was yelling, beside himself.

The clusters of the legations were watching one another, and the agitation was considerable. Zotomer, the Zangrian General, was shouting orders to his escort to repel any attack against his person. Viggo was with them, his knives in his hands, watching everything that went on. King Dasleo of Erenal remained standing beside his table, surrounded by his guard and defended by his two generals. He maintained his peace and was staring at the Zangrian General who was barking orders. Egil was beside the King of Erenal; for some reason he had been left inside the defensive perimeter formed by the Erenalian Royal Guard. He was scrutinizing what was happening at the table of honor closely.

Those who looked calmer, and therefore guiltier, were the Noceans, as they had not adopted any defensive formation. They remained quiet, sitting at their table as if the commotion had nothing to do with them. The Ambassador was talking to Astrid in a calm manner and continued eating and drinking without any fear. His personal guards were also eating, although they had one hand on their scimitars, just in case.

At the Rangers' table they were all standing. Sigrid wanted to make her way over to the King but the Royal Guard would not allow it. She was arguing with the soldiers, explaining that she could help, but they were not Rangers and would not let her through.

Gondabar saw Sigrid's futile attempts and decide to act, since he was within the protective circle formed by the Royal Guard. He tried to reach the King. He found it difficult, since when the guests had stood up from their first fright, they had toppled their chairs, but with Nilsa's help he was able to reach Raner.

"What is it?"

"I'd say poison, in the drink. They've summoned the King's surgeons and they're on their way."

"He must be taken to a room to be examined calmly, not here,"

Gondabar said.

Raner nodded.

Ellingsen heard them and nodded too.

"Your Majesty, we need to move him," Ellingsen told the King.

Thoran glared at Ellingsen with eyes possessed by pain and rage.

"No one leaves the hall! No one!" he shouted at the top of his lungs.

The legations stopped short and did not try to keep moving toward the exits.

"I want the culprit skinned alive!" Thoran was yelling.

Raner checked Orten's neck for a pulse.

"Your Majesty, he's still alive, but we must hurry to save his life."

That seemed to make the King react.

"He's not dead?" Thoran asked, his gaze lost as if he were in a dream.

"No, Sire, he's still alive," Raner said

Gondabar examined Orten's face and saw he was still breathing. Barely.

"Your Majesty, quickly. He has to be examined in another room. I'll bring the Healing Specialists."

Thoran seemed to realize at last what was happening and what needed to be done.

"Yes, let's take him, quickly."

"Royal Rangers, to me!" said Raner.

The six closest to him came over at once.

"Bring the Duke," he told them.

The Rangers picked him up and took him out by the door behind the table of honor while the guests watched.

Gondabar made a sign to Sigrid.

"Send Annika, Sylvia, and Edwina," he told her.

Sigrid nodded. "They'll need their things; I'll go and fetch them."

"Good. Nilsa, you're coming with us," Gondabar told her.

As they were leaving the hall the King turned to his guests.

"I want to know who did this! Whoever it was, have the guts to show your face!"

Everyone in the Grand Hall stood still before the King's shouts and stared at him. No one said anything or made the slightest move to confess to what had happened.

"Commander of the Guard Ellingsen!"

"Your Majesty!"

"No one is to leave this hall until I come back," Thoran ordered.

The other chiefs of state and members of the legations started to protest irately. They considered it an outrage, an affront to their honor, and they expressed it loud and clear.

"No one is going to hold me against my will!" King Dasleo's voice rose.

"Me neither!" General Zotomer of the Zangrian cried too.

"We can certainly withdraw," Princess Heulyn said, indicating her parents.

"No one is going anywhere!" Thoran yelled, beside himself.

"We are with you," King Kendryk said, looking upset.

"I said no one!" Thoran shouted at him.

"This is an outrage," Queen Gwyneth rose with Heulyn's brother, Prince Kylian.

"Commander Ellingsen, no one is to leave here!" the King repeated.

"As you command, Sire." The Commander signaled his men to stand at the doors and around the table of honor.

King Thoran left the hall through the door they had carried Orten out of and hastened to one of the rooms where several Royal Rangers were standing on guard.

Raner was at the door.

"Here, Your Majesty," the First Ranger indicated.

Thoran flew into the room like a hurricane.

"How is he?" he asked, going to his brother's side. Orten was lying on his side on a bed; to one side was a basin with vomit.

Three Royal Surgeons were tending to him. One was examining him and two were preparing tonics on one of the dressers.

"He's been poisoned, my lord," the oldest of them said, who was examining him. "We've made him empty his stomach so he could throw up the poison," he said, indicating the basin. "Let's hope he didn't assimilate much."

"Will he live?" Thoran asked, looking unhinged.

"Difficult to know, my lord. The poison looks foreign…"

"Foreign? How do you know?"

The chief surgeon pointed at the glass of beer Orten had drunk from and which was on a nearby table.

"We've analyzed the beer; it contains a poison not known in

Norghana."

"Who brought the glass?"

"I did, Your Majesty. We thought it looked like a poisoning, and in these cases it's necessary to analyze everything consumed in order to know what poison has been used," Gondabar said. He was on the other side of the room with Nilsa, Annika, Sylvia, and Edwina.

"Well thought, you old Ranger!" the King congratulated him.

"We have no antidote against it. We're combining several of the antidotes we have for the poisons most often used in other murder attempts and we're administering them to him," the Chief Surgeon explained to the King.

"Then he'll be saved, right? With all these antidotes?" said Thoran, watching how they were administering the tonics to his brother.

The Chief Surgeon sighed.

"We don't know whether the antidotes will have any effect against the poison…"

"I command you to save him!" Thoran yelled, distraught. "He has to live!"

"We're doing everything we can…" the surgeon said.

"Do more! If he dies, I'll chop off your heads! All three of you!" he threatened.

"Your Majesty…" Gondabar said.

The King turned to him.

"What!" he growled.

"Perhaps they might be able to help where the surgeons can't…" Gondabar offered, indicating Annika, Sylvia, and Edwina.

"Yes, help him! Everyone help him!"

Nilsa watched with a knot in her stomach as the three women prepared to do everything they could. When the Royal Surgeons had arrived, they had asked the women to do nothing, they were in charge. It was the usual procedure. Surgeons, and Royal ones even more so, had the authority regarding healing. The Rangers, with all their knowledge, even Leaders like Annika and Sylvia, had no power to contradict a surgeon. And often not even a City Healer. After all, the Rangers of the Specialty of Nature had knowledge of healing but that was not their only task, theirs was to be Rangers, whereas it was the healers' and surgeons' only and main job.

At that moment Sigrid appeared at the door.

"Annika's and Sylvia's things," she showed Raner two Ranger satchels.

"Come in," said Raner with a nod.

Sigrid came in and handed Annika and Sylvia their things. They started at once to work on an antidote.

"He has to live! My brother has to live!" the King was shouting with his hands to his head.

"Your Majesty, perhaps the Healer Edwina can be of help," Gondabar said.

"Healer?"

"A Healer of the Order of Tirsar, Sire. Her Gift allows her to heal."

"I've heard of them. Let her try. Let everyone try to save him!"

Edwina went over to the bed and asked to have some space. She put Orten on his back again and placed her hands on the Duke's chest. She shut her eyes and concentrated. Edwina's hands shone blue and the Healer's energy entered Orten's body. None of those present had the Gift, so they could not appreciate what was happening. They could only see that the Healer had placed her hands on Orten's torso.

"We're going to need several containers, glasses will do, two pans, and big wooden spoons," Annika asked.

"Right away," Nilsa said and ran out. She knew where to get them. The kitchens were not far from the Grand Hall, and there she would find anything she needed.

"And a fire," Sylvia said, pointing her finger at the fireplace.

"I'll make the fire," Raner offered.

Nilsa left the room like lightning and ran as fast as she could along the corridor, then she turned left, went down another corridor, and arrived at a double door that was open onto the hall of the kitchen. A large number of servants were crowded there, not knowing what to do after what had happened. When they saw her race in, they moved out of her way. Nilsa went into the massive kitchens and saw all the cooks with blank looks on their faces. They looked puzzled, frightened, and unsure what was happening.

"I need a couple of pans, wooden spoons, and half a dozen glasses, quick!" she asked.

For a moment no one moved, which surprised her. It was one thing to be confused   and a very different thing to disobey a direct order.

"Didn't you hear me? I need it now!" she raised her voice.

"Yes, yes, right away," one of the servants said and hastened to get the things for her.

The cooks though continued staring at her with restless looks.

"What's going on here?" she asked. "Something's wrong, isn't it?"

One of the cooks, who Nilsa recognized as Paulsen, the Head Cook, pointed a finger behind one of the tables at the far end of the kitchen that was rarely used.

"We had nothing to do with this, I swear," he said with fear in his voice. "We don't even know what's going on. The doors of the Grand Hall were shut and no one's given us any explanation."

"But you suspect something bad has happened?"

"Yes, something terrible. We heard the King's shouts..." he replied in a frightened tone.

Nilsa went over to where Paulsen was pointing and saw clothes on the floor, hidden behind the last table against the wall.

"Whose are they?" Nilsa asked.

"We don't know, we just found them after the commotion in the Grand Hall," said Paulsen.

Nilsa bent over and reached behind the table. She found a cook's uniform and a servant's outfit.

"Who's missing?" she demanded.

The Head Cook looked around and started to count his cooks with his fingers.

"It's hard to know, we haven't had a moment's rest all night, not one moment.... There was so much work... so many guests.... One of the new cooks is missing..."

"New cooks?"

"I didn't have enough hands to cook for all the wedding guests. I had to hire new cooks to help on the days prior to the event."

"What's the name of the missing one?"

"I'm not sure..."

"His name was Rasmussen," another of the cooks said. "He was a good cook, with experience."

"Where did he say he was from?"

"South... near the border with Duke Orten's Fortress..."

"And the other one? The servant?" Nilsa looked at Simonsen, the King's Head Butler who had called back all the servants and was counting them.

"Sandvik... Sandvik's missing..." Simonsen said.

"What do we know of him?"

"He's also new. I hired him a few days ago. Too many guests to serve... he said he was from near Bilboson. He had experience serving Eastern nobles. He knew how to carry plates and glasses; I interviewed him myself and put him on trial."

Nilsa sighed. Now she knew how the poison had entered the Grand Hall. A fake cook and a fake servant. She had to tell Raner, and fast, so they could hunt them down before it was too late.

"Paulsen, Simonsen, don't let any of your cooks and servants leave these kitchens and service areas. They'll be coming down to question you. If anyone leaves the place they'll be pursued and tried for high treason."

Upon hearing Nilsa's words all the servants and cooks stiffened and started whispering with concern. They did not know what was afoot and her words had scared them.

"No one's going anywhere," Simonsen promised.

Nilsa gathered the things she had asked for, which the servants had fetched for her, and ran off again. When she turned onto the next corridor, she met several soldiers on guard duty.

"Don't let anyone leave the kitchen area," she told them.

The soldiers nodded and went to stand at attention as Nilsa had ordered at the kitchen door. Nilsa ran toward the room where they were trying to save the King's brother's life.

"Here's... everything..." she said, breathless.

"Thank you very much, Nilsa," Annika said as she took some of the items and Sylvia took the rest.

While Edwina worked her magic, Annika and Sylvia were putting their Nature knowledge of healing to work, preparing a number of potions for the Duke to take. Although they went as fast as they could, the preparation process was long. The fire was going strong in the fireplace and they put the pans in it to heat up. They needed boiling water to cook several herbs and components to mix later.

Nilsa seized the moment to tell Gondabar and Raner what she had found out in the kitchen. She whispered so that King Thoran would not hear her. He was too upset, and hearing about their latest discovery would upset him even more.

"I'll deal with this," Raner whispered to her, and he left the room, summoning two Rangers whom he sent to the kitchens.

"Hold on, brother! Fight back! Live!" King Thoran was yelling as he paced the room from one end to the other, waving his arms with his face unhinged.

Edwina finished her healing process and took her hands away.

"I was able to heal his vital organs, but the poison is in his body and we have to fight it, or his organs will fail again," she explained.

"We have the potions ready. They'll help him fight the poison," said Annika.

"He must take them all," said Sylvia, "since we don't know which will work."

"Make him drink!" the King ordered.

The surgeons helped and Annika and Sylvia gave him the potions.

"He's a strong man. He's fighting it," Edwina told King Thoran.

"Save him. You have to save him." Thoran held his brother's head, which was drenched in perspiration.

"They're doing the impossible," Gondabar assured him.

Edwina used her Healing power again on Orten's body, healing the organs that were getting infected once again with the poison that ran through his veins while Annika and Sylvia were fighting the poison.

A long time passed during which Orten's body fought against the malicious substance, thanks to all the help the three women were providing.

Then all of a sudden, Orten's eyes opened and he cried out.

"I'm alive!"

Chapter 34

"Brother, you live!" Thoran cried.

"What... hap... happened to me?" Orten asked, half sitting up.

"You were poisoned. You nearly died," Thoran said, kneeling beside his brother and holding him up.

"Poisoned? Me? I don't remember much.... I felt very dizzy... then I fainted. I had a nightmare... I thought I was dying..."

"You've been near death," Annika told him.

Orten looked at her without recognizing her.

"Who are these women?"

"They're Annika and Sylvia, Leaders of the Skill of Nature. They've given you potions to counter the effect of the poison," Gondabar explained.

"I've been poisoned?" Orten looked in disbelief.

"That's right," Thoran said. "If it hadn't been for these two and the healer, you'd be dead."

Orten looked at Edwina with eyes open wide.

"Healer? Of those who heal with magic?"

"Indeed, my lord," Edwina said with a small curtsy.

"I'm not at all happy with magic being used on me," Orten protested. He was so weak that he tried to get up with his brother's help but could not.

"Without the Healer's intervention you would've died," Gondabar told him, making it sound not as a criticism but as praise toward Edwina.

Orten looked at Gondabar and said nothing; he was too weak. He dropped back on the bed and breathed with difficulty.

"We'll look after him, Your Majesty," the Chief Surgeon told Thoran, and he signaled the other two surgeons to help him.

Suddenly a Royal Guard came into the room, bowed his head respectfully, and spoke, "Your Majesty, Commander Ellingsen has sent me. The situation in the Grand Hall is unsustainable and requires your immediate assistance."

King Thoran stared at him.

"What do you mean unsustainable?"

"They're on the brink of bloodshed. If they're not allowed out of the Hall, lives will be lost."

"Bloody fools!"

"Go… I'm okay…" Orten said.

"I want him alive and well," Thoran said, pointing his finger at his surgeons.

"Of course, Your Majesty," the Chief Surgeon promised.

Thoran was about to leave when he hesitated. He turned to Annika, Sylvia, and Edwina.

"Make sure he recovers fully," he ordered.

"We will, Your Majesty," Annika said.

"Raner, with me!" the King shouted and went out to the corridor. The First Ranger followed him at once.

The surgeons went to tend to Orten, who had fainted again.

"Better let the Healers look after him," the Chief Surgeon said.

Edwina nodded and Annika and Sylvia got down to it. The surgeons stepped aside and let them work.

Thoran entered the Grand Hall and indeed the situation was unsustainable. The legations had gone to the doors and were threatening to kill the Royal Guards and soldiers watching them, who were preventing anyone from leaving the hall.

The exception was the Royal Family of Irinel, who remained at the table of honor with all the members standing, watching tensely what went on.

"Your Majesty, the legations," Commander Ellingsen told the King.

"Everyone, stop! No one leaves the hall!" Thoran yelled.

The legations stopped when they heard the King.

"Thoran, establish order or there will be bloodshed," Princess Heulyn said.

"Go back to your tables! Now!" Thoran yelled as if he was possessed, and he took his own place at the table of honor by the Princess.

The legations protested and tried to refuse. They did not want to go back to the tables, they wanted to get out of there alive.

"Ellingsen, take the Royal Guard, force them to stay! Raner, take the Royal Rangers. Help the Commander!"

The two saluted in unison. "At your command, Your Majesty!"

The legations found themselves surrounded by the Royal Guard and Rangers, who threatened them with their weapons.

"I don't want to turn this banquet into a blood bath!" cried the King. "Go back to your tables, all of you!"

For a long moment there were hesitations. The leaders of each legation were looking at the King and then at the other leaders. They were doubtful. They were risking their lives. A bad decision and this could end in a true blood bath. The King's soldiers were a threat, but every legation was an even greater threat to the others. If there was the least bloodshed, a massacre would follow.

Little by little, watching one another and also the Guards and Rangers with weapons ready and threatening, they all went back to their tables and sat down, reluctantly, angrily, but they did. Peace and calm seemed to return to the Grand Hall for a moment.

Nilsa came in with Gondabar and they took their places at the table of honor. Eicewald looked at Gondabar, who signaled to him that they would talk later. She looked for her friends and saw them beside the delegations' tables. All except Viggo looked as if they were having a rough time. Viggo, of course, was enjoying himself and his face showed it.

"Good!" the King went on. "Let's all sit and calm down!"

Ellingsen and Raner stood behind King Thoran with several Royal Guards and Rangers.

"My dear Princess Heulyn, Royal Family of Irinel," Thoran said making an effort to calm down." I see you all know by now, but please don't eat or drink anything. I say the same to my side of the table," he said, looking at Eicewald. "The drinks have been poisoned, and perhaps the food too."

"This is an irreparable outrage!" Heulyn said, banging the table with both hands. "My wedding's ruined!"

"Unacceptable and intolerable!" Queen Gwyneth cried. Everyone in the Irinel Royal Family was furious.

Prince Kylian had said nothing, but his eyes burnt with fury and his gaze was sweeping the tables before him, searching for the culprit.

"It is. You're all right," Thoran nodded repeatedly. "The worst thing is that the attempt has not been against my brother, it was made against me. Orten drank from my cup. Which means someone in this hall has tried to kill me."

"Who is the King of Norghana accusing?" King Dasleo said, standing up. "Is it me? Because if it is he's accusing me without evidence, and that is an affront I cannot let pass," Dasleo, King of Erenal, threatened.

"The General of the Zangrians stood at once too.

"We don't poison our rivals. We beat them in the battlefield which is where wars are decided. We haven't attempted to poison the King of Norghana. If Your Majesty is blaming us, he's making a mistake and will start a deadly quarrel with the Kingdom of Zangria, which might unleash hostilities on a large scale."

The other representatives of the legations gradually stood up with similar argumentations. They all denied attempting to poison King Thoran and all threatened armed conflict if they were accused without evidence. All except the Noceans, who said absolutely nothing. They remained peaceful and silent. But it was known by all that poisoning was a common form of murder in the Nocean Empire. They were practically the inventors of that way of killing and they had highly toxic and exotic poisons.

Nilsa was wondering whether the Noceans, knowing that the type of murder attempt pointed straight at them, were not bothering to deny it because they knew it would be in vain. King Thoran listened to everyone and then was silent. He looked at them all, one by one, each and every one of the representatives of each kingdom: monarch, general, ambassador… then at the Royal Family of Irinel, and at last he spoke.

"We are here to celebrate a Grand Royal Wedding. This attempt against my life will be investigated and I will find the culprit who, I promise, will pay dearly for this, he or she and their kingdom. They will pay with blood. But I don't want this serious offense to be an impediment for the wedding which will take place tomorrow at noon," he turned to Heulyn and offered her his hand. "If my betrothed so wishes, we well go ahead with the wedding, leaving behind this regrettable incident. What is your wish, Princess Heulyn?"

The Princess looked at her father, King Kendryk, who sighed deeply and after a brief moment of doubt nodded. Then Heulyn looked at her mother, who nodded briefly, indicating her approval. The Princess took King Thoran's hand and stood up.

"The wedding will take place as planned," the Princess announced.

Thoran smiled triumphantly.

"Very well. The wedding is on. In the morning we'll go to the

Temple of the Ice Gods to receive their blessing. At noon the wedding will be celebrated in the Throne Hall, and I expect to see you all at the ceremony. I will wed Princess Heulyn and she will become Queen of Norghana."

The legations said nothing. Their leaders nodded, some clearly reluctantly, accepting King Thoran's words.

"And seeing that we can't continue with the Gala Dinner, I bid you all good night and thank you for your presence here today," Thoran said. "You may go, let the doors be opened," he ordered.

A moment later the legations began to leave, each one headed to a door, and waited their turn to go out in an orderly way, without bumping into the other legations. The Rangers assigned to them left with the legations. Nilsa saw her friends leave and felt uneasy for them. She hoped they would have no trouble.

Thoran watched them leave with half-closed eyes. He seemed eager to find out who might have been the culprit. Once they had all left, he turned to the Royal Family of Irinel.

"I'm sorry for what has happened. Go and rest."

"This can't remain this way," King Kendryk told him, clearly furious. "It is also an offense against my family, against Irinel. It can't go unpunished."

"I know. I'll find the culprit," Thoran promised.

"And we'll raze their kingdom," Prince Kylian said, enraged.

"Why did you let them go?" Heulyn asked Thoran in an upset tone.

"I can't touch them!" Thoran cried, enraged. "Not here and now, not without evidence! If it were up to me, I'd torture them all until the truth came out. But I can't do that! They're in my kingdom on my own invitation. Nothing can happen or it will mean war. Dasleo was about to declare it. I couldn't stop him. It's within his rights as a King. In his place I might have lost my temper."

"It was Zangria, they're the ones who gain the most by killing you and preventing this alliance," said Kendryk.

"True, that might be the case. But I can't prove it for now."

"Poison is the Nocean method of assassination, and they didn't even open their mouths to deny it," the Queen said.

"The Noceans don't want strong kingdoms that cast a shadow on them," the Prince added.

Thoran nodded.

306

"My blood boils—I'd happily cut all their throats. But I can't do that. Not without evidence," he turned to Ellingsen and Raner. "Investigate the incident. Find the culprit. Don't fail me, or I swear I'll skin the both of you!" he said in a new bout of fury, clenching his jaw.

Raner looked at Nilsa.

"We'll find them," he told the King.

Chapter 35

Without wasting an instant, Nilsa took Raner and Ellingsen to the kitchens at a run. Once there she showed them what she had found out.

"What do they look like?" Raner wanted to know after hearing from Paulsen the Head Cook, and Simonsen the Head Butler.

"Paulsen spoke.

"The cook, Rasmussen, is of medium built, dark, with short hair. He could cook, he had experience."

Simonsen spoke once Paulsen had finished.

"Sandvik, the servant, is blond, tall, and thin."

"We must assume the names and information they gave are false," Ellingsen reasoned.

Raner nodded.

"Their experience was true enough; they knew how to do the jobs they were hired for. The rest of what they said was indeed false."

"I'll deal with the interrogations and finding out as much as is known about the two suspects," Ellingsen said with a wave that included all the servants held there. "Perhaps they revealed some detail by mistake to a colleague."

"I'll follow the trail of the two escapees," said Raner.

"Agreed. Let's not waste time. They can't get away," Ellingsen said, and he started giving instructions to the members of the Royal Guard who had come with him.

Raner picked up the clothes both men had worn and took them with him. He pointed to six Royal Rangers. "You, come with me," he ordered. Then he signaled for Nilsa to come as well. They left the kitchen area and moved swiftly through the corridors. Nilsa did not know what Raner was planning but he looked determined, as if he already had a clear plan.

They left the main building of the castle. It was night and everything was quiet in the large outer courtyard, with the exception of the area where they loaded and unloaded carts with supplies: sacks, boxes, crates, and barrels. About twenty men were busy working. Raner called for their group to halt and inspected the nearby buildings, then the military barracks and auxiliary posts that had been set up for the wedding.

"Two men, go to the exit gate. Make sure no one goes out," Raner ordered.

"At your command, sir," the Royal Rangers replied and left at a run. Nilsa was surprised at how fast they ran given how large they were. Not as large as the soldiers of the Royal Gard, but almost.

"Two to the stables. Check them out," Raner ordered.

Two of the men ran off.

"Do you think they'll have fled?" Nilsa asked, unable to contain herself.

"No, I don't think so... the main gate hasn't been opened during the dinner. They couldn't have left the castle. They're still here."

"You think so?" Nilsa was looking in every direction.

"Yes, they're hiding, but what we don't know is where.... The castle is huge, they could have hidden in any number of places. What's not so easy is getting out without being seen," Raner said, indicating the battlements where a large number of Norghanian soldiers were on watch duty.

"And how will we find them?"

"They're hiding somewhere, under cover of night. They must have an escape plan... a planned way out... what we'll do first is cut it off."

"The escape plan? How?"

"By surrounding the castle," Raner smiled mischievously. "If they can't get out, they can't escape."

"Oh, I see..."

"Let's go to the Tower of the Rangers," Raner said and ran off.

Nilsa and the Royal Rangers followed.

They reached the Tower. There were two Rangers on duty.

"Go inside and have every Ranger report at once, armed and in silence. We're in a situation of extreme seriousness."

"Shall I sound the alarm, sir?" said one of the Rangers on duty, reaching for his horn.

"No, I want them here at once in total silence."

"At your command," the three Rangers went into the Tower at a run.

A moment later, dozens of Rangers appeared from the Tower. Among them were the Panthers, which surprised Nilsa. She also saw

Gonars, Sugesen, Frida, and the rest.

Raner seemed surprised too. He approached the Panthers.

"Why aren't you at your posts?" he asked them.

"The legations have dismissed us, sir," Ingrid replied.

"All of us," Viggo told him. "They kicked us out," he said.

"It seems that what happened at the dinner did not sit well with them. They don't want to have any Norghanian near, not even for their own protection," Egil commented. "Something which, on the other hand, is completely understandable given the circumstances."

Raner nodded.

"Yes, it is. I wouldn't want to be in their situation."

"What do you need from us, sir?" Astrid asked.

"I want you to surround the castle on the outside of the walls and form a close perimeter so no one escapes the fortress."

"There aren't enough of us..." Ingrid said, looking around.

"Tell the rest of the Rangers who are sleeping at the back in the barracks."

"At once, sir," Ingrid said, preparing to leave.

"I need bloodhounds. Do we have any here?" Raner asked.

"Yes, sir," a Specialist said, taking a step forward and showing Raner the medallion of Man Hunter. "I'm Karlsen. I've brought my own, and Markuson's brought his too. They always travel with us," he said, indicating another Specialist standing beside him.

"Where do you keep them?"

"In the Royal Kennels, with the King's hunting dogs."

"Go get them, I want them with me in those carts," Raner pointed at them with his finger.

"At your command, sir."

The First Ranger addressed the others.

"We're looking for two men who're trying to escape the castle. They must be apprehended. I want them alive so they can be questioned. Do not kill them. That's an order."

"Understood, sir," Astrid said

Raner signaled them over and headed to the gate where the men the First Ranger had sent were speaking to the officer on duty.

"I need you to let the Rangers out," Raner told the officer.

"We can't open the gate during the night, sir," the officer did not seem very convinced.

"King's orders. We have to catch two fugitives. The Rangers will surround the castle. Tell the guards on the walls to give them support from their high vantage point."

The officer nodded.

"At your command, sir."

The gates of the castle opened and the Rangers began to go out in a single file formation. The Panthers looked at Nilsa, who indicated she was staying with Raner.

"Come on, all of you, hurry up!" Raner said.

A moment later they were all running. The gates shut behind them.

"Come on," Raner told his men and Nilsa, and ran to the carts where the men were still working.

Nilsa had thought the same thing as Raner. That was the best spot to hide and get out of the castle. The carts would leave once everything was loaded, and they would likely also carry materials outside the castle, whether it was refuse or leftovers.

Raner ordered the carts to be surrounded.

"Everyone, stay where you are!" he ordered the workers, taking them by surprise.

"Sir, we're only working..." one who looked like the foreman said.

"All of you, get on this side, in the light," Raner ordered, and he made them line up under some torches hanging from the walls.

"Are you the boss of this working gang?" Raner asked him.

"I am, sir," the man replied.

"Are these all the workers on this shift?"

The foreman looked at his gang and then at the six carts they had. "Yes, sir."

"Count them to see if they're all here."

"I'd say so..."

"Count them," Raner insisted in a firm tone.

"Yes, sir." The foreman started counting all the workers in the gang, pointing his finger as he counted and called them by name. When he finished, he turned to Raner. "They're all here, sir."

"You don't have two extra workers?"

"No... no, sir."

Raner studied them all.

"No one moves," he ordered and looked at his Rangers so they would keep them under control.

The two Specialists brought their hounds.

"Here they are, sir," Karlsen said, presenting him with two beautiful and well cared for specimens of Norghanian bloodhounds.

"What trail do you want them to follow?" Markuson asked.

"This one," Raner offered them the clothes of the two fugitives.

Carefully, slowly, giving them time to familiarize themselves with the smell he wanted them to track, the two Specialists gave them the clothes to sniff.

Nilsa watched, interested. She knew how good hounds were at following trails, and it always impressed her that they were capable of following a scent for leagues. These two beauties would find the trail to follow and lead them to wherever the two fugitives were hiding.

"Ready, sir," Karlsen told Raner.

"Get going. Find me those two traitors."

At an order from the Specialists, the two hounds started looking for the trail. Raner, Nilsa, and the Royal Rangers accompanying them watched carefully, weapons in hand.

The two hounds searched for the trail around the carts, sniffing at all the workers and the foreman, then the sacks they were unloading, but they found nothing.

"The sacks on the carts," Raner indicated.

The Specialists led their hounds up onto the carts. Nilsa readied her bow. She was sure the bloodhounds would find the two traitors hiding among the sacks.

She was wrong.

"They're not here," Markuson said.

Raner frowned. the First Ranger had also been sure they would be there.

"Check this entire area, they have to be around here somewhere," he ordered.

The Specialists did as ordered. They led the hounds all over the area and even the back part of the barracks where the soldiers slept. They tracked the whole area, and when they found nothing, they continued tracking around the main building of the castle. They did not find anything.

"Check the uncovered part up to the stables," he ordered next, sounding frustrated.

Nilsa did not think they would find anything in the clear area, because they would have seen them fleeing.

Nothing came from the outside, so the Rangers deployed there had not found anything either.

Raner had a twisted look on his thoughtful face.

Nilsa could almost read his thoughts, which were probably along the lines of, "where could they have hidden?"

All of a sudden, the hounds found the trail.

"Here, sir," Karlsen cried.

Raner, Nilsa, and the Rangers ran to where Karlsen was pointing. It was between the stable and the Tower or the Rangers. They arrived there and saw footprints behind a shed east of the stables.

"Two men squatted here, sir," Markuson indicated.

Raner and Nilsa went over to check. The place was dark and Raner asked for torches, which the Rangers hastily brought over.

Nilsa saw that it was indeed the trail of two men who had been hiding there behind the shed. Raner was looking in every direction. Behind was the wall which the wanted men could not have climbed without being seen by the guards at the ramparts, who were already studying what was going on.

"The trail goes to the stables?" Raner asked.

Karlsen and Markuson motioned the hounds to go to the stables, but they turned and followed the trail in the opposite direction.

In the direction of the Tower of the Rangers.

"What are they doing? Why are they going to the Tower?" Raner asked blankly.

"The trail goes that way, sir," Karlsen told him.

"That can't be, there were several Rangers on duty at the Tower, they would've seen them," said Raner.

"The hounds indicate that the trail hugs the wall to the back of the Tower," Markuson confirmed.

Raner and Nilsa were watching the hounds point at the place.

"There are footprints, sir. Two men," Karlsen said.

Raner was shaking his head.

"It makes no sense. Did they hide behind the Tower and risk being seen?"

"It would seem that way, sir," Markuson said.

"Where does the trail go from there?"

The hounds continued sniffing and then headed straight to the great gate that led out of the castle.

The officer and the soldiers guarding it gave them blank looks when they saw them all arrive.

"Sir?" the officer said.

"The trail ends here," said Karlsen.

Raner studied the gate, then the Tower. All of a sudden, he put his hands to his head.

"What's the matter, sir?" Nilsa asked him, concerned.

"They've fooled us," Raner said with a look of incredulity on his face.

"Fooled us? I don't understand. How have they escaped?"

Raner snorted hard.

"We let them out ourselves," he said faintly.

Nilsa's jaw dropped. It took her an instant to understand. *We, the Rangers...*

"They went out as if they were Rangers," Nilsa said out loud as she realized it.

"And Thoran is going to skin me for it."

Chapter 36

With first light, the Norghanian soldiers and the Rangers prepared to protect the course of the Royal Parade all along the way to the Temple of the Ice Gods, as they had been ordered to. King Thoran and Princess Heulyn would walk to the Temple to receive the blessing of the Ice Gods from the hands of Helge, Principal Ice Priest of the Temple.

The Invincibles of the Ice were lined up in the great courtyard at the castle. Half the regiment was instructed to go at the head of the parade and the other half at the back. They would protect the King and Princess on their way to the Temple and during their return to the castle. In the middle of the procession, the Royal Guard with Commander Ellingsen in the lead were lined up on their horses, as well as the Royal Rangers with Raner in the lead and the Royal Eagles, whom the King had specifically asked to join the parade. On the side of Irinel were Valeria and Aidan.

No other members of the Royal Families of either Irinel or Norghana would accompany the King and future Queen that morning. They would wait at the Royal Castle for the return of the couple, and the wedding would take place when they were back with the blessing of the ice Gods, in the Throne Room.

While they waited for King Thoran and his bride to appear, the Panthers chatted on their horses. They were all wearing the Rangers' dress uniform which Gondabar had gotten for them. It was not all that different from what they usually wore, but it was a little more elegant with silver edging.

"It looks like we're going to have a busy day today," Viggo commented in whispers from his saddle.

"You don't say! Blessing, Parade, and then the Royal Wedding. It's going to be fantastic," Nilsa said, shaking her hand nervously.

"Let's hope we don't have any trouble, like with the dinner..." Gerd made a horrified face.

"Everything will go well. We just have to line up and look like magnificent Royal Eagles who belong to the King," said Astrid.

"I don't know how you persuaded me into this," Molak said, who was lined up with them.

"We needed one Royal Eagle to cover for Lasgol and you were at hand," Astrid said, winking at him.

"We appreciate that you accepted to cover for him," Ingrid told him.

"I don't," said Viggo. "I agree with Captain Fantastic; I don't know why he's here."

"Because the King expects seven Royal Eagles at the parade and we're missing one," Ingrid told him.

"So? There are hundreds of Rangers here. We could've picked anyone else," Viggo protested.

"Molak is one of the best, if not the best of those here," Ingrid told him, "and you know it."

"So, what's that got to do with it?"

"It has to do with the fact that if the King asks us, we can say we've replaced Lasgol with someone perfect for the position," Ingrid said.

"This one isn't perfect for anything, and least of all to be one of our own," Viggo said adamantly.

"Don't be a dumbass! Don't you see that otherwise we'll have to explain things we don't want to explain, about where Lasgol is and what he's doing?" Ingrid replied.

"I think... I might have accepted a little too hastily..." Molak said.

"You did the right thing," Egil said soothingly. "We need a seventh Royal Eagle and you're perfect for the position. Besides, we might need you again sometime in the future if anything happens to one of us. It'll be good for you to integrate in the group, learn how we work and what we do."

"I vote for Luca, I greeted him yesterday. That's a fine Ranger, and he's more use to us than this one," Viggo insisted.

"Oh shut up, we've already decided!" Ingrid snapped.

"You make a fine Lasgol with your hood on," Astrid smiled at him. "Don't worry, everything will be all right."

"I'm not sure His Majesty King Thoran would approve of this," Molak said reluctantly.

"We have permission from Gondabar and Raner. They'll explain to the King if necessary," Ingrid told him. "We're not going to get you into any trouble, don't worry."

316

"Good. In that case, it's an honor to be a part of the Royal Eagles, even for a short while," Molak smiled, looking at Ingrid.

"A very short while, don't get too comfortable," Viggo said stingingly.

"Silence, they're coming," Nilsa warned them.

Thoran and Heulyn appeared on their magnificent white horses. Thoran's was a war courser, Heulyn's a fast mare. The Panthers were quiet as they watched them approach and got into position in the center of the retinue, in front of them. A moment later, Thoran gave the order to move and the Invincibles of the Ice started walking.

They left the Royal Castle and found the capital crowded once again, even more than during previous days. Half of Norghana was there to see King Thoran and his bride. The trumpets heralded the parade from the top of the ramparts and the crowd applauded and cheered joyfully.

The Invincibles of the Ice marched along the main avenue, the Avenue of The Snow, stepping heavily on the cobblestones to a martial rhythm. They gave the impression they were going into battle. The street was filled by Norghanian soldiers who had doubled security. Three lines of soldiers on each side of the street formed two human walls that prevented anyone from approaching the parade. The human sea pushed hard to see the monarch and his bride, but the two walls withheld the waves.

Rangers watched from the top of the buildings so that no one would dare try anything against King Thoran or Princess Heulyn. They had all the roofs and balconies under control. This time there were no Rangers in the crowd—they were all on top of buildings and the whole way was being watched. It was quite a show to see hundreds of Rangers up on the roofs and balconies, but King Thoran had requested such. He did not want to take the slightest risk. Someone had already tried to kill him once, and the culprits might try again. And outside his castle there were even more possibilities for a treacherous attempt on his life.

Thoran sat very straight in his saddle with his chin up, and he was wearing the Royal Crown on his head. He did not greet the people, unlike his subjects, who were cheering their monarch. Princess Heulyn did not greet the people either and sat as stiff as Thoran. They did not even smile. They accepted the praise without blinking.

The parade to the Temple of Ice went along the main avenue

heading to the center. The crowd did not stop cheering on their King and the one who would soon be their Queen.

As they went forward, the Panthers talked among themselves in low voices.

"They're not greeting the people..." Nilsa noted. "They're all here for them, cheering them... they should be nicer..."

"Their arrogance and presumption won't let them," Viggo commented.

"They're certainly not very friendly. The people adore them, if they just waved a little..." said Gerd, watching the crowd and shouts as the King and Princess passed by.

"Don't you find it a little strange that they're going on with the wedding in spite of everything?" Astrid commented to her friends.

"They both seem to have fixed ideas," Viggo commented back.

"What I find amazing is that the King hasn't punished Raner yet," said Nilsa in a fearful tone, looking at the First Ranger, who was ahead of them in the parade.

"For the 'escape of the Ranger'?" Viggo asked.

"Are we calling it that?" Gerd asked.

"Of course, it sounds perfect," Viggo replied.

"The King was furious with Raner and Ellingsen," Egil explained. "You could hear them shouting from the Frozen Continent, but he can't do without them right now. He needs them to go ahead with the wedding, which is what he cares most about."

"Without them to lead the Guard and the Rangers he would be unprotected and the disorganization would become chaos," Ingrid said.

"When all this is over," Astrid commented, pointing at the crowd cheering and applauding the King and his bride, "he'll deal with them."

"And with whoever tried to kill the King," Molak said.

"That's going to be hard to determine," said Egil. "There are many possible suspects."

"That someone infiltrated the castle is obvious. They knew how to get to the King and the escape had been planned very well," said Nilsa. "I was astonished when we found out how they had escaped."

"Haven't they been found yet?" Gerd asked.

"No, and they won't be. The whole thing had been planned very carefully," said Astrid. "They'll already be out of Norghana."

"You need a lot of gold for a coup like this," said Viggo.

"And lots of cunning and patience," Ingrid added.

"If they discover who it was, this is going to get pretty rocky," Viggo said with a malicious grin.

The Invincibles of the Ice arrived at the city center and turned onto a wide street in the direction of the main square which was swarming with people. It looked as if all of Norghana had come to see the parade.

The soldiers had opened a corridor through which the retinue advanced. The Panthers lifted their gazes as they crossed the center of the square to see their comrades posted on the roofs of the buildings that surrounded it. That provided some element of peace, although the crowd around them singing and cheering and applauding seemed to be capable of swallowing them up if they suddenly lunged at them. The two walls of soldiers became four lines deep in the enormous square.

They crossed the main square and entered a wide street to the north until they reached another large square that only had the one entrance. The unmistakable Temple of the Ice was in the middle. It was an entirely white construction built imitating the shape of a tall, rectangular iceberg. At a certain distance it looked like it was made of real ice. The builders had managed a special effect, as if it were a real iceberg shining snow-white under the rays of the spring sun.

The square was deserted. The soldiers had vacated everyone who had gathered in it so the retinue could reach the temple without incident. The Invincibles of the Ice split into two groups, one to the east of the temple and the other half to the west. King Thoran and Princess Heulyn were left in front of the temple with their escort.

The Royal Guard dismounted at an order from Commander Ellingsen and secured the temple's entrance. The Royal Rangers, led by Raner, headed to the back of the temple to secure it too. The Royals Eagles had orders to follow King Thoran and Princess Heulyn when they made their entrance.

Commander Ellingsen went inside with part of the Royal Guard and secured the inside of the temple. Then they came back out.

"Your Majesty, the temple is safe inside," Ellingsen reported to the King.

They waited for Raner to come back with four Royal rangers.

"The back side is secure," the First Ranger reported.

319

"Very well. Let's go in," Thoran dismounted.

The companions dismounted. Valeria approached the Queen and helped her dismount, offering her a hand. Then she looked at the Panthers and gave them a slight nod. The Druid Aidan stood behind the Princess, beside Valeria, and also nodded to the Panthers, who returned the greeting. They had not been able to speak to the Druid, and they were intrigued as to what he might be doing at the Princess' side. There had to be a reason, but they had not guessed what it was yet.

Ellingsen and Raner led the way with four Royal Rangers and half a dozen Royal Guards behind. Thoran and Heulyn went in after them. Valeria and Aidan followed them. The Panthers went in last, after the rest. They carried their bows in their hands   each with an arrow nocked, ready to release if anything happened.

They advanced along the strange interior of the building, which was mostly hollow. The walls looked like ice although they were made of granite. They reached the center with the great fountain decorated with abstract representations of the gods with indefinite shapes. The tall walls resembling ice featured long, tall windows at the back which let the light in

They saw three Ice Priests who were waiting before some sculptures that represented the Ice Gods as strong Norghanian men and women warriors, with unrecognizable features. The Priests were standing, waiting, leaning on staves of white cedar. They wore long white robes and their hair and beards were long and white, which made them look like the Ice Magi.

"Welcome to the Temple," they said. "Those who come to the temples and pray   with the Ice Priests receive the blessing of the Gods," they said in unison.

"We come seeking the blessing of the Ice Gods," Thoran replied.

The priests nodded and motioned for them to follow. They led them to a separate room at the end, slightly bigger than the others. There a priest of advanced age was waiting for them in what looked like an ice throne.

"Your Majesty, Princess, welcome to the temple. I am Helge, and I am the person responsible for the Order and the Temple," he introduced himself.

"They come seeking the blessing of the Ice Gods," one of the other priests told him, although this was well known since it had all been organized previously.

"Kings and peasants equally need the blessing of the Ice Gods for their lives to be long and prosperous," Helge said, nodding and spreading his arms wide to encompass them all.

Thoran and Heulyn stood before the priest while the rest stood behind them.

"What is the reason for requesting the blessing?" the Ice Priest asked as a formality.

"Princess Heulyn of Irinel and I, Thoran, King of Norghana, are going to be wed. We are here as the tradition of Norghana commands, to receive the blessing of the Ice Gods so that our union may be a glorious one filled with triumphs and riches."

Helge nodded.

"You seek the blessing of the Ice Gods, and I as their representative in this kingdom will grant it to you. Please, King Thoran, sit in the ice throne," the priest said, pointing at the chair.

The King sat down and leaned his back and arms on the ice structure.

Helge approached with a silver tray filled with ice water.

"Put your hands in the water of the gods and wet your head with it so the blessing may fall from the kingdom of ice and enter you," he said, looking up at the ceiling.

Thoran put his hands in the water and then wet his head with it.

"May the Gods bless you, Thoran, King of Norghana," the priest said in blessing.

"So it may be," Thoran said and stood up.

Then it was Heulyn's turn. The look on her face said she did not believe too much in that rite. But she sat in the ice throne like Thoran had.

Helge brought more water and they repeated the ritual.

"May the Gods bless you Heulyn, Princess of Irinel."

The Princess nodded and rose.

"I also want to receive the blessing of the Druid," Heulyn said, looking at Aidan.

"What blessing is that?" Thoran asked.

"I am of Druid blood. I want the blessing of my roots, of my people," Heulyn argued.

Thoran looked at Helge.

"Is there any contradiction in receiving both blessings?"

"The Ice Gods are magnanimous; they look kindly on the blessing of other minor gods. There is no problem in receiving both."

"Go ahead then," Thoran told Heulyn, although his face showed he was not happy with it.

Aidan approached the Princess.

The Druid smiled.

"The blessing of the Druids is only for those with the blood of their people."

Heulyn rolled up both sleeves of her dress, showing her pale forearms.

Aidan began to murmur under his breath, moving the wooden staff he always carried with him. The Panthers noticed he was summoning some kind of Druid Magic, which made them alert.

"What's he doing?" Thoran asked, who also felt that something was going on.

"It's Magic, Your Majesty," Raner warned him.

"Magic? Let's move back," Thoran ordered and took several steps back to the middle of the room. The Royal Rangers and the Royal Guard followed him just as Raner and the Commander did.

Valeria did not move. Neither did the Panthers. They knew Aidan. He was not going to do anything harmful to the Princess or to them. Molak, who did not know the Druid, shifted restlessly. Ingrid grabbed his arm to calm him, which did not escape Viggo's notice.

Aidan went on casting. With a light movement he touched the Princess' right forearm. And in so doing, a tattoo began to form on her skin, one in green of the style the Druids wore. He continued the spell and touched the left forearm with the tip of his staff. Another tattoo began to appear on the Princess' skin.

"The blessing of the Druids is with you. It will always protect you, since engraved on your skin it remains," Aidan told her.

"I am grateful for the blessing of my blood, of my people."

Aidan bowed deeply before Heulyn.

"May you have a full and happy future," Aidan wished her.

"May the blessings of your people, the old and the new, protect you and guide you," Helge, who had witnessed the druidical rite without blinking, wished her.

The Panthers witnessed the ritual without really understanding what was happening. They knew that the Princess had Druid blood, but she had accepted to marry Thoran, renouncing her ancestry, or so they had understood. Maybe that was not the case? Had she asked her father for permission to reconcile herself with the Druids and that was why the King had brought Aidan? Anyway, all this was very strange, and the fact that the Princess suddenly had tattoos like a Druid was even odder.

Heulyn looked at Thoran.

"I am a Druid and I will always be," she told him, showing him her tattoos.

"You'll be the Queen of Norghana, Druid or not," Thoran said.

"I will be the Druid Queen," she replied defiantly.

Thoran opened his mouth to reply.

All of a sudden, several objects fell down from the ceiling and crashed on the floor, bursting with a sound of broken glass.

A brownish smoke began to issue from the broken objects, spreading throughout the room.

"We're under attack!" cried Ingrid.

They all prepared their weapons to repel the attack.

Chapter 37

"Royal Guard! Protect the King!" Commander Ellingsen ordered.

The Royal Guard surrounded the King in the middle of the hall, protecting him by forming a circular wall with their shields. The Commander was beside the King, giving orders.

"Rangers, repel the attack!" Raner, who had been left out of the circle, shouted as he armed his bow.

The Royal Rangers aimed their bows at the brownish smoke that did not let them see who was attacking them.

"At the end of the room Valeria and Aidan stood beside the Princess.

"With me, Princess," Valeria, with her bow ready, said to her.

The Panthers were looking in every direction, ready to release, but they could see no enemies. The brownish smoke was getting more solid and started filling the whole room. What had begun as a mist was now thick smoke-like fog that kept them from seeing anything.

"Watch out!" Astrid said to their comrades.

"I can't see anyone!" Nilsa cried.

"Where are the attackers?" Gerd asked, looking in every direction.

"Back-to-back," Molak said. "Maintain physical contact with each other."

They heard new objects hitting the floor. When they broke a violet substance came out that mingled with the smoke blinding them.

"This looks bad," Viggo said.

"How bad?" Astrid asked him.

"Very, very bad."

"Get the King out of here!" cried Commander Ellingsen, and they started to retreat to the room's entrance.

All of a sudden, the door to the room was closed from their side. The Commander saw it shut as if a ghost had pushed it.

"It's a trap!" he cried.

"Break down the door!" Thoran shouted. "Get me out of here!"

The Royal Guard started hitting the door to break it down.

At the end of the room the situation was no better.

"Valeria, Aidan, protect me, don't let them kill me," the Princess ordered.

"No-one's going to hurt you," Valeria promised.

"We're here to protect the Princess," said Aidan.

"Helge, is there a back door?" Valeria asked the priest.

"No… the front door is the only way in or out."

Aidan began to cast a spell on the floor where they were. Using his druidic magic, magic of the forests of Irinel, he created a huge butterfly the size of a person. The butterfly started to flap her wings in place and with her flapping pushed back the surrounding substance. She could not push it all back, but enough for the Princess to breathe uncontaminated air.

Beside her, the Panthers were trying to decide how to get out of that situation.

"Where are the attackers? Why aren't they attacking?" Molak asked.

"They're already doing so," Egil told him.

"Where?" Gerd wanted to know, looking everywhere without seeing a shadow.

"Put on your Rangers' scarves and cover your nose and mouth," Egil told them. "Valeria, Aidan, you too, use scarves or tear your clothes, the Princess as well."

"Is it violet gas? Is it toxic?" Ingrid asked, looking everywhere, trying to see the attackers.

"It's poison," Viggo confirmed.

"Do we make a run for the door?" Nilsa asked.

"The color is more violet in the middle, if we get any closer we'll die," Astrid said.

"Then what should we do? We can't just stay here, or we'll die regardless," said Molak.

"Shoot at the windows, we have to break them," said Astrid.

"Break them so the poisonous smoke goes out," cried Ingrid, understanding what Astrid intended.

While the Panthers released at the windows, the poison started affecting the room's occupants. Several Royal Guards collapsed to the floor. A moment later two Royal Rangers fell.

"Everyone, put on your scarves!" Raner ordered. "Your Majesty, don't breathe this air, it's poisoned," he warned the King.

Thoran searched desperately for a scarf, and when he did not find one Commander Ellingsen tore a piece off his jerkin and gave it to the King to use as a scarf.

"We have to get out of here! Break down the door!"

The Royal Guard was beating on the door, but it was solid oak and it did not yield.

On the other end of the room, things weren't going any better.

"The windows aren't breaking!" Ingrid said.

"They're made of ice or a hard crystal!" said Astrid.

"Use Elemental Arrows!" Valeria told them as she was already releasing one. "The explosions might break them!"

"Good idea! Everyone, Elemental Arrows!" Ingrid said.

Egil bent over and took out a jar. He soaked his scarf in the liquid it contained.

"Pass it on and pour it on your scarves."

Nilsa nodded and poured a little on her scarf before passing the container on to Gerd.

The Panthers were releasing against the windows with Fire, Earth, and Air Arrows. The detonations against the windows were beginning to have an effect. They started to crack.

"Come on, we're almost through!" Ingrid cheered them.

Molak's arrow broke one of the windows.

"One's broken!" he said.

Nilsa burst another into a thousand pieces.

Another one broken!"

They continued to shoot and Valeria broke a third one.

Everyone, shoot at the fourth one!" Ingrid said.

Eight arrows hit the window with their multiple detonations and the glass ended up breaking.

The poisonous smoke began to escape through the broken windows.

"We did it!" cried Nilsa.

A silhouette was coming down the wall behind the group like a spider, hidden by the brownish smoke which did not let them see it descending. It was entirely dressed in white and melted into the wall. Two knives were in its hands, also white.

At last, the Royal Guard knocked down the door.

"Get the King out of here!" the Commander shouted.

The Royal Guards still standing took the King out of the room into the next one beside the great fountain. There more Guards joined them.

The King was coughing and the Commander was too.

"Is... this... area safe?" he asked his men.

"Yes, sir, this is a safe area."

"Your Majesty, are you... all right?"

Thoran was coughing.

"Bring me the... surgeons!" he ordered.

Raner came out dragging one of his men. He looked around.

"Is it safe?"

Commander Ellingsen nodded.

"Area secured."

Another Royal Ranger came out, coughing.

"I'm going to get the rest out," said Raner and, adjusting his scarf better, went back inside.

The silhouette approached Princess Heulyn from behind. The smoke still covered them up to the waist. The assassin was crawling along the floor like a white viper.

The Panthers were looking at the ceiling and the exit that had just been cleared.

"Let's get out of here," Valeria said to the Princess.

"Let's all go, we'll protect the Princess to the exit," said Egil.

Ingrid and Nilsa went ahead with Molak, the three with their bows ready. Egil approached Valeria and Aidan.

"Let's get out of here, fast!" he told them.

At that instant, the white assassin came out of the brown smoke and lunged at the Princess' back.

"Death to the Druid Queen!" he shouted.

Heulyn turned and saw the white assassin coming at her with his knives pointed straight at her heart.

Aidan started casting, but he would never be able to stop the blow in time.

Valeria lifted her bow to release.

All of a sudden, at the speed of lightning, Viggo appeared between the Princess and the white assassin. He deflected the two knives with his own.

"You bastard!" the assassin cried as he tried a counterattack. Astrid appeared at his back and stabbed him in the side with her

327

knife.

The assassin roared with pain and tried to recover.

Valeria's arrow pierced through his heart.

"Get the Princess out of here, there might be more!" Ingrid shouted.

Valeria and Aidan grabbed the Princess and took her away. The Panthers followed behind them, walking backward, bows and knives ready in case another assassin came out of the smoke that still covered the room's entire floor and reached about three feet high.

Raner arrived at their side.

"Let's get out of here, fast, the other room is clear."

They managed to get out of the inner chamber. Helge had died from the smoke.

They reached the fountain and the Princess collapsed on the floor.

Valeria assisted her and Aidan gave her a restorative tonic he carried on him with some Druid magic.

"What happened in there? I want explanations!" King Thoran was shouting as he lay on the floor.

"It was a trap," said Raner.

"To kill me? Another attempt on my life?" Thoran was looking at all of them, searching for answers.

"They tried... to kill... me," Heulyn said, panting.

"You?" Thoran's eyes opened wide.

"Yes, there's a dead assassin at the end of the room that proves it."

"An assassin? Who killed him?"

"Your Royal Eagles," Heulyn said, not looking too grateful.

Thoran looked at the Panthers.

"What's happened? Explain!"

"Your Majesty, we've fallen into a very elaborate trap," Egil said. "We survived by a hair's breadth. They used a toxic gas mixed with another to prevent us from seeing what was going on while an assassin got close to the Princess from behind to kill her. At the last instant we detected the threat and were able to neutralize it."

"Are you sure they wanted to kill the Princess and not me?"

"The Princess was their target for sure. The assassin shouted 'death to the Druid Queen.' As for Your Majesty, it might have been they wanted both of you dead," Egil finished.

"Go in there and search the room!"

The Royal Guard went in and started searching. The toxic smoke was already fading.

"And bring me that assassin. I want to see his face!"

It was not long before they came out again carrying the dead assassin. They left him to one side.

The King stood up.

"He's wearing a white mask."

"Most likely to protect himself from the poisonous smoke," said Egil.

"Take it off!"

Commander Ellingsen took the mask off his face.

"He's a Zangrian!"

The assassin's features were undoubtedly Zangrian. He had dark skin, long dark hair, and bushy eyebrows. He was short and strong.

"I'm going to destroy that blasted kingdom! I won't leave a Zangrian alive!"

"Your Majesty, the fact that he's Zangrian doesn't necessarily mean he's working for them," Egil told him in a gentle tone.

"If it's white and it comes from a cow it can only be milk!" the King roared.

"Your Majesty, that's not always..." Egil started to say, but seeing the King's irate look he stopped. He was in no mood for reasoning.

"Arrest the whole Zangrian legation! Put them all in the Royal Dungeons!"

"Your Majesty... that's going to cause a political crisis..." Commander Ellingsen said.

"They've tried to kill the King of Norghana and the Princess, who is going to be the Queen of Norghana! That's what's going to cause a political crisis!" Thoran was shouting so loud that his words bounced off the walls of the temple.

"Commander, execute my orders! Arrest all the Zangrians in the capital!"

"All of them, Your Majesty?"

"All of them! Each and every one of them!" Thoran was beside himself with rage.

"It will be as you command..." Ellingsen said.

"This is unacceptable! An attempt on my life! At my own wedding!" Thoran had his hands on the crown. He seemed unable to accept what had happened.

"They've also attempted to kill me, also at my wedding," Heulyn noted.

"We've had several casualties, Your Majesty," said Raner. "Four members of the Royal Guard are dead, as well as three of my Royal Rangers."

"They will pay for this, I swear!" Thoran promised.

"I'll go and see what the outside is like and whether there's any danger," said Raner, who made a sign for the Royal Eagles to stay. He took three Royal Rangers and went outside the temple.

They recovered while they waited for Raner to come back. Inside there was no more danger, but the Royal Guard and Rangers watched closely.

Valeria looked at the Panthers and thanked them with a gesture.

Nilsa waved at her in return.

"Everything's clear outside," said Raner. "No one has noticed anything of what happened here."

"That's good," the King said suddenly.

"Good?" Heulyn asked with a look of disbelief on her face.

"No one knows what happened here. They needn't know," the King said, more to himself than for the others to hear.

"Of course, they have to know! My father has to know!" Heulyn cried.

"And he will. But not now. Now we'll proceed with the wedding as planned."

They all stared at the King, confused.

"Your Majesty… they just tried to kill you. You can't proceed with the wedding…" Ellingsen told him.

"I can, and I will," Thoran stated.

"It's very dangerous. There have already been two attempts on your life," Raner said.

"They won't expect me to have come out alive from this one. They won't expect me to go on with the wedding even if I came out alive. That's why I'm going ahead with it."

The Commander and Raner exchanged uneasy looks.

"You're right. They won't think we'll go ahead. They won't have anything planned in that event. Let's go on with the wedding," Heulyn joined the King.

"We'll come out as if nothing has happened. Leave a few guards to control the priests so they don't blabber," said the King.

"The Principal Priest is dead," Raner said.

"They can bury him tomorrow, once the wedding's over," the King said in a tone that implied he did not care in the least.

"Very well, Sire," Raner said, bowing his head.

"You, my Royal Eagles," the King addressed them, staring at them and pointing his finger at them, which made them nervous.

"Your Majesty?" said Ingrid.

"You've saved the Princess. I entrust you with her protection until I give you new orders. Nothing can happen to her."

"No way! I don't want them beside me!"

"They saved your life and always fulfill their missions. They've never failed me, not like the rest of those here," said Thoran, looking at Commander Ellingsen and Raner.

"I hate them. They kidnapped me from my homeland. They treated me like a prisoner. They laid their hands on me. They should be dead for that."

"That was on my orders. And they brought you to me like I asked them to."

"I don't want their presence near me. You know that. I've asked you for their heads several times!"

"And I have refused. If I had granted them to you, now you'd be dead."

"I have Valeria and Aidan with me! I don't need them!"

"You'll do as your King orders!" Thoran cried furiously.

Heulyn was about to reply, but seeing that Thoran was almost beside himself, she contained herself.

"I will obey my King."

"Very well," Thoran nodded, and he turned to the Panthers. "Protect her, that's a King's order."

"We will, Sire," Ingrid confirmed.

"And now we'll go back out, parade back to the castle, and the wedding will take place as if nothing happened," said Thoran.

"So it will be done, Your Majesty," Ellingsen said.

Chapter 38

The wedding continued its course as the King had ordered. There were no more incidents during the parade back to the castle. Thoran and Heulyn rode in the midst of the Invincibles as if nothing had ever happened. The people did not know either and enjoyed the parade, cheering and applauding and shouting with joy.

The ones who were more tense were the Panthers, who were not exactly thrilled with the new mission entrusted to them by the King. Who did seem to find the situation funny was Valeria, who was smiling openly at them. Now they would have to work with her. Life took many turns.

They reached the Royal Castle, and once inside and safe, Thoran and Heulyn dismounted. The rest waited their turn.

"Commander Ellingsen, take care of the Zangrian problem," the King told him.

"Right away, Your Majesty."

"We'll go straight to the Throne Hall for the ceremony," the King announced.

"I want to change my dress. This one smells horrible, and it's not the one I have for the wedding ceremony anyway," Heulyn told Thoran.

"We're not going to take any risks. We'll be safe in the Throne Hall. If you want to change, have them bring your dress there."

"I'm not going to change in the Throne Hall in front of everyone!"

"In the back room. The Eagles will make sure you're protected."

"That's unacceptable! I'm not going to change in a back room, and least of all in front of them!"

"Yes you will, because it's safer and because the King orders it!" Thoran shouted.

The Panthers exchanged looks among themselves unobtrusively. The King was intractable, and they all knew that in these situations it was best to stay away.

Thoran entered the castle, followed by the Royal Guard with Raner and the Royal Rangers. The Invincibles remained in the courtyard all lined up. Princess Heulyn followed the King, muttering under her breath.

A short while later, while the guests of the legations and the Norghanian nobles entered the Throne Hall for the ceremony, the Panthers waited in the back room for the Princess' dress to be brought.

The hall was silent. Heulyn threw them looks of hatred. Valeria and Aidan were right beside her. At last, two servant girls came with the dress and handed it to the Princess.

"About time!" the Princess shouted at them.

Valeria took the dress and examined it in case there was anything that might be dangerous, like a poisoned pin or something similar. She found nothing and handed it to the Princess.

"Go to the far end and don't look!" Heulyn ordered, indicating the opposite end of the room.

They all obeyed at once, and the Princess began to get dressed with the help of the two servant girls while she continued muttering curses under her breath.

"Well, we seem to be working together again," Valeria whispered with a wise smile.

"It looks that way," Ingrid said, serious.

"Molak, since when are you one of the Royal Eagles?" Valeria had noticed.

"Since a short time ago, things happen…" Molak said, bluffing.

"I'm sure you make a good Lasgol," she winked at him mischievously.

"I try," Molak shrugged.

"You've chosen a good substitute," Valeria said. "Molak is very good and loyal."

"Why do you care what we do?" Astrid asked in a tone that left their enmity very clear.

"I'm always interested in whatever you do. And now more so, since we have to work together."

"It won't be for long," Astrid snapped.

"What happened at the Temple, Egil?" Valeria asked straightforwardly.

"A trap. A very well planned and executed trap."

"Do you really think it was the Zangrians?"

"It's difficult to know, although the evidence suggests it. On the other hand though, the evidence is often planted or left on purpose as a distraction."

"Isn't it too complex for it to be a Zangrian trap? The Zangrians aren't precisely known for their brains," Valeria said, tapping her forehead.

"We'd have to investigate it in depth in order to get to the bottom of it and whoever has prepared it," said Egil. "It's not going to be easy to find the culprit, I'm afraid."

"Do you think it had anything to do with the poisoning of the King at the dinner?" Aidan said.

"It might, yes," Egil nodded.

"Both attacks have been with poison," Aidan reasoned. "It doesn't seem like a coincidence to me."

"What are you doing with the Princess, Aidan?" Ingrid asked, looking out of the corner of her eye to see whether Heulyn was listening. She was absorbed putting on her elegant dress and shouting at the two poor servant girls, who were doing everything they could to please her.

"The Princess required a Druid Guide. King Kendryk assigned me for this important task."

"Druid Guide?" Nilsa said blankly.

"The Princess wants to delve into her roots. She wished to explore her potential as a Druid. Being of the blood, that's within her rights. I have come with Druid Masters to help me in the task."

"Is she going to become a Druid like you?" Astrid asked, surprised.

"How much she wishes to delve into our roots and what she wants to become is her decision," Aidan said. "My task is to guide her through the forest under the designs of Mother Nature."

"But for that, apart from Druid blood, she must have the Gift..." said Astrid.

"That's right," Aidan confirmed. "Not all of Druid blood have the Gift, but many do."

Astrid looked at Egil, who was listening closely. If the Princess turned out to possess the Gift, many things could change.

"Oh well, I'd like to see her all tattooed like you and your people," said Viggo. "Particularly the face." He grinned roguishly.

"The tattoos mark the stages of growth of a Druid," Aidan said. "Only those who reach the higher and deeper levels tattoo their faces."

"I thought that perhaps you had come to take her away," said Egil. "There are rumors that the Druids want her back."

"Those rumors are true. That's why King Kendryk is allowing me to instruct her in the Druid way of life. It's a compromise. If my people see the Princess following our laws and culture, they might be content and we might avert problems."

"King Kendryk always finds a way to negotiate a way out," said Egil in a respectful tone.

"He's an intelligent King," Aidan said.

"Don't speak of my father!" the Princess ordered. She had gotten dressed and had heard their last words. She was wearing an elegant dress of green silk with white edging. She looked regal. "Not of him, or me, or anyone in my family!" Although her yelling made her lose that regal air.

"You look radiant," Aidan told her.

"Beautiful. A true Royal Princess," Valeria said flatteringly.

"And soon I'll be a true Queen," Heulyn said with determination.

"I'll see whether you can make your entrance," Valeria said, opening the door to the Throne Hall. "They're all waiting. You may enter, Your Highness."

"Good. Let's go then," the Princess said and motioned for Valeria and Aidan to lead the way.

They entered the Throne Hall and found it bursting. All eyes turned to watch Heulyn and her escort. Half the hall was filled by members of the legations which were all together, albeit a bit separated from one another, as if they were carriers of some disease unique to their kingdom or nation and no one seemed to want to touch anyone else. There was also the risk of a dagger in the back or side. The legations all had their bodyguards with them, tense and alert.

The Royal Guard and Rangers were watching them closely. They were also posted by the four walls and by the columns of the hall, controlling everything. There were not going to be any more attempts on the life of the King or his bride.

The other half of the room was crowded with the nobles of the Court. The principal nobles of the East, like Count Volgren, Duke Uldritch, Duke Oslevan, and other important lords were in attendance. And they were accompanied by their wives, children, and close relatives, as well as minor lords who served them. The most important lords were in the first rows, near the King's throne, and the minor lords were further back.

At the back of the area reserved for nobles were the Western Nobles. Duke Erikson was there, as were Duke Svensen and Count Malason, as well as some other minor lords of the West. They had to be there, since the King had invited them and if they did not come Thoran would suspect them. Their presence would not keep the King from suspecting them, but they wanted to avoid open conflict with Thoran. The Nobles of the West had to acknowledge their King and his new Queen whether they liked it or not, and that was why they were there, and to see how the wedding ended with the crowning of the new Queen.

King Thoran waited at the throne and beside that, a second one had been set for the new Queen. On King Thoran's right was his brother Orten, as well as Commander Ellingsen and First Ranger Raner.

On the left, in front of the throne Heulyn was going to occupy, was her family: King Kendryk, Queen Gwyneth, and Prince Kylian.

The Princess arrived before King Thoran and curtseyed. She remained waiting for her fiancé to offer her the throne.

The king descended from the throne and offered his hand to the Princess, who took it, then he accompanied her to the throne and helped her settle into it.

The Panthers, Valeria, and Aidan stood to the left of the throne, in front of the Royal Family of Irinel.

The ceremony began. The Royal Magistrate, Lansen, who was to officiate the wedding, waited to one side. He was a thin man with short, scant hair in his eighties and who was always in charge of the Kingdom's most important legal business. He was rarely seen, since he spent most of his time in his study at the castle with his magistrate assistants. He approached the King and Princess and greeted them formally.

"We are here today to witness the union in matrimony of King Thoran of Norghana and Princess Heulyn of Irinel," he said, loud and grave. "Today is a glorious day in which we will crown a new Queen of Norghana."

While Lansen gave his solemn speech to the guests as part of the ceremony, the Panthers were watching the crowded Throne Hall.

What surprised them was that none of the legations had left the castle after what had happened. With the exception of the Zangrian legation, which was under arrest, locked up in the castle dungeons.

"Why are they still here?" Gerd asked in a whisper. "I would've run back to my country."

"That's what I'm wondering too," said Nilsa. "The King has yelled at them and been disrespectful to them. I'd have thought they'd all leave, or almost all."

"Perhaps they're here out of a sense of duty," Ingrid said.

"Not of duty, my bellicose blondie," Viggo said, winking at her.

"Then why?"

"Because whoever leaves will look guilty, and Thoran has his armies surrounding the city. They wouldn't get far."

"It's not that..." Ingrid said, looking at Egil for confirmation.

"I'm afraid our suspicious friend is quite right," Egil said, smiling.

"See? Think wrong and you'll always be right," Viggo smiled, proud of himself.

"The monarchs and legations don't want to leave in the middle of the wedding after all that's happened, since Thoran and Orten would immediately suspect whoever did," Egil explained. "It's only natural. If there are assassination attempts on the King and future Queen, and the legations leave in the middle of it all, they would immediately be suspects."

"Yeah... it would be suspicious..." said Gerd.

"Very suspicious," Viggo raised his eyebrow.

"Well, they could all leave at once," said Ingrid. "That way, Thoran wouldn't know who to blame. They can't have all been in it together."

"That would require them to talk among themselves and reach an agreement, something which, as you've all seen, isn't going to happen now or in a near future," said Egil.

"That's true too," said Nilsa, rolling her eyes.

"They'll be wondering what happened to the Zangrian legation," Molak said. "Do you think they know about the attempt at the Temple?"

"In this city everyone knows everything, and more so now that it's teeming with spies. They all know. They also know that Thoran believes it was the Zangrians and that's why they've been arrested," Astrid said.

Egil nodded in agreement. "Very true."

"Let's see if this ends well…" Viggo said.

"Don't you start…" Ingrid chided.

"We have to protect the Princess, and it's not going to be easy," said Nilsa.

"She adores us because of what happened in Irinel," said Gerd.

"Do you always deal with such complicated matters?" Molak asked them. "I knew you got into trouble, but I never…"

"Bah, this is nothing. Wait until we involve you in killing the dragon," Nilsa told him.

"Killing the dragon? You're joking, aren't you?" Molak looked at Ingrid for an answer.

"I'm afraid it's no joke."

Molak became more serious than he usually was.

"Captain Fantastic has choked on the conversation," Viggo whispered, chuckling.

"That would happen to anyone who comes with us," Astrid defended him. "Don't worry, Molak, you're ready for that and a lot more."

"I hope so," Molak nodded. The ceremony went on, and Lansen gave way to the traditional exchange of gifts between the bride and groom.

"Now the couple may exchange gifts, as is traditional at Norghanian weddings." Lansen announced.

"I respectfully offer you this gift," the Princess of Irinel said and called for her gift for Thoran. A servant approached and handed the gift to Heulyn so she could offer it to the King. It was wrapped in a green cloth and relatively large.

Thoran removed the green cloth and revealed a Norghanian war axe with gold and jewels worthy of a warrior king. It was a beautiful, lethal weapon, and it had obviously been crafted by a well-known artist.

"It's a beautiful weapon… magnificent," Thoran said, handling the weapon and weighing it as he inspected it.

"May this weapon lead you to many conquests in future years."

"Thank you. It will, I'm sure." Thoran was delighted with his war axe, which he was still brandishing.

Heulyn was waiting for her gift. Thoran was enjoying his axe so much that he seemed to have forgotten they were in the middle of the ceremony. His brother, who did not take his eye off the weapon, cleared his throat loudly. Thoran noticed.

"Oh yes. Here, brother, look after it for me," he said and handed him the axe.

"With pleasure," Orten said as he too studied the weapon.

"The gift," Thoran called, and a servant brought it at once.

"Your Majesty," the servant offered it to him.

Thoran took it. It was a wooden box lined with red and white velvet.

"I respectfully offer you this gift," Thoran said and handed it to her.

Heulyn took the box, which was two hand-spans by two, and opened it. She took out of it a beautiful gold necklace with a dozen huge rubies that shone red when hit by the light. The attendants muffled sighs of admiration at the sight of such a jewel. It must have cost a fortune.

"It's... it's beautiful..." Heulyn mumbled.

"My Queen deserves no less. Allow me to put it on," Thoran said as he stood behind Heulyn and placed the huge necklace around her neck. The attendants applauded the amazing gift. The King and Queen of Irinel were nodding proudly. They found the gift up to the standard they felt their daughter deserved, and also themselves as her parents.

"It's exquisite, spectacular," Heulyn said, unable to take her eyes off the valuable necklace.

"And now, the signing of the Royal Document so the wedding celebrated today is registered for future generations," Lansen announced.

Ambassador Larsen appeared, accompanied by Counselor Kacey. Larsen was carrying a Royal Scroll and King Thoran's seal, and Kacey had the King of Irinel's seal. They were followed by two servants, who carried a wooden lectern and a box with quill and ink. They placed the lectern before Thoran and Heulyn.

Larsen set the Royal Scroll in front of them with the wedding contract.

"Sign here, Your Highness," he told Heulyn first, indicating where she had to sign.

The Princess looked at her father, King Kendryk, who nodded affirmatively. Then she looked at Thoran, who waited, smiling at her.

Heulyn heaved a sigh and signed the document.

Then it was the King's turn.

"Here, Your Majesty," Larsen indicated.

The King signed.

Larsen called Duke Orten forward, who stepped up and signed the document as a witness. Then Larsen called King Kendryk, who also stepped up and signed as a witness.

Larsen gave the Royal Seal to Thoran, who softened it with a candle and then stamped it on the Royal Document. Kacey did the same with the Royal Seal of Irinel, and King Kendryk stamped the document as well.

Finally, the royal magistrate signed the document on the back with the date.

"It is official. The union is completed," Larsen announced in a powerful tone. "I hereby present you the King and Queen of Norghana!"

King Thoran placed the crown on Queen Heulyn's head.

"Long live the King!" Orten cheered.

"Long live!" cried all the nobles.

"Long live the Queen!" cried Orten.

"Long live!" everyone cheered.

Thoran motioned Heulyn to stand to receive the cheers.

"I present to you the new   Queen of Norghana!" Thoran cried.

"Hail the Queen!" the nobles cried.

"Hail the Druid Queen!" cried someone from among the legations.

There was a moment of hesitation. Then the Nobles of the West hesitated no more.

"Hail the Druid Queen!" they cried.

Thoran sat in the throne beside his Queen. He waved his hand for the cheering to continue.

"Hail the Druid Queen!" everyone cheered.

Chapter 39

Lasgol, Ona, and Camu were before the White Pearl, above the Lair at the Shelter. Loke, the Masig Specialist, was with them.

"Are you sure that's what you want to do, Lasgol?" Loke said in a concerned tone.

"I am. Don't worry, everything will be fine," Lasgol promised.

"Sigrid has entrusted me with the surveillance of the Pearl, and she hasn't said anything about you wanting to use it…"

"You wouldn't want to stop me?"

"I'm not stopping you. I'm only saying it might be dangerous, and as far as I understand, nothing must be done with the Pearl in case of what might happen. Apart from that, you outrank me. I couldn't stop you from doing anything."

"Let him use it," a voice said at Loke's back, who turned to see who it was. Enduald and Galdason were coming up from the Lair. It was the dwarf who had spoken.

"Are you sure it's the best thing to do?" Loke seemed unsure.

"It is, let him use it," Galdason said, joining Enduald.

Both Magi arrived at the top.

"Hello Lasgol, Camu, Ona," Galdason greeted them with a kind smile.

Enduald raised his hand in greeting but simply grunted a "hello."

"I'm glad to see you both in good health."

"And a little bored and frustrated," Galdason said. "No Specialists in training, and we're not making advances with the Pearl's magic."

"I assume Sigrid has told you about the Pearls and Camu, hasn't she?"

Enduald nodded.

"It was important information we needed to understand."

"We're studying it," Galdason added.

"It's good that someone else, apart from us, is investigating the power of the Pearls," Lasgol said. "Someone with the Gift. I'm sure you'll make advances," Lasgol encouraged them, happy to have help on this matter.

"I'm not that sure. Our magic isn't like the Creature's," Enduald said with a wave toward Camu.

"The Pearl doesn't respond to our magic," said Galdason. "At least it hasn't so far."

"You think that people with the Gift can interact with the Object of Power even if the type of magic is different?"

"It's one of the things we want to find out," Enduald nodded.

"Magic is universal. We should be able to find the way to bypass the type of magical restriction required to activate the Portal," Galdason explained.

"I hope you're successful," Lasgol wished them.

"How come you're here? What are your plans?" Enduald asked, indicating the Pearl.

"You see, we have to go to the Kingdom of Moontian, urgently. That's in the mid-east, far to the east. We believe that with the Portal we could get there and return quickly."

"Interesting theory," Galdason said. "It might work, indeed."

"If there's a Pearl in the east," Enduald noted.

"That's true. Do you know that there is one?" Galdason asked.

Camu shook his head.

"We don't know," said Lasgol. "That's what we want to find out. We believe that the Pearls are located all over Tremia. There should be one in the east."

"An educated guess, but a guess in the end," Enduald said doubtfully.

"Will Camu be able to find the pearl you're guessing is in the east?" Galdason asked.

I can, Camu messaged to all.

Loke threw his head back in awe.

"Well, we'll have to wait and see," Lasgol said.

"In any case, it will be good for us if Camu can open a Portal. That way we'll be able to interact and analyze the magic that rules the Portal," said Galdason.

"Yea, that's better, much better," said Enduald.

Open portal no problem, Camu messaged.

"Go ahead then," Galdason said with anticipation.

"Wait, I have something that might help you," Enduald said and headed back to the Lair.

They waited for Enduald to come back. Given his short height he was not very fast, especially when he had to go down and climb back up again from the Lair, so they waited impatiently. When he came back, he showed a tome to Lasgol.

"This old tome tells about the Kingdom of Moontian, and there's also a small map. It's not very detailed and it's many years old, but it might come in handy when you get there."

"Thank you very much! I'm sure it'll be quite useful," Lasgol glanced at the map. It was indeed quite poor and old, but it would serve them. He put the tome into his rucksack.

"Camu, please, open the Portal," Lasgol said.

I open, Camu closed his eyes and concentrated. There was a silver flash that ran throughout his body. Two more flashes followed, and Camu started sending silver pulses to the great object in a steady rhythm. He had found the correct timing in the pulses he sent to activate it, so Lasgol watched the process calmly.

The Pearl responded with a big silver flash… and shortly after the portal began to take shape above it.

Start open.

Above the Pearl, three circular silver shapes began to form. First, a circle of the same size took shape. Then a second one more elliptical and bigger, and finally, the form turned into a huge silver sphere.

Portal almost open.

Perfect. Concentrate on catching the rune that indicates the Pearl more to the east of the continent if possible.

I try. Not easy.

I know, but it's the only way we'll reach the Kingdom of Moontian fast. You need to catch a rune-destination that's on the east of Tremia.

Okay, Camu concentrated and started to manipulate the portal with his energy. *Catch rune-destination here.*

Very well. Seek other rune-destinations, Lasgol asked him.

Camu concentrated and searched for the runes in the middle of the portal.

Find rune-destination Desert. Also Reborn Continent.

Try to find a rune that points to a Pearl in the east.

Camu was silent for a long moment.

I find rune.

East? Are you sure?

East yes. No sure.

All right. We'll have to risk it.

Rune-destination chosen, he messaged Lasgol, indicating the Portal was ready.

"Loke, if you please, look after Trotter, I'm not going to take him through the Portal. Also of Milton, he's with him."

"Don't worry, I'll take good care of both of them."

"And watch that nothing comes out of the Portal that isn't us."

"Like a dragon, you mean?" Loke said, frowning.

"Yeah, like a dragon, or something similar."

"If it does, I'll alert everyone in the capital."

"Thanks. I don't recommend facing him."

"We won't. Not without reinforcements," Enduald promised.

"Our attack magic isn't very powerful," Galdason said regretfully.

"What's important is finding a way to defeat the dragon. Anything you might find on that topic is welcome."

"We'll try," said Galdason.

Enduald nodded and gave a little grunt.

"Now that the Portal is open, we'll be able to study it better."

"Good luck!" Lasgol said.

"And to you," Loke wished.

Come on, let's go in, Lasgol transmitted to Ona and Camu.

Ona was the first to go into the sphere in two big leaps. Camu followed, climbing along the Pearl. Lasgol was pushed up by Loke, and he entered the Portal.

Lasgol woke up with a terrible headache and quite dizzy. He felt terrible; it was the same feeling he already knew, as if he had been run over by a stampede of wild horses. He knew that he had probably thrown up and that it would take him a while to recover, so he did not hurry. He took it in stride.

Everything well? he transmitted as soon as he was capable of using his Gift, his eyes still closed.

Everything well. Not danger, easy, Camu messaged.

That made him feel at ease. He waited until he felt somewhat better and opened his eyes. He noticed something was off. They were in a hole beside the Pearl.

That's funny.

A little.

The Pearl seemed to be in the bottom of a deep, round depression instead of on a hill, which made it impossible to see in the distance. It was as if someone had dug out a large round hole to deposit the Pearl inside.

Let's climb out and see where we are, Lasgol transmitted after checking the hole.

Ona was already climbing the side and reached the rim in a flash. She did not make any sound of alarm, so Lasgol and Camu climbed up after her, unworried. Ona was looking around and disappeared as she moved away from the rim.

When Lasgol reached the surface, a breath of powerful breeze hit him and he almost fell back in. He had to bend over to withstand the strength of the breeze. He realized that it was not a regular breeze but a sea breeze. He looked in the direction from which the wind was blowing and the smell of the sea reached him at once. They were at the top of a high cliff that dropped into the sea.

Careful not fall in sea.

Ona was looking at the ocean from the top of the cliff with the breeze ruffling her fur.

Cliff very high. Lot of sea.

Yeah, that's the ocean, it has to be the eastern sea… and that land you see in the distance… Lasgol was thoughtful. He could see an island in the distance. Only it looked walled and had towers. Then he realized. It was the City-State of Galdar, that belonged to the Confederation of Free Cities of the East.

Know where be? Camu asked.

I think so. That must be the island city of Galdar. It's the only one of the five cities not built on the coast but on an island, I calculate we're at the end of the continent, on the east coast, off the island of Galdar. Therefore, in the upper center.

Near?

I'm afraid we've overreached our shot. We're more to the east than we wanted and more to the north. But we're a lot closer than before. Irinel is to the north and west of here. Therefore Moontian has to be south and west.

Not very far?

Not much. It'll take us a few days.

I good. Find Pearl east.

You don't say, although a little further and we would've come out in the eastern sea.

Pearl be this. I not put.

Yeah, that's true. You did very well.

Ona chirped once.

A little strange this place, don't you think? Lasgol said, looking at the hole and how close it was to the cliff's edge. There were only five paces from it.

Ona moaned once.

Pearl down not up. Weird.

Yes, very. It's as if it were hidden. You can't see it from below.

Almost in water.

That too.

I good work then.

Yeah. Anyway, we need to make sure of where we are. I don't think I'm mistaken, but I'm not completely sure either. My guess is based on what I've seen on maps and on the assumption that we're east, at the end of the continent.

How be sure?

We'll do it the old-fashioned way.

How that be?

Asking, Lasgol smiled.

Camu nodded his head and wagged his long tail, happy.

Let's follow the southwest path. Moontian is to the south and its territory reaches the Central Sea, so if we are where I think we are, we should find the kingdom or the sea if we keep going south.

Okay.

Ona chirped once.

They started going south. The landscape was not different from that of Irinel. There were some higher hills than the few they had seen there. Green landscapes of grass-covered plains were all the eye could see. There were no big forests either that they could see so far. They walked all day until night fell. They encountered a few single oaks and camped under one of them. The temperature was warmer than in Norghana, quite warmer. They did not need a fire so Lasgol did not make one. They rested peacefully. Lasgol was happy to be back out in the field, exploring new lands he did not know. He had always really enjoyed that, and having the chance to do it again was gratifying. That it was for such serious matters muddied the experience a little, but he decided to look on the positive side of the situation. They were exploring a faraway, foreign land, and that was wonderful.

With the first lights of dawn Ona was already prepared to go on, so Lasgol and Camu woke up and set out. They continued south. For two days they saw no one. Only plains and some scant forests. No villages, farms, or traces of civilization.

On the third day at last they saw people. A cart drawn by two mules appeared in the distance, and in it was a man. He looked like a peddler.

Hide, Lasgol told Camu and Ona as he went to intercept the man.

The peddler, when he saw Lasgol running over to him, stopped his cart and waited for him.

"Good morning, do you speak my language?" Lasgol asked.

The peddler shook his head and replied in a strange language.

Lasgol gave him a blank look. The peddler tried in two other languages. Lasgol felt somewhat dumb because he did not understand any of the languages. He thought they must be the languages of the City-States of the East which, of course, Lasgol did not know.

In order to be able to communicate, Lasgol asked him very slowly for Moontian. He pronounced it as clearly as he could. Realizing the peddler did not understand him, he tried to pronounce it with the accent of Irinel, which was quite peculiar.

"Moontian," the peddler said at last, nodding with an accent Lasgol finally understood.

"Where?" Lasgol asked, indicating several directions with his finger.

The peddler stood up in his cart and pointed west and a little to the south. He pointed for a long moment so that Lasgol would understand.

"Thank you! Thank you very much!" Lasgol told him, and he gave him a few coins from his pouch.

The peddler stared at the coins in surprise. He studied them front and back. Then he bit them. He seemed to like them, because he went away very pleased with a broad smile.

If the peddler was happy, Lasgol was even more so. He now knew where he had to go.

Come on, I know which way it is.

Much wonderful.

It took them several days to glimpse the large mountain range in the distance. Now there was no doubt. They were in the territory of Moontian. Those were the famous mountains of the kingdom.

They went on walking and soon they saw several farms in the distance.

People, Camu warned.

I see them. You and Ona stay back and camouflaged, I'll go and ask.

Be careful.

Don't worry, they're only farmers.

Lasgol approached the first farm and saw two people tilling the land. They looked like father and son. Lasgol had expected to find people with red hair, white skin, and   freckles, like the people of Irinel. He was completely wrong. Their skin was violet and their eyes a soft pink. Their faces were a bit rough, but the combination of violet-hued skin and pink irises made them look beautiful. They had no hair on their heads; they wore them clean-shaven and their faces were wide. They were all wide. In some funny way they looked bloated. They were of medium height, leaning toward short compared to a Norghanian, but with those bodies, they gave the impression of being very strong.

When they saw Lasgol the two farmers grew uneasy.

"Please don't worry, I just want to ask you some questions," Lasgol said, lifting his hands and showing them his palms.

Father and son grabbed their hoes as weapons. The father spoke in his language which Lasgol could not understand. They did not understand what Lasgol was trying to ask them from a prudent distance.

The exchange of words did not seem to be working, so Lasgol picked up a nearby stick and began to draw a map of Tremia. Father and son watched him and gradually realized what the drawing represented. Lasgol was pointing his stick to where he believed he was. After a while of pointing, asking, and gesticulating, it seemed the father understood Lasgol's plight.

He came over and pointed his finger at where they were. It turned out they were quite close to where Lasgol thought he was, but more to the south, almost at the sea. He thanked them for their help with smiles and thankful gestures they seemed to understand.

Now that he knew where he was, he had to find the place where Riagain and his men lived. It had to be some kind of fort or fortress type of dwelling his men could defend. The problem was, Lasgol had no idea where in the whole kingdom he might be. He needed a large city to be able to ask for someone who spoke Norghanian.

Lasgol remembered Enduald's tome and took it out. He had completely forgotten that he had it in his rucksack. He showed them the map where a majestic mountain range was drawn with several cities on its sides with strange names. Lasgol indicated to the father what looked like the biggest city, which was usually the capital of the kingdom.

The father understood. He pointed his finger to the northeast. Then he showed Lasgol three fingers, which Lasgol guessed it meant it would take him three days to reach the city.

Lasgol thanked the man again and left.

We're almost there.

Pretty people here.

Pretty? But they all look bloated and they're violet.

Much pretty.

Lasgol was puzzled.

I'm glad you like them.

Ona chirped once. She also liked them.

They walked at a good pace and in two days and a half they found themselves before the great city of Enmemounte, the capital of Moontian. The city was carved out of the side of the great mountain that seemed to have no end. Whether you looked east, west, or to the sky, it was always there: an endless mountain range. The houses seemed to be hanging from the side of mountain, piled on top of one another. It was a city built entirely on the side of the great mountain. There were thousands of houses, mostly small ones. It looked like a beehive of gray rock.

They watched the strange city for a good while from the road that led to it.

Funny city. I never in my whole life thought I'd see something like that.

Much weird. House on stone.

Ona, on the other hand, seemed to like it. She was wagging her long tail from side to side.

The time has come to find Riagain, Lasgol announced.
Find and get fire bow. That right do.

Chapter 40

Lasgol left Camu and Ona outside the city beside a stream that ran through a small forest of birches. They both wanted to go to the great city in the mountain, but Lasgol knew it was not a good idea. Better that he went first and tried to get the information they needed. He was going to draw enough attention as it was without adding Camu and Ona. Camu insisted on going under camouflage, but there were a lot of people and if Ona left the range of the camouflage, it would be dangerous. Better not to risk it.

He was not mistaken in his appreciation. Already at the entrance to the city, which was at the foot of a steep, long ramp uphill, he saw a multitude of locals crammed into the place. While other cities had streets, here they were stretches carved out of the rock of the side of the mountain which went into the mountain, or steps that went to upper levels. Everything was carved out of the side of the mountain.

The first complication arrived quickly, before he even entered the city. At the beginning of the great ramp that went up to the lower part of the capital, he encountered two huge monoliths built of rock that presided the entrance and about thirty armed guards who controlled access to the city.

He was stopped. Lasgol noticed that the soldiers had the same bloated appearance as the farmer he had met, only the muscles on their arms and legs were more noticeable. They wore golden breastplates and a skirt of metallic plates that came down to their knees. Their legs had greaves and their arms had vambraces, and the violet skin and bloated look was even more apparent in the soldiers. They also wore a square helmet, flat and without a visor so their beautiful eyes of different shades of pink could be seen. They were armed with large rectangular shields which covered them from neck to ankle. As weapons they carried picks and thick, heavy hammers which they wielded like the Norghanian war axes.

Lasgol noticed they were a people born in the mountain. The war picks and hammers they wielded indicated it. He tried to communicate with them but had no luck. No matter how much he mimed that he wanted to enter the city, he could not make himself understood, or at least that was what it looked like from the incomprehensive looks on the soldiers' faces. What was clear was that they were not going to let him in.

After a while of fruitless conversations, an old man appeared accompanied by a soldier. The old man did have hair, and it was very curly and entirely white. Lasgol could not tell his age, since with their violet skin they all looked much younger than what they really must be. By his hair and slow gait, he seemed very old. Another thing that surprised him about the old man was that he did not look bloated like the younger people, but that he had become emaciated, by age Lasgol guessed, or from some illness.

The old man stood before Lasgol and spoke to him in several languages. Lasgol did not understand, so he shook his head

"Where are you from?" he suddenly asked in Norghanian, and at last Lasgol was able to understand him.

"I'm Norghanian," Lasgol replied quickly before the man jumped to another language.

The old man smiled and nodded.

"I was running out of languages to try," he said in good Norghanian.

"They were enough, a sign that you are a cultivated man," Lasgol praised him.

"Rather than cultivated, an aficionado of foreign languages and tongues. I've always loved them."

"Unfortunately, languages aren't my thing," Lasgol apologized, feeling bad for not knowing the local lingo and, in fact, nothing of that picturesque culture.

The old man looked him up and down and noticed the composite bow Lasgol was carrying at his back.

"Are you a hunter?" he asked.

"Something like that, yes," Lasgol answered. He did not want to get into details as to who he was and what he was doing there.

"My name is Minotem. I'm the interpreter of the gate to the mountain," he said, pointing at the two large monoliths.

"I am Lasgol."

Minotem bowed his head in greeting and Lasgol imitated him.

"Our beloved city of Enmemounte," he said, indicating it behind his back, "is not open to foreigners. That's why the guards wouldn't let you in."

"Oh… pity… I needed to get in."

"May I ask what for? I might be able to help you."

Lasgol thought for a moment about what to say. The man was being kind and most likely did not mean him any harm, but it was always better to be wary.

"I'm looking for someone."

"In our great city? In the depths of the Mother Mountain?"

"Yes, that's right."

"Is it one of our own? Someone from Moontian?"

"No, he's a foreigner just like me."

"Norghanian?"

"No, from the kingdom of Irinel."

The old man nodded repeatedly.

"I understand that the person you seek lives in the city."

"I don't know whether he lives in the city, but he does live in the kingdom. I need to know where I can find him. I thought maybe someone in the city might know."

"I see… it must be something important if you've come all the way from Norghana…"

"Very important indeed," Lasgol said urgently.

"All right, let me talk to the guards."

The old man spoke to the guards in their language for a moment. To Lasgol's surprise, the guards were nodding to what the interpreter was saying, and then they moved back, leaving the way clear.

"Can I come in?"

The old man nodded.

"You can, but accompanied," he said and jabbed his thumb at himself and at the guards.

"Oh, I see, thank you."

"You are welcome. Come, I'll show you the way. Our city is beautiful, but foreigners find it a little difficult."

Lasgol began to follow the old man while he was talking and fell in stride with him. After them came three guards.

"Difficult?" Lasgol asked, looking at the houses that appeared to be hanging from the rock, as if they were glued to them by some magical means. Actually, they were chiseled on the wall's rocky face. Between groups of houses, he could see corridors that went into the mountain, and numerous stairs and passes between the different heights of the frontal constructions that went up all along the skirt of the mountain to the higher parts.

"Yes, our houses are built mostly on the face of the mountain, without going in too deep. This makes conventional streets quite difficult."

Lasgol was looking at the city as they were going up the ramp to the first houses, the ones at ground level. From there on they started surging row upon row of houses, ones on top of the others, all hanging from the great mountain. The height the higher houses had to be at, the ones that the eye lost looking up to the top of the mountain, struck him dumb.

"A most peculiar way of building," said Lasgol when he could speak.

"We, the Moontians, are the people of the mountain: the ones who live on its outer side."

"Impressive," said Lasgol when they got closer and he started to realize what they had built there. It was breathtaking.

"Isn't it indeed? Foreigners are usually awestruck. My people do not understand any other way of living and don't appreciate it in all its worth."

"They don't travel much?"

The old man stopped and laughed.

"My people never leave their sacred mountain," he said, indicating the endless mountain range that spread for leagues in both directions. "We live and die here."

"But the mountain can't feed thousands of people…"

"True. We have farmers, woodcutters, fishermen, and other professions which must live away from the Mother Mountain. But, when the time comes, they leave their houses and come here. They spend the last days of their existence resting in the depths of the Mother, and they are looked after and respected for their sacrifice. They are rewarded like this for having had to live away."

"Very interesting."

"That's why at the lower levels of the mountain, toward the inside, you'll see many old people like me," he said, smiling.

"I see. A fascinating culture."

"I would say so, yes, compared to other civilized kingdoms. Only a few travel, and it is usually for state reasons."

"Political reasons?"

"Indeed. In fact, right now our Ambassador is in Norghana, attending King Thoran's wedding."

"True. The Grand Wedding." Lasgol was surprised the old man was aware of what went on in Norghana, or that he even knew where their Ambassador was, if he was a mere interpreter of the gate.

They arrived at the foot of the majestic mountain where the first houses were. It had taken them quite a while since the old man walked slowly. Lasgol saw the women of the Kingdom of Moontian and was surprised. They had the same look, somewhat bloated like the men, although not as much, and it gave their bodies a curvy look. They appeared beautiful and delicate, their skin a pale violet with pink irises pink lips, and faces with beautiful features. They were very attractive women.

"The beauty of our women is something we are very proud of as a people," the interpreter said, noticing Lasgol's surprised look.

"Oh... forgive me... I didn't mean to offend, it's just that..."

"Nothing to forgive. It's the usual reaction of foreigners at the sight of them."

"If the older people live below, inside, who lives up at the top?" Lasgol asked, looking at the higher houses that reached the top of the range.

"At the top lives Queen Niria, at the highest point, as corresponds to her position. A little below her live the nobles. Then the craftsmen, artists, and traders. In the middle live young families with children, and further below the soldiers. At the very bottom, the old people."

"As a friend of mine would say: fascinating."

"Come, I'll take you to see Mostiais."

"Who's that?"

"He's the Officer of Permits. If there is a nobleman of Irinel living among us, he will have had to extend the permit and will know where he is."

"Oh, thank you so much!" Lasgol said.

"You are welcome. Follow me. Be careful where you step. We have to go up to the middle levels and our paths might be dangerous for you."

"I'll be careful."

Lasgol was even more surprised as they went up the stairs and stone catwalks between the countless houses that covered the whole outer side of the mountain. They did not go deep into the mountain itself, but Lasgol could see the massive number of people in the houses and squares inside. They even had waterfalls that fell from different sections down several floors to form ponds. He also saw fountains, which amazed him. He had the impression that, further into the mountain, where they had dug out the stone, they held some kind of mystery.

The people they passed by stared at him intrigued, especially the children, who followed Lasgol to look at him better. It was clear that not many foreigners came here. What was odd was that they did not need handrails, ropes, or railings of any kind to hold onto and not fall from that great height. They all moved as if it were impossible to lose footing or balance and fall into the void. That impressed him a lot.

On several occasions Lasgol had to stop and be careful where he put his foot next, because the stairs suddenly split into three, and even four new stretches of stairs that went up to various places. He wondered at the calm and steadfastness with which Minotem went up those steep stairs. It had something to do with the odd bodies they had and with a whole life living up there. Lasgol's legs were beginning to feel tired, not for the effort, but because he was not used to climbing so many stone stairs.

He also noticed that on each level or row of houses they reached there were soldiers on guard duty. They were unmistakable with those enormous rectangular shields, their flamboyant armor, and their square helmets. The picks and hammers they carried as weapons were a lot more lethal than the ones the workers carried. Also, most of the people he saw were dressed in short woolen tunics of different colors. They all wore thick boots though. Lasgol thought of how hard it would be for an invading army to conquer this city. It was like a huge wall of thirty floors which could not be knocked down, only climbed, and they would have to climb and take it floor by floor. He could not imagine any army managing that. Shooting with bows and crossbows would not work either, since the people would only need to take a couple of steps back and seek shelter in their houses of stone.

At last, they arrived at an intermediate area where Minotem turned left and went into the mountain. Lasgol followed him and noticed that, although the mountain had caves, what they had done was enlarge them to build houses of rock inside them. He could hear incessant tapping everywhere, as if they were always working to enlarge that immense city of rock.

"That tapping we hear, does it ever stop?" he asked Minotem.

"Tapping? Oh, I see what you mean. No, it never stops. We're always working on improving the city. But it doesn't bother us. We're so used to it that we don't hear it anymore."

"I can understand," said Lasgol as he watched another gang with their picks heading to a higher level.

They arrived at a stone house carved on the rock of the mountain itself and which had a slab for a door. Chiseled above the door were some strange words Lasgol could not understand.

"It's here," Minotem said, and he called out to Mostiais in a loud voice.

A moment later the slab moved to one side with a system of pulleys and chains.

Lasgol looked at the strange door with wide eyes.

They went in and Minotem spoke to Mostiais in their own language. The conversation took a while, and Lasgol could not tell whether it was going well or not because neither of the two men expressed much on their faces or tone of voice. He had to wait.

At last, Mostiais took out some scrolls and read them for a while, searching for something. He seemed to find it and indicated it to Minotem, who read it in turn.

The two men seemed to say goodbye. Mostiais examined Lasgol from head to toe.

"I have the information you wanted," Minotem said.

"Fantastic!"

"Well, not so much."

"No?"

"Let's talk outside," Minotem indicated the way out.

Lasgol nodded and let the old man go out first and then followed him outside.

"This noble from Irinel is under the protection of Queen Niria."

"Oh, I see."

"If your visit should disturb him in any way, you'll be in great trouble."

"The guards?" Lasgol eyed the escort who had followed them silently all along the ascent.

"Indeed. They will throw you into a dungeon in the deepest part of the mountains. It's not a pleasant experience. You spend a lot of time inside and there is no light."

"I see, I see," Lasgol said, using his hands to convey understanding.

"Very well. The house you're looking for is in the fifteenth row beginning at the top. It's on the left-hand side," he said, pointing upward. "You'll recognize it because it's a large house with foreign guards."

Lasgol nodded.

"Thank you very much for your help."

"I hope everything goes well."

"So do I. It's been a pleasure meeting you and your people," Lasgol said, looking around where several women were watching him, whispering while rolling their eyes and moving their pink lips.

"I will go back to my duties by the gate," the old man said. He signaled to the guard to go back with him and they vanished in a moment down the stairs.

Lasgol was left alone. He approached the edge and looked at the houses below that went down to the foot of the mountain at a great distance. The time had come to act. He had a bad feeling, as if he were betraying the old interpreter. After all, he was here to steal a priceless, bow. He justified his intentions by telling himself it was terribly important to obtain the bow, but somehow, he felt like he was betraying the hospitality he had been offered. Furthermore, once they knew what he had done, they would be even more against foreigners and letting them in.

He sighed. He did not want to steal, but he had no choice.

Or maybe he did.

Chapter 41

Lasgol went down the stairs until he reached the base of the great mountain. All the locals stared at him and whispered. The children crowded around him. He arrived at the great ramp that led to the two monoliths that formed the gate and went down a little along the ramp. Several groups of soldiers who were watching the base of the mountain eyed him warily.

He concentrated, closing his eyes. He searched for his inner energy and, once he located it in the pool in his chest, he took a good amount, more than he actually needed, and called on his *Animal Communication* skill, amplifying its reach, which consumed more than the energy required for the skill.

Camu, do you get my message? he sent as far as he could.

A moment later the answer reached him, albeit a little weak.

Get it...

Camouflage and come a little closer so we can communicate better, Lasgol transmitted.

Another moment went by.

I closer, the message reached Lasgol a lot clearer.

Perfect. Listen carefully, I have a plan.

I listen.

Good. It has two parts. Plan A and Plan B. I need you for Plan B.

I plan B, understand.

Night was falling on the great city of Enmemounte, and Lasgol was standing in front of Riagain's house. It had taken him an eternity to climb to that level, and his calf muscles were sore and knotted. Finding the house had been easy once he had reached that row of buildings. It was the only one with Irinelian guards. The torches and oil lamps had been lit and the whole cave shone with the metallic glow of thousands of small lights. It made a quaint effect.

The time had come to put his plan in action. He left his weapons and rucksack in a corner. He was not going to need them for now.

He went to the entrance of the great house, which was like a small palace, only inside a huge cave, and made entirely of rock. It had two turrets, one on each side of the main door. The only thing that made him a little nervous was the fact that the door and the turrets opened directly from the edge. If he was pushed, he would fall into the void and break all the bones in his body.

The guards in front of the door and those who were in the turrets looked at him in surprise. Lasgol assumed they had not seen a foreigner in a long time. They stopped him and Lasgol stood still before the two guards. They started asking questions, but since they spoke the language of Irinel Lasgol did not understand what they were saying, although he could guess by their gestures and looks of confusion.

"Riagain," he said calmly.

The guards began to protest and make clear denial signs.

"Riagain," Lasgol repeated, and this time he added another name: "Kendryk."

The mention of the King of Irinel caught the attention of the guards.

"Norghanian," Lasgol said, pointing at himself.

The guards exchanged a doubtful glance. That had piqued their attention. Lasgol was trying to create doubt and interest with the mention of the King's name and saying he was Norghanian. The guards might think that something had happened to the King in Norghana, and that would interest their lord. Besides, the fact that a Norghanian had appeared there, knocking at his door in that remote corner of Tremia, was most disconcerting, so their lord would want to know the reason.

They signaled him to stay where he was and one of the guards went inside. Lasgol had to hold back a small smile of triumph. The plan had worked. The guards were looking at him grimly, but that was to be expected in any case. The guards who had gone inside soon came back out.

He was ushered into the stone palace and taken to a large patio with a big fountain in the middle of a small pond. Lasgol was amazed once again by the skill of the people of the mountain, who were capable of guiding water anywhere in the depths of the mountains and creating fountains like this one.

From there he was led to the upper floor up some stairs. The stone palace was bigger than it looked from the outside. Being built inside the mountain, the optical effect made everything look smaller than it really was. The lights of the torches also helped create this effect. They arrived at a great double door where two soldiers stood on guard.

The guards who had accompanied him knocked on the door and received the order to enter. They ushered him in. It was a huge, long room with a carved oak table before which a man was standing, waiting. Lasgol had no doubt it was Riagain as soon as he saw him. He was a nobleman of Irinel, tall and slender, with pale skin, red hair, and light-brown eyes.

There was a lit fire on one side of the room between two large cupboards, and on the wall above it Aodh's Bow was hanging. It was unmistakable. A bow that looked made of gold with strange inscriptions carved along its body. It shone with the light glow of gold which made it impossible not to notice and stare at it.

Lasgol went to stand near the nobleman. Four guards stood behind him.

"Well, well, life's full of surprises," Riagain commented in Norghanian with an Irinelian accent.

"You speak Norghanian, that's going to make things easy," Lasgol smiled.

"I was brought up to be King of Irinel. I studied many things, among them the languages of the most important rival kingdoms," he said with a bitter smile.

"I haven't been that lucky, and the truth is I'm beginning to realize that knowing languages is quite important in life."

"I see that the journey to this peculiar kingdom has impressed you."

"Everything in this kingdom has impressed me, a lot."

"The truth is it's very picturesque indeed, which brings me to the question of   your name and your business here."

"My name's Lasgol Eklund, and I'm a Norghanian Ranger."

"Interesting, more surprises still. A Ranger no less."

"You know us, sir?"

"Yes, I know of you and of your missions. A Specialist, I guess."

"I am." Lasgol nodded.

"How interesting. You may leave us," he waved the guards off. "Wait outside until I call you."

The guards nodded and left.

"You mentioned King Kendryk, and that interests me. What's up with the dear enemy who usurped my throne?"

"Well… I mentioned him so they would let me in. My mission has nothing to do with the king. He's in Norghana attending his daughter's wedding."

"Yes, I had heard that. I hope it goes wrong and becomes a blood bath. I hope they tear at one another's throats at the banquet."

"It might happen, yes," Lasgol was hoping it would not, but it would not be the first time a wedding ended in a bloody event.

"So, you're saying you used the King's name to get to me. Well played. And what does a Ranger Specialist want with me?"

"It's a pretty complicated matter."

"Well, I have time. It's not as if lots of things happen here. The thing is, I'm quite bored."

"If you let me, I'll tell you the reason for my visit. You might find it difficult to believe."

Riagain smiled.

"As I said. Entertain me. Take me out of my boredom in this forced exile."

"Very well, I'll tell you everything."

Lasgol told the nobleman all about Dergha-Sho-Blaska, without getting into too many details. He explained how they had found him, the orb, the sects, his reincarnation in the fossilized dragon, the weapons that could kill it, and his Bow. He explained as well as he could and tried to make it as credible as possible. As he told the story the face of the nobleman remained impassive, so Lasgol could not tell whether Riagain believed him or not. Most likely he did not—who would without having been in the midst of it all? —but he had to try.

Once he finished, Riagain watched him for a long moment with his eyes half closed. Lasgol thought he must be deciding whether it was all a bad joke or if a madman had come to see him.

"That is a wondrous story, if I've ever heard one," he said, nodding. "An amazing story."

Lasgol looked at him. He still was not sure whether the man had believed him or was mocking him.

"I swear it's the truth."

"It's an extremely difficult truth to believe."

"I'm not saying it's not, but it's true."

"I'd like to believe you, more than anything else because of how twisted the story is, but I can't, I'm sorry."

Lasgol had already feared that reaction. He sighed.

"Even if you don't believe me, will you lend me the Bow? I'll return it once we don't need it anymore."

"I'm afraid not. That bow is unequaled. A treasure, even if it's not magic as you claim, but it is quite light and accurate. I've used it hundreds of times, I can assure you," he said, pointing at it over the fireplace.

"We need the Bow. The dragon is about to appear, I know it, I can feel it. The Bow is the only weapon we can defeat it with."

"I don't know what you intended to accomplish by coming here, to my exile, and asking me for my most precious possession. I don't know whether this is some twisted plan of Kendryk's against me. What I can assure you is that you won't achieve anything," said Riagain, and his tone was now one of annoyance.

"I swear it isn't…"

"Guards!" Riagain called.

Four guards came into the hall armed with the shields and javelins typical of Irinel and hastened to where Lasgol was standing. They surrounded him with their javelins aiming at his body.

Lasgol raised his hands.

"Take him and throw him out. Don't let him bother me again. Take him to the Mountain Guards and explain that he's upset me."

Lasgol sighed again.

"I want it to be noted that I tried the nice way…"

"What do you mean?"

"That I came and asked for the Bow nicely, explaining how grave the situation is. You leave me no choice but to take it away anyway. I'm sorry it has to be like that."

The soldiers stiffened but Lasgol did not move.

Camu, Plan B, Lasgol transmitted.

Plan B ready, Camu messaged at once.

"Take him! And if he tries anything skewer him!"

At that instant Camu became visible behind the soldiers. He had come into the room through the door the soldiers had left open.

"What… is… that…?" Riagain muttered at the sight of Camu, and he unsheathed his sword with eyes filled with terror.

The soldiers did not know what to do when they saw Camu, whether to attack, defend themselves, or run away.

"Don't just stand there! Attack!" Riagain shouted to his men.

"I wouldn't do that..." Lasgol warned them.

Two of the soldiers stepped forward and prepared to throw their javelins.

Camu opened his mouth and used his Ice Breath skill. There was a shrill hiss followed by a great gust of frozen breath steam that came out of Camu's mouth at great speed and froze the two soldiers where they stood before they could throw their javelins. They were both turned into two ice statues.

"For Irinel! What's that?" Riagain cried.

Camu moved toward the other two soldiers, who cowered behind their shields. This time he used his Tail Whiplash skill, and with it he threw the two soldiers in the air. They crashed against the far wall and nearly took Riagain with them. They did not get back up from the tremendous blow. The nobleman had taken cover behind his desk.

"I'm sorry things have to be like this," Lasgol said as he went over to the fireplace and carefully took down Aodh's Bow. As he grabbed it, he felt the hair on his nape stand up.

"Take the bow, but tell the monster not to kill me," Riagain begged without coming out from behind the desk.

"He won't kill you. And those soldiers won't die either. They'll thaw around dawn, although they might be quite touched and may take weeks to recover fully."

"Leave, I don't want any more trouble."

"You won't. One thing you must know, you are wrong. The dragon exists, just like my friend here exists, and this Bow has magic, although you can't feel it."

"Leave," he said and crouched behind the desk.

Come, you did very well, Lasgol transmitted to Camu.

I put fierce face.

I noticed, a full-fledged monster.

Be difficult.

To make a monster's face?

Yes, I too handsome.

Lasgol had to laugh out loud.

364

Chapter 42

Lasgol and Camu left the great city of Enmemounte. Camu went down camouflaged along the outer face of the houses carved into the great mountain. Since he could cling to anything it was easy for him, he was like a giant lizard. Luckily no one could see him, or more than one would have had a heart attack. Lasgol did not have his skill, so he had to walk down the thousand and one steps until he reached the lower area. He rubbed his calves when he reached the ramp that went to the monoliths that formed the entrance gate.

He took one last glance to the great city on the mountain with its thousands of lights, rock houses, and violet people with pink irises. A most curious civilization—he would have to come back one day and spend more time there. He made the decision to return. The guards did not give him any trouble leaving; it was very clear they were not fond of foreigners.

Ona was waiting for them not far away and quite upset. She had not been able to take part in the recovery of the Bow and she was annoyed. She expressed it with several growls, which Lasgol readily calmed with caresses and sweet words. A moment later Ona was no longer upset and she was back to being the usual good and obedient panther.

Lasgol stopped to contemplate the beautiful golden bow he had in his hands. It was very light; it barely weighed anything at all. It was not made of gold, that much he knew. Gold weighed more. He did not think it was made of any known light gold-plated metal, although that might be the case. He had the feeling that the metal used was that golden color and that it was some metal they did not have in Tremia, or that which they had not yet discovered. He would have to let Egil and Eicewald examine it and see what they thought.

The string was also special. It was not the string of a regular bow. It looked like some kind of gold elastic wire, although that was impossible. The feeling it gave when touching the string was metallic, another mystery of this wonderful weapon. The inscriptions engraved along both sides of the bow were beautiful but incomprehensible. He wondered who had engraved them and what their purpose was. They certainly did not resemble any rune he had ever seen before.

What do now? Camu asked him.

Now we go back to Norghana.

Portal?

Yes, we'll go to the eastern Pearl and you take us back home to the Pearl at the Shelter.

Okay.

The return to the Eastern Pearl, as they had called it, was uneventful. The three friends made the journey as fast as they could with the intention of getting back to Norghana, the sooner the better.

When they arrived at the Pearl above the cliff, where the sea broke, Lasgol saw the island city in the distance and felt the urge to visit it someday. There would be a time, but now was not it.

They went down into the enormous hole where the Pearl rested.

All yours, Camu. Open the Portal.

I open.

Camu used his power. He sent the pulses at the Pearl at the exact rhythm and the Pearl responded with a silver flash. A moment later the great silver Portal was taking shape above the Pearl.

Lasgol was watching the Portal and how Camu was searching for the rune of the Pearl at the Shelter.

Don't get it wrong and send us to another Pearl.

Not worry, I know.

Lasgol sighed, *I hope so.*

Done, Camu said.

Very well, let's go then.

Ona took a great leap and then another to enter the Portal headfirst.

Lasgol smiled. He called upon his *Cat-like Reflexes* and, imitating Ona, he went in head first with two big leaps.

The last one to enter was Camu who, since he could cling to the surface of the Pearl, did not need to take a leap.

Lasgol woke up in a bed with a slight headache. He was in a room. For a moment he was worried, then he realized that the place was vaguely familiar. He was alone. He half sat up in the bed.

The door opened and Enduald came in with Galdason.

"At last, our sleeping beauty has woken up!" Enduald said in a whining tone.

"Where am I?"

"In the Cave of Winter in one of the guest rooms," Galdason explained. "We couldn't leave you lying by the Pearl."

Lasgol realized he did not feel half as bad as he usually felt after crossing the Portal.

"Have you given me something?"

"Yes indeed," said Enduald.

"Does it work?"

"Yeah, it does."

"Well, you can thank Annika when you see her. She created the potion to alleviate the effect of traveling through the Portal based on the symptoms you all experienced before."

"Well, she was spot-on."

"We're happy to see you safe and sound."

"And with the Bow," said Enduald.

"The Bow, do you have it?"

"Yes, don't worry. We've been studying it to see what we could find out about the weapon and its power. Also, to see whether it really is a special weapon or simply a charmed or enchanted one, which is more common."

"And? Is it special?"

"Definitely special. We've analyzed its magic and it's one that's not common at all. It's ancient," said Galdason.

"We've concluded that it's not simply a charmed weapon," Enduald said. "Which is something we were afraid of, but it's not that."

"Then it might really work?"

"There's more," said Galdason.

"And that's what?"

"Remember that when we analyzed your magic, we discovered something very interesting and puzzling at the same time?" Galdason said.

"Yeah…" Lasgol did not feel too comfortable talking about it.

"We discovered that in your magic there are two types of different basic energies," Enduald explained. "If you remember, the first, more modern energy we traced to its origin about three thousand years ago. The second type of magic we traced to over five thousand years ago."

Lasgol nodded.

"You told me that my magic is composed of two types of magic of ancestral origins."

"And the one that dates back five thousand years is similar to Camu's," Enduald noted.

"Exactly," Galdason confirmed. "Let's say that you're an arcane oddity, something very uncommon. Two different magics, and very old ones, run through your veins."

"I remember…" said Lasgol, who had not finished fully assimilating the implications of it all.

"Well," Galdason went on, "the magic of the Bow is similar to one of your base magics.

"The one three thousand years old," Enduald told him.

Lasgol's eyes opened very wide.

"Similar?"

"Almost identical," Galdason said.

"I don't understand… what does that mean?"

"That those who created the bow are the Gods who disappeared three thousand years ago and whose magic runs through your veins," Enduald said.

"Are you sure?"

"Yes, we've studied it in depth while you were resting. We were in for a big surprise," said Galdason. "The weapon is authentic. It dates from that era. It was created by the Gods that are supposed to have lived in that era, and it has strong traces of their magic."

"But… if it's a weapon to kill dragons… shouldn't it have been created with dragon magic?"

"You mean the other base magic we found running through your veins? The one that's like Camu's? Galdason asked.

"Yeah, well, it would make more sense, wouldn't it?"

Galdason and Enduald looked at one another. Their eyes opened wide as if they had reached some conclusion.

"On the contrary, Lasgol. Think again. The Bow is made with the magic of the Gods who fought the Dragons. That Bow is a weapon created with their own magic to fight against dragons," Galdason said.

Lasgol thought about that.

"Yeah, it makes more sense that way. Since all the magic we've encountered—the Pearls, Portals, Orb, everything—has Drakonian magic, I had assumed the weapons would have that too."

"What's important is that this weapon is really a weapon built with the magic of the disappeared gods," said Galdason.

"That leads us to believe that it was created to that end, or at least that thanks to that type of magic, it's capable of killing dragons," Enduald concluded.

"But we won't know until the moment comes…"

"I'm afraid we won't," said Galdason.

"It can only be tested on a dragon," said Enduald.

Lasgol was thoughtful.

"Have you tried the Bow?" he asked all of a sudden.

"Loke has tried it."

"And what happened? Did its magic activate?"

Both magi shook their heads.

"Loke shot with it and it behaves like any other bow. It's very light and precise, but its magic did not activate," Galdason said.

"Great…" Lasgol said woefully.

"But, here's where your magic comes into play," Galdason told him.

"My magic?"

"We believe it's very possible that in order to use the weapon and call upon its power, the wielder must be like its creators, or one of their descendants," Enduald said.

Lasgol watched the two magi, who were looking at him, very excited.

"Oh… I see. You think that since I have that magic, I'll be able to use the bow."

"That's what we believe, yes," they both nodded.

"There's only one way of knowing," Lasgol got to his feet. "Come on."

They went outside the Lair and found Loke with the bow in his hand. Beside him were Ona and Camu.

You already well?

Yes, very well.

Much great.

Ona licked the back of Lasgol's hand and stood close beside him.

"An exquisite weapon," Loke told him, handing it to Lasgol.

369

"I'll see whether I can activate its power."

They all watched Lasgol nock an arrow in the fine golden bowstring. He aimed at an oak about two hundred paces away. He concentrated and tried to connect with the Bow. He used his *Arcane Communication* skill for this, since it allowed him to communicate with magical objects and objects of power.

For a long moment nothing happened. He could not interact with the bow's magic. He released the arrow to see if anything happened. The arrow flew straight to the tree and hit it right in the center where Lasgol had aimed. Yet, there was no magical effect associated to the shot. Lasgol did not feel like he had activated the weapon's magic either.

He wrinkled his nose and tried again. He called on his *Arcane Communication* skill, but this time he gathered a large amount of his inner energy to maximize the effect. Eicewald had taught him how to do that, and perhaps it would work. He had the feeling that the weapon had been created by and for beings with great magical power. He was not at that level—there was still a long road for him to travel.

He pulled the string back to his nose and aimed. He concentrated on the weapon and this time he felt the strange tingling feeling of a skill activating. There was a green flash that ran through Lasgol's body and then the Bow. In reply, the Bow gave off a golden flash. It was a small, weak one; Lasgol felt like the flash could be a lot more powerful. He released and the arrow left the bow. The Bow seemed to catch fire, as did the arrow. It was a mixture of fire and gold. The visual effect was amazing. The arrow hit the tree, and when it did there was a bang and the arrow went straight through the oak and continued on until they lost it in the distance.

"That was amazing," Loke said. "It went through, leaving a huge hole."

Lasgol looked at the Bow, which was shining and burning in gold. "It was."

"Does it burn?" Galdason asked, pointing at the weapon.

"No, I feel nothing."

"Let me try something," said Enduald as he reached out to take the Bow.

"Ouch!" he withdrew his hand at once. "It's burning hot!"

"Is it? I don't feel anything." Lasgol switched the Bow to his other hand to make sure he had not scorched his hand and could not feel with it. No, he had not burnt it, even if the Bow was on fire.

"Impressive," Galdason said.

"It certainly is, but we still don't know whether this will be enough to kill the immortal dragon."

I be Drakonian. You try on me, Camu volunteered.

Lasgol threw his head back.

No way! Under no circumstance.

I brave. You shoot, aim tip of tail.

No, I'm not going to shoot at your tail.

No kill. Sure no hurt much.

We don't know that.

"True, that would be risky," said Enduald. "We don't know the effect of the Bow's magic. It might create an unbearable pain until it caused death, like the Magic of Curses does. Or it could poison you with a toxin that kills Drakonians."

"Enduald's right. We don't know what effect the Bow's magic has on a Drakonian. We can't risk it."

You heard them, Lasgol told Camu.

I resist all that, sure.

Sure, but we're not going to try.

"What are you going to do then?" Galdason asked Lasgol.

"I have to go back with the Bow. I want Eicewald to examine it too. Perhaps he'll be able to help with the weapon's power. I have the feeling that I only managed to activate a minimal part of its power. I don't think that would be enough. It's only a feeling I have, but my intuitions don't usually fail me."

"That's a clever idea. The Ice Mage will be able to help you better than we can," said Galdason.

"Eicewald is wise, and much of his magic is attack-based. He's spent years studying and focusing on war magic, he'll be able to help with the Bow's magic, which will also be to that end," Enduald said.

Lasgol nodded.

"You have my owl, Milton?"

"Yes, we looked after him together with Trotter," Loke told him.

"Thanks a lot! I'll send Milton and ask Eicewald to meet me in the Forest of the Green Ogre. There we can experiment in peace with the bow until we master it."

"I think that's an excellent plan," said Galdason.

"Good luck!" Enduald wished him.

"Thank you very much, all three of you, for everything," Lasgol said.

"Always at your service," Galdason replied with a big smile.

"Magical service," Enduald noted.

Lasgol smiled.

"See you soon!"

Leave? Camu messaged him.

"Yes, we're going back."

Much great.

Lasgol smiled.

My thoughts exactly.

Chapter 43

Lasgol, Camu, and Ona were sitting in front of the tent by the pond in the Forest of the Green Ogre. Trotter was drinking quietly on one side of the pond. Lasgol had Aodh's Bow on his crossed legs. He had been practicing all morning. By now he was able to call upon the magic of the Bow with every shot he tried. It was a significant improvement, since only a day before he had been missing half the time and the Bow only performed average shots.

He was greatly looking forward to seeing Eicewald to explain everything to do with the Bow and also so the Mage could help him with the matter of activating its full power. He was also dying to know what had happened during the wedding, which was already over and which he had missed. They had gone straight to the forest without passing through the capital to show Eicewald the Bow, so Lasgol had no information of the latest events.

It was late afternoon by the time Eicewald finally arrived. The Ice Mage approached the tent, leaning on his white staff with a big smile on his face.

Eicewald! Happy! Camu messaged, along with a feeling of joy at seeing the Mage their friend and master.

"Camu, Ona, Lasgol! What a joy to see the three of you!" the Mage replied.

"The joy is all ours!" Lasgol said, smiling from ear to ear at seeing the Mage who had taught them so much and whom they considered a true eminence in everything to do with magic.

Eicewald hugged Camu first and then Ona and Lasgol.

"What happened at the wedding? Did everything go well?" Lasgol wanted to know.

Eicewald looked resigned.

"Let's say it went as well as we could expect."

"There's been trouble then?"

"Quite a lot, yes. Serious trouble."

"Do we have a Queen?" Lasgol asked, almost doubting whether he should ask and fearing the answer.

"We have a Druid Queen."

Lasgol's eyes widened.

"I'll explain everything later. The Panthers are all well and had a star performance. So good, in fact, that King Thoran has now entrusted them with the safety of his Queen."

"Oops… that's not good…"

"Yeah, that's what awaits you on your return. That, and a war."

"War?" Lasgol was struck dumb.

"We're about to start a war against Zangria. It's Thoran's thing. I'll explain everything."

"I see you've been most entertained."

Eicewald nodded, smiling.

"And what about you? How are you? Did everything go well?" the Mage asked them.

"We're fine. The journey has been an experience. The Kingdom of Moontian and her peoples are fascinating."

People violet. Eyes pink. Very pretty. Live in great mountain. Houses hang from mountain, very funny.

Eicewald smiled.

"I see you liked it."

"Very much, honestly."

"And Aodh's Bow? Did you get it?"

Lasgol pointed at the bow that was leaning against his rucksack.

"We got it."

"Is it that one? Is it authentic?" Eicewald went over to examine it.

"It is."

"It looks like a magnificent weapon," Eicewald touched it with his magical staff of ice and shut his eyes. "I can feel its magic. A very old and powerful one."

"I need your help to use it. I'm not capable of using its full power."

That's because the blood of its creators doesn't run strong in your veins, a voice sounded, powerful and deep in the minds of all four of them.

Lasgol looked at Eicewald.

The Mage shook his head.

"Trouble…"

Drakonian magic! Camu warned, very agitated.

Lasgol took Aodh's Bow and nocked an arrow from his quiver. He called on his power; he was looking everywhere but saw nothing. Trotter was shifting restless by the pond but they could not see anyone.

Eicewald started to cast protections on himself. He conjured a protective sphere of hard ice against physical attacks and then another protective translucent sphere against magic.

Lasgol realized when he saw him doing this that real trouble was approaching, and he called upon all the skills that could help him in combat, one after the other and as fast as he could. He finished with *Woodland Protection*, which covered him entirely from head to foot.

Ona was looking and growling toward the east of the lake, as if she could see something there, but in reality, there was nothing there.

Drakonian magic here. Close! Camu warned them, together with a feeling of great unease.

All of a sudden, as if it came from another dimension to materialize before them, there appeared the head of a horrific dragon right in front of their faces.

"Dergha-Sho-Blaska!" cried Lasgol, recognizing him at once.

That's right, you insignificant human. I am Dergha-Sho-Blaska, immortal dragon, king among dragons reborn in a new body.

Lasgol aimed at the head. There was no doubt it was Dergha-Sho-Blaska. He recognized at once the yellow reptilian eyes that shone with new life, the horns above them, and the crest that crowned his head. Also, the huge and lethal jaws he was showing off to intimidate them.

Eicewald, like Lasgol, aimed his staff at the huge horrendous head floating in the air in front of them.

Is he here? Lasgol asked Camu, thinking that perhaps it was a vision since all they could see was the head.

Yes be. Magic camouflage.

The little Drakonian is intelligent, Dergha-Sho-Blaska transmitted to them with his powerful voice that hurt their minds as if he had shaken them.

Lasgol squinted while he bore the negative effect in his head.

"Show yourself," he demanded.

The eyes of the great dragon flashed and suddenly the body of the monstrous creature began to be visible, as if it came from another world, only he was there right before them. The colossal body, over a hundred and fifty feet long, became visible little by little. A crest went down from his head and along his back and the long and powerful tail. His whole body was covered with reddish-black scales. Four short, powerful legs supported the great body and ended in claws that looked as devastating as they were sharp. The enormous wings were folded along his sides.

Now that you see me, kneel before your lord, he ordered with a mental message sent with such force that it was like a blow to their minds.

Lasgol felt it like Ona and even Trotter, who protested. Eicewald seemed to bear it thanks to the anti-magic protection he had raised. Camu created a dome of magic-denial to protect himself and Ona, who was beside him.

"Our lord is the King of Norghana," Eicewald replied in a quiet tone, as if establishing a fact, not refusing to obey.

Ha! Ha! Ha! A deep, powerful laughter reached their minds, shaking them. *Your ignorance and blindness are ridiculous. I am Dergha-Sho-Blaska, the Immortal Dragon, he who sleeps and doesn't die. King among the dragons.*

"What is it you want?" Lasgol asked, careful so that his tone would not offend the dragon.

To recuperate what is mine by right, my kingdom. To rule over this world, the world of those of my blood.

"That kingdom was a long time ago. The world has changed. Now human kings and emperors rule over Tremia," Eicewald explained, trying to talk to the dragon without provoking his anger.

That's irrelevant. This world belongs to those of silver blood; it always has and always will. I will recuperate what is ours so that my people can fly through the skies of this world and rule like they did ten thousand years ago.

"There's no need for bloodshed. We can reach some kind of understanding," Lasgol offered.

There's only one understanding. I will rule over this world, and all humans will kneel before me and pay homage to me or be exterminated.

The humans are many and of different kingdoms," Eicewald told him.

Humans are insignificant. A bother that soon will stop being one.

"The humans didn't cause the dragons to leave. We had nothing to do with that, and we shouldn't be punished for something we didn't do," Lasgol argued, trying to make it clear that they hadn't had anything to do with the war against the dragons.

Dergha-Sho-Blaska laughed again with that deep, derogatory laughter.

Humans can do nothing against dragons. They were not who defeated us.

You forget I was there when it happened. Your small, simple mind can't assimilate that I've lived thousands of years. I've flown these skies long before the arrival of men in Tremia.

"There must be a way to avoid confrontation. We can find a way to understand each other, to work together and agree on terms of peace between humans and dragons for the future," Eicewald said in pleading tone.

There's only one way to avoid confrontation. All humans will surrender to me.

"The human kings and emperors won't surrender that easily…" Lasgol said. "They won't renounce their thrones."

"Unfortunately, they'll fight," Eicewald added.

In that case they'll die, and with them all those who contest my power. It's useless to offer any resistance. They can do nothing against me.

"They have armies of thousands of soldiers and powerful magi to send into a fight," Lasgol said.

The human armies and magi can do nothing against Dergha-Sho-Blaska. Their weapons can do nothing to me. Their magic is weak—they'll never manage to defeat me.

"Not even if all the kingdoms should unite?" Eicewald asked.

They would only manage to be a nuisance and prolong their agony. The humans can do nothing against those of the silver blood. If I have to kill them all, I will.

"If that's the case… why hasn't the Immortal Dragon begun his conquering campaign?" Lasgol asked, raising an eyebrow. Something did not make sense. If Dergha-Sho-Blaska was so powerful that he could destroy whole kingdoms, why was he not doing so already?

Dergha-Sho-Blaska stared fixedly at Lasgol.

Only a fool reveals his plans to the enemy. Your small minds are incapable of understanding my plans and their execution.

"It must be because he needs something he doesn't have yet," Lasgol told Eicewald.

"Or because he's not telling us his real plan and there's another, very different one he's hiding," Eicewald replied.

Dergha-Sho-Blaska laughed again, and this time he laughed so hard Lasgol thought his mind would burst.

Oh you, inconsequential humans, trying to understand the plans of a superior being. Pathetic.

"Then… why are you here?" Lasgol asked. "What does the great dragon want from us?"

You are interesting, human. You have silver blood and gold blood in your veins. Something that surprises me, and I am rarely surprised. I've lived thousands of years and have seen a lot.

"Are you here for me?" Lasgol asked blankly.

No, not for you. I'm here for the little one, he transmitted, staring at Camu.

I not little one.

You are. You're still a pup who has yet to grow and develop to become a true, powerful Drakonian.

I grow in time.

I want you to do so by my side. I am your kin. Your blood and mine are related. You shouldn't be with humans, they're inferior to us. Very inferior. You must be with those of your kind.

I happy with humans.

It is an aberration that you are with them. They can't help you to develop. I can. With me you'll reach your full potential and be able to rule.

I king?

I'll give you a part of this world. Choose the kingdoms you want and they'll be yours. You'll be the lord of Norghana, Rogdon if you want them. Everyone will fear you and worship you like a god.

Camu was thoughtful.

Camu, don't let yourself be fooled, Lasgol transmitted only to Camu, but somehow Dergha-Sho-Blaska intercepted it.

Don't you dare put the little one against me, he sent to Lasgol, and he did so with such force that Lasgol suffered an instant migraine.

Eicewald, seeing Lasgol writhing in pain, conjured an anti-magic defensive sphere around him.

Mage, don't push your luck. If you conjure again in my presence, I'll kill you, he threatened Eicewald and turned his enormous head toward the Mage.

Camu blinked hard.

These humans my friends. I stay with them.

That's a bad decision. I was expecting more from a Drakonian.

Be my decision.

Remember, you are not a dragon. I don't have to respect your life.

I stay with friends.

Wrong decision.

"Will you leave us now?" Lasgol asked him, fearing it would not be so.

I haven't come only for the little one.

"What are you looking for?" Eicewald asked, and Lasgol thought he knew the answer.

I've come for what you hid in the bottom of that pond, he transmitted to them, looking toward the great pond at his back.

Dergha-Sho-Blaska flashed in red-black and suddenly the pond began to tremble as if there were an earthquake. The water of the pond started to rise toward the sky like a geyser. At the top of the geyser, which rose thirty feet high above the surface of the water, there appeared the Silver Pearl.

With a movement of his head, Dergha-Sho-Blaska directed the pearl until it settled beside his front left leg.

Lasgol was watching in awe. How had he known the Pearl was hidden there? And how was it possible he could move objects like that, with his mind?

"The Silver Pearl, that's what you were looking for ..." Eicewald murmured.

That's not its name, but that's irrelevant. Tell me, Mage, where have you hidden the twelve lesser pearls?

"I don't know what you mean," Eicewald pretended.

Lasgol knew he was referring to the necklace of silver pearls.

Last chance. Where are the twelve lesser pearls?

Lasgol looked at Eicewald. Only the Mage knew where he had hidden them. He had not even told Lasgol yet.

"I think you're mistaken..." Eicewald began to say.

You think wrong, inferior mage.

Dergha-Sho-Blaska spread his immense wings and gave a thundering roar that made everyone cower. He extended his wings of over sixty feet of width, flapped them hard. The push of the whirl he created lifted Trotter into the air and made him crash against the trees.

"Trotter!" Lasgol cried out, worried.

Ona lunged into attack with all the power of her strong legs.

The dragon hit her with one of his wings and sent her flying in the air against the same trees.

"No!" Lasgol cried in horror.

Dergha-Sho-Blaska launched a strong mental attack against Eicewald. Lasgol could see the dragon's magic attacking like a red cone that came out of the dragon's mind and was bathing the Mage. He was surprised he could see the dragon's magic.

Eicewald's defense, the anti-magic sphere, seemed to hold off the attack for a moment. But a moment later the Mage was forced to send more and more energy to strengthen his defense, which was being destroyed with the power of the dragon's attack.

"Leave him alone!" Lasgol shouted at him.

Insignificant, inferior creatures. You're going to learn to respect a superior being.

Lasgol could see how Eicewald's sphere was coming apart under the influx of the attacking cone. Although the Mage was sending all his energy to strengthen his defense,   it would not last long. The strength of the dragon's attack was impossible to withstand, not even for Eicewald, one of the most powerful Magi of Tremia.

Eicewald changed his tactic and conjured an offensive attack. He moved his staff and out of it flew a dozen missiles of ice in the shape of sharp stakes which headed straight to Dergha-Sho-Blaska's torso. Lasgol witnessed with incredulity how the ice stakes hit the dragon's body. A cloak of red energy became visible, enveloping the body of the dragon at the moment of impact. The missiles did not pierce it.

"He has anti-magic protection!" Lasgol warned Eicewald, who continued fighting to maintain his defensive barrier.

I told you that if you conjured you would die. It's your end, Dergha-Sho-Blaska transmitted with a strong mental blow.

Lasgol withstood it because of the sphere Eicewald had raised around him. He had to help the Mage or the dragon was going to kill him. He raised the Bow and aimed where he supposed the dragon's heart was.

Don't be ridiculous, human. You can't even control that bow.

Lasgol concentrated and used all the energy he could to activate the power of the Bow and thus overload it. There was an intense green flash and then another gold one from the Bow. Lasgol released. The Bow caught fire and the arrow that flew out of it did so too, both fire-colored and with a golden glow.

The arrow flew straight to Dergha-Sho-Blaska's body, who saw it and moved his great left wing, putting it in the path of the arrow's trajectory. The arrow hit the wing and there was a golden burst. The arrow pierced the wing and remained stuck in it.

Dergha-Sho-Blaska opened his yellow reptilian eyes and Lasgol felt the dragon's disbelief at once. He was staring at the arrow in his wing and could not believe it.

You've wounded me. That's impossible, Dergha-Sho-Blaska sent, more puzzled than furious.

Lasgol hastened to nock another arrow in the Bow, seeing they had a chance.

Dergha-Sho-Blaska leapt toward Lasgol and hit him with his wounded wing. The blow was so tremendous that Lasgol was sent flying through the air and fell thirty paces away, landing with a sharp blow. Luckily, he was wearing his *Woodland Protection,* which absorbed the force of the blow and its impact. The dragon had gotten rid of Lasgol as if he were swatting a mosquito.

When Camu saw Lasgol was hit he attacked. He opened his mouth and used his Ice Breath skill. The frozen stream headed straight to the dragon's body and hit him squarely. But once again the cloak of red energy that protected the dragon stopped the attack. Camu persevered and continued sending more Ice Breath. But the frozen stream died on the protective cloak without affecting the dragon.

Eicewald seized the moment when the dragon was not focused on him and conjured a powerful winter storm over the creature, which should freeze him to the marrow with its low temperatures and strong freezing winds. All the Ice Magi knew that nothing could survive a storm of ice of maximum power like the one Eicewald had just conjured up, using almost all the energy he had left. Keeping up his defense had consumed too much energy already.

Your magic is so inferior and futile it's simply laughable.

Dergha-Sho-Blaska stood under the winter storm without flinching. His magical protection absorbed it completely just as he was absorbing Camu's frozen breath. He flapped his wings as if he were basking in the frozen storm.

It's your end, mage, Dergha-Sho-Blaska said as he attacked with another powerful mental blow. This time the barrier did not hold and the mage fell to the ground on his knees, his defenses broken. He put his hands to his head and cried out in pain. Dergha-Sho-Blaska was killing him, destroying his mind.

Camu ran to the Mage's side and protected him within his dome of magic-denial. Dergha-Sho-Blaska's mental attack could not penetrate the dome.

Surprising. The little one is more powerful than it seems. It doesn't matter. You have no escape.

The dragon took a great leap forward with the help of his wings. As if a giant eagle were descending upon them, the dragon fell on Camu and Eicewald with his claws. Camu's anti-magic dome was no use against physical attacks. The dragon's claws hit Camu and Eicewald.

Lasgol was getting back on his feet when he saw it.

"No!"

The claws could not get through Camu's tough scales, but he was thrown to one side with a tremendous blow of the dragon's strong back legs. Eicewald was not so lucky. The claws of a front leg tore through his defense of ice and the other one tore his body apart.

Lasgol nocked a new arrow in the Bow.

Dergha-Sho-Blaska looked at him and sent him a mental attack with a blow of power, which Lasgol received equally in mind and body. He was sent backward about ten paces and was left lying on his side with blood dripping out of his mouth and ears.

The colossal dragon shook his wings triumphantly and roared to the skies with a thunderous sound. The dragon dropped Eicewald, who turned to Lasgol with the last of his strength. He smiled at him.

"No…" Lasgol reached out his hand.

The light left Eicewald's eyes. He was gone.

"Why…?" Lasgol asked in despair.

Because I am a superior being, supreme. I will rule over all this world. I will destroy the kingdoms that oppose me. I will annihilate all resistance.

"We could… live together in harmony…"

Dergha-Sho-Blaska gave another leap and stood over Lasgol. He stared at him for a moment as if deciding what to do with him.

I'll spare your life because you're of my blood, the silver-blooded ones. But if you confront me again, I'll kill you. I don't forget that you are also of the gold-blooded, my enemies.

Lasgol had the dragon's maw above his face. The mental messages thundered in his head and he was about to lose consciousness.

"Wait…"

Dergha-Sho-Blaska spread his enormous wings, gave a powerful leap, and took to the air, flapping his wings hard and raising a hurricane under his body.

Don't you ever cross paths with me again, and with this warning the colossal dragon flew away, taking the Silver Pearl in one of his claws.

Lasgol looked at Camu, who was gasping for breath. He looked wounded.

"Camu..." and he fainted.

Chapter 44

Lasgol woke up three days later in the Tower of the Rangers in a room that was not the one they usually shared.

"I see you never cease getting into trouble," a feminine voice he recognized said.

"Healer Edwina, what? Where? How?" Lasgol muttered, trying to understand the situation.

"And I also see you can't refrain from asking questions," she smiled kindly at him. "Don't move. You've received a horrible beating, both physically and mentally."

"Eicewald!" Lasgol cried. Flashes of what had happened at the confrontation with Dergha-Sho-Blaska were going through his mind...

"I'm very sorry, Lasgol. Eicewald is dead."

"No!" Lasgol put his head in his hands.

"Take it easy and don't move so much. I've healed the physical damage your body sustained but I couldn't do much about the harm your mind has sustained. You must rest and stay quiet, no sudden movements."

More flashes passed through Lasgol's mind.

"Camu, how's Camu?"

"Don't worry." The Healer put her hand on his chest so he would not sit up on the bed. "Camu's recovering. He has a broken leg and several broken ribs, but he's all right."

"Where is he, can I see him?"

"He's at the Shelter with Annika and Sigrid, who are looking after him. Don't worry, he'll fully recover. We couldn't bring him to the castle."

"And Ona and Trotter?"

"Ona is with Camu, she didn't want to leave him. That Snow Panther must have nine lives because nothing happened to her, although the bruises she had were huge."

"And Trotter?"

"Well... Trotter..."

"No!"

384

"It's not what you think, don't fret. He's recovering at the Royal Stables, but he fractured his left hind leg. I've healed it, but his days of adventuring with you are over. If he should break that leg again, and he might, because my healing can only repair to a point, he'd have to be put down."

"Oh no!"

"I'm afraid so. You'll have to find yourself another mount."

"Poor Trotter," Lasgol covered his eyes. Tears were running down his cheeks.

"It's not so bad. He'll have a quiet retirement at the Royal Stables and you'll be able to visit him whenever you visit the castle."

"Everything's gone so, so wrong..."

"Look on the bright side. You and Camu are bruised but still alive. You could've died."

"Yes, I know. It was close."

"Your friends are dying to see you. I'll give you a moment to compose yourself and let them in. They're very insistent."

"Yes, I'm sure they are."

"I'll come by later to see how you're doing," the Healer said as she went to the door of the room.

"Edwina," Lasgol called her.

"Yes, Lasgol?"

"Thank you very much, once again."

The Healer smiled.

"Just make sure we don't see one another like this in a long time," she said with a smile.

Lasgol nodded. "I'll try, don't worry."

The Healer could not keep the Panthers out for a second longer. Astrid came in like a wind, and after her came Nilsa, Ingrid, Gerd, Egil, and Viggo.

"Lasgol!" Astrid hugged and kissed him profusely. "We've been so scared!"

Astrid," Lasgol smiled while she covered him in kisses.

"Let the rest of us hug him too," Nilsa said to Astrid, who was reluctant to move aside. A moment later all the Panthers were hugging Lasgol one by one, showering him with love and attention.

"I'm fine, really," he kept saying.

"That's because you haven't seen your face," Viggo said.

"That bad?"

"It looks like you were hit in the head with a war axe," Gerd said.

"You look very handsome with those black eyes," Nilsa joked.

"Do you feel all right?" Egil asked him.

"I think so," Lasgol looked at his friend, and his eyes showed what he had been through.

"Well, weirdo, once again you've proven that we can't leave you alone for a moment without you getting into the biggest trouble," Viggo told him as he offered him an arm, which Lasgol took gladly.

"Do you know what happened?" Lasgol asked.

"We know," Ingrid said.

"The bug told us everything," Viggo told him. "In his own way, of course."

Lasgol nodded.

"How did you find us?"

"Eicewald had told us he was going to meet with you. Since you didn't come back, we got worried and went looking for you," Astrid said. "What we found there nearly broke our hearts."

"Dergha-Sho-Blaska?" Lasgol asked.

"Not a trace, he vanished into thin air," said Ingrid.

Lasgol looked at Egil.

"He's planning something, I don't know what it is yet, but he's planning something. He wants the Silver Pearls."

Egil nodded.

"That's why he's not letting himself be seen. There's something else he wants to do before revealing himself to the world."

"Maybe he's shy," Viggo joked.

"He wants to conquer the world and for all humankind to kneel before him because he's a superior being," Lasgol explained. "I don't think 'shy' describes him properly enough."

"If that's what he wants to achieve, he's missing something," said Egil.

"What are we going to do about the dragon then?" Ingrid asked with concern.

"The loss of Eicewald is irreparable," Egil said ruefully.

"He was a great man," Nilsa said, her eyes still moist.

"I still can't believe he's dead," Gerd said with great sadness in his tone and face.

"We have to keep fighting against Dergha-Sho-Blaska. We have to stop him before he manages to carry out his plans," said Lasgol.

"We owe it to Eicewald, who fought and died trying to stop him."

"Yes, we owe it to Eicewald, and we will stop Dergha-Sho-Blaska!" Astrid said confidently.

"Between all of us, we'll find the way," Ingrid said.

"What happened at the wedding?" Lasgol asked suddenly.

"Oh, you missed a good one," Nilsa said.

"With murder attempts on the King and Queen," Gerd added.

"Who tried to murder them?" Lasgol asked, surprised.

"Come on, Egil, admit that it was you who poisoned Orten, although what you were after was to kill Thoran," Viggo said.

"Don't speak nonsense, dumbass," Ingrid chided.

Egil was silent and they all looked at him.

"Egil, it wasn't you, was it?" Nilsa asked him, looking worried because of Egil's silence.

"No, it wasn't me…" Egil said.

"See? Sometimes you say the stupidest things," Ingrid scolded Viggo.

"Let him finish. There's more here than meets the eye," said Viggo.

"Is there?" Gerd wanted to know and was now beginning to worry.

Egil was silent for a moment, thinking.

They were all staring at him, waiting for his reply.

"I'm going to have a heart attack if you don't explain yourself," Nilsa told him, beginning to hop in place.

"It's complicated…" said Egil.

"We know complicated. Tell us what's going on," Astrid told him.

Egil nodded.

"The Western League is tired of waiting and has begun to act, against my recommendation to wait for a better moment to intervene."

"Was it them?" Ingrid asked.

"That would make sense. The Nobles of the West want to see Thoran dead more than anyone, more than Zangria, Rogdon, the Nocean Empire, or other kingdoms," Nilsa said.

"Egil, was it them?" Ingrid insisted.

"Or was it any of the other kingdoms?" Astrid asked.

"It was the League. The attempt on Thoran's life during the

honor dinner before the wedding was them. I tried to talk them out of it but they wouldn't listen. The odds that it would succeed were very low, as it turned out in the end. The plan was good, but almost any plan would've turned out wrong in those circumstances."

"That's bad news," Ingrid said. "If King Thoran finds out, we'll have another civil war."

"Thoran believes it was the Zangrians, so for now there's no danger of that," said Astrid.

"Tell them everything, Egil," Viggo told him.

"Is there more? What does he mean?" Ingrid asked, looking from Viggo to Egil.

"Is there anything else we should know?" Astrid asked.

Egil sighed.

"I helped with the escape plan. The idea of how to get the cook and the servant out of the castle was mine," Egil admitted.

"Why did you get involved?" Ingrid cried in disbelief.

"I had no choice but to get involved," Egil said with a shrug. "Sometimes in life you can't simply stay on the side and watch events unfold."

"Did they make you in any way?" Astrid asked him.

"Yes and no. They made me because they were going to do it anyway. It was already planned. If I didn't intervene it was going to be a disaster. They would've been caught and we would've had a new civil war with thousands dead, and we would've lost it because Thoran would've had the support of Irinel. I had to stop that from happening. Since I couldn't stop the coup, because they didn't tell me how they were going to do it and I wouldn't be able to stop it, I decided that the best thing to do was to get involved and save the situation."

They all listened to his explanation and were then silent, thinking.

"Well, you did save the situation. They weren't caught. There wasn't a civil war," said Gerd.

"That's right. You did the right thing," said Nilsa.

Egil shook his head.

"I didn't do the right thing."

"I don't understand. You saved the situation by stopping them from being caught," said Ingrid.

"There's the 'no' part of the previous question," Viggo said. "Explain yourself."

Egil smiled at Viggo.

"Nothing escapes you." Viggo made a face that meant "of course." "The 'no' part is that I also took part because I didn't want to be left aside, off the throne."

"They were going to leave you out?" Astrid asked. "How?"

"My cousin Lars Berge has entered the political game. They had him hidden and protected. If I didn't step forward as leader of the League and fought for the throne, they were going to cast me aside and continue with him."

"But do you really want the throne?" Gerd asked him. "Because if you don't, let your cousin and the League keep it. You don't need to shoulder all that responsibility."

"Yeah. You don't need to be king unless you want it with all your heart," said Nilsa. "You've already done a lot for the kingdom. Being king and everything it would take to get the throne by taking it from Thoran and his people is a tremendous load."

Egil heaved a deep sigh.

"That's the question. Do I want the throne or not?"

"Only you can answer that. Your heart must tell you," Astrid said.

"I've thought about it a lot. Long and thoroughly. All this time I've been trying to postpone the inevitable, the decision I had to make. If I want to be king, I need to take action. Assume the risks, both mine and those of all the people of the West, and lead the way with determination, guiding the League and my people. If I don't do it, someone else will do it for me, and the results might be terrible for the west and for Norghana."

"Are you saying what I think you're saying?" Nilsa asked.

"He's saying he's going to fight for the crown," said Gerd.

Egil nodded repeatedly.

"It's what's best for Norghana."

"But you're not saying that you really want it, that it's the best thing for you," Astrid told him.

"Because it's not," said Viggo. "The truth is that the know-it-all doesn't want the throne. He does it because he knows that, if he doesn't, whoever takes the throne will cause a catastrophe."

"He does it to avoid another civil war that the West will lose, and to stop a foreign kingdom from invading us when we're bleeding out half dead," Astrid said.

"I don't want to be king. I never have. But I can see that if I'm not, all Norghana will suffer. Because of that, I accept being king."

"We have to think this through carefully. We'd become traitors once again," said Ingrid.

"Thoran will hang us if he has the merest suspicion," said Nilsa.

"This is starting to get fun," Viggo said, rubbing his hands together and grinning mischievously.

"I'll understand that you don't want to be involved in this," Egil said, offering them a way out. "It's high treason."

"It wouldn't be the first time," Astrid winked at him. "I'm with you. Thoran will lead us all to ruin eventually. Of that I'm positive."

"I think the same as Astrid. Thoran is going to destroy the kingdom, and he's not a king I want to follow to the death," Nilsa said, shaking her head.

"Count on me. You'll need someone to cover your back," Gerd said with a slap on his shoulder.

"I wouldn't miss it for anything," said Viggo. "It's going to be so much fun."

Egil looked at Ingrid, who was debating with herself inwardly.

"My honor tells me that I can't commit high treason. On the other hand, I agree with Astrid and Nilsa. There's nothing I'd like more than to see a worthy king on the throne of Norghana, an honorable and intelligent one, who makes the kingdom prosper," she sighed deeply. "I'm with you, Egil. I'll support you."

Lasgol was the last one to speak. He had been listening to everything he had missed.

"I'm with you, Egil, I always have been and I always will be," he told his friend.

"Thank you. Thank you all. It means a lot to me to be able to count on you."

"One thing still isn't clear," Nilsa said all of a sudden. "If the attempt at the dinner was by the League, who tried to kill the Princess at the temple?"

All looks turned to Egil.

"I haven't solved that mystery yet," he said.

"But it wasn't the League then," said Astrid.

"No, it wasn't the West."

"So, the Zangrians then," said Ingrid. "The murderer was a Zangrian."

"That's too obvious and easy," said Viggo. "It wasn't the

Zangrians."

"Then who?" said Nilsa.

"That's what we'll have to find out. We have a new player in the game, and he's betting high," said Egil. "Who it is and what he's after we don't know. For now, he's managed to make Norghana and Zangria go to war, and that will also drag Irinel into it because of the new deal signed."

"So, it must be someone who hates Zangria," Nilsa guessed.

"Or someone who wants to weaken Norghana, even Irinel. Wars waste nations," Ingrid said.

"There are many players in the game with different interests and many hidden hands at work. They might cause cannon balls which right now we can't see," Egil said.

"Do you mean that whoever has caused this hasn't even been identified?" Astrid asked.

"It's very possible that until the next play we won't know who he is," said Egil.

"I can't wait to see what play that is," Viggo said, smiling.

"However it turns out, and come what may," Lasgol started to say as he continued lying in bed with Astrid sitting at his side," we'll face it together, like we always do."

"And we'll come out victorious," Ingrid raised her fist.

"Without a doubt, since you have me," Viggo said with a big smile.

"For the Panthers!" Nilsa cheered.

"For the Panthers!" they all joined in.

The adventure continues in the next book of the saga:

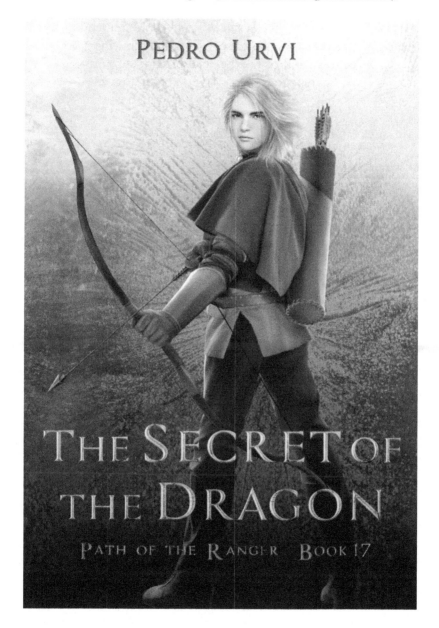

Note from the author:

I really hope you enjoyed my book. If you did, I would appreciate it if you could write a quick review. It helps me tremendously as it is one of the main factors readers consider when buying a book. As an Indie author I really need of your support.

Just go to Amazon end enter a review

Thank you so very much.

Pedro.

Author

Pedro Urvi

I would love to hear from you.
You can find me at:
Mail: pedrourvi@hotmail.com
Twitter: https://twitter.com/PedroUrvi
Facebook: https://www.facebook.com/PedroUrviAuthor/
My Website: http://pedrourvi.com

Join my mailing list to receive the latest news about my books:

Mailing List:
http://pedrourvi.com/mailing-list/

Thank you for reading my books!

Other Series by Pedro Urvi

THE ILENIAN ENIGMA

This series takes place several years after the Path of the Ranger Series. It has different protagonists. Lasgol joins the adventure in the second book of the series. He is a secondary character in this one, but he plays an important role, and he is alone…

THE SECRET OF THE GOLDEN GODS

This series takes place three thousand years before the Path of the Ranger Series

Different protagonists, same world, one destiny.

You can find all my books at Amazon.
Enjoy the adventure!

See you in:

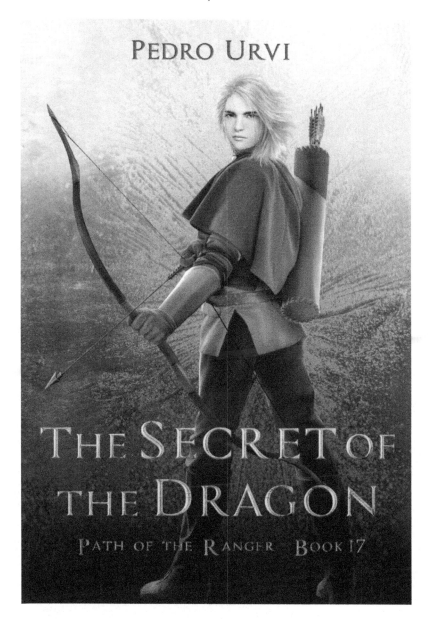

PEDRO URVI

THE SECRET OF
THE DRAGON

PATH OF THE RANGER - BOOK 17

Made in the USA
Las Vegas, NV
10 November 2023

80592649R00223